SEARCHING FOR BRANDON BASON

LANCE MOSHER

Searching for Brandon Bason
by Lance Mosher

Cover design by Vesna Tišma and Lance Mosher

Edited by Julie Frederick

ISBN: 978-0-9897041-4-4

Library of Congress Control Number: 2020911852

LanceMosherBOOKS.com
FOR YOUR JOURNEY

To my wonderful wife, Kristen,
who has always supported me in my writing

PROLOGUE

FRANCINE LOOKED OVER HER SHOULDER EVERY MINUTE OR SO AS she walked down an East Nashville sidewalk. The events of the past few months had put her on edge. But tonight was a break. She crossed over an old stone bridge and glanced at her watch. It was late, but Genevieve would understand. She climbed the four steps of her friend's porch, a small wooden box tucked under her arm, peeked over her shoulder again, and knocked.

The door opened, revealing Genevieve's worried face. "Hi, Francine. Come in," she said, forcing a smile. "Coffee?"

"No. I can't stay long. Barry's shift will be over soon. Brandon's asleep."

Genevieve stepped aside, ushering Francine in. They both sat down at the dining table.

"I came to bring you this," Francine said, sliding the old cigar box toward her friend. "If anything were to happen to me..." She paused and took a deep breath before continuing. "I need you to give this to Brandon."

Genevieve frowned. "Frankie—"

"I'm serious. Promise me you'll do it."

"Fine." She sighed. "I promise. But how long are you going to put up with this?"

"It's just a phase. You know Barry's job is stressful. He works hard for us."

"A phase? Phase or no phase, you don't deserve any of this."

"Maybe I do, you know? I haven't been a good wife lately—"

Genevieve reached over and pulled up Francine's sleeve. "You're not a good wife? Tell me, what kind of husband does that?"

Francine jerked her arm back. "I'm not here to talk about this. Just keep it safe. Got it?"

"Girl, you know I'm here for you," Genevieve said gently. "When have I let you down?"

"Never. Thank you." The corners of Francine's mouth curled up a bit. She stood. "I've got to get going. One more thing."

Genevieve also stood, cradling the box in her hands. "Anything."

"How's your shoulder?"

"Fine," she replied, a note of surprise in her voice. "Fully recovered. Surgery was almost a year ago."

"Good. I was wondering, do you still have your medicine? You know, the stuff that helped you sleep in the beginning?"

CHAPTER ONE

A JOLT OF PAIN SHOT THROUGH BRANDON'S FRESH WOUND AS HIS tongue traced his gums and bottom lip. The events of the previous night replayed in his mind. Waiting for his ride, he idly picked blades of grass, pulling them taut between thumb and forefinger until they snapped. He was thankful his lip hadn't busted on the outside. But his arms, now hidden under his coat sleeves, hadn't fared so well.

It was nearly summer, but no one would have guessed by the way Brandon was dressed. As usual, he had opted for his trench coat, rather than explaining once again to his two best friends why he hadn't called the cops on his stepdad. If getting the authorities involved was the right thing to do, surely his mother would have gone that route when she was alive. No, Brandon had to put up with Barry for another month or so, and then he'd be able to figure something out.

A 1988 beige Chrysler New Yorker came into view, prompting Brandon to stand. Matt was more reliable than the school bus. As Brandon stood, his long black bangs fell over his brown eyes. The car pulled up. Justin was in the passenger seat, so Brandon climbed into the back. "You got it?" he asked Matt.

"You know it!" Matt said, holding up the latest nü-metal album. "You guys have no idea how hard it was for me to wait until we were together to listen to it." Matt slipped the CD into the aftermarket player. The heavy guitar intro played through the car's stereo speakers. He cranked up the volume and sped forward.

After a few minutes, Matt shouted, "This is the first day of the rest of our lives!"

Justin put down his window a few inches, which tousled his dirty blonde hair. He pulled out a cigarette, lit it, and took a drag. "You've been saying that for weeks," Justin said.

"But it's true! Hasn't it hit you yet? We—the class of 1999—graduate in less than a month."

Matt pulled over. He put the car into park, turned down the volume, and faced Brandon and Justin. "But then what? Are you guys going to come with me or not?"

Brandon raised his eyebrows and looked back into Matt's blue eyes. "What? To the Grand Canyon? You're seriously going?"

Matt gave Brandon an expressionless look. "Am I serious? I've only been talking about this trip since the fifth grade!"

"But we were kids," Justin said. "You're telling me that you've saved enough money to go to somewhere you researched for a middle-school project?" He blew a puff of smoke out the window.

Brandon held his sleeve over his nose as some of it came into the back seat. He wished Justin didn't smoke. At home, the house reeked of cigarettes. He'd learned fast not to press the matter with Barry.

"Well, no," Matt admitted. "But I've got a good chunk saved, and I think I'll get more for graduation. My mom wants me to spend it on college stuff. But it's my money. I've got to see the GC before I get into the real world." He met Brandon's eyes. "To answer your question, Brandy, yes, I'm serious."

"All right," Justin said. "We'd go anywhere with you, but where do you think me and Brandon will get the money? My grandma wouldn't care if I go, but she's not gonna fork out the cash to pay for it."

"I've got a bit of money," Brandon said.

"No." Matt and Justin barked in unison.

Brandon used to work bagging groceries at the local store. Barry had taken most of his paycheck, saying it was his right to charge him rent. But Brandon had been able to stash away a bit of money without Barry's knowledge. He didn't have plans for it yet, but Brandon expected that someday it could help him get far away from Barry. Matt and Justin knew how hard he had worked. One day, Barry had passed out drunk just before Brandon's shift was due to start. Barry was his only way to the store, and missing work had cost Brandon his job.

Matt sighed. "You guys are downers. But you're right. I've heard my whole life that I need to be more realistic. I guess I just needed to hear it from you to believe it."

"Who knows?" Justin flicked the cigarette out the window. "Summer's not here yet. Maybe something will happen."

Matt put the car into drive and turned up the volume. A few minutes later, they pulled into Matt's assigned parking spot at the high school.

As they stepped out of the car, Justin fixed his eyes on Brandon. "You know you can't wear that coat anymore," he said in a hushed tone. "Plus, it's like eighty degrees out here."

Brandon shrugged and closed the car door. He looked Justin up and down, eyeing the spikes around his wrist and the JNCO jeans that nearly covered his shoes. "I'll let you know when I'm ready for your fashion advice." He slung his backpack onto a single shoulder.

As they approached the school doors, Brandon said, "At least it's Friday. What are we gonna do tonight?"

"You know I can't," Matt said.

"Right," Brandon said, deflated. "Basketball game." Matt was first trumpeter in the school band. None of the trio enjoyed sports, but the school band was expected at all of the home games.

Brandon turned to Justin. "Wanna ride the bus to my place? Since it's Friday, Barry will be going to the bar after work, so you can probably stay till nine or so."

"Sweet," Justin said. A few years ago, Justin's parents had gotten themselves into financial trouble. Their solution? Leave Justin and his sister at Grandma's house indefinitely, which didn't bother Justin, since he never had a good relationship with his parents. His grandma didn't care what he was up to, so long as he checked in with her once in a while. Instead of resenting his parents, Justin was grateful for the freedom their bad decisions gave him.

"You ready for the first day of the rest of our lives?" Brandon teased. Matt rolled his eyes and pushed open the school door.

Brandon had forgotten about the upcoming basketball game, but clearly, his fellow students hadn't. The school team had made it to the championships, which was apparently a big deal. The halls were full of green and white decorations—the school colors. Streamers hung from the ceiling. Many of the students wore specially printed shirts to celebrate the day. Brandon felt like he had to wash himself of all the school spirit in the air. He opened his locker, and something smacked him in the back of the head. As he turned, he saw a half-eaten apple fall to the ground.

"Don't forget to have three servings of fruit a day!" A burst of laughter came from across the hall. It was Cody, the star basketball player, with a few others of his kind: preps.

Brandon turned back to his locker, trying to ignore the bullies.

"Oh no, Cody, he's going to fetch his book of spells!" one of the preps said, which earned another round of laughter.

Brandon looked farther up the hall and spotted Principal Vernon. The commotion caught the principal's attention, and he looked directly at Brandon. Cody ducked out of view.

"Mr. Bason," Principal Vernon called.

Brandon swore under his breath.

"Meet me in my office, please."

"Yes, sir." Brandon slunk back to the front of the school. He cursed himself for being so careless. He had told himself over and over to watch out for Vernon. The teachers wouldn't care so much, as the policy about trench coats was still new—the result of a nationwide attempt to make schools safer after a school shooting in Colorado had rattled the world less than a month prior.

Not sure why this makes the school safer, Brandon thought. *It doesn't make me safer.* But Mr. Vernon was a stickler for policies.

The front office was bustling with activity. Brandon stood, hands in pockets, waiting. "Morning. How may I help you?" one of the receptionists asked.

"I'm here to see Mr. Vernon."

"You can go in." She gestured toward the principal's office door. "I'm sure he'll be with you in a moment." She turned to assist another student.

Brandon stepped in, and the door *clicked* closed behind him. He sat down and waited. The bell for first block rang. *Great,* he thought. *Now I'm late.*

After a few minutes, the principal stepped in. Tall and balding, with a sandy mustache decorating his upper lip, Mr. Vernon had a kindly but authoritative air about him. He didn't acknowledge Brandon's presence right away. He sat down at his desk and rubbed his eyes beneath his glasses.

"Brandon..." Principal Vernon began. He met Brandon's gaze and breathed heavily out of his nose. "I know it's been tough for you since your mother...well, for the past couple of years. I don't want to make things harder for you. But you know the new policy about trench coats. No exceptions."

Brandon sighed. "Yes, sir."

"You're a good young man, Brandon. I don't want your circumstances to convince you otherwise. More importantly, I don't want to see you throw your own future down the drain. I'm not sure why you think the rules don't apply to you. I'm going to have to ask you to hand over your coat."

Brandon sighed again. For a moment, he just sat there. Then, slowly, he removed the dark gray—almost black—coat. Underneath, he wore a black t-shirt.

Mr. Vernon extended his hand over his desk. Brandon reached to pass the coat to him. The principal grabbed it and then paused, seeing Brandon's arms. He sat back down, coat in hand. "You want to talk about that?"

"No, sir."

"In confidence," Mr. Vernon assured. "You're safe in here."

Brandon shook his head and looked down.

Mr. Vernon stood up and walked to the office closet. He hung Brandon's coat on a hanger and closed the door. "I'm sorry, Brandon, but I'm going to have to keep this until after graduation. These are the superintendent's rules, not mine. You're lucky she hasn't put a uniform policy in place yet."

Brandon sat, motionless.

"Just a moment," Mr. Vernon said. Then, he stepped out of the office. Through the receptionist's window, Brandon watched Mr. Vernon as he walked out of the main office and exited the school. When he came back in, he handed Brandon a sweater. "Look, I know it's not goth—or metal—or whatever your look is called. But it's probably better than nothing."

Mr. Vernon was right. Walking out of the office in just a t-shirt in Brandon's state was like throwing a steak to the dogs. The preps, who always seemed to have perfect lives, targeted those who didn't look, dress, or talk just like them. Apparently, making other people's lives worse made the preps' lives better.

Brandon took the sweater with pursed lips, then slowly put it on. It smelled old. On second thought, he wondered if he would be better without it. But the act of compassion was not lost on Brandon. Standing awkwardly in the oversized, scratchy sweater, he mustered a weak smile of thanks. The principal, back behind his desk, was busying himself with some papers and didn't appear to catch it.

"You're free to go, Mr. Bason. And remember," he added, "you can always talk to me if you feel like it."

For the rest of the day, Brandon made sure he was more careful. Avoiding the preps was usually harder than avoiding the principal, but with the basketball game on everyone's mind, he was able to finish the day without incident.

He headed out the school's front doors after the final bell. Justin and Matt were hanging out near bus number five. As Brandon approached, Justin raised his eyebrows. "What kind of fashion statement is that?"

"Shut it," Brandon retorted.

"Vernon take your coat?"

Brandon huffed.

"Told ya."

"Actually," Brandon began, "this *is* a fashion statement. I call it 'The Burnin Vernon.' Whatcha think?" Brandon mocked a catwalk and turned around.

"Hmm..." Matt touched his chin, playing the ever-critical judge. The three cracked up.

"Ditch the game tonight," Brandon tried to coax Matt.

"Wish I could. But there's no way. Not this close to the end of the year. Mr. Renkins would have my head. And I've got to keep up my grades. Check it out." He held up a piece of paper for Brandon and Justin to see. "SAT scores are in." He had made 1450.

"And that's good, right?" Brandon didn't mean to be insensitive. Growing up, Matt was always the brainy one.

"Good?!" he responded. "That means if I can keep up my GPA, I should be able to get a full scholarship to UC!"

Justin let out a sigh. "It'll be a bummer when you're in Chicago." He leaned against the bus and looked away.

"I know. But it would be nice to have the support of my two best friends," Matt said.

The bus driver sounded her horn for the two-minute warning.

"You've got it, man," Brandon said. He looked Matt in the eyes. He admired his friend. In reality, Matt was his hero. Smart and musically talented, he was also down to earth. He never let his abilities get to his head. Matt had everything going for him. Despite struggling financially, his parents were always supportive, and he had a great future to embrace. Brandon was not about to stifle any of that. "For real. We support you," he said. "I mean, it will be a bummer not having you around. But besides the Grand Canyon, we know this college has been on your radar since forever."

The three were silent for a moment. "That just means we need to make the best of this summer," Brandon said. "One last summer of shenanigans before you become Mr. College Boy, and Justin and me become, well, whatever we become."

"Thanks, guys. This summer's gonna rock. GC-bound! Right?" Matt smiled, waiting for an answer.

"Sure, dude. Whatever you say," Justin said.

"You never know," Brandon said.

"That's what I'm talking about! Here," Matt said, pulling off his backpack and setting it on the ground. He retrieved a tattered folder and handed it to Brandon. "You guys look it over tonight. Tell me what you think tomorrow. You'll be convinced we have to do this."

Although Brandon and Justin had seen this folder dozens of

times over the years, this was the first time Matt had encouraged them to look at it, let alone given it to them. It was thick in Brandon's hands. The front cover used to have an abstract galaxy printed on it, but most of it had been scratched or rubbed off from use. The words "GC-BOUND" were written in permanent marker below "MATTHEW STEELE."

"Sure," Brandon said, placing the folder into his own backpack.

"See ya tomorrow," Matt said.

"Tomorrow!" Justin held out his fist. The other two bumped theirs to it at the same time.

"The first day—" Matt began.

"—of the rest of our lives," Brandon and Justin finished together. They stepped onto the bus, while Matt walked back toward the school.

The driveway was empty when Brandon and Justin arrived at Brandon's house. Relieved, they went inside and threw their bags into Brandon's room. While there, Brandon paused to consider whether or not to keep wearing Mr. Vernon's sweater. After a moment, he shed it and threw it onto his backpack. He then remembered Matt's folder, making a mental note that he and Justin should look over it to humor Matt. Otherwise, they would have nothing to say when Matt asked about it tomorrow. Brandon went to the kitchen and made some popcorn. Then, he and Justin plopped onto the couch in front of the TV, hoping to find a horror film.

An hour or two later, Brandon looked at the clock. "After this movie, remind me I've gotta make Barry's dinner."

"I thought you said he'd be out late tonight."

"He will. But if he happens to be hungry when he comes

home, so help me if I don't have dinner ready. I guess I'll make some patty melts. Want one too?"

"Sure. Thanks."

"Man, Matt's been working hard lately," Brandon said.

"It feels like we haven't seen him much at all."

"He really wants us to be happy for him, you know."

"I am," Justin said. "I guess I should say it more. I just get upset when he starts talking about college stuff. I still have no idea what I'm gonna do after graduation. He's got his whole life figured out."

"Yeah..." Brandon trailed off, his attention fixed on the gory scene playing out on the TV.

Brandon's reminder to make Barry's dinner never came. Hours after the movie had finished, both of them were sound asleep on the couch. Brandon started awake at the sound of a car pulling into the driveway. "Get up!" He slapped Justin on the shoulder, who scurried to Brandon's room.

"He'll probably pass out soon," Brandon called to Justin. "You can head out the back door then."

Brandon ran to the kitchen, leaving the TV on. He turned on the stove and dug around the freezer for the frozen patties. *Brandon, you idiot! First Mr. Vernon, now Barry!*

There was a knock at the door. *Strange,* Brandon thought. *Why would Barry knock?* Another knock. He looked at the clock. Nearly eleven. He closed the freezer and approached the door.

He opened it and saw a police officer and another man standing on the doorstep. "Brandon Bason?" asked the officer.

"Yes, sir..."

"Are you Barry Sharp's son?"

"Stepson."

Brandon's mind raced. Had Vernon contacted the police

after seeing Brandon's arms? What would Barry do to him when he found out?

"Brandon, my name is Officer Schaefer. I'm with the Davidson County Police Department. I am sorry about the late hour. There's been an accident. We need to talk to you. It might be best if we come in and discuss it."

Brandon felt a rush of relief. *An accident,* he repeated in his mind, moving aside to let the two men in. He gestured toward the dining table. He turned off the stove and sat down at the table too.

"Is Barry okay?" Brandon asked the officer.

"He'll be fine," he answered.

Brandon didn't know how he felt about that answer. Disappointed? He met the eyes of the other man, who gave a gentle smile in return. He was much younger than the police officer—maybe in his twenties—with brown hair and a face covered in freckles. Brandon gathered he wasn't a police officer himself, since he wore a bright orange button-down shirt, instead of a uniform. Brandon looked back at Officer Schaefer. "So, what happened?"

"Nearly two hours ago, your father—"

"Stepfather," Brandon corrected.

"Right. Your stepfather caused an accident in the middle of town. A few people were injured, and it looks like one person has died. Barry was intoxicated, and he's been taken into police custody. By the look of things, he's going to be locked away for a long time."

Barry's killed someone again? Brandon thought. As horrible as it was, Brandon couldn't help but think of his luck. "How long?" he asked.

"Typically, there would need to be a trial—and there will be. He'll appear before a judge soon. But all of the witnesses' stories are the same, and even Barry eventually confessed to being at fault. He will most likely be convicted and receive the full punishment of the law, which means it could be several years before he's released."

Brandon started thinking of what life would be like free of Barry, subconsciously moving his tongue between his bottom lip and gums. He knew he should feel bad. People had been hurt because of Barry—nothing new about that—and one person was dead. Still, Brandon couldn't help it. He felt justice had finally come. Whatever the cost, Brandon was free. Barry couldn't hurt people anymore. He couldn't hurt him anymore.

It was Barry's fault Brandon's mother had died two years ago. Brandon was the one who had found her. She was meant to pick him up after school, since none of his friends had their driver's licenses yet. When she didn't come, Brandon had walked home, opening the door to an eerie silence. She lay motionless in the middle of the living room floor. That image still haunted him in his dreams at times. The coroner had officially labeled it a suicide, claiming there were drugs in her system. Brandon knew his mother would never do that to him. She would never have left Brandon alone in Barry's custody. No, whatever the truth was, Brandon knew if Barry had never entered the picture, his mom would still be alive to take care of him. And now, justice had finally been served.

Officer Schaefer broke Brandon's train of thought. "Brandon, this is Ronald Fitzgerald." Officer Schaefer was talking about the man who had come with him.

Ronald extended his hand toward Brandon. Brandon shook it. Ronald looked down, noticing the bruises on Brandon's arm. Brandon snatched his hand away and crossed his arms over his chest.

Officer Schaefer continued. "We have on record that you're seventeen years old. Is that right, Brandon?"

"Yes, sir. I turn eighteen in July."

"The reason I brought Ronald with me is—"

Justin entered the room. Brandon had forgotten about him.

He must have figured out it wasn't Barry who had pulled into the driveway.

"Oh, this is my friend Justin," Brandon told the visitors.

"Good evening," Officer Schaefer said.

"And now for our eleven o'clock news..." the TV blared in the background. "A car accident caused by a drunk driver has left two people hospitalized and one local high school senior dead."

"Could you please turn that off for us?" Officer Schaefer asked Justin.

The news anchor continued. "Julie is on the scene. Julie?"

Justin moved toward the TV in the living room and froze. He looked at Brandon, horrified.

"What?" Brandon asked, stepping into the living room. He glanced at the TV. A 1988 beige Chrysler New Yorker lay mangled in the middle of an intersection.

Matt's 1988 beige Chrysler New Yorker.

CHAPTER TWO

Brandon melted to his knees. Officer Schaefer stood up.

"Are you okay, son?"

"Who was it that died in that car accident tonight?" Brandon asked, stone-faced.

"I've not been informed yet," he replied.

Brandon looked back at the TV, his mind numb. The report was already over, and they were showing highlights from the basketball game that night.

"Was it..." Justin trailed off. "Can you find out who it was?" he asked the police officer.

"I wouldn't have the authority to tell you—"

"Please, can you just find out?" Brandon pressed.

The officer peered into Brandon's horrified eyes before saying, "Give me a moment." He stepped outside. Brandon could hear him speaking into his radio.

Ronald rose from his seat and walked over to Brandon and Justin in the living room. He crouched down and put a hand on Brandon's shoulder.

Brandon put his head in his hands, trying to make sense of the night's news. First, Barry was going away, freeing Brandon of any future pain and abuse. Justice would finally be served. But at what cost? Justin was motionless, his face pale. Brandon looked up at Ronald, who still had a hand on his shoulder. "Why are you here?"

Ronald removed his hand and apologized.

"I mean," Brandon continued, "why did you come here with the police officer?"

"Oh. Right. Well, seeing that your legal guardian would no longer be able to take care of you, I was sent to inform you what the next steps are. I work for Child Services." Ronald looked at Brandon's arms again.

Brandon felt the urge to hide, the image on the TV screen etched into his mind as a freeze-frame. *Was that really Matt's car? Surely there are more cars like his out there. What did the reporter say? "High school senior..."* He tried to visualize the parking lot at school on a regular school day. Who else had a beige car? The front door opened. Officer Schaefer stepped in. Brandon stood and turned toward him, pleading for answers with his eyes.

"Why did you ask me who was killed?" Officer Schaefer asked Justin.

"The car on the TV—it looked like our best friend's car. Matthew Steele," Justin said, voice cracking.

"I am not able to confirm anything until the family has been informed," the officer said, but his face said it all. "I'm so sorry, boys."

Brandon felt dizzy. This couldn't be happening. What did this mean? He thought back to the momentary relief he'd felt at the news that Barry had done something to get himself locked away. Guilt started pricking his heart, and his legs buckled beneath him. Then, he was on his knees again. Panic-stricken, he tried to control his breathing.

After a few moments, Officer Schaefer and Ronald gently lifted him to his feet. "Justin," Officer Schaefer began, "where do you live?"

Justin blinked and swallowed. "Not far from here."

"What were you doing here tonight?"

"Just hanging out. It's Friday night."

"Is everything okay at home? Are your parents there?"

Justin nodded. "Me and my sister live with our grandma."

"Let me call her. Do you think you two can stay there tonight?"

While Officer Schaefer used Brandon's house phone to call Ms. Sanders, Brandon went back to his room to put on Vernon's sweater. Afterward, he got into the back of the police car with Justin. Brandon was dazed during the short drive to Justin's house.

They pulled into the driveway. Officer Schaefer walked Justin and Brandon to the front door, Ronald in their wake. Justin's grandma was waiting for them. She hugged Justin and then met Brandon's eyes. "I'm so sorry about Barry," she whispered. Letting Justin go, she stepped aside. "Come in. Jessica's in bed."

"Thank you, ma'am," Officer Schaefer said. He motioned for everyone else to go in first. "I know it's late," he said to Ms. Sanders. "These boys have had a rough night, especially Brandon. Ronald and I still need to speak with him. Is there a place we can do so?"

"Of course." She poured three glasses of water and put them on the dining table. Ronald asked her a few questions and wrote something on a clipboard. Then, Ms. Sanders and Justin went upstairs.

Officer Schaefer, Ronald, and Brandon sat down. "You must have a lot of questions for us," Officer Schaefer said. "You should be able to visit Barry tomorrow."

Brandon pulled the sleeves of the principal's sweater down further. "I don't want to visit him."

"All right," Officer Schaefer said. "In that case, you take it from here, Ronald."

"Brandon," Ronald began, "is it true you have no living grandparents?"

"Both my mother's parents died years ago. I don't even know who my father's parents were." Brandon spoke slowly and quietly with unfocused eyes.

"No aunts or uncles?"

"Not that I know of."

"We have had a file on you since your mother's death. I am so sorry for what you've been through in the past couple of years."

Still dizzy from the roller coaster evening, Brandon took a deep breath as he tried to process the emotions of the past couple of hours—the fear that Barry had come home and caught Brandon asleep, the thrill that Barry was going to prison, the horror of the sight of Matt's mangled car. Brandon could hear the sound of the reporter's voice and how she had announced Matt's death as if it were just a part of her job: "... one local high school senior dead." *Matt...is...dead,* Brandon thought to himself. *Barry...killed...Matt.* Brandon's cheeks flushed in anger.

Ronald was still talking about something. Brandon considered telling Officer Schaefer he had changed his mind; he did want to visit Barry. He had never been punished for his crimes against Brandon's mother. He likely didn't even know it was Matt he had killed tonight. *Would he even care?* Brandon imagined giving Barry the news and watching him shrivel in shame and remorse. But then Brandon shrunk from the idea. Barry never felt sorry for hurting others. Instead, he would find a way to humiliate Brandon. And once again, Brandon's fear of his stepdad would paralyze him; he would be caught in his snare—same old story.

"It's not an orphanage," Ronald said.

Brandon snapped back to reality. "Uh, what?"

"It's not an orphanage, Brandon. It's just a home for boys

until you turn eighteen and can find your own place," Ronald repeated.

"What's not an orphanage?"

"The home you'll be staying in, Brandon," Ronald said. We can complete the paperwork tomorrow. It's called Grand Junction Home for Boys."

"What? Why can't I just stay at home? I'll be eighteen in a couple of months."

"We understand, Brandon," Officer Schaefer said. "We know you're not a child. For the most part, we know you can make your own decisions. But there are laws—"

"Maybe I can stay here?" Brandon offered.

"That is possible," Ronald said. "But that's something that takes time. Now that you have no legal guardian who can take care of you, and you have no next of kin, there would be some lengthy steps to take to put you under a new official guardian. By the time those steps were completed, you'd likely be of age anyway. Grand Junction is already in our system and has a vacancy."

Brandon huffed and clenched his fists beneath the table. He turned away from the men.

"And as I said, it's not an orphanage," Ronald repeated. "It's an actual home with a few other boys in similar situations. Mr. and Mrs. Jenson will see you through graduation and help you get on your feet."

"Do we have to talk about this tonight?" Brandon asked.

"I'm afraid so," said Officer Schaefer.

"But we're almost done," said Ronald. "We can come at ten tomorrow morning to take you back to your house to get some belongings. Then, we'll take you to Grand Junction."

Brandon was silent for a moment. "And I have no say in this?" He looked at Officer Schaefer.

"Unless you have any other family, then, no."

"I think you'll like the Jensons," Ronald said. "You'll still be in

East Nashville. Finding a home in the same school district is normally unheard of, but you lucked out. I know it probably doesn't sound that way." He smiled gently. "It's just until you can establish yourself, and we will help with that too. Now, get some rest. We know it's been a long night."

Officer Schaefer and Ronald stood up, their water glasses untouched. They bid Brandon goodnight and let themselves out. It was past one in the morning, and Brandon was exhausted. As he dragged himself up the stairs, the weight of the day pressed down on him.

Noticing Justin's light was still on, Brandon inched the door open to find Ms. Sanders sitting on the bed, stroking Justin's hair. He was asleep. Brandon guessed Justin had told Ms. Sanders about Matt. She stood and gave Brandon an apologetic look before asking, "Need anything?" She had made a pallet for him next to Justin's bed.

Brandon shook his head. He wanted to thank Ms. Sanders, but his throat was constricting. Knowing he would break if he spoke, he simply looked her in the eye and managed a grateful smile. She smiled kindly and left the room.

Brandon slept like the dead, grateful for the few hours of escape from reality. Before he knew it, Ms. Sanders was waking him and Justin for breakfast. They said nothing to each other as they went downstairs and ate their pancakes, the only sound coming from the TV Justin's sister Jessica was watching in the living room.

Ms. Sanders broke their silence. "I'll be going to see Matt's parents this afternoon. It would be good for you to go with me."

Brandon looked at the clock. 9:40. Relieved, he said, "Sorry, Ms. Sanders. I'm getting picked up in twenty minutes."

"I'll go," said Justin.

Brandon remembered the visitors who had come to see him after his mom died. They were pitiful. They treated him like a baby and said things like, "Everything happens for a reason," and "God just needed another angel." *What's that supposed to mean, anyway?* Brandon thought. *Did God need her more than me? Does God need Matt too?* He subconsciously narrowed his eyes. *You can keep your needy God! Don't bring him around me,* he said to those people in his mind. If those people actually cared for him, they would have stuck around. He hadn't seen them since the funeral, when they had left Brandon in Barry's hulking shadow. Even his mom's best friend, Genevieve, had vanished from his life.

Brandon was still wearing Mr. Vernon's sweater when Officer Schaefer and Ronald came. He thanked Ms. Sanders, then slipped out of the house and got into the car. The ride to his house was quiet, which was fine with Brandon; he wasn't in the mood for any small talk.

When they arrived at Brandon's house, Officer Schaefer pulled two empty suitcases from the trunk and offered them to Brandon. "Personal items only please. Someone else is taking care of Barry's things. You'll have a chance after a few weeks to gather the rest of your belongings. We will wait out here."

Brandon grabbed one of the suitcases and entered the house alone, the stillness making his pulse quicken. Reminded that Barry wasn't home—and possibly would never be coming home —Brandon resisted the temptation to flex his freedom by stomping through the house and slamming cabinet doors. The urge disappeared when Brandon saw the TV—a reminder of the previous night's newscast.

Brandon made his way to his bedroom. It was dark in there, just like always. He had never owned curtains; instead, his mom had hung sheets over the windows years ago. Sheets were not as easy as curtains to move back and forth, so he always left them covering the windows. Still, a bit of sunlight peeked through, giving Brandon enough light to see.

His backpack on the bed caught his attention. Unzipping it, he took out Matt's folder and peered at Matt's name on the front. He lay the folder on the blanket and opened it. A map folded accordion-style extended toward him. Matt had cleverly turned his folder into a pop-up book. Still, the map needed to be manually unfolded twice more, making it eight times the size of the folder as it spread across the bed; it was a map of the United States. A bold red line traced a route from Nashville to the Grand Canyon, with different cities along the way highlighted and marked with numbers. Four pockets were glued onto the map, and Brandon noticed each pocket had numbers on it: "1–3"; "4–6"; "7–9"; and "10–12." He opened the first one and pulled out a postcard. It was labeled "1." "JACKSON, TENNESSEE" was scrolled across the front, with a photo of a steam engine train at a place called Casey Jones Village. He turned it over and read a hand-written note.

> *Dear Matt,*
>
> *Thanks for your letter. I'm happy to oblige! Here's your postcard. We hope you'll turn in and visit us on your way to the Grand Canyon!*

It was signed by the mayor of Jackson. Brandon pulled out the rest of the contents of the first pocket—a couple of smaller maps and two more postcards. Each postcard had a number, which corresponded with a city highlighted on the map. He opened the next pocket and discovered the same thing. Some of the postcards had dates going back several years to when Matt, Justin, and Brandon were in middle school. Another pang of guilt stung him. Brandon and Justin had never truly known how serious Matt was about the trip to the Grand Canyon. Thinking back, it should have been clearer to them. But Brandon never took the time to ask about it or to share in Matt's excitement. Matt had been Brandon's hero. Did Matt know that? What must Brandon have been to Matt? *Some friend, huh?*

He stuffed the contents back into the pockets and carefully

folded the map. The creases were well worn, reinforced with tape in several spots; it must have been folded and unfolded hundreds of times. He closed the folder and put it into his backpack.

Looking around at his meager possessions, Brandon wondered what he should take. He pulled some clothes out of his dresser and unceremoniously stuffed them into the suitcase, then packed some toiletries. The single suitcase was still half empty. But there was one more thing. Lifting his mattress, he grabbed the envelope that had his cash in it, then walked out of the house with his backpack and the suitcase. He opened the door to the car and didn't look back.

CHAPTER THREE

THEY HAD TO DRIVE PAST THE HIGH SCHOOL TO GET TO GRAND Junction. It was a Saturday, so the campus was empty. Brandon could see where the bus was parked yesterday—the last place he had spoken with Matt. What would Brandon have said or done differently if he had known at that moment that it was the last time he would ever see his friend? Brandon averted his gaze, his mind and body still numb from the shock of last night. A few minutes later, they pulled up in front of a white two-story house. It looked like it was pulled straight from a storybook, with its white picket fence and perfect siding.

A middle-aged couple came out to meet them as they got out of the car. "You must be Brandon," the woman said. She was tall and pretty with long, brown hair. "I'm Mrs. Jenson," she continued warmly, extending her hand, "and this is Mr. Jenson."

Mr. Jenson was shorter than Brandon. His hair was graying, as was his trimmed beard. "Come inside, bud."

He ushered them in, explaining that the rest of the residents were out doing various things, but Brandon would meet them all later.

"There are six bedrooms," Mrs. Jenson said. "Yours is the second one on the right." She gestured up the stairs.

Brandon went to his room while Officer Schaefer, Ronald, and the Jensons stayed downstairs discussing things.

The door to his room was ajar. He tentatively opened it. A bed, flanked by a nightstand, was made up for him with neatly ironed sheets. In the corner stood a dresser. It was basic but comfortable.

Brandon sat on his unfamiliar bed, motionless and replaying the past twenty-four hours in his mind. His suitcase remained closed.

He lifted the sleeve of Mr. Vernon's sweater, eyeing his bruises; they were still there, although the pain wasn't as sharp when he pressed on them. The yelling the other night had started when Barry had complained about the taste of dinner. Brandon said he had done the best he could. Drunk, as usual, Barry had seen that as talking back. Soon, the yelling turned into a backhand, and Barry dragging Brandon to his room for the night. Brandon didn't fight back. He never even resisted. He knew it would just cause more pain, his slender frame nothing compared with the mass of Barry's.

He felt drained sitting on the bed, although he had hardly done anything all morning other than come to this place. He wondered if Justin had gone to Matt's house yet. Before he knew it, Brandon lay down and drifted off to sleep.

He woke to a gentle knock. "Brandon?" It was Mrs. Jenson.

Brandon sat up and rubbed his eyes. The daylight in the room had shifted to a warm orange while he slept.

"Dinner's almost ready."

Brandon hadn't eaten since breakfast. He was hungry but not interested in being with people, except Justin. For some reason, though, he felt no urge to talk to him. What would he say?

"Are you coming?" Mrs. Jenson's voice was gentle, which

must come with a job of dealing with orphans. "It's okay if you're not hungry—"

"Yes, ma'am," Brandon said wearily, picking himself off the bed and following her downstairs.

The dining table was full of food and surrounded by mostly unfamiliar faces. There were a couple of boys Brandon recognized from his own school, but he had never talked to them before. He hoped they didn't recognize him. Dinner was accompanied by small talk and chatter about the other boys' days. Keeping his head down and avoiding eye contact, Brandon quickly got his point across that he wasn't interested in talking just yet.

After dinner, Mrs. Jenson took Brandon to the family room. She filled him in on the conversation with Officer Schaefer and Ronald. Counseling would be available for Brandon the following week if he felt he needed it. In the meantime, she gently explained, she or Mr. Jenson were always available to listen. Brandon sensed she was genuine, and although he didn't show it, he was grateful. She also laid out the house rules. All of the kids were sixteen or seventeen, so they were granted quite a bit of freedom. They were expected to work hard in school, but if the schoolwork was done, they could come and go as they pleased. A few of them had after-school jobs. Curfew was 9pm.

Back in his room later that night, he heard Mr. Jenson calling him. "You've got a phone call, Brandon." He went downstairs and picked up the receiver. It was Justin.

"How did you get this number?" Brandon asked.

"That Ronald guy gave it to me. He said something about supporting each other." He paused. "So, how's it going?"

Brandon told him about his new arrangements, then asked about Justin's day.

"It was so sad at Matt's house," Justin said. "Nobody knew what to say. We just sat there for like a half-hour saying nothing. The funeral is on Tuesday. They want us to be pallbearers. I told them we'd do it."

Brandon had been a pallbearer for his mom's funeral. The casket had been a lot heavier than he had first expected, but he had mustered his strength to show Mom how tough he was. Thinking back, it was a bit childish. What a hypocrite he was. At school, he was pushed around. At home, he was a wimp. But among the dead, he was tough.

There was silence on the phone for a minute. "You'll do it, right?" Justin asked.

"Yeah."

More silence.

"Well, I guess I'll let you go," Justin finally said.

"Okay."

Brandon went back to his room. It was nice of his friend to call, but he still wasn't in the mood for talking. What was there to say? *Sorry my stepdad killed Matt, who had his whole life ahead of him and never even got the chance to see the Grand Canyon...* His backpack lay on the floor. He wondered when he could show Matt's folder to Justin. Lying down, he closed his eyes. Tears rolled down into his pillow before he drifted off into a fitful sleep.

The following day, Ronald showed up to talk to the Jensons. He had worked it out so Brandon could be excused from school for the next two days—Monday and Tuesday. The Jensons agreed to drive Brandon to the funeral on Tuesday. Ronald had also explained there would be an assembly at school on Wednesday to honor Matt, and he thought it important for Brandon to be there.

Brandon wondered what Justin was up to, but he couldn't find the energy to call him. Justin didn't call Brandon either. But

Brandon knew Justin had his grandma and sister. Who did Brandon have? He kept a low profile, emerging from his room only at mealtimes, until Tuesday morning.

Tuesday finally came, gray and rainy—fitting, as far as Brandon was concerned. Mr. Jenson had organized a suit rental for Brandon for the funeral.

When they pulled up to the small church, Brandon noticed a graveyard behind the building. A tent stood over a freshly dug grave. He was expected at the church early to be filled in on his role as a pallbearer. Mr. Jenson offered Brandon an umbrella, but he declined. What difference did it make if he got wet? They entered the building, making it Brandon's second time in a church. The first, of course, was for his mom's funeral two years ago. Walking into the foyer, Brandon saw the pulpit in the front, which seemed large for such a modest building. Next to it was a closed casket. The rows of pews stood empty except for one. Justin sat on the front pew next to Ms. Sanders and Jessica. Brandon wanted to join them, but Mr. Jenson motioned for Brandon to come with him to talk to a man standing on the far side of the foyer.

After receiving pallbearer instructions, Brandon excused himself and went toward the front of the church. Ms. Sanders gave him a weak smile. He sat down awkwardly next to Justin. Neither of them said anything to each other.

"Come on," Ms. Sanders whispered to Jessica. The two got up, leaving Brandon and Justin alone.

"Know what you're supposed to do?" Justin asked.

"I've done it before."

Justin grunted.

Then, it was quiet again. Brandon swallowed. His throat was constricted, and he felt oddly uncomfortable next to his friend, despite their long history. Although Justin was usually considered the "quiet one" at school, when it was just the three of them, conversation had always flowed easily. *Three is down to two now.*

Brandon studied the casket—satin black with wooden accents. His mom's casket had been open. The car accident must have damaged Matt badly for them to have kept his closed. Still, he wanted to see his friend. Maybe it would help him come to grips with reality. Seeing his mom's cheekbones unnaturally jutting out of her face, her motionless chest, her folded hands—it had made it real to him.

People started entering the church, and Brandon straightened up. He watched the preacher step behind the pulpit. As far as he knew, Matt's family never went to church. This guy probably just came with the funeral package. He stood silently, looking toward the back of the building as if waiting on something. Brandon was shocked to see the room quickly filling up. He noticed a few people his own age, likely relatives excused from school for the funeral. Soon, the church, which could have perhaps held two hundred people, was full. People folded their umbrellas and continued coming in from the foyer.

With standing room only, the preacher began. He started talking about death, calling it a mystery. Brandon found it hard to focus, the image of Matt's twisted car invading his thoughts. He remembered the last moments he'd had with Matt at the bus stop. *This is the first day of the rest of our lives...* Stricken, Brandon began to silently cry, as he knew his friend's goals would go forever unmet.

The preacher held up a Bible and said something about God and heaven. Brandon felt the heat rise into his cheeks. He cursed God. *If God actually cared, he would have left Matt alone,* he thought. *Why didn't he just take Barry instead?*

Soon there was an opportunity for close friends and family members to get up and say something. The family probably expected Brandon and Justin to participate, but the two remained seated. Matt's dad choked a few things out. So did a couple of other relatives.

Afterward, Brandon and Justin followed their instructions, lining up in front of the casket with the family and the rest of the pallbearers. As people passed them, Brandon could hear their pitiful words of sympathy all over again: "It must have been God's plan." "Everything happens for a reason."

After what seemed like an eternity, Brandon took his post next to the casket. Together, the six guys carried it out the side doors of the church, the rest of the family following closely behind. The rain had eased, but it was still coming down in drizzles. Brandon and Justin were at the back of the casket, Matt's lifeless body suspended between them. Brandon could see that Justin was focused on his task, a vein in his neck bulging.

They turned the casket toward the churchyard. Staring straight ahead, Brandon noticed someone already out there, standing next to a large oak tree. When she saw the funeral procession, she dodged behind the tree, but not before Brandon recognized her. *Aunt Genni?* Brandon hadn't seen her since before his mom's death. She never even checked in on him. She couldn't even be bothered to attend his mom's funeral. *What is she doing here?*

Distracted, Brandon slipped on some mud, nearly losing his footing. The entire casket jolted, and the others struggled to keep it steady. A couple of the guys in front glared back at him. He regained his balance and gave an apologetic look, breathing a sigh of relief that disaster had been averted.

Brandon shook his head to get back on task. Still, his mind drifted. *Why is Aunt Genni here?* he asked himself. She only knew Matt as Brandon's childhood friend. She wasn't close to anyone in Matt's family, as far as he knew. *And why is she sneaking around?* Brandon decided it didn't matter. He had more important things to think about.

They approached the massive hole in the ground. There was a machine that had green straps across the grave. The pallbearers carefully placed the casket onto the straps and backed away.

As the graveside service was intended only for close family and friends, the tent easily covered all who were there. The preacher said a few more words. Then, a machine began unrolling the straps, which lowered the casket into the hole. Once it was at the bottom, the preacher grabbed a handful of dirt and threw it onto the casket—the beginning of a complete burial.

After the service, there was silent hugging as the mourners dispersed, heading to their cars. Brandon shuffled over to Matt's parents. Did they know it was Barry who killed their son? Of course they did. That's why he'd avoided saying anything to them all day. How could he face them as the stepson of the man who had killed their son? He stood in front of them and met Mr. Steele's eyes. Neither of Matt's parents was crying. Brandon recalled the numbness he'd felt at his mother's funeral; like he was watching events unfold, but not processing them. He wondered whether Mr. or Mrs. Steele had yet to accept what had happened to their son.

Brandon saw Matt's blue eyes staring back at him. He steadied himself against the sudden surge of grief. He looked at Mrs. Steele, who forced a smile. *Say something,* Brandon told himself. *But what?* He searched his mind for anything that seemed right, but he came up blank. He considered things others had said to him in his grief. Thankfully, he stopped himself before any of that came out of his mouth. In the end, he simply said, "I'm sorry for your loss."

Mr. Steele gave a curt nod and patted Brandon awkwardly on the shoulder. "I know, son," he managed to choke out. "You were a good friend to Matt."

Brandon stood there, tears welling up unexpectedly, before smiling weakly and muttering, "I guess I'll see you around."

He turned and stepped out from under the tent into the rain, welcoming the drizzle. The silence that had descended on his life since Friday night threatened to suffocate him. He watched Justin approach his grandma's car. His friend had barely said a word to him. Did Justin somehow blame him? Brandon didn't know what to think. Friends were meant to support each other during times like these, but that didn't seem to be the case today. *Give it time*, Brandon thought. No, he didn't want to give it time. He needed a friend right now.

Brandon was about to call out to him when someone grabbed his hand from behind. Brandon whipped around to see Genevieve's stricken face. Her dark olive skin was soaked. Her black hair that was usually kinked in thousands of tiny, unruly curls was plastered against her head. He noticed a few streaks of gray, which hadn't been there the last time he had seen her. Crow's feet decorated the edges of her large, dark eyes.

"What are you doing here?" he asked her brusquely. She was a bit shorter than he was. He didn't remember that. He looked back at Justin, already getting into the car. He tried to move toward him, but Genevieve tugged on his hand to get his attention.

"I heard about all that happened," she said quietly in her southern accent.

"What do you care?" he said.

"I am so sorry about everything. I wanted to come earlier, but I knew that I wouldn't be able to see you at Grand Junction."

He cocked his head at her. "How do you know where I'm staying?"

"That doesn't matter. I came to give you something."

"Why can't you visit me there?"

"The restraining order," she said, hushed. She glanced around.

Brandon looked at her, puzzled. The rain began to run down his face.

She pulled on his hand. "Come."

Genevieve led Brandon to the oak tree she had been hiding behind earlier. She picked her jacket up off the ground, revealing a small wooden box.

"What restraining order?" Brandon said.

Genevieve looked deep into his eyes for a moment, searching for something. "You're upset with me."

Pain swelled in Brandon's heart. "Are you surprised?"

"No. But I'm wondering why."

"Let's see. Where have you been for the past two years? You were Mom's best friend. You helped raise me. Where were you when Mom died? Why didn't you come to her funeral? I needed you then!" He paused. "But I've needed you even more lately."

Genevieve closed her eyes and touched her temples. "Of course they wouldn't tell you. They insisted on treating you as a child. After all, you were only fifteen." She opened her eyes and looked back at him.

"What are you talking about?"

"There's more you need to know. You deserve to be mad at me—to hate me. But you also deserve to know why you should hate me. It's not for the reasons you think. Do you remember where I live?"

"Of course I do."

"Can you come to my house tonight? I'll fill you in."

"I don't know," Brandon said, running his fingers through his drenched hair. He looked past her to see Justin's family had left. He sighed.

She picked up the box from the ground and shoved it into Brandon's hands. "I'll see you tonight." Drops of rain fell to the ground as she shook out her jacket. "Don't tell the Grand Junction people." She peered around the tree once more, then raised the jacket over her head and slipped away.

Brandon looked down at the wooden box in his hands. It had a clasp holding it shut and two bronze hinges on the opposite side. A word had been etched on the top, faded but legible: "DEAN."

"Dean" was Brandon's middle name.

It had also been his father's first name.

CHAPTER FOUR

THE RIDE BACK TO GRAND JUNCTION PASSED IN SILENCE. MR. Jenson tried to engage Brandon in conversation, but he wasn't in the mood. The funeral didn't occupy his thoughts; his mind whirled from the unexpected meeting with Genevieve and the mysterious box bearing his father's name.

He didn't know his father; he had died before Brandon was born. His mom hadn't talked much about him, and Brandon had learned over the years it was best not to ask questions, although he was desperately curious. On the few occasions when Brandon mustered up the courage to ask, he could tell his mom still hadn't come to terms with the loss; she'd said it had been the worst thing that ever happened to her.

"What's that you got there?" Mr. Jenson broke Brandon's train of thought.

"I'm not sure, really," Brandon admitted. "Something from a friend." Instinctively, he pulled the suit jacket over the box, hiding it from view.

When they arrived, Brandon thanked Mr. Jenson and headed to his room to shed the soaked suit. After changing into new clothes, he picked up the box and sat on the bed. He still hadn't peeked inside. A strange reluctance came over him. He was curious, of course, but also hesitant to find out what lay hidden within. He examined the outside of the box; it had some weight to it. After sliding his fingertips across his father's name, he unlatched the clasp and opened it.

His mother's beautiful smiling face beamed back at him. The picture Brandon saw must have been taken years ago—perhaps before Brandon had been born, and before the stresses and strains of life could be read in the wrinkles on her face. Her strawberry blonde hair looked like it was freshly permed. Brandon couldn't recall her ever looking this happy as long as he had known her. She was held at the waist by a young man wearing an army uniform, whom Brandon judged to be just a little older than he was. His hair was jet black, just like Brandon's, although not as long. The young man bore an equally happy smile to Francine's under a nice, well-trimmed mustache. Around his neck was a pair of silver dog tags. Brandon had never seen a picture of his father, but he was sure this was him. The need for guessing vanished when he turned the photograph over and read the inscription.

My dearest Frankie,

Every moment we're apart will be torture to my soul. But I'll be back. Until then, let us count the minutes.

Your love forever,

Private Dean Bason

The date stamped on the back was November 29, 1980—exactly eight months before Brandon was born. He turned the photograph over again to look at it closer. His father's eyes were dark brown, just like his. Brandon had his mother's nose and mouth, but as he searched the young man's eyes—inscription or not—there was no question that he was staring into the eyes of his father.

He placed the photo on the bed and looked back into the box to find what he guessed must have been the same dog tags that his father wore in the photograph. He picked them up by the chain, and they *clinked* together. They hardly seemed used. Underneath his father's name and social security number, the dog tags read, "O Pos" and "CHRISTIAN."

Brandon looked up and exhaled. "O Pos" didn't make any sense to him. But he felt that final word in the back of his throat —"Christian." He didn't know whether to swallow or spit. He dropped the tags back into the box and raked his fingers through his hair. It was surprising enough to learn his father was in the military, but a *Christian*? Maybe personnel were forced to pick a religion.

Brandon thought back to what Genevieve had said at the graveyard. She had more to tell him, but he felt that had to do with her situation, not his father's history. Yet she was convinced he would come and see her after he'd opened the box. Brandon still seethed at having not seen her for the past two years. And of all places to show up, she came to Matt's grave to...to what? Simply give him this box? Why couldn't she have done this earlier? Genevieve didn't tell him how or when she had come across the box. Of course, not knowing the contents at the time, he didn't think to ask her. Why did she have it in the first place?

There was something else inside—something black. He reached for it.

"Brandon?" It was Mrs. Jenson. "Dinner's ready."

Brandon quickly replaced the contents and closed the lid, leaving the box on the bed as he went downstairs. Questions continued to swirl in Brandon's mind while he wolfed down his dinner. He looked at the clock. 5:30pm.

"Mr. Jenson?" Brandon spoke up.

"Yes?"

"Would you be able to drop me off at Justin's house?" Justin's house wasn't far from Genevieve's place. For whatever reason, the Jensons were not supposed to know about Genevieve. "It's about a ten-minute drive from here."

Mr. Jenson wore a concerned look. "How are you feeling?"

"I'm okay," Brandon said, giving what he hoped was a reassuring smile.

"Sure. No problem. It'll be good for you to be with a friend this evening."

After dinner, Brandon went upstairs to get ready to go. The bruises on his arms were starting to fade a bit. Still, he longed for his trench coat imprisoned in Vernon's office closet. He glanced out the window; the rain had cleared. He placed his father's box into his backpack, grabbed the hanger that held his suit, and headed downstairs.

"Sorry that it's so wet," Brandon said, handing the suit to Mr. Jenson.

"I'm sure it'll be fine. It's unavoidable on days like this."

As Mr. Jenson was dropping Brandon off at Justin's house, he said, "So you'll call me if you need a ride back tonight?"

"Yes, sir."

"Sounds good. See ya later, bud." Mr. Jenson pulled away.

Brandon stood at the edge of the driveway and looked at the house; a light was on in Justin's room upstairs. Brandon considered knocking on the door. He wanted to reconnect, since they had hardly said two words to each other since Friday night. He wanted to tell Justin about the box. But instead of walking down the driveway, he peered down the road to ensure Mr. Jenson's car had vanished. Then, he started toward Genevieve's house.

Nearly there, Brandon stepped onto the old stone bridge over the creek where he had spent many an afternoon playing while his mom and Aunt Gemi jabbered. Then, he remembered the black item inside his father's box. Sitting on the bridge barrier, he pulled the box out of his backpack and opened it once more. The sound of rushing water filled the air, the creek higher than usual because of the day's rain. Beneath the photograph and dog tags was the black thing. It filled the bottom of the box from edge to edge. He pulled it out—it was an old book. He ran his fingers over the worn leather cover, searching for a title, but couldn't find one. Brandon opened it to find a handwritten dedication.

To our beloved Dean,

Congratulations on the best decision of your life. May the words of life guide you home. We are so proud of you.

Love,
Mom and Dad
June 3, 1978

Brandon opened the book to a random spot. It had a strange layout; big numbers and smaller numbers interspersed between lines of text filled the page. He read the first thing he landed on.

My son, do not forget my teaching,
But let your heart keep my commandments;
For length of days and years of life,
And peace they will add to you.

What is this? Brandon thought. *A poetry book?* He kept reading.

Do not let kindness and truth leave you;
Bind them around your neck,
Write them on the tablet of your heart.
So you will find favor and good repute
In the sight of God and man.
Trust in the LORD with all your heart,
And do not lean on your own understanding.

He thumbed through the pages and saw words upon words next to countless numbers. He went back to the front of the book and turned past the dedication. *No, not a poetry book,* Brandon thought as he landed on the title. "HOLY BIBLE."

None of this made sense. Why did Genevieve have this box? What kind of person was Brandon's father? He picked up the dog tags from the box and ran his finger over the word "CHRISTIAN." Something else in the box caught his eye. In the space where the Bible had been was an envelope. He picked it up and opened it. To his surprise, he found a stack of bills. He quickly counted them: $550. Brandon stuffed the contents back into the box, slung on his backpack, and kept walking to Genevieve's—faster this time.

The sun was low in the sky as Brandon climbed the four steps to Genevieve's porch, his father's box tucked under his arm. He knocked. Genevieve peeked out and looked up and down the street. She quickly let him in and hugged him. He didn't hug back.

"It doesn't seem like so long ago when your mother came with that same box," Genevieve said. "I don't suppose you have any questions about it?" she asked with a playful tone.

Brandon dropped his backpack, placed the box on the dining table, and sat down.

"Sorry, that was meant to be a joke. Of course you do," she said more seriously.

The house smelled like it always had. He looked into the living room. The same TV he always remembered sat in one corner. In the opposite corner, where his toy box had once stood, was an end table with a plant on it.

Genevieve sat across from him. "I am so sorry about Matt, Brandon. I can't imagine what you and Justin have been going through—especially you. I guess Barry's gonna be locked away for a while."

Brandon grunted.

"Hey," she said, reaching to place her hand on his.

Brandon looked into her eyes. Concern burned deep in them. "Where have you been?" he asked, almost in a whisper. "You're right—you can't imagine what I've been through. And I've had to face it on my own. And now, even me and Justin are drifting apart."

She took a deep breath. "I am so sorry I haven't been there for you since your mom died. I wanted nothing more than to sweep you away from Barry. But the last time I tried to help you and your mom…" She paused and gripped his hand tighter. "…I ended up killing my best friend." Concern was replaced with despair in her eyes.

"What are you talking about?"

"Let me ask you. How do you think your mom died?"

"They said she killed herself. With drugs or something. But maybe Barry…or…I don't know. She wouldn't have done that."

"You're right. She wouldn't have. She didn't. Brandon, I haven't been around these past two years, because the court put a restraining order on me against you until you turn eighteen. The night your mom gave me that box, she asked me for some of my painkillers." She paused. "It looked like your mom could use some relief—just to be able to sleep. I didn't think much of it. I thought I was helping her. I was so stupid!" Tears began to well in her eyes. "A couple of weeks later, the police showed up." She began to cry.

Brandon sat there, motionless.

"Of course, they found my name on the pill bottle. They asked me a lot of questions. In the end, they said that I was no good for your family, and I am not allowed to see you anymore. I'm so sorry, Brandon. If I had just—" She stood and went to the corner of the kitchen, weeping.

Brandon tried to take in this new information. Was his mom's death really Genevieve's fault? He watched as she covered her face with her hands and began to slump to the floor. "I'm so sorry, Brandon," she said through sobs. "This shouldn't have happened. I should have been there for you. That's why your mom came to me in the first place. It was like she knew things were getting out of hand. She expected I would be there for you if something ever happened to her. But I wasn't." She looked up at Brandon through her tears. "I'm so sorry," she whispered again.

"That's all I've heard for the past few days," said Brandon. "People are sorry for me." He got up and walked over to Genevieve. He grabbed her hand and lifted her to her feet. It was strange being able to do that since she had always been the grownup, and he the kid. A lot had changed in the past two years.

"You must hate me," she said, a quiver in her voice.

He wrapped his arms around her, which evoked another round of sobs.

Brandon pulled away to look at her again. "No, Aunt Genni. I don't."

The corners of her mouth curled up a bit, but the smile didn't reach her eyes.

"I do have more questions," he said.

Her eyes found the box on the table. "Of course you do. I knew you would. Sit down." She and Brandon sat back at the table. She took several seconds to regain her composure. Once she did, she said, "Your mom came here just a couple of weeks before she died. She gave that box to me, asking if I'd give it to you if something ever happened to her. Things weren't going well for Barry at work, and he was taking it all out on her. I tried to help—I really did. But she didn't want to talk about things, and she told me if I told anyone about it, I would just make things worse. I didn't know what to do." Tears once again threatened to roll down her cheek. She shook her head and wiped her eyes with the palms of her hands. "Of course, the court order prevented me from coming anywhere near you.

When I heard about Barry's accident the other day, I knew I needed to find you. I learned you were being placed in Grand Junction, but I couldn't just show up there. I figured Matt's funeral would be the best place—well, not really the best, but the easiest way—to get this to you." She pointed at the box. "Did your mom ever tell you about it?"

Brandon shook his head. He opened it and pulled out the photograph. "And this is Dean. This is my father," he said, more as a statement than a question.

"Mm-hmm. I got to meet him a couple of times. Now you can see where your hair comes from." She reached over and moved his bangs to the side. "And your beautiful brown eyes."

Brandon pulled out the Bible. "And this? Why did you give this to me?"

She shrugged. "It came with the box. Apparently, your mom wanted you to have it."

"She never believed this stuff." Brandon tossed the Bible onto the table.

"But your dad did."

"I guess so," Brandon said. He picked up the dog tags. "It looks like Dean was a Christian." Brandon resisted the urge to roll his eyes. His father seemed like a respectable man—he apparently adored his mom, and he was a soldier. Brandon thought about how it would have been growing up if his father had not died. "How did Dean die?"

"It was an accident in Basic Training. I don't really know the details. All I know is me and Frankie were having the summer of our lives in 1980." She smiled at the memory. "A couple of months after we graduated high school, a few of us girls went to hang out at Crewley's Ridge." She paused with a grin on her face. "Do the kids still go there to make out and get into trouble?"

Brandon looked away. "How should I know?"

"You devil." She reached over the table and gave his shoulder a playful push.

The truth was, Brandon did know; kids were probably there right now, despite their parents' warnings. But he didn't run with the crowd that went there—the preps. If he ever showed up there, he'd be dead meat.

"Anyway," Genevieve continued, "that's where we were when we met Dean. He also had just graduated—from somewhere in California. He was backpacking across the country when he met some of our friends. Dean immediately swept your mom off her feet." She laughed. "I had never seen her so happy."

"Me neither," Brandon said, picking up the photograph from the table. "I never saw her smile like that." Brandon couldn't help but smile back at his mom. He glanced at the clock over Genevieve's shoulder. 7:30pm. He needed to be back at Grand Junction in an hour and a half.

"Anyway, after meeting your mom, he stuck around. He said he was backpacking to see the world, but Frankie had become his world. He was sweet to her. Sure, he was a bit of a partier, but we all were back then. If I was a worse friend, I could have even been jealous." She gave a sheepish smile. "How I wish things would have worked out, Brandon. She was so happy. But, as they say, all good things must come to an end. Before he set out from California, he had enlisted in the army. He was due in Fort Worth for Basic Training a few months after meeting your mom. The day he left was the last time we saw him."

"So, how did my mom get this stuff?" Brandon asked.

"A few weeks after Dean left for Basic, Frankie learned she was pregnant." Genevieve met Brandon's eyes. "With you, of course. She wrote to Dean right away. It took a while for her to get a response, which scared your mom. But she eventually heard back. Then, it seemed there was no stopping Dean. The letters started coming nearly every day. He told her about his past and how he had been raised as a Christian. I think it took so long to get that first response because he wasn't sure at first if he was gonna tell her all of that. But in the end, he explained to your mom how meeting her was a blessing from God or something. You see, after he had graduated high school, he enlisted in the army and left California against his parents' wishes. I guess he was sowing his wild oats, as many of us do. But getting the news that he was gonna be a dad was a wake-up call for him. He wanted to raise his family right."

Again, Brandon considered how it would have been to be raised by his father.

Genevieve continued. "He wrote to your mom, telling her how he had started getting into his Bible again, and he couldn't wait to share his beliefs with her. Honestly, it kinda freaked her out at first, but she knew Dean had only good intentions. She was still smitten." She smiled again and shook her head. "After Basic Training, Dean planned to come back here and take your mom to California. He still hadn't told his parents about her, much less about the fact that he was gonna be a daddy. He even started talking about marriage in his letters." She took a deep breath. "All of a sudden, the letters stopped coming. By then, it was like March or April. She kept writing to him, but she didn't get a response. Then, out of the blue, a package came in the mail. It was Dean's Bible and dog tags, along with a letter from some of his friends at Basic. They explained that there had been a freak accident, and Dean was dead. Your dad had apparently talked to these guys about Frankie all of the time. Since your parents weren't married, the military would not have felt obligated to tell your mom about it. Technically, even Dean's dog tags should have been mailed to his family, but his friends reported them lost and shipped them to your mom instead. Dean had apparently been saving his cash for his new family." She tapped the envelope at the bottom of the cigar box.

Brandon picked up the photograph again. It was the first and only one he had ever seen of Dean. He had wanted to be a good father. But then, just when things were going well, he was killed.

"You wouldn't believe the heartbreak that package brought with it," Genevieve said. "Your mom was absolutely devastated. It threatened to destroy her. I don't know how she survived, except that I guess you kept her going. She knew she had a child to bring into the world and raise. But she was never the same after that day. There was no way for her to get to Dean's funeral. She didn't even know Dean's parents' names. It was like he never existed, except—" Genevieve reached across the table and put a hand on Brandon's cheek, "—she had you."

He picked up the Bible and ran his fingers over the rough edges, which told of years of use. He thumbed through the pages. "You're telling me," he began, "that after Dean decided to trust in God, then God killed him?"

Genevieve's eyes widened. "Uh, well, I don't know if I would put it that way."

"It must have been part of God's plan, huh? Tell me one thing that makes sense in all of this. A man grew up believing in God, and as soon as he left the house, he felt free to actually live. He found the love of his life and was gonna be a dad. Then, he turns back to this Bible, and God kills him."

"Well, I don't think it works like that," Genevieve said.

"When Mom died, people said God needed her. No doubt, people are saying the same thing to Matt's parents right now."

Genevieve shifted in her seat. "I don't know, Brandon. I've never been religious. All I know is your dad planned to teach that to you." She gestured toward the Bible. "And, for whatever reason, your mom thought you should have it. Maybe you should try to read it. Your mom tried, but it didn't make a lot of sense to her. I guess she could have tried harder, but she had you, and her focus shifted. You were a handful." She grinned and tapped Brandon's nose, something she used to do when he was a boy.

Brandon scoffed. He glanced at the clock and began to replace everything in the box. It would be an hour or so walk back to Grand Junction, so he needed to get going. "Thanks, Aunt Genni. It's good to know all this stuff. I wish Mom would have been more open to talk about it when she was alive."

"Me too," she said.

Brandon stood. "I've gotta go. I'm sorry I was so upset with you."

"You have every right to hate me."

"Never." He gave her a warm smile.

CHAPTER FIVE

Ronald and the Jensons agreed that it would be best for Brandon to go back to school as soon as possible. Brandon wasn't so sure. He had only missed a couple of days, but it felt like a lifetime. He didn't have much choice as he awoke the next day, Wednesday, and reluctantly got dressed and packed his things. He opened his backpack. He removed Matt's folder, numbly placing it under his bed, then went through the motions of eating breakfast and walking to the bus stop.

As the school bus entered the parking lot, Matt's parking spot sat empty. Brandon thought about how someone else would be given that same spot next year, oblivious to its history. Pain stabbed at Brandon's heart. *Matt is dead,* he told himself. Tears pricked his eyes. He thought of Francine. *Mom is dead.* He thought of his father. *Dean is dead.* He thought of Barry. *And Barry is alive.* Of all the people, Barry was the one to keep living. His cheeks grew hot as the tears began to roll down. He quickly wiped them away and checked to see if anyone had noticed. No one, thankfully. As the bus came to a halt, he grabbed his backpack and stepped off.

For the first half of the day, Brandon mindlessly walked

from class to class, speaking to no one. The hallways were noisy with inane chatter and the slamming of lockers, the classrooms full of restless kids sitting through lectures. Brandon wondered why any of it mattered. Life had come crashing down, and there he was: sitting in Mrs. Cooper's algebra class.

The intercom interrupted the teacher. "Remember, there will be an assembly in the gymnasium after this block to honor the memory of Matthew Steele. All students and staff are expected to attend."

Around him students spoke in hushed tones. Were they whispering about him? Brandon wondered whether they knew about Barry; whether they would blame Brandon for his friend's death. The bell rang.

As Brandon approached the gymnasium, he saw Justin for the first time that day. "Hey," he said.

Justin bobbed his head.

For a moment, they stood at the entrance of the gym, students stepping around them. Brandon looked inside. Some students sat somberly on the front row of the bleachers. The rest of the student body noisily scrambled for seats and sat chatting with their friends, thankful for anything that got them out of class.

In the center of the court was a wreath decorated with flowers propped up on a stand. A table displaying a few photos of Matt stood next to it. Behind the table was a projector screen.

"Crazy, huh?" Justin said.

Brandon grunted.

"Guess we should go in."

They walked in, and Brandon noticed Cody and some other preps huddled nearby on the front bleacher. They started snickering at Brandon and Justin as they passed them. Cody said something that Brandon didn't catch, but it earned some laughter from Cody's minions.

"Come on," Justin said. They ascended a few rows of

bleachers and found their seats as the rest of the school flowed into the gym.

A few minutes later, Principal Vernon came to the center of the court and picked up a microphone. "All right, students. Let me have your attention, please." The loud chatter gradually eased, but the principal had to call for attention one more time before it was quiet enough for him to continue. "As you all know," he began, "we lost Matthew Steele, one of our own, this past Friday. We have all felt the absence his loss brings. Before proceeding, I am calling for a moment of silence to honor the memory of Matthew Steele." He turned off the microphone and placed it on the table. He stepped away, closed his eyes, and bowed his head. The gym was hushed.

Brandon thought about the last time he'd seen Matt. He thought of Matt's folder, currently stowed under his bed at Grand Junction, right next to Dean's box. Brandon heard snickering—Cody and the preps again.

Mr. Vernon picked up the mic. "We know the pain that death can bring. We are all experiencing it now. The school counselor, Mrs. McMillan, is available this afternoon for those who need to speak with her." He paused, allowing Mrs. McMillan to stand, then continued. "In a moment, we are going to play a slideshow of photos from Matt's life. We're thankful to Matt's parents for their help putting this together. Seeing as Matthew was the victim of an accident caused by a drunk driver, as part of today's assembly, we will also have a presentation by Police Officer Schaefer from the Davidson County Police Department."

The image of Matt's car on the TV screen flashed into Brandon's mind. He tried to blink it away.

Vernon continued. "He's going to talk to us about some of the tragedies related to alcohol he's had to deal with while on duty. But without further ado, let us begin the slideshow."

The gymnasium dimmed. A flickering light projected images

of Matt's childhood onto the screen, from his earliest days as a baby and then a mischievous toddler, to elementary school photos of him smiling broadly for the camera. There were family photos of him with his parents and grandparents; Christmas photos; vacation photos. There was one of him with a homemade rocket ship composed of boxes and toilet paper rolls. A photo of when he won the middle school spelling bee. And finally, a photo of Matt, Justin, and Brandon together—the three of them wearing jean jackets and their tough-guy faces.

Brandon heard a sniff from Justin and turned to see his tear-streaked face. As another photo of the trio beamed onto the screen, he heard more sniggering. Cody was turned around, pointing at Justin. When he saw Brandon looking at him, he mouthed, "Aw," and pretended to rub his fists in his eyes like a baby. It was then that something in Brandon began to unravel. He looked away from Cody, sat up straight, and smoothed out his shirt. Focusing on the screen, he tried to forget about the bully. Still, his cheeks began to heat up.

Justin finally realized that Cody was mocking him. "That jerk," he whispered, wiping his eyes with the back of his hand. "He made fun of Matt his entire life, and now he doesn't even have the decency to respect him when he's dead."

Brandon breathed in deeply, his heart racing. Still, Cody continued his childish mocking, wiping pretend tears from his eyes and sniffling loudly. Next to him his prep friends stifled their laughter.

Justin swore. "Forget this. He's the dead one now." He sprung to his feet and pushed through some seated students. Justin jumped down two rows of bleachers at once, his feet landing with a loud *thud*. Principal Vernon noticed and started to approach them from the center of the court. Justin didn't slow or stop. He made it to the gym floor.

Cody jumped up. "Oh, I guess you're gonna have to defend your pal, seeing as he's—well, not here." The preps laughed. All eyes were on Justin marching toward Cody, the lights in the gym still dimmed. Brandon followed close behind. Justin closed the distance faster than Cody could prepare for and shoved him with all his might. As if in slow motion, Cody windmilled his arms, then he tumbled to the floor in front of the bleachers. At that second, all the rage and all the pain rushed to Brandon's head. Whatever had begun to unravel now snapped. Shooting past Justin, he jumped on top of Cody, his fists taking on a life of their own as they pounded Cody's face. One, two, three blows—that was for Matt. For the years of humiliation Cody and his crew had dealt to him, he landed another blow. And another. As Cody cried out, students around them stood to see the commotion. Brandon didn't take notice. For the fear and anger he'd bottled up against Barry, for years of abuse he'd endured at the hand of a man he hated, Brandon reached up. Cody tried to block it, but he was too slow. Brandon brought his fist down and heard—and felt—a sickening *crack*.

Hands reached under Brandon's arms, peeling him off Cody. His lifelong bully rolled over, holding his face. He moaned, his blood dripping onto the gymnasium floor. Around him students gasped in excited horror at the sight.

His arms pinned to his back, Brandon tried in vain to shake the person off him. Exhausted from the adrenaline rush, he was no match. He looked over his shoulder to see it was Officer Schaefer restraining him, Principal Vernon at his side. Brandon stopped resisting and breathed out deeply.

Cody still lay on the floor, a group of teachers kneeling next to him to assess the damage.

Officer Schaefer eased his grip and let go of Brandon. He spoke sharply. "You're lucky you didn't kill the boy," he warned. Was that what he had been trying to do? Brandon certainly hadn't planned on fighting Cody; but what choice did he have?

Mr. Vernon nodded to the police officer, then grabbed Brandon and Justin by the shoulders and led them to the basketball coach. "Please assist them to my office." Matt's slideshow still played in the background, but the entire school was focused on the commotion.

Firmly holding Justin's arm on one side, and Brandon's on the other, the coach marched them to Vernon's office. "Stay here," he said sternly, shutting them inside to wait for the principal.

"Well, that was cool," Justin said, letting a small laugh escape. "Did you break his nose?"

That's when Brandon felt the pain pulse through his hand. Holding it up, he said, "Either that, or I broke my hand. Ouch."

"How long has Cody had that coming?"

"Since birth," Brandon said, also laughing a bit.

"You're gonna be in so much trouble though."

"Me? I'm pretty sure you're the one who pushed him down!"

"But I didn't make him bleed all over the floor! I hope it leaves a stain. You'd be a legend."

Brandon breathed deeply again. "Matt would have done the same for us."

"Definitely," Justin agreed with a smile.

After a moment, Brandon said, "Can you believe he's gone?"

Justin shook his head. "It just doesn't seem real."

"I know what you mean."

They both sat down to wait for the principal. Looking around, Brandon saw the closet where Mr. Vernon had stashed his trench coat. He also spotted a large map of the United States on the wall. He stood and walked over to study it. He found Arizona. Then, he found the Grand Canyon. Putting his left index finger on the Grand Canyon, he slid his other hand toward Nashville. Halfway there, another city caught his attention: Fort Worth. It was just outside Dallas, Texas, almost exactly halfway between the Grand Canyon and Nashville.

"What's up?" Justin asked curiously, peering over his shoulder.

Brandon stepped aside, finger still on the Grand Canyon.

Justin looked closer and understood. "He'll never make it there."

Brandon took his hand down. "You remember Matt gave us his folder on Friday? I still have it. You've gotta see it."

The office door opened. Principal Vernon stepped in, and Brandon and Justin quickly found their seats.

Mr. Vernon sat at his desk without speaking. He sighed heavily and began rubbing his eyes beneath his glasses. "Boys," he began, "you know what's hard about my job?"

Brandon was unsure if he was supposed to answer.

The principal stopped rubbing his eyes and looked at Brandon and Justin. "I have no doubt you feel you were doing the right thing today. If all details were considered, I would probably side with you. But I don't have that luxury. Our school system has a no-violence policy. And from my vantage point—" he nodded toward Brandon, "—Mr. Bason, you mercilessly battered a fellow student after you—" he turned to Justin, "—knocked him to the ground. Do you have anything to say for yourselves?"

Brandon avoided his glare and shook his head. He flexed his hand, which was aching and had started to swell. Justin didn't say anything either.

Mr. Vernon continued. "Brandon, it looks like you broke Cody's nose. The nurse is assessing him now. If there are medical bills, the family can press charges. This is a serious matter. You know that, right?"

Brandon didn't say anything, but of course he knew. Why else would he be ushered into the principal's office?

"You know that, right?" Principal Vernon repeated.

Brandon met his piercing gaze. "Yes, sir." He pursed his lips.

Mr. Vernon sighed. "The typical punishment for fighting is three weeks' suspension. Seeing as there are less than two weeks until graduation, I have no other option." He paused. "Boys, you're suspended for the rest of the school year."

Justin straightened in his chair, concern on his face. It looked like he wanted to say something.

"And," the principal continued, robbing Justin of any chance to speak, "you're banned from walking the stage. Both of you."

"Seriously?" Justin said, unable to hide his shock.

"You can still receive your diplomas—so long as you pass your classes, that is. School staff can drop off your remaining assignments each day until the end of the school year. We will be in touch regarding your final exams."

Brandon stayed silent, indifferent to the news. He didn't regret pounding Cody, if that's what Mr. Vernon was trying to get him to do. Brandon bit his lip to conceal a smile. *How long has Cody had that coming?*

Justin huffed and sat back in his chair.

"I know you don't think I'm being fair. I'm guessing you were acting out of nobility for Matthew, huh?" Mr. Vernon stood and walked toward the door. "I wish I had the liberty to judge by motives. But these are the school's rules, not mine." Brandon was reminded of how Principal Vernon had said something similar when he took his trench coat last week. Brandon guessed it was still in the office closet. "Stay here while I go and arrange the paperwork." The principal walked out of the room.

"Can you believe this?" Justin said. "I mean, four years of this prison just to be told I can't graduate!"

Brandon started laughing.

"This is funny?"

"Well, getting in trouble, no. But we beat up the most popular kid in school." He flexed his aching hand again. "You're right. We will be legends."

"It's all you, dude; you're the one that broke his nose!"

Brandon grimaced when he thought of the *crack* beneath his

fist. "I was so angry. It was all adrenaline. It's probably a good thing the cop pulled me off him."

Justin chuckled and shook his head. "You're right about one thing, Brandy. Matt would have done the same for us. I can't believe those preps were laughing!" He swore.

Brandon leaned back in his chair, thinking about his situation. It felt like he and Justin were back to normal. Even if it had taken a few punches and a suspension, it was worth it. Brandon had never been particularly excited about graduating, anyway. Sure, he looked forward to being finished with school. But, for one, no one would come to his graduation. For another, he had no idea what he was going to do afterwards. Grand Junction was supposed to help him get on his feet in the real world, but nothing was in place for that yet.

But what if...? An idea was forming in his head. He sat for a minute or two, letting the idea take shape. Then, he craned his neck to see into the receptionists' office. Satisfied no one was looking, he walked behind the principal's desk and unlatched the window that opened to outside.

"What are you doing?" Justin asked.

"Meet me here tonight at 8:30."

"What?"

"I'm serious. Can you meet me here—" Brandon pointed out the window to the grass outside, "—at 8:30 tonight?" He walked back to his seat.

"Why?"

"Shh!" Brandon could see Vernon was coming.

The door opened. The principal handed Brandon and Justin the paperwork and ordered them to give it to their guardians. "The assembly for Mr. Steele has ended. Mr. Bason, Coach Newman will escort you to your next class. Mr. Sanders, please go with Mrs. Peters." Principal Vernon busied himself with papers on his desk. "That is all, boys."

CHAPTER SIX

BRANDON DIDN'T GET A CHANCE TO TALK TO JUSTIN FOR THE REST of the day. Neither of them was allowed to go anywhere unescorted. Coach Newman even insisted on watching Brandon board the school bus, as if he were a ticking time bomb that would go off at any moment if left to his own devices.

On the ride back to Grand Junction, Brandon worked out the details of his plan. When he arrived, he hurried to his room but was stopped by Mr. Jenson.

"Everything okay, bud?" he asked, concern etched on his face. "It was your friend's memorial today, wasn't it?"

"Yeah," he replied curtly, edging past Mr. Jenson. He knew that Mr. Jenson was only trying to help, but he didn't need his help; he had a plan.

Back in his room, he found the cash that he had saved and put it inside the envelope with Dean's money, making the total nearly one thousand dollars. He stuffed his toiletries with a few clothes in his backpack, along with Dean's box and Matt's folder. After ensuring he hadn't left anything important, he went downstairs to get ready for dinner.

As he sat down for dinner, he apologized to Mr. Jenson for

his rudeness and tried to act as normal as possible, even making some small talk with another of the residents. Then, he thanked Mrs. Jenson for the meal and went back upstairs. He sat on his bed and waited. The sun started to bathe his room in orange. *This is it,* he thought, pulling on Mr. Vernon's sweater. He grabbed his backpack and went downstairs, making a beeline for the door.

"Where you headed?" Mr. Jenson said.

Brandon turned. "For a walk," he replied, a little too quickly.

"It's not that cold out there." Mr. Jenson was looking at the sweater. He spied the backpack Brandon wore and gave an expectant look.

"Oh, yeah. I'm meeting Justin. School project." The note from the principal was still in his back pocket. He had no intention of giving it to the Jensons. He had nothing against them. They were kind and generous. But his life wasn't their business.

"Okay, bud. No problem. Just remember curfew."

"Yes, sir," Brandon said, stepping out the door.

Brandon took his time walking to the school. He needed to arrive after sunset. He held out hope that Justin would show. But what if he didn't? He pushed the thought from his mind.

A little less than an hour later, the sun was well below the horizon, and the school came into view. Brandon expected it was close enough to 8:30. He walked the outskirts of the parking lot, avoiding stepping into the security lights that flooded the parking spaces. When he came near the spot just outside Principal Vernon's office, he saw a shadow sitting under the window. *He did come!* There was just enough ambient light to make him out.

"Dude, what is this about?" Justin asked, standing up. "I see you're sporting the Burnin Vernon again." He stomped on his smoldering cigarette butt.

"Thanks for coming." Brandon set his backpack down and looked around. The coast was clear. "Keep a lookout, will you?"

"For what?"

Brandon didn't answer. He wiggled the principal's office window, and it came loose. Brandon stole one more look at Justin, raised his eyebrows, gave a quick smile, and slipped in.

"So, you want to get us in trouble with the law too?" Justin whispered through the window. "We've spent enough time with the cops lately."

Brandon ignored him. Then, everything was dead quiet. He took a couple of tentative steps forward. It dawned on him that the school could have had a security system. *Too late now,* Brandon thought as a bead of sweat formed on his forehead. He walked over to the closet and opened it. There it was, still on the hanger. He pulled off Mr. Vernon's sweater and snatched his trench coat. He slipped it on and gave a sigh of relief. Before closing the closet, he picked up the sweater and put it on the hanger.

He turned back to the window, and out of the corner of his eye, he spotted a figure by Vernon's desk. He froze. Why was someone in the principal's office at this time of night? And why were they sitting here with the lights off? Surely, no one expected him. No alarm had sounded. Or had he been seen earlier when unlatching the window? He continued to stare at the figure. It wasn't moving. His eyes adjusted, and he took a step forward. He let out the breath he was holding. It wasn't a person; it was the memorial wreath from Matt's service.

Brandon approached it. Photos had been pinned all around the wreath. Among them was the picture of Brandon, Justin, and Matt in their jean jackets. He grabbed it and stuck it in the breast pocket of his trench coat.

He climbed out of the window and stumbled to the ground. Straightening, he smoothed out his jacket and spread out his arms in victory.

Justin gave him a scolding look.

"I can breathe again," Brandon said.

"All this for a jacket?" Justin asked. "You're a doof." He shook his head.

"Hey, you didn't have to come," Brandon said, still smiling at his victory.

"And if I would have known your plan, I wouldn't have!"

"Relax. No one saw us. Plus, there's more."

Justin stared at him, waiting for him to finish.

"Not here," Brandon said. "Let's go. By the way, how did your grandma take the news about graduation?"

"She wasn't happy, but once I told her about what the preps were doing, she said we did the right thing. Then, she said this could be a good thing. I could get a head start looking for a job before the rest of the graduates." He rolled his eyes.

During the fifteen-minute walk to Genevieve's house, Brandon filled Justin in on the box and what he had learned about his father. As her house came into view, he pulled the principal's note out of his back pocket and tossed it in the creek. They arrived, and Brandon knocked on the door. Genevieve answered, a smile spreading on her face as she took in her visitors.

"Hi, Aunt Genni."

She gave Brandon a warm hug. "What a great surprise."

"Remember Justin?"

"This is Justin? How you've grown!"

"Hi, Ms. Genevieve," he said, inclining his head.

"Come in. What brings you here at this time of night? Not that I mind. You know you're always welcome."

Brandon walked over to the dining table and set down his backpack in a chair. Then he sat in the chair next to it. He pulled out Matt's folder and opened it; as he did so, the map unfolded itself. Brandon unfolded it twice more, revealing the map of the United States with its red route, numbers, and pockets.

Justin eyed the map over Brandon's shoulder. "No way."

"Way," Brandon replied.

"What is that?" Genevieve asked, walking over to the table.

"Matt was planning a trip to the Grand Canyon," Brandon explained. "Just before he died, he gave us this folder. He was sure it would convince us to go with him. Look at this." Brandon opened up the first pocket and spread out the post-cards and mini-maps. "Each one of these corresponds to the different numbers on the map." Brandon pointed to the post-card for Jackson, Tennessee, and then to the city on the map. He traced his finger along the red line. He stopped in Texas, where Dallas had been labeled "4." He pulled Dean's box out of his backpack and opened it. He laid the photograph of his parents over Texas and looked up at Genevieve. "And Dean was stationed at Fort Worth, right?" Before she could reply, Brandon added, "I'm going."

"What?" Justin said.

"You heard me right. I'm going. I'm taking Matt's map, and I'm going to follow it to the Grand Canyon. Since Fort Worth is halfway there, I figured I could stop and learn more about my father. Maybe I could find my grandparents and, well, let them know that they are grandparents."

"Okay, Daniel Boone, what have you done to Brandon?" Justin said.

"Sit down," Brandon said, looking at Justin and Genevieve. Justin hesitated and then obeyed. Then, so did Genevieve. "Listen—my entire life things have been happening to me. Mainly bad things. Things I have no control over. And every one of them has left me bruised and wondering what there is to live for. I'm tired of things happening to me. I'm ready to start doing. If I don't, I don't know if I could handle whatever happens next."

Brandon could tell by their raised eyebrows and bemused expressions that they were listening. Maybe they were the only two people in the world he could talk to so honestly. He had to give it a shot; what choice did he have? He glanced at the clock. Fifteen minutes past his curfew.

He continued. "Just look at this." He spread his arms over the map. Pain shot through his hand. He grabbed it and flexed it. "What were we willing to do for Matt on an impulse today? And he didn't even ask us to do it."

"Brandon," Genevieve interrupted. "What happened to your hand?" She must have noticed it was starting to turn purple.

Brandon shrugged off the question and continued before she could press him on it further. "But Matt did ask us to do this." He landed a finger on the Grand Canyon. "I'm going. You coming?"

"When? Now?"

"That's the plan. What's left here for you? We're not allowed to graduate. What would you be doing anyway? Oh, right," he smirked, "looking for a job."

Justin didn't say anything.

"Let's do this for Matt."

Genevieve spoke up. "Okay, so you're going to the Grand Canyon. With this map, right?"

Brandon nodded.

"Any idea how long of a drive that is?"

"Uh…" said Brandon.

"It would probably take a normal person over twenty hours. But look." She followed the red line. "Matt didn't plan for a straight shot. He planned to go through Mississippi and Louisiana. And after Dallas, he wanted to avoid the interstate altogether. With this route, we're talking days. And that's just counting the driving."

Brandon considered it for a moment. She was right. He shrugged. "Doesn't bother me."

Justin sat with his mouth somewhat agape. He looked back at Genevieve, likely wanting her to keep trying to talk sense into Brandon.

She didn't disappoint. "And how are you going to get there? Do you have a car?"

Brandon straightened. "Well, no. I've got the money from Dean. And some I saved up myself. I'll take the bus." He met eyes with Justin. "I mean, we'll take the bus."

"The bus?" she said incredulously. "Sounds like you've really thought this one through."

Brandon ignored her comment. "What do you say?" he said to Justin.

"I don't know, dude. I've never done anything like this."

"And you think I have? We've got to honor Matt. He would do it for us." Although Brandon believed that with all his heart, he had an ulterior motive as well—to learn more about his father.

"So, you're suggesting we go to the Greyhound station and just ask for a bus to the Grand Canyon?"

"All the cities are marked. We just need to look for the bus going to the next city at each stop."

"No," Genevieve said decisively. Brandon didn't blame her for trying to get him to consider this sensibly, but for her to act like his mother was going too far. He was about to tell her as much when she continued. "You don't have to take the bus. Take my car."

Brandon widened his eyes. "No. That's crazy! You can't give us your car."

"How long is this trip going to take you? A few weeks? Maybe a month?"

"No idea," Brandon said.

"I can manage the summer without a car. The grocery store is just down the road. Plus," she reached over the table and moved Brandon's bangs to the side, "I need to make up the last two years to you. It looks like you're not gonna be talked out of this. You might as well take my car."

After a moment's pause, Brandon said, "Okay then." He turned to Justin. "No Greyhound needed. But I am in need of a friend."

Justin sighed and sat back. "What am I gonna tell my grandma?"

CHAPTER SEVEN

BRANDON AND JUSTIN CLIMBED INTO GENEVIEVE'S CAR JUST before ten o'clock.

"So, does she know that we don't have our driver's licenses?" asked Justin. Genevieve stood on the front porch of her house, her arms folded across her chest.

"What she doesn't know won't hurt her. It's fine. Driver's Ed, remember?"

"Sure," Justin said, securing his seatbelt.

"We'll be fine," Brandon reassured.

Justin smiled and sighed. "I guess so. Let's do this." He lifted his fist, and Brandon bumped it. Brandon waved at Genevieve as he put the car in reverse and turned onto the road. The old blue Buick drove like a boat, every bump bouncing the vehicle like it was riding waves. It made a clicking sound when Brandon turned the steering wheel to the right, and the brakes whined when he slowed down. But it was their ticket to freedom, and better than taking the bus.

They pulled into Justin's driveway. "I still can't believe we're doing this," Justin said.

"Don't be long," Brandon ordered. "And don't you dare think about backing out now."

Justin got out of the car and walked inside. A few minutes later, he returned with a backpack.

"What'd you tell her?" Brandon asked.

"She was in bed. I told Jessica to say that I'm staying with you, and I'll call her in the morning."

"You weren't supposed to mention my name."

"Don't have a cow. I'm just buying time until I can think of something. I'm not sure why it has to be a secret. I doubt my grandma would care if I went to the Grand Canyon with you."

"Even if she knew we were driving illegally?" Brandon paused. "Let's just say I didn't exactly work this out with the Jensons."

Justin gave Brandon a questioning look.

"It'll be fine. Now, how do we get to Jackson?"

They pulled out Matt's folder. Once unfolded, the map crowded them out of the front seats. Justin opened the first pocket and pulled out the first mini-map. "I guess it's obvious, but we need to head west on the interstate." Brandon started the car and pulled out of the driveway.

As they headed out of town toward the interstate, they looked for signs that pointed them in the right direction.

"Keep your eyes peeled," Brandon said.

Then, Justin shouted, "No!"

"What?!" Brandon tensed and looked around.

"No CD player! What am I gonna do with these?" Justin pulled a sleeve of CDs out of his bag.

"Man, I thought we were going to crash or something. Don't scare me like that! Go to 105.9 on the radio. They should have something decent."

"There!" Justin pointed to a sign that said, "I-40 W MEMPHIS."

Brandon swerved the boat of a car to the right toward the onramp. At the end of the ramp, he tried to merge onto the interstate. Halfway into the lane, another driver blew his horn and nearly collided into them. Brandon swore and weaved the car to the shoulder at speed. The other driver honked once more. After he passed them, Brandon slid the car into the right lane and let out his breath. "We'll get used to it," he said, adjusting his grip on the steering wheel. He reached inside his breast pocket and pulled out the photo of the trio. "Hey—look what else I snatched from Vernon's office." He passed it to Justin.

Justin laughed at the memory. "I don't know what's gotten into you. Since when have you been the breaking-into-the-principal's-office-let's-go-on-a-spontaneous-road-trip type?"

"I don't know, man." The traffic had eased, and Brandon was cruising at a comfortable fifty-five miles an hour. "Something snapped this afternoon at school. Something besides Cody's nose, that is. I realized that everything I've ever done has been because I was expected to do it—not because I wanted to do it. And if I didn't do what I was expected to, I got punished, you know?"

"Well, that is how society works," Justin responded. "You're born, and your parents tell you what to do. Then your teachers at school. Then the government, right?"

"I guess so, but I started asking myself why Matt wanted to go to the Grand Canyon. I always thought it was childish for him to hold onto a silly school project all these years."

"So did I."

"But maybe we shouldn't have tried to squash that dream," Brandon said as he moved the car into the center lane to pass an old Chevy, then settled back into the right lane. "He felt free enough to make plans—to do something he wasn't expected to do. And what did I do? Roll my eyes and call him a dreamer. Do you remember what he called us on Friday morning?"

Justin flicked a cigarette out his window.

"He called us downers," Brandon said. "He was right. We should have done all we could to get him to go on this trip. And after all these years of calling him silly, he still wanted us to go with him."

The two of them sat with their regrets while "Wonderwall" by Oasis played on the radio.

A few minutes later, Justin held up the photo of the three of them to the window, allowing the interstate lights to illuminate it. "Matt, buddy," he said to the picture, "ready for the first day—night—of the rest of our lives?" He leaned over and slid it behind the steering wheel to display it next to the speedometer.

They continued to make their way west on the interstate. According to the signs, Jackson was 120 miles away. They would be there in a couple of hours. Traffic lessened as the night grew later. They left Nashville behind.

It was nearly one in the morning when they saw the first exit for Jackson. "Finally," Brandon said wearily, rousing Justin from his brief sleep. "Let's find a place to stay." Brandon pulled onto the exit ramp. He turned a hard right into the parking lot of the first motel they saw, causing the car to click the entire time.

"Have you ever checked into a motel before?" Brandon asked.

Justin shook his head.

They grabbed their backpacks and entered the lobby. A guy who looked to be in his twenties was at the front desk reading a magazine.

"We need a room," Brandon said.

"With two beds," Justin added.

He put down his magazine. "Sure. Got some ID?"

Brandon looked at Justin.

He fished in his pocket and produced his student ID and showed it to the clerk.

"High school students?"

"Seniors. I'm eighteen," Justin said.

"I'm gonna need more than this."

Justin looked back at Brandon and shrugged.

"No ID, no room."

"Look," Brandon began. "We won't say anything. We just need a room for the night. We won't cause any trouble, and we'll be gone before you know it. Promise."

"Sorry," the clerk said, pointing to a sign outlining the motel's policy.

Brandon pursed his lips. "Now what?"

The clerk pointed through the lobby window. "They serve minors over there."

Brandon and Justin turned to see where he was pointing. Across the street stood a shabby building with a half-illuminated sign above it. The clerk was already back to reading his magazine.

A couple of minutes later, they entered the other motel's lobby, the air soaked with the stench of cigarette smoke. "Kinda late to be checking in, don't ya think?" a sandpaper voice greeted them. "Name's Roger." A cigarette bobbed in his lips with every syllable.

Brandon stifled a cough. "Can we get a room with two beds, please?"

"You betcha. We've got a $19.99 special just for ya."

Brandon pulled out his envelope and paid the man. "Thanks," he said reluctantly as Roger passed him the room key.

If Brandon had hoped for cleaner air when they arrived at their room, he was mistaken. The place reeked of stale smoke and mildew. He clicked on the desk light.

Justin threw his bag onto an old chair. He wrinkled his nose at the stained cover on his bed before throwing it on the floor.

Then, he kicked off his shoes and crawled into bed. "I'm beat," Justin said. "See ya in the morning." He pulled the sheet over his shoulders and turned toward the wall.

Brandon sat on his bed and opened his backpack. Finding his father's box, he pulled it out and retrieved the Bible. Genevieve had advised him to try to read it. His stomach churned at the thought of the brainwashed Christians he knew from school—the ones who always seemed so artificially happy and who sometimes spent their lunchtimes praying for who knows what. He ran his fingers through his hair and looked over his shoulder. Justin seemed to be fast asleep already. He opened the book at a random place and read the first words his eyes landed on.

> *And when He had entered Capernaum, a centurion came to Him, entreating Him, and saying, "Lord, my servant is lying paralyzed at home, suffering great pain." And He said to him, "I will come and heal him." But the centurion answered and said, "Lord, I am not worthy for You to come under my roof, but just say the word, and my servant will be healed. For I, too, am a man under authority, with soldiers under me; and I say to this one, 'Go!' and he goes, and to another, 'Come!' and he comes, and to my slave, 'Do this!' and he does it." Now when Jesus heard this, He marveled, and said to those who were following, "Truly I say to you, I have not found such great faith with anyone in Israel. And I say to you, that many shall come from east and west, and recline at the table with Abraham, and Isaac, and Jacob, in the kingdom of heaven; but the sons of the kingdom shall be cast out into the outer darkness; in that place there shall be weeping and gnashing of teeth." And Jesus said to the centurion, "Go your way; let it be done to you as you have believed." And the servant was healed that very hour.*

"Pssh. Yeah, right," Brandon whispered. *People can't really believe this junk,* he thought. *Bunch of sheep.* He placed the Bible on the desk, took off his coat, crawled under the covers, and fell asleep.

Bang, bang, bang, bang! "Get up, kids!"

Brandon blinked. He turned over and saw Justin rubbing his eyes.

Bang, bang, bang, bang! "Come on!" came Roger's scratchy voice. "It's a half-hour past checkout. I should be charging extra!"

Brandon shot up, sunshine streaming through the grimy curtains.

Bang, bang, bang, bang!

"We heard you!" shouted Justin. "Just a minute!"

Brandon got out of bed. He pulled on his coat, stuffed his father's box in his backpack, and opened the door.

Roger was standing there with a cigarette in his lips. "This is how ya pay back my hospitality?" There was a lady with a cleaning cart next to him.

"Sorry!" Brandon said. "We're leaving, okay?" He pulled the motel room key out of his pocket and handed it to Roger.

Justin grabbed his bag, and they stepped outside. Roger stormed back to the front office, while Brandon and Justin began walking to the car.

"Wait!" Brandon said. He thought for a second and turned to see the cleaning cart disappear into the motel room. He bolted across the parking lot and grabbed the door just before it closed. Then he slipped in, sidestepping the cart, and grabbed the Bible off the desk. Arriving back at the car, Brandon put the Bible into his breast pocket, which was just big enough to hold it, although the top of the Bible still stuck out a bit.

Justin raised his eyebrows.

"What?" Brandon said, putting up his hands in defense. "It was my father's. I can't just leave it behind."

"I didn't say anything."

They got into the car and drove to a nearby gas station to refuel. Brandon went to the counter to pay.

"Are you a KJV kind of guy?" said the clerk.

"Huh?" Brandon responded.

The clerk was eyeing Brandon's pocket. "That's a Bible, right?"

"Oh. What did you ask?"

"KJV?"

"Sorry, I have no idea what that means."

"Just asking what translation it is." He handed Brandon his change.

"It was my father's. It's in English. Thanks." Brandon left the store scratching his head. On his way out, he spotted Justin huddled in a phone booth. Brandon got into the car and waited.

Justin looked back at the car, the phone's receiver glued to his ear. He nodded and hung up. "It's all taken care of," he said after opening the car door.

"What did you tell her?"

"That I'm with my cousin job hunting and that it will take a few days, and I'll be staying with him."

"What if she calls your cousin?"

"Not likely. But I'll call him sometime soon and fill him in. I'll tell him to grab some applications around town for safe measure."

"So, where do we go now?" Justin asked.

"I guess we find some grub." Brandon drove the car toward what seemed to be the busier side of the interstate. After they'd grabbed some food, he pulled out Matt's map and retrieved the postcard from Casey Jones Village.

"Do we really want to go look at an old train?" Justin asked.

Brandon found the location labeled "2"—Memphis,

Tennessee. He pulled out the corresponding postcard. It was from a place with a guitar in its logo called Sun Studio. Brandon turned it over and read the back.

Dear Matt,

So, you like rock music? Sun Studio is the birthplace of rock 'n' roll. We look forward to seeing you when you come through Memphis!

"Now, that sounds more interesting than a train museum!" Justin said.

Brandon couldn't agree more.

CHAPTER EIGHT

IT DIDN'T TAKE THEM MUCH EFFORT TO CLOSE THE DISTANCE between Jackson and Memphis. The time passed in a comfortable silence, both boys alone with their thoughts. Occasionally, Justin fiddled with the radio dial, searching unsuccessfully among the static for some decent tunes, then switching it off with a sigh. Brandon didn't mind; he liked the quiet and found his confidence with his driving skills growing as the odometer clocked up the miles.

Matt had certainly done his research with the mini-maps. On paper, finding Sun Studio seemed straightforward; they just had to get onto Union Avenue and look out for the big guitar. It quickly became clear, however, that it was easier said than done. They found Union Avenue easily enough, but it was bustling with activity. Brandon felt the need to suck in his stomach as he tried to carefully navigate the colossal car down the narrow lanes of one of the busiest streets in downtown Memphis. Cars weaved in and out of traffic. He had no idea what the speed limit was, but that seemed irrelevant. If he went too slow, they would be run over. At least the red lights every few feet gave him a moment to catch his breath and refocus.

"There it is!" Justin shouted, pointing to a massive guitar on the side of a corner building. "Turn here!"

The Buick *clicked* as Brandon swerved onto Marshall Avenue. With a bit of careful maneuvering, Brandon managed a passable parallel parking effort on the street only a short walk from Sun Studio. After stepping out of the car, he held up the postcard. "So, this is the birthplace of rock?" He regarded the guitar on the building. "Looks legit!" They headed to the entrance and pushed open the door.

On the back wall behind a milkshake machine was a large black and white photo of some guys around a piano. Brandon thought he recognized the one at the keys. "That's Elvis, right?" he said to Justin.

"I think so."

"Of course it is!" said a jubilant voice. A man holding a tray in his hand with empty milkshake glasses introduced himself as the owner of Sun Studio. He had been clearing a table in the café. "That's the Million Dollar Quartet. The other three are Jerry Lee Lewis, Carl Perkins, and the Man in Black himself." He pointed to each one in order.

"I know that's a black and white photo," Justin said, "but it doesn't look like he's wearing black."

"That's his nickname, son. You're telling me you boys don't know Johnny Cash when you see him?"

"I've heard of him," Brandon said.

The owner rushed to the bar to put down the tray. Returning, he asked, "What do you know about rock 'n' roll?"

"For one," Brandon said, trying to hide a smile, "we don't call it rock 'n' roll. It's just rock. We listen to Korn, Staind, Disturbed, and Rammstein."

"Show a little respect," he said playfully. "Grab a seat, boys." He gestured to an empty table. They all sat. "I like modern rock too. Driving beats. Precision guitars. Slick bass lines. And yes, the occasional scream is okay." He gave them a sideways smile.

"But all the artists you listed a moment ago owe their careers to guys like Elvis." He pointed to the Million Dollar Quartet. "Ask anyone in the rock 'n'—er, *rock* industry, and they'll agree."

Brandon and Justin turned to see the photo again.

"Are you familiar with any of the songs recorded in this studio? 'Blue Suede Shoes'? 'Great Balls of Fire'? 'Folsom Prison Blues'?"

Brandon and Justin exchanged a bemused glance. "Maybe 'Blue Suede Shoes,'" Justin said, a little embarrassed.

The owner stood up and walked behind the counter. He handed them a CD. "Here's a sample. Take it; listen to it when you get the chance. It's about time you learn your heritage."

"Thanks," Brandon said, turning the CD case over.

"And you'll be surprised what else you have in common with singers like Presley and Cash," the man continued.

Brandon looked up. "What's that?"

"They weren't just rock stars. They were gospel singers too." The owner pointed at the Bible poking out of Brandon's pocket.

Brandon resisted the urge to roll his eyes. He'd forgotten to return the book to Dean's box.

"Have a look around," the owner said. "The tour is eight dollars. If you're interested, let Lizzy know." He nodded to a young lady behind the counter and got back to work.

Eight dollars was a fair price, so they took the plunge and gathered with the small group of tourists waiting for the tour to begin. What did they have to lose? A few minutes later, an enthusiastic, twenty-something-year-old guide named Nick led them into the open studio room where, he explained, the first rock 'n' roll songs of history were recorded. The very microphone used in those early recordings stood in the middle of the room. Guitars and amplifiers—both old and new—lined the walls. The tour guide asked if anyone had a dollar bill. A middle-aged man produced one, and the guide took it. He picked up an acoustic guitar and wove the dollar bill between the strings. He muted the strings with his left hand and strummed the guitar with his right, producing a rhythm that sounded like a train coming down the tracks. "Anyone recognize that sound?" he asked.

"'I Walk the Line!'" someone called.

"That's it!" Nick gave the dollar back. "When Johnny Cash came in to record, he didn't have a drummer. So, this is how he recorded his percussion."

Brandon had never thought about the history of rock music —he never would have thought that he cared to know. But standing in that room, among the awe-struck tourists, there was no mistaking that he was in a place of great significance. The walls were covered with what looked like white cork boards, likely for dampening the sound for recording. As Nick told them his rehearsed spiel of the history of rock, no doubt with some embellishments, Brandon couldn't help but imagine well-dressed men of the 1950s breaking all their mothers' rules to record songs that would revolutionize the music industry. He pulled the CD out of his coat's inside pocket and looked at it again. *I'll give it a shot,* he thought. Then, he remembered Genevieve's car didn't have a CD player. As the tour ended, Brandon surprised himself by asking the guide a few questions and reading some of the placards spaced around the studio.

"That was pretty cool, wasn't it?" he asked Justin.

"Yeah, I guess Matt really did do his research."

By the time they left the studio, the sun was low in the sky. Back in the car, they consulted the map. From Memphis, instead of going west on I-40, they were to turn left onto Union and right onto South Bellevue Avenue. It would eventually turn into Highway 51. Location "3" on the map was New Orleans, Louisiana—a much further drive than Memphis was from Jackson. Soon after crossing into Mississippi, they found some dinner and a place to rest for the night.

The next morning, they got on the road toward New Orleans. Less than two hours later, they started hearing a noise from the car—a knocking from the engine. "What is that?" Brandon asked. It didn't sound good.

"Beats me," Justin replied.

Brandon ignored it, hoping it would go away. It didn't. It grew louder. The knocking turned into a loud *clang*. Then, they heard a *bang*, and smoke began rolling out from under the hood. Blinded by the smoke, Brandon slowed the car down and pulled over. Thankfully, the brakes still worked.

"Uh..." Justin muttered. "What just happened?"

"Your guess is as good as mine." The engine had cut out. Brandon got out of the car and walked to the front. Smoke continued billowing from the front of the vehicle. "Pop the hood!"

"How?"

"I think it's a lever under the steering wheel!"

Justin found it. The hood unlatched, and Brandon lifted it. The remainder of the smoke engulfed his face, choking him. Sputtering, he walked away from the car, waving his hands wildly in front of him. Justin stepped out and joined him. When the smoke cleared, they peered at what must have been the engine. *Or is that the transmission?* Brandon thought. *Or maybe it's the radiator?*

"What do you know about cars?" Brandon asked.

"That this one's broken."

Brandon swore. "What am I gonna tell Aunt Genni?"

"That's important and all, but my question is, what are we gonna do?"

CHAPTER NINE

THEIR OPTIONS LIMITED, THEY BEGAN WALKING ALONG THE ROAD toward the next town. Brandon tried to suppress his panic by humming the Johnny Cash melody that the Sun Studio guide had played. Justin shuffled along quietly behind him, kicking the gravel as he walked. About an hour later, they came upon a small garage on the outskirts of Winona, Mississippi. It had a Mexican restaurant attached to it. "Mmm. Smell that?" Brandon said. "Maybe we can get some food after we find out about the car." They entered the garage office.

Brandon had to squint as his eyes adjusted to the dark of the office. The only windows were in the front door and the door behind the counter that led to the equally dark shop. In here, the smell of Mexican food was no match for the pungent smell of oil. Car part catalogs were sprawled over the grimy counter.

A man behind the counter wore a blue jumpsuit with the sleeves partly rolled up, revealing his hairy arms. "What can I do fer ya?" he said.

"We broke down a few miles up the road," Brandon said.

"Need a tow?"

"I guess. How much will that cost?"

"What's wrong with it?"

"Well, we were driving, and we started hearing a knocking, and then a loud noise. It started smoking—dark, black smoke."

"That don't sound too good. Just down the road? You boys walk here?" he asked, a note of concern in his voice.

Brandon nodded.

"The tow's on the house. Roy!" he shouted. The door behind the counter opened. Country music flowed into the room as an older man came inside from the shop. His wispy white hair was accented with engine oil, as were the wrinkles on his face. "Take these boys to their car," the man ordered. "Just down the road. They'll show the way."

The three of them piled into the cab of the tow truck, which smelled exactly like the room they had just left. On the way, Brandon asked, "How much do you think it'll cost to fix the car?"

"I won't have a clue till we look at her," Roy said. "We can tow 'er back to the shop, and I'll have a look there."

A half-hour later, they were back at the shop with Genevieve's car. "Go next door and grab a bite," Roy said. "I'll come on over when I've got the diagnosis."

Brandon and Justin retrieved their things from the car and walked into the restaurant. The orange interior walls had paintings of desert landscapes. Brandon thought maybe that's what Arizona kind of looked like. He now wondered if he would ever know. Most of the tables were occupied with customers chatting and enjoying their food. It smelled delicious, and he was starving. "Let's just get some chips and salsa until we know how much this is gonna cost," Brandon said.

"I hope it won't cost too much. I couldn't bear smelling this all day and not splurging a little bit."

Brandon threw his bag in a booth and sat down. They ordered some water.

Fifteen minutes later, the mechanic found them. He sat down next to Justin. "I've got good news and bad news."

"Give us the bad news first," Brandon said.

"Your crankshaft's busted. The connecting rods for a couple of your pistons are torn to bits. Looks like your car hasn't been oiled in years."

Brandon cringed. That did sound bad. "That's part of the engine, right?"

Roy chuckled. "Yep. But the good news is I've got the parts in stock."

That sounded better. "Good. So, what's this going to cost?"

"That's the rest of the bad news. The parts don't cost too much. But I'm gonna have to take her engine apart to fix it. Lots of labor. Prolly be done on Monday. We're lookin' at somethin' like nine hundred."

Brandon coughed. "Nine hundred dollars?"

"Dude, what are we gonna do?" Justin asked.

"I don't know, but I don't think we can afford that. And even if we could, there'd be nothing left."

"Talk it through," Roy said, standing up. "You can come over and use our phone if ya need to." He walked out.

Brandon pulled out the envelope and counted the money. Eight hundred and thirty dollars. He started looking in his pockets, telling Justin to do the same. Suddenly, Brandon had an idea. He took out the Bible and started thumbing through it.

"What are you doing?" Justin asked.

"I read something the other day that claimed Jesus healed a paralyzed guy. If he can do that, then maybe he can give us some money." Brandon laughed. "Maybe Dean used some money as a bookmark." He tossed the Bible onto the table in frustration.

"There might be a Greyhound station nearby. We can do the bus thing," Justin said.

Brandon sat in silence for a moment. "You've finally come

around to that idea? I guess we don't have much choice. But what do we do with the car?"

Justin seemed to be distracted by something.

Brandon started to laugh. "How did we get it into our heads that we could drive to the Grand Canyon?"

"Wait a minute. *We?* It was in *your* head. But we've started this. We can't give up. Matt wouldn't give up."

"Okay. But what do we do about the car? Just leave it behind and hop on a bus?"

Justin wasn't listening. He was looking behind Brandon.

Brandon started to turn around, and Justin kicked him under the table. "What in the—"

"Don't look," Justin said.

"Don't look at what?"

"There's a guy over there who's been staring at us for a few minutes."

Brandon turned around and saw several people.

Justin sighed and threw up his hands. "Or you could look. That's fine too."

"That guy in the hat?" Brandon asked.

"No. That Black dude over there with glasses in the green shirt."

Brandon stole another look and met eyes with the guy Justin was talking about. He had short hair and a goatee. He seemed to be in his twenties.

"And you're looking again," Justin hissed.

The guy smiled, acknowledging the eye contact. He stood up, grabbed his plate, and walked over to their table. He stood there for a moment with his toothy grin. His shirt was dusty, and he had some dried paint on his hands. "Got room for one more?" He had a deep voice that suited his physique.

"Uh, sure," Brandon said. He moved over.

The guy set his plate down and sat. "I'm Anton."

"Brandon."

"Justin."

After an awkward few seconds, Anton asked, "What are you up to?"

"Just having lunch," Justin said.

"You've been sitting here for twenty minutes. You haven't ordered anything. Chips and salsa are your lunch?"

"We haven't made up our minds yet," Brandon said.

"I see," Anton said, eyeing their closed menus on the table. "You eaten here before?"

Brandon picked up a menu.

"Lisa!" He motioned for a server to come over to the table. "Lisa, these are my friends, Brandon and Justin. Will you bring them two of my usual?"

"No problem, Anton."

"What are you doing?" Brandon asked.

"Problem solved," he said, winking. "You couldn't make up your minds. You'll love the creamy chicken enchiladas. Best thing on their menu."

"The thing is, Anton," Justin began, "we're not sure if we'll be able to pay for creamy chicken enchiladas—hence the water and chips."

"Don't worry. My mama taught me that when I order, I pay. Lisa!" He got the waitress' attention again. "And two sweet teas, please."

"Why are you doing this?" asked Brandon.

"Anyone with two eyes could tell you fellas were stuck. And I've got two eyes. I saw how you counted your money after the mechanic came in. Afterward, you didn't order any food." He pointed to the Bible. "And the Lord has blessed me to work with my hands. 'Let him who steals steal no longer,' you know."

The boys looked at each other skeptically.

"You used to steal?" Brandon asked.

The waitress brought their two glasses of tea.

"No, but I thought you..." Anton trailed off. "Sorry, Ephesians chapter four."

"I'm not following," Brandon said.

"It's a passage in the Bible. It says that we ought to work with our hands, so we can have enough to help people in their time of need. I was encouraged you got your Bible out when you were in trouble."

Now Brandon understood. "No, we're not—I mean, I'm not —It was my father's Bible. I don't know anything about it, really. No offense, but I'm not interested either. It's just a memento."

"Sorry to have assumed," Anton said. "My bad."

Brandon expected Anton to go back on his offer to help now that he knew he and Justin weren't like him. He thought about the few Bible-thumpers he did know. They always stuck together and never showed interest in people who weren't like them. Or if they did, they were fitting in with Cody and company, mocking the losers around them—losers like Brandon. But Anton showed no sign of budging. Was this guy for real?

It wasn't long before the waitress arrived with two steaming plates of food, which looked and smelled delicious. Brandon picked up his fork and eyed Anton suspiciously, searching for something. Deceit, maybe? A hint that this was a joke?

Anton smiled. "You like cheese, don't you? Dig in!"

Justin took a bite. Brandon hesitated and then followed suit. "This is amazing!" Justin said. Brandon agreed, but he kept it to himself.

Anton finished the food that he had brought over from his table. Wiping his mouth and putting the napkin on his plate, he said, "I've learned it's the restaurants off the beaten path that are the best. I find them everywhere I go. I've been in Winona for about a month. I must have had lunch here fifteen times already."

Brandon assumed Justin was thinking the same thing he

was. *Who is this guy, and what does he want?* For the time being, Brandon was thankful for his kindness. Still, he kept his guard up.

"You guys do much traveling?" Anton asked.

"We're actually traveling now," Justin replied. "Or maybe more accurately, we *were* traveling."

"Really?" Anton said.

"Our car's broke," Justin said. "Not sure what we're gonna do yet."

"Is there a Greyhound station around here?" Brandon asked.

Anton touched his goatee in thought. "Dunno. Where are you heading to?"

"Arizona," Brandon said.

"Whoa! Where'd you come from?"

"Nashville."

Anton thought about that for a moment. "Winona doesn't seem like a place you'd pass through on your way to Arizona. What's waiting for you in Arizona? Family?"

"Look, Anton," Brandon said. "We appreciate lunch and all. Very nice gesture to help some guys in need. But me and Justin need to work some things out, if you don't mind."

"No, no, no. All good and understood. I'll settle up this bill and let you fellas be." He stood up.

"Thanks, dude," Justin said. "You were right. I think these are the best enchiladas I've ever had."

"No problem. I hope you two have a great trip." He walked to the cash register.

"That was interesting," Justin said in a hushed voice.

"If that's what you want to call it. Hypocritical, if you ask me," Brandon said, cutting his eyes toward Anton.

"Hypocritical?"

"He's probably glad we gave him an easy out. You saw how he was only interested in talking to us when he thought we were reading the Bible or whatever. Too bad he had already offered to pay for our lunch before he found out we weren't his kind."

"Come on," Justin said. "He seems like a nice dude. You really think he bought our lunch because he thought we were Christians?"

"I'm sure of it."

Anton started walking back to their table. "All settled up. And I got the tip too. Have a good one." He gave a warm smile and walked out.

"Now he's just trying to look good," Brandon said.

As they finished their meals, Brandon and Justin continued to try to come up with ideas of how to get back on the road. In the end, they admitted defeat. They went next door, and the garage agreed to a payment plan for the nine hundred dollars, so long as they put half down now. That left them enough money to stay in a nearby motel, and what they hoped was enough money to cover food and gas until they got home.

"I guess I'll call Aunt Genni," Brandon said.

"Better wait until the car's fixed," Justin suggested.

"Good idea."

"But I do need to call my cousin." Justin asked the man behind the counter if he could use the phone.

Brandon stepped outside.

A few minutes later, Justin came out. "My cousin's cool with telling my grandma that I'm job hunting. When we get back to Nashville, you can drop me off there, and I'll fill out the applications he picks up."

"Fine with me."

With backpacks slung across their shoulders, and Dean's Bible sticking out of Brandon's pocket, the two of them walked toward Winona. They found a motel, not unlike the one they had stayed at in Jackson. At least this one had microwaves in the rooms and provided cereal and bagels in the lobby each morning. They checked in for three nights.

Brandon sat on the stiff bed—the fourth new bed in a week. Exactly a week prior, life had been normal. Matt was getting ready to play his trumpet at a basketball game. Barry was on his way to the bar. Brandon and Justin were sitting on the couch in front of the TV that would soon produce an image that Brandon would never forget. And now, Brandon sat on a bed in...where were they? Somewhere in Mississippi, the farthest he had ever been from home. Which was sad, really. Most of the people from school at least went to the Gulf during summer vacation. In their grand plan to honor Matt, Brandon and Justin had only managed to make it to the next state.

Whatever had woken up in Brandon two days ago when he jumped on Cody, pounding his face into the gym floor, was retreating back to where it had come from. It was excruciating. That afternoon at school, he'd thought he was so courageous, so invincible. He even had the guts to break into the principal's office. Brandon laughed to himself and shook his head. Now that it was time to turn back, he knew he was letting Matt down. *We'll try again some other time, buddy. I promise.*

"What're we gonna do for dinner?" Justin said, coming out of the bathroom.

"Remember that small grocery store we passed? They've probably got some Hot Pockets and peanut butter and jelly."

"Works for me. Let's go."

As hot as the afternoon sun was, Brandon continued to wear his trench coat. He had wondered how they would wash their clothes, but he knew he could hold off for a few more days till he got back to Grand Junction. Were the Jensons worried about him? Before the car broke down, he'd felt he was doing them a favor disappearing like that. He put the thought out of his mind for the time being, not wanting to think about what he would say to them when he returned in a few days. At least he didn't have to face Barry. Anything was better than that.

CHAPTER TEN

CHECKOUT FROM THE MOTEL WAS AT ELEVEN ON MONDAY morning. This time, Brandon ensured he left with his father's Bible tucked in his coat pocket. He and Justin walked back to the garage to see if they were finished fixing Genevieve's car. About a half-hour later, they arrived, and Justin stomped out his cigarette.

"You never answered my question!" a familiar deep voice called from across the parking lot. It was Anton. "What do you want in Arizona?"

Brandon scoffed. "Is this guy for real?"

"The Grand Canyon!" Justin called back to him.

Anton was wearing sunglasses and leaning against a late-model maroon sedan. "I've never been there. I've heard it's beautiful. Still looking for a Greyhound?"

"Nah," Justin said. "We've gotta head back home."

"Let's go," Brandon urged, stepping toward the garage.

"It's the money, isn't it?"

"That's none of his business," Brandon whispered as he stepped closer to the garage.

"Got a map on you?" Anton asked.

"Yeah." Justin tugged Brandon by his backpack. "Come on."

Brandon hesitated, then followed Justin to Anton's car. Justin nodded toward Brandon's backpack. Reluctantly, Brandon unzipped it and pulled out Matt's folder. "Last week, Matt hadn't even shown it to us," Brandon whispered. "Now, we're just going to show it to anyone who asks?"

Justin extended his hand. "Just give it to me." Brandon sighed. Justin set the folder on the hood of Anton's car and opened it.

"This is incredible!" Anton said, taking off his sunglasses and replacing them with his eyeglasses that had been hanging on his shirt. "You guys make this?"

"A friend did," Justin said.

Anton found Winona on the map. "We're here. It looks to me that going back up to I-40 is the best way to the Grand Canyon. But what's this red line?"

"That's what our friend planned out," Justin said. "He wanted this to not just be about the destination, but also the journey, you know?"

Brandon stood with his arms crossed, watching Justin and Anton pore over Matt's map.

"For sure," Anton said. "Looks like your friend's done his homework. Where is this friend?"

Brandon spoke up. "Six feet under."

Justin scraped the ground with his feet, while Brandon stood defiantly, hands on hips. *And none of your words of wisdom are gonna bring him back,* he thought.

"I'm sorry, fellas." Anton straightened up and looked at them with concern in his eyes.

"We've got to get going," Brandon said. He reached between Justin and Anton and began folding up the map. He picked up his bag, stuffed the folder in it, zipped it up, and slung it on his shoulder. "Thanks again for lunch the other day," he said with as much sincerity as he could manage. He started to walk toward the garage.

"How long do you have?" Anton asked.

Brandon stopped and turned to Anton. "Huh?"

"How long do you have? When do you need to get to Arizona?"

"Didn't you hear us?" Brandon took a step toward Anton. "We're not going anymore." He slowed his speech, as if talking to a child, each syllable staccatoed. "We're on our way back to Nashville."

"Before you head back home, hear me out," Anton said. "I came to Winona to help a family renovate their basement. I put the baseboards up this morning. I'm here—" he gestured toward the Mexican restaurant, "—to celebrate the finished job. If it's the money thing, I'll take you. We could leave after lunch." He said it matter of factly, as though it were the most natural thing in the world to drop everything and escort two strangers halfway across the country.

Brandon took another step forward and squared up with Anton. Anton was a bit taller and much stronger than Brandon, but with Justin's help, he could take him down if he tried anything. "What do you want?" Brandon finally asked.

Anton raised his hands in a gesture of mock defeat. "Only to help—and maybe to make a couple of friends. I know it seems strange, some random fella offering you lunch and then a ride to the other side of the country and all. But seriously. I know what it's like to have major plans crumble on you. A broken car shouldn't stop your dreams. Do you think it's an accident we're here at this place together again? I just finished the last job that I had lined up before school starts in August, and I was just wondering what I was gonna do with my summer."

Brandon backed off. Maybe this guy was genuine. But more than once Barry had appeared genuine too, when he had vowed for the millionth time that he wouldn't drink anymore. Brandon had fallen for it in the beginning, but in the end, it only resulted in blood and bruises—and death. And if this guy was the real thing, Brandon thought, then he must not be right in the head. Justin, on the other hand, looked interested.

Anton continued. "An adventure is just what I need. And like what my mama taught me about lunch—since I'm offering, I'm paying. I made a good chunk of spending money this spring, and I'll pay for the gas and stuff along the way. It seems to me to be a win-win: You get your Greyhound; I get an adventure. Or I can help you pay to fix your car, if you prefer. Your call, I guess."

Brandon could see Justin chomping at the bit, clearly under Anton's spell, a huge grin on his face. "We need to talk about this," Brandon said curtly, as he dragged his friend back toward the garage. "What is up with this guy?" he whispered.

"I think he's legit. He's trying to be nice."

"But who does this—does he know how much it will cost him to pay for everything? And we can't just go with some stranger," Brandon said.

"What's your problem?" Justin said accusingly. "This trip was your idea, remember? You're the one who convinced me to go across the country on a whim, and you also almost had me convinced that the first bind we got into meant we should give up. But now we get a free ride, and you say no?"

Brandon shrugged.

"Wait," Justin said, a sudden knowing look on his face. "It's not because he's..."

"No!" Brandon said. "I can't believe you. Of course not. You know me better than that." Brandon pursed his lips. "It's just... that Bible thing the other day."

"Well, you did have a Bible on the table. You can't help him for wanting to talk about it."

"But he doesn't even know us. It's just a ploy for him to get us in his car and bash us with his religion. Can you imagine? It would be so awkward." He paused. "But I like his last idea about paying to fix the car."

"Are you for real? First, we can't take advantage of someone like that—just take his money and drive off into the sunset. Second, I think all this is in your head, Brandy—he's just a nice guy who wants to help some poor kids. Third, I bet Anton has his driver's license. And fourth, look at his car." They glanced over. Anton had his sunglasses back on as he leaned against the Nissan Maxima, apparently minding his own business. "I don't think it would break down on us, and it probably has a CD player. Are you ready to go to the Grand Canyon? Or do you want to go back to your orphanage?"

"It's not an orphanage," Brandon said defensively.

"Whatever."

Brandon swore. Justin had a point; there was nothing for him back home—he didn't even have a proper home anymore. "Fine. But if he gets weird, don't say I didn't warn you. I'll be hitchhiking back to Nashville." For a moment, an image of his father hitchhiking across the country popped into his mind.

"Fair enough." Justin raised his fist for Brandon to bump it. "First day of the rest—"

"Let's go," Brandon said.

CHAPTER ELEVEN

THE MECHANIC WAS NEARLY FINISHED REPLACING THE crankshaft on Genevieve's car. Brandon and Justin worked it out with the garage that they would pick it up on their way back through in a few weeks.

"You guys hungry?" Anton asked, nodding toward the restaurant.

"Definitely," Justin replied.

As they started walking, Brandon stopped abruptly. "Be right with you," he said.

He walked back to the car and snagged the photo from behind the steering wheel, then jogged to catch up with Anton and Justin. They studied the map over a quick lunch.

They had barely exited the restaurant when Justin brought a cigarette to his lips and pulled out a lighter.

"One rule," Anton said. "No smoking in the car."

After Justin finished, they piled into Anton's car, which indeed had a CD player. Justin sat up front, while Brandon took the back seat. The seats were soft, the interior spotless, and the car had a pleasant smell to it. Anton started the engine, and The Marvelettes' "Please Mr. Postman" blared through the speakers.

Justin feigned being sick and looked back at Brandon, who mouthed, "strike one."

Justin covered his ears. "I'm melting!"

Anton laughed. He pressed stop. "You two will remember that this is my car, right?"

"Sure," Justin said. "But we signed up for a ride, not torture."

Anton turned around in his seat. "It appears your friend over here is a little drama queen," he said to Brandon. "How would you like to sit up front?"

Justin reached into his backpack and grabbed a CD from the sleeve. "I think the one riding shotgun should get to pick the music. Keeps the driver's eyes on the road, you know. You wanna know what real music is? We'll ease you into it. Try this one."

Anton looked at Fuel's *Sunburn* album for a moment before popping it into the player. The three were hammered with heavy guitars accented with hard snare drum hits.

"That's what I'm talking about!" Justin shouted.

"I can dig," Anton said. He lowered the volume. "Tell ya what. You explain to me why you like this music, and I'll tell you what there is to like about Motown. Then, you'll need to give my music another shot. I'll convert you before we reach the Grand Canyon. Actually, you'll learn to love it by the time we leave Louisiana."

Justin wore a thoughtful expression. "Sounds fair to me. But the odds are against you on this. Don't get your hopes up for converts."

Anton smiled and put the car in drive. "Nawlins, here we come."

Justin and Anton chatted for a while about what made nü-metal so appealing. "It's the natural evolution of music from the early '90s," Justin said. "And it's so much more. It's like putting funk, metal, and grunge in a blender. You like poetry? We've got it. How about rap? Got it too. DJs? Heavy guitars? All over the place. Now, this album—" Justin pointed to the stereo, "—is what I call a gateway album." He smiled at Anton. Brandon knew this side of Justin well. He wasn't being pretentious. This was his element, and he lived to have these types of conversations. "This band isn't fully nü-metal. They're more post-grunge. But they're heavy enough. And they've got some catchy stuff." Justin turned up the volume.

As the music pumped and Justin and Anton continued to chat about genres, Brandon retrieved the final postcard in the first pocket of Matt's map. It read, "JACKSON SQUARE," under a statue of a man on a horse. He turned it over and saw another personalized message to Matt, this one beckoning him to learn about the Civil War and the French Quarter, the oldest neighborhood in New Orleans. It sounded dreadfully boring to Brandon. Yet Brandon admired Matt for it. When there was an opportunity to learn, Matt paid attention, even if the information had no apparent use. What was the point of people his age learning about a fight that happened over a century ago? Brandon didn't know. But Matt had always been curious, so he tried to see it from Matt's perspective: an opportunity to discover something interesting. After all, going to Sun Studio ended up being more of an educational trip than Brandon had expected. And he was grateful. He thought of the train museum in Jackson they'd skipped over. Should they have stopped? Brandon shook his head. *Nah.*

It was going to take them over four hours to reach the edge of New Orleans, giving Brandon a lot of time to think. He pulled Dean's box out of his backpack and found the photograph of his mother and father. Brandon wished he could have seen his mother that happy just once. He held the dog tags and thought of his grandparents. What were they like? What were the chances that he could find them? Would they be happy to learn they were grandparents? Were they Christians too? That idea didn't exactly excite Brandon, but he was willing to look past it. They were from a different generation. Brandon put the stuff back in the box and let the gentle movement of the car rock him to sleep.

He awoke on the outskirts of New Orleans as traffic slowed to a stop-start speed. Rush hour had begun. Thankfully, most of the traffic was heading out, not in, so the congestion gradually eased. With the help of Matt's mini-maps, finding the French Quarter was a cinch. Parking, however, was a different story. Brandon felt himself tense up as they circled the blocks, vainly searching for a space. He'd been in similar situations with Barry, who seemed to think that if he swore loudly enough, someone would move. But Anton didn't seem bothered in the slightest. Fifteen minutes later, they finally snagged a spot near a street market.

"And here we are," Anton announced. He walked around to Justin's side and opened his door, ushering him out like a chauffeur would.

Justin smiled. "What service!" he exclaimed.

Brandon let himself out and managed to crack a smile.

There were things of all sorts to look at and purchase at the market—colorful fruits and vegetables (some of them completely alien to Brandon), textiles, knick-knacks, hippie-style clothing, New Orleans souvenirs, including what looked like Tarot cards and voodoo dolls. Justin couldn't resist picking up a voodoo doll and holding it up to show Brandon. "Let's call him Cody," Justin said. "Or Vernon."

Brandon laughed. "How about Barry?"

Justin showed it to Anton. He gently grabbed it and put it back on the table. "Come on. We're on a mission, right?"

They walked toward Jackson Square. On their way, they could see an open-air café packed with people. The line to the counter zig-zagged and ended on the sidewalk. As they got closer, Brandon read the sign—"CAFÉ DU MONDE."

"I've heard of this place!" Anton said excitedly. "I've got

family upstate. They visit New Orleans every few years, and they always come back talking about these doughnut things. We've gotta try them!"

"What was that about being on a mission?" Brandon asked.

"Sure!" Justin said. Then, he whispered to Brandon, "Let's not be downers, okay?"

The smell of coffee filled the air. Brandon looked at a nearby table and saw people eating some powder-coated food. "They do look good," he admitted.

They went to the back of the line. Although it was long, it moved fast, and a few minutes later, Anton was ordering a plate of the doughnut things, which were called beignets. Just like parking, it took them some circling to find an empty table. Once they did, they sat down to enjoy their dessert. They reminded Brandon of a funnel cake he'd once had when Matt's family had taken him and Justin to the county fair.

"So, what number is New Orleans on your friend's map?" Anton asked with a powdered sugar mustache.

"Three," Brandon said. "Jackson, Memphis, New Orleans."

"And Dallas is number four?"

"I think so."

"My family upstate lives just outside Shreveport," Anton said, "which is between here and Dallas. My Aunt Mavel's always got people staying at her house. I bet she'd let us bunk there tomorrow night. If she doesn't have room, she'd at least feed us."

Brandon finished his beignet, dusted off his hands, and pulled out Matt's folder. Since their table was so close to the next one, there wasn't enough room to unfold the entire thing, but he opened it enough to find Shreveport. Matt's red line crossed right through it. The distance from New Orleans to Dallas looked more than twice as long as the distance between Memphis and New Orleans. "Yeah," he said, folding up the map.

"Good idea. Break up the trip a bit. Think she'd let us wash some clothes?"

The day was still bright, but the sun was inching toward the horizon. They finished their treats and stood. Regaining their bearings, they made for Jackson Square, which wasn't far from the café. They knew they'd arrived when Brandon spotted the statue of the rider and his horse. Behind the statue stood an ornate church. He pulled the postcard out of his pocket and handed it to Justin, who held it up, so the image and the real thing were beside each other.

There were plaques and signs to read all over the place in Jackson Square; Matt would not have been disappointed. Anton walked toward the statue and started reading its inscription. Afterward, he found another plaque to read. And so he went for the next few minutes—bouncing around Jackson Square, learning its history. Matt would have been doing the same thing. Brandon settled on learning about the statue, which was of Major General Andrew Jackson. That name sounded familiar. *Was he a president?* Brandon couldn't remember.

He heard music coming from the direction of the church. He gave into the impulse to follow it, Justin and Anton a few paces behind him. As they approached the space in front of the church, they saw a six-piece band exploding with energy and sound. Four Black guys and two White guys hammered on a snare drum, strummed a standup bass, and blew through a trumpet, trombone, and saxophone. One of them played a small piano on wheels. A crowd was gathering around them, stepping to the beat. Before Brandon knew it, his head was bobbing too. His feet soon followed. Justin also seemed intoxicated by the sound.

"Look at you fellas!" Anton exclaimed, coming up next to them. "You're more open-minded than I thought! Behold!" He extended both arms toward the street band. "The foundation of Motown!" Anton started stepping to the beat and walked a bit beyond the musical group. Still bouncing, he entered the gates of the massive church, Justin at his heels.

Brandon hesitated, then followed them through the gates and the massive doors.

Anton was reading another plaque—this one about the history of the building. He looked at the votive candles. He frowned, and Brandon thought he saw him shake his head slightly.

Brandon stepped past him into the cathedral. His jaw dropped as he peered into the vast space. It was massive. He guessed Grand Junction could fit inside the cathedral four or five times. Directly in front of him were rows and rows of pews. A handful of people sat on them—spread out—a person here, another there. Some had their heads down, presumably praying. Beyond the pews stood a platform with structures and statues on it that Brandon didn't understand. This place was much different than the church where Matt's funeral was held. It commanded silence, although a loud footstep or a cough broke the silence every few seconds, echoing off the walls. Then, Brandon noticed the columns. His eyes followed them to the second level, and then to the ceiling. Elaborate paintings dotted the surface over one hundred and fifty feet above him. He stared at them until he began to feel dizzy.

Out of the corner of his eye, he saw Justin walk to the right behind one of the columns. Brandon followed. There were stained glass windows in the side walls. Between two of the windows was a painting on an easel. Brandon stepped closer. It was of a woman holding a newborn. Under the picture, the sign read, "The Virgin Mary with Child." Despite the reverence the place commanded, Brandon laughed quietly. He thought of the Christmas songs he had heard. He always chalked it up to part of the Christmas fun—Santa Claus, elves, and a virgin mother. But to see people actually devoted to such a tale...

Brandon spotted Anton—still reading plaques and signs,

frowning the entire time—and followed Justin at a distance. He didn't know why, but this place seemed to be the type where people kept to themselves. Conversation felt forbidden. Step-by-step, they made the loop around the cathedral. They saw more stained glass and paintings, as well as ornaments and candles on every platform.

The three of them finished the circle and stepped outside, squinting. After their eyes adjusted to the early evening sun, Anton said, "How about we get more adventurous tonight?"

Brandon gave him a bemused look. "Meaning?"

"Something other than Mexican food." Anton started looking for a place to eat, receiving no help from Brandon and Justin.

It wasn't Brandon's place to offer suggestions; Anton was paying after all. As they walked, he thought of the day. That morning, they had been planning to head back to Nashville. If they had, they would have missed out on all this. He looked around at the buildings in the oldest neighborhood in New Orleans. Whatever Anton's deal was, he was kind. Brandon could give him that. And, in some funny way, he reminded Brandon of Matt.

They happened upon a seafood grill. "Work for you?" Anton asked Brandon and Justin.

"That *is* more adventurous," Justin said with a sour expression.

"Sure," said Brandon.

After being seated and placing their order, Brandon said to Anton, "You were giddy in the square, bouncing from plaque to plaque. What's your interest in all this stuff?"

"'Never stop learning.' It's what my granddad always said. He came from a different generation; didn't have the opportunities we do. He planted within me the desire to learn something new whenever I can. Listen when people speak. Ask more questions than I answer. How do things work? What happened in the past? That kind of thing."

"Matt was like that too," Justin said quietly.

"Who's Matt?"

"He was our friend who made that map. He died less than two weeks ago."

There was silence.

"Were you three supposed to make this trip together?" Anton asked.

"Sort of," Justin said. "Matt had planned for all of us to go—"

"No," Brandon interjected. "Me and Justin were jerks to Matt about this trip. In the fifth grade, we were assigned a research project in social studies on the Grand Canyon. Matt did most of the work."

"All," Justin corrected. "He did all the work."

"He ate it up," Brandon said. "When he learned about the Grand Canyon and stuff, he got it in his head that we were all gonna go together. We didn't help with the project. We thought the hype would fade, but it didn't. All we did was shoot down his dreams."

"Or ignore them," Justin added.

"And he never got to see the GC," Brandon said, his voice wavering.

"I'm so sorry about your loss, fellas," Anton said gently.

"Thanks," Justin said.

"I also noticed you changed your attitude when we went into the church," Brandon said, regaining his composure. "I thought you would be even more excited in there, but you seemed upset. What's up with that?"

"You noticed?" Anton said. "Well, the building and artwork are beautiful—stunning." Anton stroked his goatee before continuing. "As beautiful as all of it is, to quote the apostle Paul, 'they have a zeal for God, but not in accordance with knowledge.'"

Brandon had no idea what he meant by that. *Paul who?* Their server brought their drinks to the table. After a moment, Brandon said to Anton, "So, you think all this stuff happened?"

"What stuff?"

"This New Orleans stuff. Civil War and General Jackson."

Anton narrowed his eyes. "Of course I do. It's our history, right? Do you?"

"I do, but I don't remember any of the details. I'm sure I've heard teachers explain this stuff from history books." He pulled the Bible out of his pocket and set it on the table. "But you also seem to believe *this stuff* actually happened."

"What stuff, exactly?" Anton asked, smiling.

"Do you have to ask? A virgin getting pregnant. A man healing people just by speaking."

"Ah, I think I understand. You're asking how someone so interested in history can believe the Bible."

"I guess that's it. You said it yourself that you want to know history and how stuff works. Well, I don't think I've ever read anything in a science book about how virgins can have children and paralyzed people can be healed. How can you be consistent? You believe in history, yet you also believe in this ancient book filled with myths and fairytales."

Anton leaned back in his chair. "I wish everyone in the world was asking that question."

"Really?" Brandon raised his eyebrows at Justin, as if to say, *Can you believe this guy?* Justin silently sipped his soda.

"Sure. Most people who aren't religious go on assuming what they want about Christians and Christianity. You've gone a step further and asked a believer why they believe. I guess my question for you is, are you honestly searching for answers?"

Brandon thought that was a strange response. He was starting to warm up to Anton, especially since he hadn't tried to force anything on them...yet. But Brandon was curious to see whether his temper would flare when someone questioned his religion. From Brandon's experience, if someone was religious, the best way to find out who they truly were was to mock or question their beliefs. Brandon didn't want to push too hard, however, since the last thing he needed right now was an argument. However, Anton had praised Brandon for questioning his beliefs. And Brandon was pretty sure he wasn't being sarcastic. "Am I searching for answers? If there are any, why not?"

CHAPTER TWELVE

"OKAY. ANOTHER QUESTION," ANTON SAID. "YOU CLAIMED THE Bible is an ancient book of myths and fairytales. What do you mean by that?"

Brandon thought for a moment before replying, "You want me to speak my mind here?"

"Absolutely," he said without hesitation.

"It makes sense for the people of hundreds of years ago to be religious. A thunderstorm scares someone? Must be the gods." Brandon raised his hands, feigning fear. "A society needs order? Write a book and claim the rules come from a higher power who will judge you if you don't mindlessly obey. Need a crutch? Invent some guy who will forgive you if you swear at your parents. Or hit your stepson." Brandon frowned. "But we've gone past that, don't you think? We can explain what causes lightning without inventing higher powers. We don't need a virgin to give birth for us to feel good about our decisions."

Anton appeared to take in what Brandon was saying. "That crutch you speak of—is that Jesus?"

"In Christianity, yeah. In other religions, it's probably some other guy. And before I come off as some intolerant jerk, I should say I think it's fine for people to have their own beliefs and all, so long as they mind their own business. My dad was a Christian." Brandon paused, realizing that this was the first time he had referred to Dean as his dad, rather than his father. "But it just seems inconsistent to me to read these plaques about historical events and believe them, and then read this—" he landed a finger on the Bible, "—and believe it too. No offense."

"I told you, fellas," Anton began, "that I was looking for a couple of friends on this trip. I think I've found them." He smiled at Justin, who was playing with the condensation on his soda glass, and then at Brandon. "If I'm going to return your friendship, then I won't be offended when you speak your mind to me. And I'll assume you're not just being truthful, but also interested in the truth."

Brandon didn't say anything, but he allowed the corners of his mouth to curl up a bit. Anton seemed one of a kind. Who else would drive a couple of stranded strangers to New Orleans? Who else would choose to spend their hard-earned money buying food for some careless kids? Who else would not explode at someone —friend or not—after he tried to undermine his religion?

Anton continued. "Since you mentioned other religions, let's put them on the table too: Buddhism, Islam, Hinduism, just to list some of the big ones. What separates Christianity from all other religions?"

Brandon shrugged. "Jesus, I guess."

"You guess right," Anton said. "Now, if your claim is true—that Jesus is a myth—then what does that do for Christianity?"

"Destroys it. But that hasn't stopped people from believing the myth."

Justin showed no sign of contributing to this exchange; he seemed content to spectate.

"Sure," Anton agreed. "If Jesus never existed, then Christianity falls flat. Other religions are based on ideas. Christianity, however, depends on history. It stands or falls on whether or not what the Bible claims is historical fact."

Brandon leaned in subconsciously. "So, why do you keep believing it?"

"Simple. Because what the Bible claims happened actually happened." Anton smiled.

"Ha! You believe what the Bible claims because the Bible says so?"

"You misunderstood me. I don't just believe all this because it's in the Bible. I believe it because I believe the Bible is a credible source to claim such things."

"Pssh!" Brandon pushed on the table, leaning back in the booth. He said to Justin, "You're hearing this, right?"

Without looking away from his glass, Justin said quietly, "But it seems like he's not finished. Maybe you should hear him out."

"Justin's right," Anton said. "I'm not finished. There's an important lesson we all need to learn right here and now." Anton spoke with controlled determination. He didn't raise his voice, yet his speech commanded attention. "And I'm not just talking about the lesson on why I believe this stuff happened." He gestured toward the Bible. "The lesson is in keeping each other accountable. As you get to know me, you'll learn that I am passionate about talking about what's in this book. But no one does anyone any favors by forcing their beliefs on others. Instead, they should ask questions and listen. And if anyone makes any claims—that includes me—we need to ask for evidence."

Brandon leaned in again, curiosity piqued. "Okay. So this is me asking for evidence."

"All right then. What year is it?" Anton said.

"Last I checked, it was 1999," Brandon said.

"And next year will be?"

"2000," he replied, wondering where this train of thought was leading.

"Hmm," Anton said. "We're counting up in years. The following year will be 2001. 2001 years since what?"

Brandon was silent. Was this a trick question?

Anton continued. "Apparently, about 2000 years ago, something happened. Something important. Something major enough to change the entire way people measure the passing of time. And every time someone has written the date since then, they have, in some small way, acknowledged that event. Let me show you. Pick up the Bible and turn to Matthew chapter one."

Anton was more intelligent than Brandon had first judged him to be. He had a strong build, and with a job remodeling houses, he must be good with his hands. Intellectuals usually didn't fit that model. They were all clean-shaven and cravat-wearing. Brandon stared at the Bible in front of him. "I don't know how to work this thing. Do you?" Justin shook his head.

"No problem." Anton picked it up, turned to a passage, and gave the Bible to Brandon, pointing. "See the top of the page?"

Brandon looked down. "Matthew." He had no idea the name "Matthew" was in the Bible. He wondered if Matt's parents had known that when they named him.

"That's the book—the Bible contains sixty-six books. This one is the book of Matthew. The big numbers are the chapters. The small numbers are the verses. Simple."

"Sure," Brandon replied.

"Read verses twenty-four and twenty-five for us."

Brandon hesitated and glanced over at Justin, who seemed to be waiting for him to comply. "Okay."

> *And Joseph arose from his sleep, and did as the angel of the Lord commanded him, and took her as his wife, and kept her a virgin until she gave birth to a Son; and he called His name Jesus.*

Brandon abruptly closed the book. "This is what I'm talking about. Angels? Virgins giving birth? Come on. What evidence do we have to believe this stuff?"

Their server came to the table with their plates of food. Brandon grabbed the Bible and stuffed it back into his pocket while she set a platter of fried shrimp and cocktail sauce in front of him. Justin had opted for a burger. The server handed Anton a bowl and left to fetch silverware. "That chowder looks g—" Brandon began, but stopped when he noticed Anton had his head bowed and eyes closed. Anton looked up. "Sorry," Brandon said.

Anton smiled. "No prob. Where were we?"

"Angels and virgins," Brandon said a little too loudly, just as the server returned with the silverware.

"Let me know if you need anything else," she said with a bemused smile, her eyes wide from what she'd overheard. As she left the table, Justin flushed a shade red.

Anton and Brandon laughed. "That's right," Anton said. "But the Bible claims it happened. So, what do you make of that?"

"Of course it does. Whoever wrote the Bible had an agenda."

"And who wrote the Bible?" Anton asked, gently blowing on a spoonful of chowder.

"Beats me," said Brandon, taking a bite of shrimp. "Maybe Matthew?"

"You mean to tell me that you know the author had an agenda, but you don't even know who he is?" Anton remained calm. He simply asked a question.

"Well," Brandon said. "Come on. It's clearly biased. They want to paint a good picture of this Jesus guy."

"I don't disagree," Anton said. "There were about forty men who wrote down the words that would come to make up the Bible. For now, let's consider the historical accounts of Jesus. That's Matthew, Mark, Luke, and John. These four men wrote about the life of Jesus on earth. Two of them personally knew him. And all four claim that Jesus was a real person and performed miracles. In other words, they painted a good picture of this 'Jesus guy.' Were they biased? Absolutely. But just because it's biased, is it wrong?"

Brandon didn't say anything.

"We saw that statue in the square today," Anton said. "Who was Andrew Jackson?"

Justin spoke up. "President."

"That's right," said Anton. "Seventh president of the United States. The earliest information we have on him was written by people who knew him—and by Jackson himself. Those people were biased, and they spoke favorably of him. But who do you think is most qualified to write such things?"

"The people who knew him," Brandon answered, getting Anton's point.

"A court of law still calls eyewitnesses to the stand, even if such witnesses are biased and friends with the person on trial."

"All right," Brandon said. "I see your point. So I won't fault the Bible for being biased. But no matter how closely a person knows you, I'm not gonna believe them if they tell me your mother's a virgin."

Anton cracked a smile while chewing on some bread. "I wouldn't either. But you leave my mama out of this." Anton finished his bite. "We're now talking about two different subjects. Whether or not Jesus of Nazareth was a historical person, and whether or not a God capable of performing miracles exists."

Brandon thought about that for a moment. "I thought they went hand-in-hand."

"In one sense, they do. The Bible claims both are true—Jesus really lived, and God exists. However, just because one is true, it doesn't automatically mean the other is also true."

Justin sat silently, enjoying his burger. For once, Brandon wished he would speak his mind.

"The God of the Bible exists," Anton said.

"Okay," Brandon said.

"That's it?" Anton asked, putting down his spoon. "You agree with me?"

"Well, not really, but you're entitled to believe that."

"Sure I am, but we're friends, and such a claim brings with it huge implications. Remember what I said? When someone claims something, we should ask for what?"

"Ah," Brandon said, feeling a little like he was in school. "Evidence. So, what evidence is there that this God exists?"

"I thought you'd never ask. Think of something you've seen —anything at all."

"Uh," Brandon said, "that statue of the president."

"Perfect. Has that statue been here since forever, or did it have a beginning?"

"It had a beginning, of course." Having thought he was starting to understand Anton's way of thinking, Brandon once again felt adrift.

"Of course. And that's true for every material thing. We have three options." Anton counted on his fingers. "Either a thing in question has always existed, it created itself, or some outside force created it. Scientists used to think the big exception to that was the universe itself. But now, we know the universe had a beginning. And that's why the scientific world has been so interested in trying to answer this question: How did the universe begin? What do you think?"

"I don't know," Brandon said with a shrug. Now this was turning into a science lesson. "My teachers talked about the Big Bang."

"Sure," Anton said. "But what was that Big Bang? A common theory is that a tiny ball of matter packed densely with an insane amount of energy exploded ages and ages ago to form the universe as we know it. My question is, where did that ball of matter come from? We still have those three options: always existed, from itself, or something else. If you take God out of the equation, you're always left with the question, 'But where did that come from?' It's the law of cause and effect." Anton took another bite of bread.

Again, Brandon was thrown off by Anton's intellect. It was like he had been preparing for this moment or something, like he had a script. Brandon had to think about what Anton was saying for a minute to fully grasp it. He considered the statue of Andrew Jackson. Indeed, it had a creator. But was the answer to life's biggest question really that simple? Of course it wasn't. Otherwise, every sane person would unquestionably believe in God. But he knew several people much smarter than him who didn't. Brandon realized what Anton had missed. "You're right. We are left with that question. And now I'll turn it on you." He paused before asking, "Where did God come from?"

Anton smiled. "Now you're getting it!"

"Really? It seems to me that you're in checkmate." Brandon grinned and leaned back in his seat again. He popped a couple of shrimp in his mouth while Justin chewed on some fries.

"You're using your noggin." Anton knocked on his head. "You're trying to poke holes in an argument, which is the only way to test something's integrity. If I am going to place my confidence and set sail on a ship, I want it to have been tried, tested, and held up under the greatest scrutiny."

Brandon's smile faded. He raised an eyebrow at Anton.

"Will you get your father's Bible out again?" Anton finished off his clam chowder and pushed the bowl aside. "Humor me for a moment, will you?"

Brandon slowly reached for the Bible, suspicion etched on his face.

"This time," Anton said, "we're looking for a book called John."

Brandon thumbed through the Bible, glancing at the top of the pages.

Anton guided him. "Keep going. You've gone a bit too far. There! Now, turn to chapter four, and read verse twenty-four for us."

Brandon did so.

God is spirit, and those who worship Him must worship in spirit and truth.

He closed the Bible.

"That verse said God is what?" Anton asked.

"God is spirit." Brandon ate his last shrimp. "What's the point?"

"That means God is not part of this material world. God is not subject to the laws of physics."

"Oh, right," Brandon said sarcastically. "That's convenient."

"Trust me; I know it sounds like a cop-out, but it's not. Turn to Psalm ninety. It's in the middle of the Bible."

Brandon found it right away, feeling an unexpected sense of pride. But he kept that to himself.

"Good," Anton said. "Now, verse two, please."

Before the mountains were born,
Or Thou didst give birth to the earth and the world,
Even from everlasting to everlasting,
Thou art God.

"Don't let the older language distract you," Anton said before Brandon could mock it. "The Bible says that God is what?"

Brandon still had the Bible open. He looked closer at the verse. "From everlasting to everlasting."

"And what do you think that means?"

"It claims God has always existed."

"Right. God is spirit, and he has always existed. He is not subject to the laws of physics. And here's why that's important."

Anton leaned in to make sure he had both Brandon's and Justin's attention. "People these days are talking about fossil fuels and running out of resources, right?" Brandon nodded. "It's because we live in a limited world. Stuff is limited; time is limited. Stuff and time had a beginning. Therefore, whatever the source of the universe is must be unlimited and timeless. God—as spirit, from everlasting to everlasting—fits that description." Anton leaned back in his chair. He wiped his mouth and put his napkin in his bowl.

Although Justin had been quiet the entire time, Brandon noticed the way he seemed to hang on every word. Brandon wondered what he was thinking. Was he buying what Anton was saying? Brandon didn't even know if he himself was buying it. Sure, Anton had made a moving speech, but could it hold water?

Anton got out his wallet and put some money on the table for the server's tip. He pointed at the Bible. "One more verse before we get out of here. Hebrews three." Anton helped Brandon find the chapter. "Verse four."

Brandon read it out loud.

> *For every house is built by someone, but the builder of all things is God.*

"Would you believe me if I claimed this restaurant just popped into existence?" Anton asked. That was a rhetorical question if Brandon had ever heard one. He didn't respond. Anton continued. "Would you believe this restaurant came about by unguided mutations?" Brandon noticed Justin crack a smile. "I'm not trying to insult your intelligence, fellas," Anton said. "You don't believe that because, as the Bible states, every house has a builder. One more question: Who built this restaurant?"

"How should I know?" Brandon said, not meaning to sound rude.

"Was he White? Black? American? Truth be told, it was probably more than one person. But you and I don't know, do we?"

"What's your point?" Brandon asked.

"The questions, 'Where did God come from?' and 'Who created God?' have been thrown around for as long as people have been having these types of conversations. They're undoubtedly good questions to ask, but people usually ask them assuming they somehow take away from the argument for the existence of God. But they don't. I don't have to know where the builder of this restaurant came from to say, 'I believe without a shadow of a doubt that someone made this restaurant.'" He paused before adding, "I believe without a shadow of a doubt that the universe had an intelligent designer. Asking questions about that designer —like who is he, what is the nature of his love, and where did he come from—is a different matter altogether. A worthwhile endeavor, to be sure. But a different matter." When Brandon and Justin didn't say anything, he said, "Who's up for dessert?"

They all agreed that the beignets from earlier were enough dessert to last a few days and headed back to the car. The sun had set while they were in the restaurant, which surprised Brandon. It didn't feel like they had spent that much time in there. On the other hand, he was also surprised when he considered that it was just this morning he and Justin had taken Anton up on his offer to drive them halfway across the country. As he got into the car, his mind was still whirling from the conversation over dinner. It was the most in-depth discussion he had ever had about religion, and not a single word of it was said with a shout. Only the closest of friends could speak their minds like that on such a touchy subject without losing their temper. Right?

All the hotels near Jackson Square were either pricey or

close to collapse. They drove about twenty minutes away and found a tidy one at a fair price—certainly nicer than the previous place he and Justin had stayed in. They rented a room with two beds and a cot. Anton insisted on taking the cot. When he was in the shower, Brandon asked Justin, "What'd you think of all that tonight?"

Justin shrugged.

"That's it?"

"No, that's not it. But I also think there's more to it." He sighed. "Anton reminded me of Matt today."

"Me too." Brandon raked his fingers through his hair.

"Anton said his grandfather taught him to never stop learning. That is so like Matt. During dinner, I kept thinking, 'What would Matt do?'"

"Quietly observe," Brandon said. "I see."

"Look," Justin said, situating himself on the edge of his bed. "I know the Christians at school have been jerks to us. None of them would have given us a second thought if they saw us stranded in the middle of nowhere, much less offer to drive us to Arizona. This guy is clearly different. Hear him out."

"Sure, man," Brandon said, a little disappointed in the lack of support from Justin. Brandon grabbed his backpack and sat on his bed with his back to the wall. He retrieved Dean's box and pulled out the dog tags. He ran his fingers over the word "CHRISTIAN." Was his father more like the kids at school, or was he like Anton? Was he a judgmental jerk, or was he selfless and patient? He picked up the photograph, studying his father's face, then settled on the idea that Dean had definitely been like Anton. Anyone who had made his mom as happy as she was in this photo must have been like Anton.

The next morning, they had breakfast in the hotel dining room before checking out. This time, Brandon called shotgun. They spent some time wandering through the city, driving under bridges, passing massive cemeteries, and noting the number of colorful houses. The shop faces looked like they came from a world Brandon had never seen, but inside the shops, they sold modern, everyday things. "Nawlins sure does have a different culture, huh?" observed Anton.

By mid-morning they were on their way to Shreveport. Once outside the city, Anton found a gas station where they could fill up. He stepped out of the car, but quickly opened his door and handed Brandon a twenty-dollar bill. "It's prepay. Can you put this on pump seven?" Brandon entered the gas station and gave the clerk the money, then he walked back toward the exit. Just before the door, he stopped at a newspaper stand; something about this newspaper had caught his eye. What was it? He scanned the front page. His heart skipped a beat when his eyes landed on a photo in the top-right corner.

It was a photo of him.

CHAPTER THIRTEEN

IT COULDN'T BE, COULD IT? BRANDON PICKED UP THE NEWSPAPER and studied the picture, confirming what he already knew. His stomach tightened. What had he done to land on the front page of a newspaper outside of New Orleans? Even worse, it wasn't a local newspaper—it was a national one. It must be a mistake. Under the photo, the inscription read, "The search continues for missing Nashville teen. P6." Brandon hesitated and then turned to page six to find a small corner article below his senior yearbook photo.

> *SEARCHING FOR BRANDON BASON*
>
> *It has been six days since Brandon Bason went missing from his foster home in Nashville, Tennessee. If you have seen him, please contact the local police or call the toll-free number below.*

"Yo! Brandon!" Anton called from the gas pumps. "All good?"

Brandon looked up with a start and gave Anton a thumb's up. He noticed the clerk staring at him and felt conspicuous, like there was a neon sign flashing, "Here he is—the runaway kid!" Trying to act as natural as possible, he folded up the newspaper and replaced it on the stand.

As he sat back down in the front seat of the car, his head spun. *Searching for Brandon Bason?* he thought. It didn't make sense. Why would they be searching for him? *I'm nearly eighteen years old. I can make my own decisions. Isn't that what Officer Schaefer had said?* Was he in trouble? What would happen if they found him? He tried to push the idea out of his mind.

"My turn today!" Anton said, sliding into the car. He flipped down the sun visor above his seat, revealing a sleeve of CDs. He grabbed one. "This is what I call—" he turned to smile at Justin, "—a gateway album." Justin groaned. "*Motown's Greatest Hits.* The Four Tops. Stevie Wonder. Jackson 5." Anton slid the disc into the player. The first song started playing, and he sang along, holding a pretend microphone.

"Are we there yet?" Justin whined.

"Still not converted, huh? And even after Nawlins." He shook his head. "I've got my work cut out for me. Well, we've got four or five hours on the road today—plenty of time to change your mind." Anton steered the car toward I-10 and began their journey to Shreveport.

Song-by-song, they made their way through *Motown's Greatest Hits.* Brandon recognized a few of them from the times his mom would listen to the oldies station in the kitchen. Grateful for the distraction, he let his mind drift. He unzipped his backpack that was on the floorboard between his feet and pulled out Matt's folder. Unfolding the map a single time revealed enough to see New Orleans. He traced his finger on the red line to where he thought they were driving at that moment—somewhere between New Orleans and Baton Rouge. Staring out the window, he saw nothing special. Just miles of highway surrounded by low-hanging trees. Still, this was something Matt had wanted to see. He tried to appreciate it.

Anton was singing quietly as he drove, gently drumming the steering wheel to the beat. He couldn't be any more different than Brandon and Justin. But he was turning out to be an all right guy, and he reminded both Brandon and Justin of Matt in an odd way. Brandon thought about how quick he had been to dismiss, and even insult, Anton. He had assumed Anton was like the rest of the Christians he knew—only interested in being around "his kind." Instead, he sought friendship with some random goths stranded in small-town America. Brandon tried to rehash their conversation over dinner last night. Anton felt he had logical reasons to believe in religion—in a God—who could make virgins give birth. He presented some compelling arguments. *Every house has a builder.* Brandon accepted that. *But does that really mean the world has a creator?* It seemed many of the people he had grown up with believed in God, but they never did what Anton had done for him and Justin. Instead, they used their God as a crutch for themselves or a way to condemn others. In Brandon's book, "Christian" and "hypocrite" should be under the same entry in the dictionary, with one possible exception—Anton. What was it Anton had asked him? *Are you honestly searching for answers?* Was that what he was doing —searching?

Then, his mind returned to his photo in the newspaper. His pulse quickened as he continued to wonder what kind of trouble he was in. He glanced in the side-view mirror and ran his fingers through his hair.

"All right, carefully listen to this next song," Anton said. An upbeat song with a piano melody started, and a man and some backup singers began singing about money.

After the song played for a couple of minutes, Anton asked, "So, what is it you want, Brandon? Barrett Strong didn't even try to mask it. He wanted money. What about you?"

"I wouldn't mind some money," Brandon said.

"Ditto," Justin echoed from the back seat.

"You would agree with people like Mr. Strong that money is what you want?" Anton asked.

"Well," Brandon began, "I guess it's not money itself. I've never had much. But it's the things money can get. And don't give me that 'Money can't buy happiness' stuff. I know that. But a lack of money can definitely bring unhappiness."

Anton considered that before asking, "What are you willing to do to get money?"

"Work, I guess, like everyone else. Get a decent job. Is that what you mean?"

"Work is a good option. Why not steal it?"

"Steal it?" Brandon asked, wondering where this was leading.

"I've already told you why I don't steal," Anton said. "Remember? It was when we first met."

"I remember," Brandon said.

"But why don't you and Justin just steal the money you want? You guys are sharp. You could probably hit up a bank in some small town we pass through, and you'd never get caught."

Justin seemed just as confused as Brandon felt. "What are you getting at, man?" Brandon asked.

"What's stopping you? I want to know."

"Uh, because we're not thieves," Brandon said.

"That's right!" Justin agreed.

"But why not?" Anton asked. "Why don't you just con some money out of an old lady, or maybe snatch a fella's wallet? Better yet, kill someone for their money. That way, there are no witnesses."

"Because that would be wrong, of course," Brandon said.

"Exactly!" Anton said. "Here's another question: Why are stealing and murdering wrong?"

"Are you saying they're not?" Justin piped up.

"Of course they're wrong. You know it. I know it. But why?"

Brandon thought that was a strange question. It was also a simple question, yet he couldn't come up with a simple answer. He finally said, "Because it is."

"Because it is," Anton repeated. "That might satisfy a three-year-old, but you can't pass that one off on me. Let me rephrase the question. We agree that theft and murder are wrong. Is that objective or subjective?"

"Huh?" Brandon said.

"That's kind of a fancy way of saying fact or opinion. For example, you and I had seafood last night. Justin didn't. Why?"

"'Cause it's gross!" Justin said.

"That's subjective," Anton said. "The information comes from the opinion of the person—the subject. However, when I say the speed limit is sixty-five—" he pointed to a speed limit sign they were passing, "—I am providing objective information. The truth is found in the object rather than the subject. It's Justin's opinion that seafood is gross. But if we go a hundred, and I try to tell a cop that it's all a matter of opinion, he's going to appeal to a standard outside of us, and even himself—namely, the state law. So, when the three of us say murdering someone to steal their money is wrong, is it objective? Is the moral truth outside of us? Or are we just stating our opinion, and we all just happen to agree?"

"How can you think so deep this early in the morning?" Justin asked.

Anton chuckled. "It's nearly lunchtime!"

Brandon thought. "I think the answer is objective," he said. "I mean, it's just like the speed limit. If I killed someone and told the police that it's my opinion that murdering is okay, they'd still lock me up. It won't matter what I think."

Anton nodded. "You got it. But somewhere, this comparison will break down, won't it?"

"What comparison?" Justin asked, clearly trying to get his head around the debate.

"Breaking the speed limit and murdering someone. Why is the speed limit sixty-five here?"

"I guess because the people who made the law thought that's the fastest safe speed we can go on this road," Brandon reasoned.

"What would you think if I disagreed with that? What if I said to you, 'I see their point, but it's my opinion you could go seventy and be just as safe'?"

"Doesn't matter to me," Brandon said.

"Yep. And I wouldn't care if you argued for sixty. But what if Justin said, 'It's my opinion that murder is fine'?"

"Hey, why do I have to be the murderer?"

"Because you turned your nose up at my chowder last night!" Anton looked at Justin in the rearview mirror. "And my Motown!"

"I wouldn't mind knocking some sense into him," Brandon said with a smile.

Anton laughed. "Just not too hard, or else you'll be tried for murder. Back to my point: Is that just a clash of opinions? It's illegal to go sixty-six on this interstate. It's also illegal to kill someone. But if Louisiana decided to change the speed limit law, we wouldn't care. However, let's see what happens if they remove the prohibition for murder."

"So you're saying," Brandon began, "that the speed limit, although more objective than liking seafood, is still subjective in nature?"

"You could say that. But, more importantly, I'm saying things like murder and stealing are morally and objectively wrong. No matter what the state law is, no matter when or where we live—Asia, Africa, America—murder and stealing are and will be wrong." Anton paused for a moment, giving Brandon some needed time to soak that in. Justin had his face scrunched up as though he too were deep in thought. "But we still haven't answered the question why. *Why* is it wrong to kill an old lady and snatch her purse? It's not just our opinion. And it's not just because the law says so."

"Well," Brandon began, "I guess it's because it's not good for society. If we went around murdering each other, then we'd kill each other off. I think I remember learning in kindergarten to treat others the way you want to be treated. Do that, and things go smoothly."

"Looking to benefit society makes sense at first. There's the idea that morality is merely cultural. And some laws certainly are based on location. For instance, some roads have a limit of forty-five, and others sixty-five. But there are a couple of problems with the idea that all morality comes from society. First, you say that it's good for society to not murder people. Define *good*."

Brandon wasn't sure if Anton was setting an intellectual trap, so he stayed silent.

"Whatever works," Justin said. "Like, if it brings about good—"

"Didn't you ever learn not to use the word itself in the definition?" Anton said with a smile. He continued. "Again, good can be a matter of opinion. You might say more people alive is good. Another person might say fewer people allow for more resources, and therefore, that's good. Who's to say who is right? And if there is good, then there is better. And if there is better, then there has to be best. Where does that best standard come from?"

Brandon closed his eyes tightly, trying to mentally catch up to what Anton was saying. He turned to Justin. "I don't think we ever would have had conversations this deep on a Greyhound."

Anton smiled. "I'm not finished. Second, let's pretend your suspicions are right. There is no God—no creator. That means the three of us are here merely because of a series of unguided accidents. That also means any value humanity has is self-assigned. In other words, outside of our own minds, we're really no more valuable than house flies or mosquitoes. And when one insect kills another, there's no remorse. There's no justice. It's just the way of life."

"I'm confused now. Are you saying it doesn't matter if people kill each other?" Brandon asked.

"If there is no God, that's the logical conclusion. If life truly ends when our bodies die, it doesn't matter. Life is snuffed out, and justice is never served. However, if God does exist, then there will be justice, and it matters what we do in this life. With God, we can have a moral standard. Without God, an objective moral standard cannot exist."

Now it made sense to Brandon. There was the trap. "Oh, so you think people who don't believe in God can't be good. I see." If Christians believed non-Christians couldn't be good people, then they had God-given reasons to mistreat people around them. Perhaps Anton wasn't as different as Brandon had thought. Maybe he was just as judgmental as all the other religious fanatics.

"Not at all," Anton responded, surprising Brandon. "I know plenty of people who don't believe in God who are morally upright people. In fact, they probably haven't made many of the same mistakes I've made. Yes, of course people who don't believe in God can be good. However, they have to borrow from God to prove that objective morality even exists. In other words, you can be good without believing in God, but good cannot exist without God."

Brandon's ears grew red. *Now who's the judgmental one?* he thought. He realized the corner he had put himself in, but he had an out. "In that case, I don't believe objective morality exists."

Anton let that simmer for a moment. "So, you really think it is just opinions?"

"Sure. I think your point was to convince me that God exists. Instead, you convinced me that objective morality—something I hadn't heard of until this morning, by the way—doesn't exist."

"Think about that school shooting that's been all over the news. Has this all been just a clash of opinions? If someone killed your best friend, you'd shrug it off and chalk it up to different points of view? After all, who are you to impose your opinion on another? You like seafood; he likes killing people."

Brandon felt the blood rush to his cheeks. Someone *had* killed his best friend. His first instinct was to lash out at Anton, but Anton didn't know anything about what Brandon had been through. He wouldn't understand, anyway. Did Brandon just happen to disagree with Barry's actions? No. His stepdad had killed his mom and his best friend, and that was wrong. No matter what the law said, no matter what others thought, whether Barry felt guilty or not, it was wrong. Brandon also thought of the school shooting. It dawned on him that he wasn't the only one suffering because of injustices at that moment. Many others were also mourning the loss of their best friends.

Anton continued. "You can't tell me you've never looked at a situation and said, 'That's not fair,' or 'He shouldn't be doing that.' I know I have. And every time we say things like that, we are appealing to a higher, unchangeable, objective moral law. And wherever a law is, there must be a lawgiver. So, it follows that the moment we say any other person ought to act a certain way, in a roundabout way, we are acknowledging the existence of God."

The three of them went quiet as they made their way toward Shreveport, *Motown's Greatest Hits* still playing. Anton seemed to be giving Brandon and Justin time to think more about what they had discussed. Then, Brandon broke the silence. "But you're jumping to conclusions."

Anton arched an eyebrow.

"You make a good point and all. If objective morality exists,

God must exist. But how do you know we're even talking about *your* God? There are hundreds of religions in the world. You can't just assume that your God is this lawgiver."

Anton held up a finger. "You're also assuming I'm assuming. You see, I'm looking at this systematically, just as you are. Got your dad's Bible handy?"

Brandon patted his breast pocket.

"Look for a book called Romans."

Brandon closed his eyes and sighed. He just had to open his mouth again. Dutifully, he obliged and started to thumb through the Bible. "Got it."

"Find verse twenty of chapter one. What's it say?"

Brandon read it out loud.

For since the creation of the world His invisible attributes, His eternal power and divine nature, have been clearly seen, being understood through what has been made, so that they are without excuse.

"Thanks," Anton said. "Last night, we talked about how design demands a designer. The verse says three things about God are evident just by observing creation. Number one: God's invisible attributes. Two: God's eternal power. Three: God's divine nature."

"I think I speak for both of us when I say you're talking over our heads," Brandon said. He turned to Justin, who nodded his agreement.

"Let's break it down, fellas. When we look at the world and everything in it, we can notice a few things about who made it all. For example, if you look at a beautiful painting, you can say the painter is creative and has a good eye for this or that. You can say those things, even though you've never even seen or spoken to the artist. The world is God's canvas, and it is full of beauty, the people and animals in it are relational, and love makes it go 'round. Almost all people agree that without love, life has no meaning. Creativity, relationships, and love all point to the one who created such things. Those are God's invisible attributes. The creator of the universe is creative, relational, and loving. The Bible agrees, but I don't need the Bible to tell me that. I can learn it from creation."

Brandon thought more about what Anton was claiming. If his God was powerful enough to create the world and heal people, then he could have stopped Barry from abusing others—from killing others. If God was powerful and loving, both his mom and Matt would still be alive. "You say your God is loving?" Brandon asked. "This God, who also has the power to create and control the universe?"

"Of course," Anton said. "I know it from experience, I know it from the Bible, and I know it from observation. The world is full of God's love."

Brandon scoffed. "It seems easy enough for you to say. But what about us who know from experience and observation that the world is full of ugliness and hatred?"

"I don't deny that," Anton said. "However, the ugliness caused *by* hatred comes from people breaking objective moral laws, which is going against God. But we're getting ahead of ourselves. Remember how you asked where God comes from?"

Brandon's cheeks grew hot. Asking about God's power and love seemed to Brandon like a perfectly reasonable question, and he sensed Anton was being evasive. He could also see out of the corner of his eye that Justin was leaning forward in his seat, listening carefully to the conversation. "Yeah, sure," Brandon said.

"We talked about how God is infinite and timeless," Anton said, moving on from the question about God's love. "That's not just a cop-out. That must be the case. The creator of time and material things must exist outside of time and be made up of non-material stuff. That's God's eternal power."

He continued. "And finally, there is God's divine nature. Since such a powerful, unlimited being exists, and since he created us to be loving and relational, it only makes sense for us to dedicate our love and relationships to him. I don't expect you to fully understand or agree with all this. It's just my answer to your question."

Brandon thought for a moment, then laughed. "I forgot what that question was."

Anton chuckled. "That's my fault, not yours. I took this deeper than I intended. You said we were jumping to conclusions to assume that the moral lawgiver is the God of the Bible."

"Oh, that's right," Brandon said.

"But I don't want to jump to conclusions. I want to look at this systematically. Design demands a designer. Moral law demands a moral lawgiver. What else can we learn about this creator? And is there something out there that already tells us about such conclusions?"

Brandon looked down at the Bible in his hands. He placed it back in his pocket.

"By the way," Anton said, "I don't think that's what you really want."

"What's not what I want?" Brandon asked.

"Money." He pointed to the stereo, although the song about money had ended a while ago. "Or the things you can buy with money."

"And why do you think that?"

"I think you're searching for something else. Something bigger. With more meaning. A fella who just wants money and stuff doesn't get in a car with a stranger that has nothing more to offer than a trip to a big hole in the ground." Anton grinned at Brandon.

There was that word again. *Searching*. Brandon shifted in his seat with the thought that people were searching for him. There was something else making him uncomfortable, but he couldn't put a finger on it. He let that word continue to roll through his mind. *Searching*.

It was late afternoon when they pulled into Anton's aunt's driveway. The driveway was long enough that they couldn't see the house from the road. They drove through a long row of trees that opened up to a large field of crops. In the distance, and beyond the field, Brandon could see a two-story farmhouse next to a massive oak tree. Several cars were parked in front of the house. As they approached, Brandon noticed a few kids playing on a tire swing that hung from the tree. Four adults sat on the front porch. Anton stopped the car, and as Brandon stepped out, it felt like the humidity had doubled between New Orleans and Shreveport. He saw sweat beginning to bead on Justin's forehead. The sound of cicadas and children's laughter filled the air until Brandon heard a shriek.

An older woman with graying hair was running down the steps toward them. "It's my Anton! Ooo, thank you, Lord! I can't believe it! It's my Anton!"

"Hi, Aunt Mavel," Anton said warmly, returning her embrace. She hugged him tightly while holding a glass of what looked like sweet tea, the condensation rubbing off onto Anton's shirt. "It's good to see you, Aunty."

She stepped back from the hug and grabbed his face with her free hand. "Boy, why didn't you tell us you were coming? Oh, never mind that! How's your mama?"

"She's good. I want you to meet my friends." Anton motioned for Brandon and Justin to step forward. "This is Brandon, and this is Justin."

"Well," Aunt Mavel said. "It's a blessing to know you fine boys." Brandon extended his hand, and Aunt Mavel pushed it away. She hugged him, and Brandon stiffened, not knowing how to react. He had never been called a "blessing" before. He loosened up and gave her a weak hug in return. She smelled nice. Then, she hugged Justin just as enthusiastically. She turned to Anton. "I know you're planning to stay for suppa. Look—" she turned toward the front porch, "—Aunt Margie and them are here too."

"Actually, Aunty," Anton began, "we were hoping to stay for longer than supper."

CHAPTER FOURTEEN

Aunt Mavel didn't hesitate to agree—to insist—they stay for as long as they needed to, her sincerity evident in the broad smile on her face. Brandon marveled at her unquestioning generosity. *Must run in the family,* he thought. Brandon and Justin were given a room with two beds at the end of the hallway upstairs. Brandon retrieved his backpack from the car, and the moment he set it on his bed, he heard, "Wash up! Suppa's on!"

"Suppa" looked and smelled delicious. The table was covered in platters of roast beef, gravies, greens, and roasted vegetables.

"It's like she knew we were coming or something," Justin whispered to Anton.

"I told you," he said. "She always has people staying at her house. I can't remember a time here when she didn't prepare this much food. Just wait until dessert." He winked.

Soon, twelve people—the three of them, Anton's uncle, his aunts, and the five kids who had been playing in the yard—were gathered around the large dining table. Brandon sat between Justin and Anton. His stomach rumbling, he couldn't wait to reach for some of the food, but he paused when he noticed a hush fall over the table. He looked around. No one had put anything on their plate yet. Anton held out his hands to his sides, palms up. A man Brandon had learned was called Uncle Jarvis, on the other side of Anton, grabbed his hand. Everyone else began doing the same. Justin extended his hand to Brandon awkwardly. Brandon reached out and held Anton's and Justin's hands, completing the hand-holding circle around the table.

"Oh Lord, our Lord," Uncle Jarvis began in a husky voice. Brandon saw that everyone in Anton's family had their eyes closed and their heads bowed, including the kids, a couple of them looking no older than four. "How majestic is your name!"

"Mm-hmm," said Aunt Mavel.

Uncle Jarvis continued. "We thank you for these thy gifts, which thou hast bountifully bestowed on us tonight."

"Mm-hmm."

"What a blessing it is, too, Lord, to have Anton and his friends with us tonight. May we receive these thy gifts with thanksgiving. And may you, oh Lord, receive all the praise and glory. In Jesus' mighty name..."

"Amen!" the family said in unison.

Then, there was an explosion of motion and sound, which caused Brandon to jump a little. Arms extended across the table this way and that, reaching for and passing food. Everyone used manners, saying things like, "Please, may I have the gravy after you?" and "Will you please dish me some of that?" Before Brandon could reach for anything, someone had plopped a large serving of greens on his plate, then some roast beef, and then some sweet potato. Justin was given the same treatment. They looked at each other, and Justin gave a half-smile.

"Hey, Anton!" Uncle Jarvis said after everyone had finished passing the dishes. "How old are you now?"

"Twenty-five."

"You finish that apprenticeship with the construction guy?"

"Two years ago. I've been able to finish many paid jobs since then, allowing me to save enough to start preaching school this coming August and also go on this trip with my friends."

"Boy, that's great," Uncle Jarvis said with pride in his eyes. "A gospel preacher in our family. If you would have told me that twenty years ago...Boy." He shook his head. "You know Aaliyah would have been proud."

A preacher? Brandon had never thought to ask Anton what kind of school he was going to in the fall. He was smart, so Brandon had assumed it would be some academic thing far beyond his own comprehension. *And who is Aaliyah?*

"What about you, boys?" Aunt Margie said in a soft tone that contrasted with Uncle Jarvis' booming voice. She smiled at Brandon and Justin. Brandon felt all the eyes at the table on him. He flushed at the sudden attention.

Justin spoke up. "We just finished high school. Well—"

"I thought you looked young!" Uncle Jarvis said with a chuckle. "You got your whole life in front of you."

"Why don't you plan to stay an extra night with us, Anton?" Aunt Mavel asked. "It would be nice to have you come with us tomorrow evening."

"I don't think that's such a good idea, Aunty. Plus, we've got to get back on the road."

"It'll be fine. Brother Jones would love to hear about your plans."

"Sorry, Aunty."

"Well, I hope that school also teaches you to settle down. Stay in one place. You could make a big difference, ya hear?"

The family continued their meal, chatting and laughing their way through the platters of food until there was nothing left. Brandon and Justin enjoyed their food to the last bite in silence. Anton's family was loud, which put Brandon on edge a little. He was not used to people who expressed themselves so effusively. But the more he watched, the more he believed there was no pretense in these people—these people who seemed so different from him. Anton knew and loved them, that was clear. But somehow, Anton also seemed a bit out of place around them.

Anton was right; dessert *was* worth waiting for—warm apple pie with Bluebell vanilla ice cream. After dessert, the family piled back onto the front porch to enjoy some sweet tea, coffee, and a lot more talking.

By that time, Brandon was mentally and physically exhausted. It had been a long day. He sensed Anton watching him as he tried, yet again, to stifle a yawn on the front porch. Anton got the message and tactfully excused himself, along with Brandon and Justin, to show them the laundry room. He then went back to join the family.

While they waited on their load of laundry to finish, Brandon asked Justin, "Did you hear what Anton's uncle said? Anton's going to be a preacher."

"I'm sure the neighbors heard what Uncle Jarvis said." They both laughed. "This is a nice family. I like them."

"What about Anton being a preacher?"

"Makes sense to me," Justin said, shrugging. "I mean, he always finds a way to talk about the Bible and stuff."

"You would think he would have told us, wouldn't you?"

"Why? We didn't ask. Besides, so what?"

"I don't know," Brandon said. Justin was right. What difference would it have made if Brandon knew Anton was going to be a preacher? It probably would have made things worse, causing extra tension between them. Truth be told, he likely wouldn't have gotten in the car with Anton in the first place. "Where do you think they're going tomorrow?" he asked.

"What do you mean?"

"Anton's aunt wanted us to stay another night so Anton could go somewhere with them tomorrow. He seemed to know what she was talking about."

"Beats me."

Their load of laundry finished. There was no dryer, so they

had to hang the wet clothes on the clothesline out back. It was early evening, and the sun was still hot. Yet Brandon wondered how wet clothes could dry in these conditions. If it were possible, the air seemed even more humid than before. While they were behind the house, Justin took the opportunity to sneak in a smoke break.

Brandon woke the next morning to sunshine pouring into the room. He had rested well. Rolling over, he noticed the window was wet. Looking outside, he saw that not just the window, but everything else, was wet too. It must have rained last night. Brandon swore.

Justin shot up. "What?"

"The first time in my life I hang clothes on a clothesline, and it rains!"

Brandon and Justin slipped on their shoes and went downstairs, the smell of bacon wafting from the kitchen.

They were almost to the back door when Aunt Mavel spotted them. "Mornin'! Leaving so soon?" she said from the kitchen. She wore an apron as she stirred something in a bowl.

"Good morning," Brandon said. "No, ma'am. Breakfast smells delicious. We've just got to go check on our clothes. I think it rained last night."

"It came a monsoon. You boys didn't hear it?" She started chuckling.

They ran outside, their shoes squelching in the wet grass. They made it to the clothesline to discover their clothes weren't soaked. In fact, they were almost dry. Brandon felt his shirts to confirm, while Justin reached for some jeans. They looked at each other, puzzled. As they stepped back inside the house, they kicked off their shoes. Aunt Mavel began chuckling from the kitchen again, still stirring. "What's a matta, boys?"

"It's strange," Brandon said. They walked to the kitchen together. "We hung our clothes out last night, and we were sure they'd be soaked through. How did they get so dry already?"

"I'll tell you how." She chuckled some more and put down the bowl. "I knew it was gonna rain. I could smell it in the air and feel it in my knees. I brought your clothes in last night and put 'em back out this mornin'. That's how." Her mouth turned into a warm smile.

"Wow," Justin said.

"Thank you, Ms. Mavel," Brandon said.

"No, no, no! That's Aunt Mavel to you."

"Thank you, Aunt Mavel," Brandon said, smiling back.

Just then, they heard someone pounding down the stairs. Reaching the landing, Anton was scrambling to get his shoes on. He opened the front door and ran outside. Brandon looked out the kitchen window to see Anton reach his car and put his hands on his head. He seemed frustrated.

"Ooo-wee," Aunt Mavel said. "I saved your clothes, but I didn't think to check Anton's windows."

Anton came back inside. "They're soaked! The entire front seats of the car are soaked."

"It'll dry, honey," Aunt Mavel said. "It's gonna be another scorcher today. Don't you worry."

Anton looked at Brandon and Justin. "You guys seemed to enjoy Aunt Mavel's cooking."

"We did," Justin said, rubbing his stomach.

"It was amazing," Brandon said, making sure Aunt Mavel could hear the compliment too.

"Looks like we'll be having dinner here again tonight," Anton said. "We need to let the seats air out." Aunt Mavel clapped her hands, clearly happy about the proposal. Anton went outside. He popped the hood on his car and unhooked the battery. Then, he opened all four car doors.

After breakfast, Anton started clearing the table. "Come on," he told Brandon and Justin. They looked at each other and started picking up the bowls. When they arrived in the kitchen, Anton was already running water to wash them. "You'll soon get the hang of it," he said.

"So, Anton," Brandon said, rolling up his sleeves. "You never told us you were going to school to be a preacher."

"Brandon, you wash. Justin, you can dry. I'll put them away, since I know where they go. What's wrong? Don't think I'm preacher quality?"

"It's not that..." Brandon started washing the first plate.

"Of course it's not. The first preachers for Jesus were backwoods fishermen. If they could do it, I can do it too. So, what's the problem?"

"Nothing. That's cool, man."

Justin looked at Anton and raised his eyebrows.

"Okay, I'll come clean," Anton said. "I could tell when I met you, Brandon, that Christians weren't your favorite people. Why would I make it more difficult to become your friend by telling you you're going on a road trip with a future preacher?"

"Yeah..." Brandon said, handing a dish to Justin. He hoped that Anton could see that he didn't feel that way toward him. At least, not anymore. "I just wanna say that me and Justin really appreciate what you're doing for us. There'd be no way for us to honor our friend if you hadn't offered to take us."

"And you've got a really cool family," Justin added.

"I hear that." Anton chuckled. "They're good folk here. They're not without their faults, but who is? Speaking of your friend, why don't you guys tell me about him?"

Brandon stared into the soapy water before answering. "He had everything going for him. He was a genius. He had a great family. He was talented."

"And—" Justin smiled at Anton, "—he liked good music."

"Oh, now that was low. I thought you were coming around yesterday afternoon. I saw your head bouncing."

"Sure, if that's what you wanna tell yourself," Justin said. "For real, though—other than the music thing—you remind me of him. That, and, well, he was White."

"Sounds like he was a pretty decent fella," Anton said with a laugh. "His name was Matthew, right?"

"Yeah, how'd you know?" Brandon asked.

"It's on the front of the folder with the map."

"Oh, that's right. Yeah, Matt Steele," Brandon said.

"Was he your age?"

"Mm-hmm," Justin said. "We were all supposed to graduate together."

"So," Anton said, "losing him was unexpected?"

Brandon's heart dropped to his stomach as the image of Matt's smashed-up car came to mind. He closed his eyes and placed his hands on the edge of the sink to steady himself.

"Hey—you okay?" Anton asked.

"Yeah, sorry...It just all happened so recently."

"You don't have to apologize for anything, Brandon," Anton said.

While they finished up the dishes, Justin described to Anton what had happened to Matt. Anton was quiet the entire time.

Once the last dish had been put away, Anton said, "Come with me." They all slipped on their shoes, Brandon pulled on his trench coat, and they walked outside. "Isn't it a little hot for that thing?" Anton asked. "If it's a fashion statement, you've already made it. You can take it off now."

Justin lit up a cigarette and took a drag. "Don't bother asking. He's never been able to give me a good reason. Plus, Brandy already knows I'm able to make the best fashion statement without a coat."

Brandon resisted the temptation to lash out at Justin for using that name around Anton. The more he thought of it, the more he realized he didn't mind.

Anton smirked at Justin's JNCO jeans and black Rammstein shirt. "Right."

Brandon shifted in his coat while they walked. The truth was, it had merely become a habit. As Barry grew more violent at home, the coat served two purposes—it covered most of the bruises, and it somehow helped Brandon feel less insecure. However, it was a lot easier to blend in during winter.

Anton led Brandon and Justin to the back yard past the clothesline and into a field. "Watch for snakes," he warned as they navigated through the neat green rows of a crop that Brandon didn't recognize. The crops were surrounded by trees.

"What is this?" Justin asked.

"Soybean," Anton said. "I think this property has grown soybeans for all history. My great-great-great-grandfather was sold to the owner, Alexander Davis, when he was fifteen. His name was Anthony."

"Sold?" Justin asked, then flushed as the meaning dawned on him. "Oh, yeah."

Anton shrugged. "The family treated him well—for slave-owners. He was included as part of the family. When slavery was abolished, he had nowhere to go, so he asked to stay here on a wage. It worked out, I guess. The Davises had big plans when they moved here, but they couldn't have children. Their dreams were shattered. So, when they died, Anthony, who had found a wife and started having children of his own, learned the house and property were willed to him. That's how we have it."

They made it to the edge of the field, where a path meandered through the trees. Anton started walking down it; Brandon and Justin followed. Their footsteps were soft on the path, and Brandon could hear birds in the trees. It was nice to be out of the sun, but it was still humid in the small forest. The birdsong soon mingled with the sound of running water. The path led them to the top of a steep embankment, which went down to a creek. It looked just deep enough to swim in.

"The Davises taught Grandpa Anthony how to read," Anton said. "They used the Bible as their textbook. The first words he ever read were straight from the word of God."

Anton had deep conviction etched on his face. Suddenly, Brandon felt out of place. Although he had begun seeing Anton as a friend, he had no clue how he could relate to him in this moment. He didn't know what to say. Justin was staring into the creek. What was this all about, anyway?

"Grandpa Anthony spent all his spare time learning to read —learning to read the Bible. My granddad, who was his grandson, said Grandpa Anthony was a craftsman with his hands. He didn't know much academically. In fact, learning to read the Bible was his only education. But that's all he needed. He taught his family what he learned in the Bible, and they lived it. They really lived it. I kid myself sometimes and make excuses for my shortcomings. I look at the faith Grandpa Anthony and even my granddad had and say things like, 'Life was simpler back then.' But was it really?"

Was life simpler back then? Brandon wondered. *Especially for someone like Anton's great-great-great-grandfather?* Brandon couldn't imagine what it would have been like to be a slave. But when he thought about life portrayed in the olden days on TV, maybe life did seem simpler.

"No," Anton said, answering his own question. "Life was certainly different. But it wasn't easier. They had difficulties you and I will never know. And they were tempted in the same ways we are. When it comes down to it, they had to search for the same answers we do, but with a lot less formal education."

"Are life's answers in the creek?" Justin asked, flicking his cigarette butt into the water. "Why'd you bring us here?"

"This is where Grandpa Anthony died. And his wife and his kids. This is where Granddad died too."

Brandon wasn't expecting that. Had there been an accident?

It seemed like a solemn thing to say, yet Anton said it with a smile.

"This is where I died too," Anton continued. Now, Brandon knew Anton wasn't speaking literally. But instead of helping his understanding, it only added to his confusion. "It's also where I was raised to life. I know it doesn't really mean much to you fellas. I don't blame you one bit. But I thought since we were on the farm, I'd show it to you. If you were to follow this creek, it would lead you to the Red River, which has always seemed appropriate to our family."

"Why's that?" Justin asked.

"The Red River gets its name from its color. When it floods, it turns red because of the clay and soil that spill into it. But to us, it reminds us of blood."

"Is that a Civil War thing to you?" asked Brandon.

"No. It reminds us of someone else's blood—Jesus'. And this creek is where Granddad baptized me into Jesus Christ."

CHAPTER FIFTEEN

Brandon mulled over Anton's words. He had heard of baptism before, but this idea of being "raised to life," as Anton had put it, messed with his head. And what was the Christian obsession with blood all about? It sort of put him on edge.

"So, where does Aunt Mavel want you to go this evening?" Justin asked Anton on their way back to the house. Brandon was grateful for the change of subject.

"Looks like we are going to be staying that extra night after all, huh?" Anton said. "Bible study."

"Bible study?" Brandon said.

"Every Wednesday evening, the local church gets together for Bible study."

"Sounds right up your alley," Brandon said, trying not to sound sarcastic. "But it seemed to us that you didn't want to go. You said it wasn't a good idea or something."

Anton was quiet for a moment, deep in thought. "Last time I went, I caused a bit of a scene."

Brandon stopped walking. "You? Caused a scene?"

Anton laughed. "Not a fight or anything. We had a great study on what Jesus teaches about hypocrisy. I pointed out something that I thought was a bit inconsistent with them." Anton and Justin had stopped walking too. "People think Jesus is all about 'don't do this' and 'don't do that.' But really, he wants us to have the best life possible. That's why what he condemned the most in all his teachings was hypocrisy. And it's so difficult for us to see the hypocrisy in our own lives, but it's easy to see it in others. You know what I mean?"

Brandon could relate.

"One Wednesday, when we all gathered to study Jesus' words on this issue, their hypocrisy in a certain area stood out to me. It was so clear since I was a visitor—albeit a regular visitor. But then they turned it back on me. It turned out I had a log in my eye."

Brandon furrowed his eyebrows in confusion.

"Right," Anton said. "Sorry. When Jesus first taught against hypocrisy, he encouraged his disciples to help their neighbors out with their shortcomings. But first—" Anton landed a thumb on his chest, "—you must evaluate your own life with honest judgment. He said that if your brother has a piece of sawdust in his eye, make sure you first address the log sticking out of your own eye. Then, you'll be able to help the guy struggling with a bit of sawdust. It's a humorous way to make the point."

"Simple, but profound," Justin said.

"That's a normal reaction to Jesus' teachings. Anyway, I saw a piece of sawdust, and I called them out on it, but I didn't do it in love. I was ignoring the log in my own eye. I was doing some fill-in preaching in my local congregation, which wasn't good for a young, hot-headed ego. I was fresh out of high school, telling everyone I was going to be a full-time preacher in no time. But after that episode, I knew I needed to spend a bit more time meditating on the character and teachings of Jesus. I put off my preaching plans, studied the Bible as much as I could, and started working with my hands. Now, I'm going to be wise about it. I'll go to preaching school to learn at the feet of men who have been preaching for longer than I've been alive."

Anton began walking toward the house again, Brandon and Justin in his wake. By the time they made it to the back yard, Brandon's and Justin's clothes on the clothesline were dry; however, the seats in Anton's car were still wet, ruling out the possibility of getting back on the road anytime soon. Brandon and Justin retrieved their clothes and took them up to their room. While they were packing them into their bags, Anton appeared in the doorframe.

"I'm ashamed," he said, shaking his head.

Brandon and Justin stopped packing and gave him their attention.

"That's what's holding me back from going tonight. They're good people. And Brother Jones, their preacher, is a great fella. He teaches the truth. But I haven't been back since I upset them. I've been thinking about it, and I don't know if I'm ready to show my face again." He paused. "May I come in?"

"Sure," Justin said, sitting on his bed. Brandon followed suit.

"Thanks," Anton said, staring at the floor. He sat in a chair stationed in the corner of the room. "In my shame, I've tried not to think about that incident since it happened. But it's stuck in my head today. I just don't know if I'm ready to go back."

Brandon felt strange seeing Anton like this, battling with himself over a decision. So far, Anton had been full of resolve. Indecisiveness didn't seem to be one of his traits. Yet, here he was, obviously tormented by the choice.

"Hey," Justin said. "You said it yourself. They're good people. Seems to me you've gotta suck it up and just go." Anton looked up. "Plus," Justin continued, nodding to Brandon, "me and Brandon will go with you." Brandon widened his eyes. "Right, Brandon?"

Brandon huffed and ran his fingers through his hair. "Why do you have to rope me into this?"

"Because our friend could use our help, that's why."

Anton brightened a bit at Justin's offer. "Would you really come?" he asked.

"Yeah," Justin said. "It's gonna be weird for us, no doubt about it, but we should be there for you."

Anton smiled. "Thanks. That means a lot."

When it was time to leave that evening, the interior to Anton's car had finally dried. As they got in, Anton took a deep breath and said, "I'm ready. I already feel strengthened knowing you guys got my back." Brandon smiled politely, although he really wasn't looking forward to it.

After a ten-minute drive, they arrived at the church, the parking lot fuller than Brandon had expected for a Bible study; he counted twenty-five cars in it when they pulled up, including Aunt Mavel's minivan and Uncle Jarvis' truck. The cathedral in New Orleans had made it seem that extravagant artwork was part of their religion. The people who met here clearly had other ideas. The church was a nondescript building with gray cladding. If not for the sign out front, and maybe the large parking lot, no one would have guessed it was a church. The building was about the same size as the one where Matt's funeral had been.

They parked and approached the front doors. Anton hesitated, as did Brandon, who peered into the foyer through the glass doors. There were several people talking to each other, most of them smiling. He spotted Aunt Mavel laughing with someone.

"We're not gonna chill outside all night, are we?" Justin said behind them.

Brandon and Anton exchanged a glance. They both took a breath. Anton opened the door for Brandon, and he stepped in.

"Hello," a young woman said to Brandon, extending her hand. She was holding a Bible. Brandon shook her hand. It was soft. He smiled back. He found her very pretty. There was something about her gentle demeanor, shoulder-length hair, and large, dark eyes. She gave a start when she spotted Anton next to him. "Anton? Is that really you?"

"Hey, Sophia. It's good to see you."

"How long has it been?" she asked. "Five years?"

"Just over six." The two of them hugged. Anton seemed to relax a bit. Justin was busy looking around. Brandon still felt tense. He stole another glance at Sophia just before she went into the auditorium, where more people had gathered. Rows of pews, all facing the same direction, filled the place. Brandon guessed maybe fifty or sixty people were there in total. It was then he realized he and Justin were the only White people in the building. He rubbed the back of his neck and continued to look around.

"Let's go in," Anton said a minute later. The three of them stepped into the auditorium.

"Anton Prayther," bellowed a large man with a huge smile. He grabbed Anton's hand and shook it vigorously.

"Hey, Brother Jones," Anton said. "These are my friends, Brandon and Justin."

Brother Jones shook their hands just as enthusiastically. "I'm so pleased you came tonight."

Anton put his hands in his pocket. "Brother Jones," he said, "I wanted to apologize for the ruckus I caused the last time I was here."

"Don't you worry about a thing." He put his arm around Anton. "All is forgiven. And I hope you found it in your heart to forgive the nasty things that were said in return. We're all brothers and sisters here, and we need to be united—just like you said that night, right?"

"Yes, sir." Anton nodded. He smiled as he watched the pews filling up around him. "It doesn't look like much has changed, though," he said.

Brother Jones pulled away and addressed Anton in a serious

tone. "A lot has changed in the past few years. You'd be surprised. But we don't have the time to talk about it now. How long are you in town? Staying with your Aunt Mavel, I assume?"

"Yes, sir," Anton said. "We'll be back on the road tomorrow."

"Well, you'll just have to take my word, then. Some good things have happened. Unity, my boy. Unity." He gave Anton a broad smile, then glanced at the clock on the wall. It was seven o'clock. "Better find a seat," he said to them.

Brandon and Justin followed Anton to a vacant pew near the front. Instead of standing behind the lectern, Brother Jones grabbed a folding chair and sat in the aisle between the two rows of seats.

"Who remembers where we were last week?" he asked.

An older lady raised her hand, and without waiting on Brother Jones to call on her, she said, "The temple at Passover."

"That's right. In Luke two, Jesus stayed behind at the temple when he was twelve. Now, turn to Luke three, and we fast forward nearly twenty years. Who will read the first twenty verses for us?"

A young man stood up. "I will." He began to read. The passage began with a list of people who were ruling different regions at the time the story supposedly took place. *Great,* Brandon thought. *I came to be bored to death.* The young man reading had trouble over some of the complicated names. He seemed embarrassed, but no one snickered or elbowed their neighbor the way people would in school. Most of them had their own Bibles open in their laps as they followed along. Brandon reached for the Bible in his pocket.

"Where is he reading from?" Brandon whispered to Anton.

"Luke three." Brandon handed Anton the Bible, and he quickly found the spot. He gave the Bible back to Brandon. By then, the young man had made it to verse three.

And he came into all the district around the Jordan, preaching a baptism of repentance for the forgiveness of sins.

Brandon thought about the creek behind Aunt Mavel's house, where Anton said he had been baptized. Brandon didn't know what baptism was exactly, but it apparently involved water. Now, Brandon noticed it had something to do with forgiveness.

He continued to listen, following along as the young man read. The guy who was doing this baptizing in the story turned out to be a pretty bold preacher, calling his audience a bunch of snakes. Then, he talked about wrath and fire. *So, this is where Christians learn to be judgmental,* Brandon thought. In the end, the prophet of the story went to jail for his preaching. *Serves him right. He should have minded his own business.*

After the reading, the young man sat down. Brother Jones thanked him, then started giving a history lesson about all the people listed at the beginning of the passage. Bored, Brandon let his mind—and eyes—wander. He looked around at the auditorium. It had some of the same features of the first two churches he had been to—pews with Bibles in the backs of them, a lectern up front, and a sound system. Unlike the cathedral, there were no stained-glass windows or paintings. It did, however, have some unique features. For one, it was much darker inside than the other churches. At first, Brandon wondered if that had more to do with the time of day than anything else, but then he noticed there were not as many windows as in the church where Matt's funeral was held.

It struck Brandon that this was the first time he had gone to a church for what it was built for—learning about the Bible. Why had he come? Definitely not out of personal interest. Justin was right that they should support Anton. But Anton seemed to be doing fine and in no need of support. He was paying close attention to whatever Brother Jones was saying about the Bible passage. Justin shifted in his seat, as he also appeared to be listening. Brandon couldn't help but wonder what all these people thought of him and Justin. Sure, they had greeted them with smiles, but Brandon knew that everyone had a fake face they gave to people when they first met them. What were they really thinking right now of these grungy White guys sitting in their pews? He felt even more self-conscious when he spotted Sophia across the aisle from him. He watched her tuck her hair behind her ear while she followed along in her Bible. Maybe not everyone wore a fake face. *Sophia probably doesn't,* he thought.

Something Brother Jones said brought Brandon back to reality. "…And that's one more testament to the reliability of the Bible. It's not just an instruction book on how to live. It is a collection of documents rooted in history. Through the Holy Spirit, Isaiah said this over five hundred years before it happened, and it happened just as he predicted."

Yeah, right, Brandon thought. *Whoever Isaiah is just got lucky.* Brandon thought back to his discussions with Anton about the existence of God. He conceded that it made sense that someone created this universe. Anton claimed the creator was loving. Now, Brother Jones was also claiming this God empowered people to predict the future. If that were the case, then why didn't God look ahead at the destruction Barry would cause and stop him before he ever had the chance?

These thoughts occupied Brandon's mind for the rest of the session, and he felt his cheeks growing hot, despite the air conditioner in the building blowing right on him in the pew. When the Bible study was over, everyone stood up and started mingling again. Anton didn't waste any time. He made straight for the door, and Brandon and Justin followed him.

"Anton, my boy! Just a sec." Brother Jones approached them from the water fountain in the foyer. He stuck out a massive hand to Brandon. "And you two—" he looked Brandon and Justin in their eyes, "—it was so good to have you here."

Brandon shook his hand. "Be safe on the road tomorrow. Say, where are you going?"

"Dallas," Anton said.

Brother Jones grunted. "I wouldn't go there if I was paid. The traffic would be the death of me. What's in Dallas?"

"Adventure," Anton said with a smile.

"Oh, to be young," Brother Jones said. "Hey, I do hope you'll remember us in prayer. Good things are happening around here. I wish I had the time to tell you. And be safe, ya hear?"

"Yes, sir," Anton replied. He turned toward the door.

"Thanks for having us tonight," Justin said as he followed Anton out the door.

"You betcha," Brother Jones said. Brandon snuck another glance in the auditorium, but he didn't see Sophia. He turned to follow Anton and Justin. "Hey, son," Brother Jones called, getting his attention. Anton and Justin were already in the parking lot. "That Anton—" he pointed out the church's glass front door, "—he's grown into a fine young man. Comes from a fine family too. You be a good friend to him, okay? He couldn't have too many, and the Lord knows he's been through a lot in the past few years."

Brandon peered into Brother Jones' eyes. He saw nothing but authenticity. "Yes, sir." Brandon smiled. "Anton's been a good friend to me. And Justin."

"Come back anytime, boy," he said, winking. "Anytime."

As Brandon exited the church, he watched Anton get into the car. *Been through a lot?* he wondered. All this time Brandon had been thinking only of his own miserable existence and had never once considered that Anton had anything other than an easy life. Clearly, there was still a lot more to learn about his new friend.

CHAPTER SIXTEEN

SITTING SHOTGUN AGAIN, BRANDON LOOKED IN THE SIDE-VIEW mirror, watching Shreveport disappear. Every mile marked a new record for him—the farthest he had been from home. Lifting the sleeve of his coat, he noticed his arm was finally free from bruises. He flexed his hand, and there was only a hint of pain left from when he pounded Cody's face. Then, he remembered the sample CD the owner of Sun Studio had given him and pulled it out of his bag. "Do you mind?"

Anton ejected the Motown CD and placed it in the sleeve on his sun visor. "Go for it."

Brandon inserted the disc. "That's All Right" by Elvis Presley began playing. "Just so you know," Brandon began, "this isn't my choice. It's something someone else—"

"Hey, fella," Anton said, "whatever rocks your boat." He smiled. "Get it—rocks? Never mind."

"Anton," Justin said from the back seat. "Can I ask you a question?"

"Sounds like you already did," Anton said with a smile, looking at Justin in the rearview mirror.

"Ha ha, you're on a roll this morning," Justin said. "I don't want to sound...well, I don't want you to be offended—"

"I think I've told you both that you can speak your minds to me. I doubt I'll be offended. Shoot."

"Thanks, dude," Justin said, then seemed to hesitate before asking, "Are there not any White Christians in the Shreveport area?"

"Ah. So you noticed that, did you? I imagine you both felt a bit out of place."

Brandon shrugged. "Didn't bother me. But I admit I'm a bit curious too."

"Of course there are White Christians back there." He pointed back with his thumb. "But they meet separately. They'll get together for special events, but other than that, they keep to themselves. What do you think about that?"

"Sounds old fashioned to me," Justin said.

Brandon agreed with Justin. "Don't you see?" he said with a frown. "That just shows that the Bible is just an ancient, superstitious book."

"Why do you say that?" Anton asked.

"We've moved past segregation. At least we should have. But it seems the Bible fanatics won't let it go."

"And that's the lesson we need to learn," Anton said.

"What lesson?" Justin asked.

"Christians are not always the best representatives of the Christ."

"What do you mean?" asked Brandon.

"You need to know, Brandon," Anton glanced at him before focusing back on the road, "that the Bible does not endorse segregation or racism. The message of Jesus calls Christians to be like him. We're supposed to love people the way he did. We're supposed to ignore social and racial barriers to build relationships and help people. It's because of what the first page of the Bible says." Anton looked over expectantly.

"That's my cue, huh?" Brandon said. Anton smiled. Brandon pulled the Bible out of his pocket.

"Find verse twenty-seven on the first page and read it, will you?"

Brandon complied.

> *And God created man in His own image, in the image of God He created him; male and female He created them.*

"Thanks," Anton said. "When God created humans, he created them like himself. And we are supposed to treat people with the dignity of God. When we see someone weaker than us, the message of Jesus says we are to help them in their weakness."

Justin spoke up. "But what does this have to do with us being the only White people at church last night?"

"I'm getting there," Anton said. "When people are down, God wants them to be lifted up. And he wants people who believe in him to be the ones to do that, because, well, we're supposed to represent him. Check out Jeremiah chapter twenty-two, verse three. Find the middle of the Bible and go just a bit further."

It took a moment, but Brandon found the passage and read it.

> *Thus says the LORD, "Do justice and righteousness, and deliver the one who has been robbed from the power of his oppressor. Also do not mistreat or do violence to the stranger, the orphan, or the widow; and do not shed innocent blood in this place."*

"This was spoken to the people who lived in Jerusalem a long time ago. God was explaining to them why their entire nation had failed. They didn't consider the helpless. It happens all the time because people—that includes all three of us—are selfish. When we see someone's weakness, instead of lifting them up, we often take advantage of them. So, how does this relate to last night? Well, how do you think race is connected here?"

"Just because someone is a different race doesn't mean they're weaker," Justin said.

"Exactly!" Anton said. "However, as you are well aware, there was a time when people thought that minority meant inferiority. That's one of the things that spurred on slavery and racism among our ancestors, right? That's all behind us now—at least, that's what people want us to believe. However, we've not done a good job fixing it. People thought that simply removing Jim Crow laws would fix things. Instead, those who had been oppressed started demanding back what had been taken from them and their parents."

"Fair enough," Justin said.

"Sure," Anton said. "But it's 1999. We need to move past that and really work together—and that should be especially true for Christians."

As Johnny Cash's "I Walk the Line" began playing, Brandon recalled the dollar bill Sun Studio's tour guide had used. He wondered what it would have been like to live back then when this song was recorded. What would people have thought about him befriending someone of a different race? "How does dividing the church by race help?" Brandon asked.

Anton frowned. "It doesn't. Remember how I stirred the pot a little bit a few years ago? This is what I called them out on. Look, I understand most people like being around those who are similar to themselves. It's natural to navigate toward a people group that you identify with. But the gospel of Jesus tells us to break free of natural gravitation and proclaim that the kingdom of God is here. The early Christians had trouble with that too, because there were also racial barriers in the first century. Still, Jesus' messengers—the apostles and prophets—were sent out to tell the masses that Christ had broken those barriers down. Check out Galatians three, verses twenty-six through twenty-eight."

Brandon handed the Bible to Justin in the back seat. "Your turn."

Justin held up a hand to stop him. "No, thanks."

"Fine," Brandon said. "What page is that on?"

"It'll be toward the end of the Bible. And it's a small book, so it's easy to miss. It's called Galatians because the apostle Paul originally wrote it to the Christians who lived in a place called Galatia."

After a bit of flicking, Brandon found it.

"Good," Anton said. "Chapter three, verses twenty-six through twenty-eight," he repeated.

Brandon read out loud.

> *For you are all sons of God through faith in Christ Jesus. For all of you who were baptized into Christ have clothed yourselves with Christ. There is neither Jew nor Greek, there is neither slave nor free man, there is neither male nor female; for you are all one in Christ Jesus.*

"Did you catch that?" Anton asked. "The Bible says that your race is irrelevant when it comes to living in Christ. If the apostle Paul were writing this to American Christians, perhaps he would have said, 'There is neither White nor Black.' I don't know what it was like for my grandparents, or even my parents, who grew up in a segregated society, being forced to use different water fountains and all. I won't pretend to know how painful it would have been for the law to class you as a lower member of society. But, for whatever reason, many Christians back then just went with it. They ignored what the Bible says about this, and they acted like race makes a difference in Christianity. And we've done a poor job rectifying it. Is there anything wrong with one church being predominantly Black, and the church across town being mostly White? Not necessarily. But when you have someone who lives literally next to the 'White church building—'" Anton used air quotes, "—drive ten miles or more to meet at the 'Black church building,' or vice versa, it seems that social comfort is more important than serving Jesus—the one who died to break down such barriers. See what I mean?"

It did make sense to Brandon.

Anton was gripping the steering wheel and looking straight ahead. "I should be more patient and understanding." There was a quiver in his voice. "At least, that's what they told me six years ago. So, why were you two the only White people there? Tradition."

"You could have just said that to begin with, dude," Justin said. "I didn't mean to reopen a wound or upset you."

"No. It's good that you asked. You needed to know. Maybe one day, you'll truly see who Christ is. You'll understand how much he loves everyone, and things like race and social class mean nothing to him. Your best bet is to simply read that book." Anton pointed at the Bible in Brandon's hand. "But God knew that not everyone will have—or take—the chance to do that. Instead, he told his people to live in a such a way that, when others see them, they see Jesus. But we're pretty bad at that sometimes. Maybe most of the time. The people you met last night are good people. They really are. And I am blessed to have them as my brothers and sisters in Christ. But even the best people are good at making bad decisions. I'm the one who had a short temper a few years ago. Since then, I've asked God to kill that part of me. By his grace, I am who I am today. But even when good people fail to represent Jesus, don't take it out on him."

Even the best people are good at making bad decisions, Brandon repeated in his mind. Christians were meant to represent the God of their Bible, yet they sometimes did a lousy job. Because of that, people blamed God for the hypocrisy they saw in Christians. Wasn't that what Brandon had been doing his entire life? Brandon considered himself a pretty good person, yet he could relate to what Anton had just said. He had displaced his anger, his fear, his venom. For a moment, he considered taking back all the bad things he had said about the Bible and God. But once again, Anton had claimed that this God also loved everyone. If God was who he claimed to be, then things would have turned out differently. It wasn't just the Christians who were hypocrites. Brandon was sure God had some bad decisions to answer for too.

"So, what's the plan for Dallas?" Anton asked, changing the subject.

Brandon opened the backpack between his feet and got out Matt's map. He pulled out the first postcard from the second pocket. It had the Dallas skyline pictured, but no particular attraction on it. Brandon shrugged. "Not sure. There's not even a mini-map to go along with Dallas." Brandon looked at the big map a little closer. "We could shoot straight for Fort Worth. It's just past Dallas."

"What's waiting in Fort Worth?"

"Army base."

Brandon put the map back in his bag and retrieved his father's box. He pulled out the dog tags and let them dangle from his hands in front of him.

"Your dad's?"

"I want to go to the base to find out more about him, and maybe even learn who his parents—my grandparents—are. I don't know where they live, or even if they're still alive."

Anton noticed the photo in the open box.

"Is that your dad?"

"Yeah. With my mom." Brandon held it up for Anton to see better.

While still trying to pay attention to the road, Anton looked at the photo the best he could. "You've got your dad's eyes—and definitely his hair. What happened to your parents?"

Brandon took a deep breath and returned the photo to the box. "They're gone," he said.

Anton stared ahead. "I'm sorry about that."

"Dean—that's my father—died before I was born. I never knew a thing about him except his name. And that's only because Dean is my middle name. I just got all this stuff, including this Bible, a week ago. That's how I found out he was a Christian. And an 'O Pos,' whatever that means."

"An O Pos?"

Brandon held up the dog tags again. "Says right here: 'O Pos, Christian.' Is that a sect of your religion or something?"

Anton stifled a laugh. He took a moment to compose himself. "I'm sorry. No, that's not a sect. That's a blood type."

"Blood type?" Brandon brought the tags closer to his face.

"Mm-hmm," Anton said, still smiling.

Laughter erupted from the back seat. "You're such a doof, Brandy!" Justin said. "I could have told you that!"

Brandon's ears turned red. "Well, why didn't you?"

"Uh, 'cause you didn't ask."

"Sorry for laughing," Anton said. "It's standard for military ID to have a soldier's blood type on it in case he's ever found unconscious but needs medical help or something."

Of course that made sense. Brandon had learned about the different blood types in junior high biology, but he hadn't made the connection. Ears still burning, he shoved the tags into the box. He picked up the map again. "Let's just get to Fort Worth."

It was after lunchtime when they reached the edge of Dallas. Brother Jones was right about the traffic. They climbed a large bridge that extended over several other highways. The bridge curved around, and then Anton hit the brakes to avoid causing a pileup. They saw nothing but taillights for what seemed like miles. Inch by inch, they made their way through the metropolis, following the signs to Fort Worth. An hour later, they saw a green sign so small that it would have been easy to miss if they were traveling at speed. It was for the Fort Worth Army Base.

As soon as they exited, Anton let out his breath. The road ahead was clear. "It feels like I can breathe again." They continued for a few miles, until the signs instructed them to turn right into what looked like a gated community. An office building stood next to two lanes blocked by boom gates and a security booth. Beyond the gates were rows of houses. Anton navigated the car into the right lane, slowing to a stop. They were about twenty feet from the lane barrier and the booth when he pointed to a sign above the boom gate.

United States Army

Welcome to Fort Worth.

Please have your Military Identification Card ready.

"What's your plan?" Anton asked.

"I guess we try to get inside and talk to some of the officers who might have known Dean," Brandon said. "Or maybe there's a record of his parents."

"You mean we drove through all that traffic to get here, and you had no idea what to expect?"

"I've never been to a military base," Brandon said defensively.

"Me neither," Justin said.

"Well, how do we get in without an ID?" Anton asked.

Brandon fished the dog tags out of Dean's box. "Show them this."

Anton hesitated for a moment and then took them. He rolled down his window and inched the car toward the booth.

The lady inside the booth seemed to be in her fifties. She set down her newspaper, slid open her window, eyed the trio in the car, and then stuck out her hand. "Welcome to Fort Worth. ID, please." Anton extended the dog tags out his window. She screwed up her face and looked back at him. "And what am I supposed to do with those?"

"The soldier these belonged to was stationed here some time back. This is his son." Still holding out the dog tags, Anton leaned back to allow the lady to look closer. She didn't.

"And your point is?"

"Sorry, ma'am. We're just here to learn more about that soldier. You see, Brandon here—"

"You don't have a military ID or visitor's pass?" she cut him off.

"A visitor's pass? How do you get one of those?"

She pointed to the office building. "Tell the visitor's center who you're here to see. So long as they notified their superior officer before 5pm yesterday, your names should be on the list. Each of you will need to provide a photo ID and your social security number. Come back when you have your passes." She closed her booth window.

Anton rolled up his window. "Do you know anyone else here?" He handed the dog tags back to Brandon.

"Let's just go back to Dallas."

Anton put the car in reverse and found a parking spot near the office building.

"What are you doing?" Brandon said. "I don't know anyone else."

"Maybe they can look up some info on your dad." Anton stepped out of the car, and Brandon and Justin followed him into the office. A middle-aged man sat behind a desk. Brandon half-smiled at Anton, who said, "Don't look at me. This is your gig. Go on." He pushed Brandon in front.

"Uh, hi," Brandon said.

"Hello, sir," the man said, standing up as rigid as a board. "What can I do for you?"

"My name is Brandon, and I, well…My father was Dean Bason." Brandon handed the tags to the man and continued. "He was stationed here eighteen years ago. Did you know him?"

The man smiled. "No, sir. Eighteen years ago, I was at Fort Hood. I was a rookie then, and we didn't come this way all that often."

"Oh," Brandon said, accepting the dog tags back. "Thanks." Brandon turned.

Anton spoke up. "Sir, is there any way you could tell us anything about him? Brandon never had the chance to meet his father, and we're searching for some answers. Could you look up some records? Maybe Brandon's grandparents' names? And possibly their address?"

The man pursed his lips and gave a quick shake of his head. "I'm sorry, gentlemen. Even if I could access that information, I wouldn't have the authority to give it to you."

"Thanks anyway," Brandon said, reaching for the door.

"Sir," Anton said. "These dog tags and a photo are all he has of his dad. What can we do to learn more about his family?"

"There is the National Personnel Records Center," the man said. Brandon turned to look at him. "If you really are the next of kin, you should have no problem accessing his records."

"That's great," Anton said. "Where can we find that place?"

"Saint Louis, Missouri."

CHAPTER SEVENTEEN

THEY STARTED BACK FOR DALLAS, BRANDON IN THE BACK SEAT with his arms crossed, and exited the interstate at Arlington for a late lunch. "Let's get away from the interstate. Remember," Anton said, tapping his head, "it's the places off the beaten path that are the best." He looked around. "Although it seems all the paths around here are quite beaten." There were businesses and restaurants as far as the eye could see. A few minutes later, Anton spotted a café on the corner of a side street called the Cravings Cart. "That place probably has the greasiest burgers," he said, turning into the parking lot. Justin rubbed his hands together in anticipation. The Cravings Cart was certainly a unique-looking building. The side of the café had a mural of Usher having coffee with Bill Clinton. The door was green, round, and wooden with a large brass handle in the middle.

"It's a hobbit hole!" Anton shouted, pounding the steering wheel in excitement. Brandon jumped in his seat.

"A what-it hole?" Justin asked.

Anton froze and stared at him. "You can't be serious. Hobbits?"

Justin gave Brandon a puzzled look. "You know what hobbits are?"

"Sorry, never heard of 'em."

Anton dropped his jaw. "They only come from a couple of the best-selling novels of all time!" He pointed at the round, green door. "This is meant to look like the front door to Bag End from *The Hobbit* and *The Lord of the Rings*."

"Sorry," Justin said. "Still don't have a clue what you're talking about."

"That's a shame," Anton said, exiting the car. Justin and Brandon followed him to the door. "An actual shame. I'm not much of a fiction reader. And when I do read fiction, I normally don't reach for fantasy. But my ninth-grade reading teacher made us read them, and I'm glad she did. I reread *The Hobbit* last year."

"Sounds amazing," Brandon said in a flat tone. "Let me add that one to my running list of books I should read. So far, there's the Bible—" he held up one finger, "—and the one with the round door." He held up his second finger for emphasis. "That will make for some fun summer reading." He didn't mean to be rude, but his mind was on other things. The closer they got to Dallas that morning, the more Brandon had admitted to himself that this trip was not just about honoring Matt. It was also about searching for information about his father, and maybe even his grandparents. And it looked like that search had ended before it had even begun. He was reminded of the newspaper headline: SEARCHING FOR BRANDON BASON—a fact he still hadn't shared with Justin or Anton. He realized at that moment that the physical search for Brandon Bason was irrelevant. So what if he'd run away and hitched a ride across the country? He'd go back eventually and be reunited with—well—whoever had been looking for him. For him, it was a search of a different sort. This trip was supposed to help him figure out who he was, without the trappings of life in East Nashville defining him.

After they'd left the base in Fort Worth, Brandon had found Saint Louis on the map. They had been traveling in the opposite direction the entire time. He reached for the doorknob. The hobbit door looked like it weighed a ton, but it swung easily on its single hinge.

Crossing the threshold into the Cravings Cart was a little like walking into a different world—maybe this was some sort of portal, like Anton was suggesting. The café was crammed with people from all walks of life enjoying food and coffee. There was a guy with an afro wearing oversized headphones reading a book. Brandon couldn't help but sneak a peek at the title. It wasn't either of the books Anton had mentioned. A woman with her arms covered with tattoos was finishing a burger. And a tall guy at the counter ordering his food wore a large cowboy hat. He looked to be about Brandon's age, maybe a little older, with blonde hair and a mole on his left cheek. They stepped in line behind him, studying the menu board.

Anton tapped the cowboy on his shoulder. "Hey, do you eat here often?"

He turned and smiled. "A couple of times a month." Brandon was expecting to hear a thick, southern drawl, but there was only a hint of southern in his voice.

"What are they known for around here?" Anton leaned back and said to Justin and Brandon, "This is how I found out about the enchiladas at that Mexican restaurant."

"You asked a cowboy?" Justin smiled.

"Get the number five," the cowboy said. "You won't regret it. Unless you're afraid of a little spice."

"I'm not," Anton said.

"Sounds good to me," Justin said.

"I'll just go for a greasy burger," Brandon said. "Do they have those here?"

"You bet." The cowboy pointed to the section on the menu board to the far right. "I'd go for number eighteen."

"Thanks very much," Anton said, dipping a pretend hat.

The cowboy struck a pose that screamed, "I'm proud to be a Texan." Brandon rolled his eyes.

The three of them sat down and waited for their food. It turned out the number five was hot wings with a side of spicy macaroni and cheese. The burger the cowboy recommended came with a fried egg and beets on it. Brandon had never had an egg on a burger before, so he went for it, but he asked the lady at the checkout to hold the beets.

"It's too bad we'll have to eat our macaroni with our hands," Anton said to Justin, who stared back in confusion. "You see, if this is Bag End, then there's no silverware anymore," Anton said, giggling to himself.

"Another hobbit thing?" Justin asked.

Brandon heard a snort behind him. He turned around to find the cowboy. "No, I think Lobelia Sackville-Baggins returned them," the cowboy chimed in, still chewing a hot wing. His cheeks were dotted with sauce. He picked up a fork to show them. "That was great," he said to Anton, chuckling.

"Were you eavesdropping?" Anton questioned him playfully.

"I wasn't dropping no eves, sir. I promise." The cowboy snorted again.

Anton laughed. Brandon was not amused. "Another hobbit thing. Sorry, guys. Hey, Cowboy Gamgee, why don't you join us?"

Without hesitating, he picked up his tray and sat next to Brandon. "What translation do you use?" he asked him, eyeing Brandon's pocket. "I couldn't help but notice it earlier."

"It's in English," Brandon said.

When Brandon didn't offer anything else, the cowboy said, "Right. I assumed as much, but…never mind. Anyway, the name's Devin," he said. The group made introductions. "I'd shake your hands," Devin said, "but…" He raised his sauce-covered fingers for them to see. "So, you guys never had Cravings Cart before? Are you new in town?"

"We're passing through," Anton said. "A road trip of sorts. We came from Shreveport this morning."

"Cool," he said, scooping up some macaroni. He paused and then put the fork back down, "Sorry. You haven't gotten your food yet."

"Don't wait on us," Anton said.

"No, it's fine," Devin said. "This is Texas. I was raised with manners. Anyway, since you came from Shreveport, and you're in Arlington now, you must have already explored downtown Dallas."

"Good try, Sherlock," Anton said. "But no. We just came here from Fort Worth. Try to figure that one out." Anton smiled at Brandon.

"Sorry, you'll have to give me something to work with," Devin said.

Brandon pulled the dog tags out of his pocket and tossed them onto the table.

"Ah. Military family," said Devin. "Must have been to the base. Who'd you go to visit?"

"No one," Brandon said.

"Brandon's trying to learn about his grandparents," Anton explained. "The fella at the army base said we should go to some records place in Saint Louis."

"You don't have to go to Missouri," Devin said, just as the server appeared with the rest of the food and refilled their drink cups. Before Brandon could ask him what he meant, Anton had bowed his head in prayer. Justin leaned over to Devin. "He does this every time we eat."

"Me too," Devin whispered back. "He must have been raised in Texas." He winked at Brandon. They waited for Anton to finish. Then, they all started eating.

Brandon took a bite of his burger. He had to admit the egg was a nice touch.

"You weren't very forthcoming with info earlier," Devin said. "I just couldn't help noticing the Bible in your pocket, yet you didn't pray with Anton. Are either of you religious?" He pointed his fork from Brandon to Justin. "Just curious, guys. I know we're not supposed to talk religion in America. But remember, this is Texas." He grinned.

"It's fine," Brandon said with a sigh. "I shouldn't be surprised. I don't even know why I carry this thing around. Sentimental reasons, I guess. But ever since I started to, all kinds of strangers have commented on it. If you're asking if I believe in a collection of fairytales that claims to predict the future and to be written by a guy who makes virgins give birth, then no. I'm not religious."

Devin widened his eyes and looked at Anton. Sadness crept into Anton's eyes, and he looked down to poke at his macaroni with a fork. "I don't mean any offense," Devin said.

"Don't mind Brandon," Justin said to Devin. "He's been pouting for hours. You're just reminding him that we've finally met a Christian who knows what he's talking about and actually lives out his religion. Brandon's learning that the arguments that he's depended on for so long maybe aren't as bulletproof as he once thought."

Brandon's cheeks grew hot. He put down his burger and scowled at Justin.

Justin didn't scowl back. Still looking at Brandon, he said, "It seems it's easier for us to insult the religion than to come up with real arguments against it."

"Oh, are you going to join them now?" Brandon asked Justin. The same feelings he'd had before pounding Cody's face began to surface. Surprised, he tried to push them back down. But something inside continued to unravel.

"What?" Justin raised his hands in defense. "I'm just saying the things Anton has been saying have made sense."

"So, you're now some Bible-thumping sheep who believes in a loving guy in the clouds who drove my mom to kill herself and allowed Barry to kill our best friend?!" Brandon stood up, his emotions getting the best of him. "Think about it, Justin. Two weeks ago, Matt was all starry-eyed, looking forward to his graduation and taking us—*us*, Justin—on this trip. But look around. Where is Matt now?" He paused, letting the moment hang in the air. No one said anything. A few people in the restaurant had noticed the commotion and began to stare. "Yeah. I don't see him either. Instead, I see a couple of guys who think their God is loving because of what they read in *this*." Brandon pulled the Bible out of his pocket. "You think I don't have a real argument against their religion?" he asked. "How about this?" He flung the Bible at Justin. It hit his chest and landed on the table, an inch from a plate of hot wings. "If you want to convert to some God who has the power to both control the universe and predict the future, be my guest. You'll be just as foolish as my father." He leaned forward and planted his fists onto the table hard, causing Devin to jump. Brandon looked at Justin and then Anton. Peering into Anton's eyes, he said, "But don't you dare tell me your God is also loving."

They continued to lock eyes for a moment, not saying anything. Anton showed no anger. Instead, the sadness that had crept into his eyes earlier became more prominent. Brandon broke the stare, grabbed his backpack, and turned toward the ridiculous hobbit door. Again, it swung easily on its single hinge, and Brandon slammed it closed behind him.

CHAPTER EIGHTEEN

THE TEXAS SUN SHONE DOWN ON BRANDON AS HE WANDERED THE streets of Arlington. Paying no attention to where he was going, he knew only that he needed to get as far away from the café as possible—away from Justin, away from Anton, away from the arrogant Christian cowboy, and away from their hypocritical beliefs about a God who cared. With all Anton's talk about looking at evidence, where was the evidence in Brandon's life that anyone had ever really cared about him? His mom had, but she was gone. And now, one of his best friends was dead, and the other had betrayed him. Pushing back angry tears, Brandon walked and allowed his mind to wander.

He remembered the first time his mother had introduced Barry to him. If only there were a way to travel back to that day and warn his mother, and even himself, of the torment she was bringing into their lives. She had assured him that Barry was the answer to all their problems; that he would bring them some security.

Brandon thought of the good times he'd had with Matt and Justin. There was hardly a happy memory from his childhood that didn't include them. They had always been his refuge from life with Barry. How many times had Brandon shown up at either of their houses, his signature trench coat hiding the latest bruises, only to be welcomed in, no questions asked? Brandon picked up the pace, turning onto yet another unfamiliar street.

Frustration welled up inside him as he thought of Anton, and how easy it had been for Anton to inject himself into Brandon's and Justin's lives. Was Brandon angry at Anton? He sighed. How could he be? The guy seemed faultless. Of course, Brandon didn't like being preached at, but nothing Anton had done or said could have been classified as "preaching."

Then, there was the cowboy. Devin had blamed his lack of etiquette on being a Texan. Even Brandon had been brought up to know that religion and politics were never neutral topics of conversation. Yet, Brandon couldn't put his finger on anything the cowboy had done wrong either.

Brandon's ears began to burn, but the Texas sun wasn't to blame. What had come over him? Justin—the person who knew him the best—had every right to call Brandon out in the middle of that restaurant. Ever since his mother's death, Brandon had struggled with displacing his anger. On second thought, no, Justin didn't have the right to humiliate Brandon in front of Anton and a stranger. It was Justin's duty to be on his side. How dare he sympathize with them? Conflicted, Brandon sighed and looked around. It slowly dawned on him that he had no idea where he was, except that he was in a strange Texan town. The landscape had changed. Businesses and restaurants no longer made up the scenery. Instead, houses and apartments surrounded him. Apparently, he had wandered into the suburbs. *Great,* he thought. *Not only am I friendless; I'm also lost.*

At least he had his backpack. Maybe Matt's map could lend some guidance. Thinking of the map brought an image of Dean's box to his mind. It was then Brandon remembered he had left the dog tags on the lunch table. What had Devin said? He didn't have to go to Missouri to learn about his family. So, where did he need to go? Devin never did finish that thought. But even if he had, Brandon probably needed the dog tags. They had Dean's social security number on them. Brandon pictured returning to the restaurant to retrieve them. No doubt, the guys were probably still hanging out, glad to be rid of him. He couldn't walk back in looking like a sad puppy with his tail between his legs. No, he would count the tags as a loss, just like his friends. Just like his ride. What should he do? What would Justin and Anton do? Would they carry on without him? *I would if I were them,* he thought.

The sun was casting a deep orange glow onto the apartment faces around him. He must have been gone for hours. He lifted his head a bit, listening for sounds of the city. They seemed to be coming from behind him and to the right. He turned around and attempted to retrace his steps. The more he thought of it, the more convinced he was that he needed to veer toward the left, now that he had turned around. There was an alleyway coming up, which looked like it would cut straight into the direction he needed to go.

The alley was wide enough for a single car to pass through, allowing the homeowners to access their rear driveways and garages. With no sign that it was a dead end, he entered. Halfway down the alley, he spotted a large garbage can tipped over into the middle of the path. Knowing it would stop anyone from trying to drive through, he bent down to lift it back up. With his hand just shy of the handle, he noticed a bulk of brown and black fur sticking halfway out of it. Before he could react, a rottweiler backed out of the bin with some refuse in its mouth, clearly not expecting to see a person face-to-face. Brandon froze, as did the dog. *Run!* his mind told him, but his feet remained glued to the ground. A heart-stopping growl emanated from the dog's chest. *Run!* He locked eyes with the dog. Despite everything inside of him wanting to flee, his body remained motionless. The dog was preparing to pounce. Finally, Brandon's feet moved. He turned and bolted.

The dog wasted no time and was immediately on his heels. Brandon weaved back and forth, but there was not enough room in the alley to do any good. Even if it were wider, Brandon doubted he could outrun the dog. *This is it,* he thought. *I'm going to be dinner for a street dog.* Brandon was jerked back, and he stumbled, almost landing on his bottom. The dog was pulling on his coat, and it began to rip. Just then, Brandon saw someone entering their back door. "Help!" he screamed. The stranger paused and glanced back, but he didn't see Brandon. Brandon grabbed a handful of his coat and yanked on it. It tore the rest of the way, leaving a chunk of fabric in the dog's slobbery mouth. He sprinted toward the house. The stranger had already stepped inside, but the door was still open. Brandon nearly plowed into him as he jumped over the threshold and slammed the door behind him.

Once again, he found himself face-to-face with a stranger, albeit a human one, who was clearly not happy to see him. This one was an older man. His face screwed up in anger. He looked up and down Brandon's sweaty trench coat. "What do you think you're doing barging in my home—" The answer came with a thump and a growl, as the dog lunged itself against the door, barking viciously. The man's eyes widened. Brandon stood with his backpack to the closed door, not moving or saying anything. The dog gave up quickly, apparently knowing there was a more accessible snack waiting for him back at the garbage can. The man exhaled, seeming to relax. "Black and brown dog?" he said. Brandon nodded. "He's a regular. Everyone knows to stay away from him. Everyone except you, apparently."

"I'm sorry," Brandon whispered. "Can I just sneak out the front?"

The man grunted and led Brandon to the front of the house.

"Thanks. I guess you saved my life," Brandon said with a nervous chuckle.

"It's a good thing I was saving your life. Otherwise, I might have ended it. This is Texas, boy. I hope you don't make it a habit barging into houses." He closed the door.

Brandon crossed the street, hoping to put extra distance between himself and the alley. *What is it with Texans?* he thought. *Do they just use their state as an excuse to do whatever they want?* He felt his knees would give way. His legs shook from the adrenaline coursing through his body. He paused to steady himself, trying to get his bearings. The city sounds seemed closer, but he was still unsure of where he was. Deciding on a direction, Brandon picked up his pace. As the adrenaline wore off, reality set in: He was stranded somewhere outside Dallas with no idea of what to do next. He longed to see Justin and Anton.

Sometime later, he emerged on what looked like the main street. It seemed familiar—perhaps where they had exited the interstate. At first, he felt excited, like he was closer to where he needed to be. But then he remembered Anton had veered away from the main street to find food off the beaten path. He sat on the curb, wondering what he should do next. He briefly considered looking for a police officer or police station, but then thought better of it. If the newspapers knew he was missing, so would the Dallas police, right? What would happen if the police did find him? He ran both of his hands through his hair, clasping them behind his head.

Not only was the fading daylight telling him it was dinnertime; his stomach was too. He had only taken a single bite of his egg burger before storming out of the restaurant. He was hungry, friendless, and lost. He had failed at finding answers about his father—about himself. He no longer felt he could honor Matt since he had thrown away his friendship with Justin so easily.

And on top of that, his coat was ruined—the only thing he owned that he cared about. He picked up the part that was ripped. The hem was starting to unravel. His head in his hands, he continued thinking through options. He could call Genevieve—she didn't even know the fate of her car yet. Even though he dreaded explaining things to her, he realized she was the only person left who cared for him. He took a deep breath and stood, resigning himself to the only choice he had: to find someplace with a phone and ask directions to the local Greyhound station.

"There!" a familiar voice called out of a passing car's window. It was a white minivan. The driver was wearing a cowboy hat, and Justin hung out the passenger window, pointing at Brandon. They pulled up next to the sidewalk, and the door of the van slid open.

"We've been searching all over for you!" Anton said as a look of relief washed over his face.

"Where've you been, dude?" Justin asked.

Brandon blinked at them, a mixture of emotions welling up inside him. He hadn't realized how desperate he was to be found until the wave of relief hit him at that moment. His anger from earlier succumbed to thankfulness—thankfulness for friends who would spend their afternoon looking for someone who had not only disrespected them, but also abandoned them, causing them no end of stress and panic. Had he really thought they would just carry on with their meal and forget about him? He had been so selfish. "I'm sorry, guys."

"Dude, don't worry about it," Justin said, still hanging halfway out the window.

"Really?" Brandon said.

"Really," Anton said. "It's completely understandable. Justin told me what you've been through." He paused. "I'm sorry, and I'm so glad we found you. Do you really think Justin could cope with me and my Motown on his own?" He smiled. "Come on.

We're crashing at the cowboy's house tonight. Tomorrow, we're going to the library."

Brandon narrowed his eyes. "The library?"

"I never got the chance to finish my train of thought at lunch about your dad," Devin said from the driver's seat. "You don't have to go all the way to Missouri to learn about your dad's family. All you have to do is go to the net."

"The internet?" Brandon asked.

"There's a company out of Utah that's been collecting names for years," Devin said. "They've started putting them on their website. I don't have a computer at home, but they just upgraded everything at the library downtown. We can go there when they open up in the morning."

Brandon regarded the three guys in the van. If he were them, he would have ditched himself by now. But instead of resenting him, they eyed him with concern. They genuinely wanted to help him. He couldn't believe what a jerk he had been. He stepped toward the van.

"First, we need to go to the police," Devin said.

"The police?" Brandon stopped just short of the door.

"Yeah," Anton said. "We wanted to look for you, but we expected you would eventually go back to the Cravings Cart. What would you do if you didn't find us there? We assumed you would go to the police. So, we let them know the situation."

"It was kinda weird too," Justin said. "At first they gave us a sheet of paper to report a missing person. But the sheet said they wouldn't do anything until forty-eight hours after you went missing."

"Which is a bit ridiculous," Devin said.

"But once we turned in the sheet, they were jumping at the chance to help us. They said they would do what they can to find you. They asked if we would just stay at the station, but Devin insisted we drive around too. They couldn't keep us there, so they said if we find you, we should report back to them. Let's go."

"Well," Brandon said, trying to sound casual, "that's probably not necessary. Dallas is huge. Everything's fine. We don't need to bother the police with this anymore. Besides, I'm starving."

Devin looked at his watch. "Do police stations close?"

"Dunno," Anton said.

"Well, if they do, they're probably closed by now. Plus, the other guys should already be at the house."

"And you say you've got food at your place?" Justin asked.

"You bet!" he said.

"Then what are we waiting for?" Justin said.

Brandon climbed into the van next to Anton. He would have to tell them the truth at some point.

Just not yet.

CHAPTER NINETEEN

DEVIN'S HOUSE WAS ONLY A FIVE-MINUTE DRIVE AWAY IN A NEARBY suburb. As they arrived, Brandon noticed Anton's car already parked next to a couple of others. They piled out of the van, and Devin led them into his home. It was a small, but nice, ranch-style house with beige siding and a neatly mown front yard. Devin took them to the basement, which he called his "pad."

"I still live with my mom," he said. "I'll be going to college in the fall, so I get to move out of a smelly basement to a smelly dorm room. Come and meet the guys." They rounded a corner and found two guys their age sitting on a couch playing a video game. They paused it just long enough to greet the newcomers before resuming. "We do this every Thursday night," Devin said.

"Thursday?" Justin asked. "Why not Friday or Saturday?"

"Jake," Devin said, pointing at the first guy on the couch. He wore glasses and had red hair and freckles. "Works at the bowling alley, and he's always scheduled to work weekends. Same for Scott." Devin pointed at the other guy. He had short black hair and stubble on his chin. "But he works at a movie store. That's how we can always score these video games. He's allowed to rent them for free." He pulled up three chairs next to the couch for Brandon, Justin, and Anton, then sat on the couch next to Jake. "This one is a role-playing game. We've been waiting for it to be available. That's the one thing about it. Customers come first, so we're usually about six months behind. But at least we don't have to pay for them!"

Brandon watched Jake maneuver a character on the screen dressed up as a knight. From what he could gather, it was the knight's job to transport a pink baby monster safely from one kingdom to another. Brandon had played video games here and there growing up. His family had never had the money for them. Neither he nor any of his friends cared much for being shut into a room for hours on end staring at a television. Still, he watched the TV now with interest, although he was a little distracted by his hunger. He thought it would be rude to ask for food as soon as he arrived at the cowboy's house, so he watched in silence.

The doorbell rang. "Cowabunga!" Devin said, standing up. Jake and Scott didn't budge. Devin grinned at Brandon's puzzled look before going upstairs to answer the door. Almost immediately, Brandon felt his stomach growl as the familiar smell of freshly cooked pizza wafted into the room, followed by Devin carrying four pizza boxes. Still smiling, Devin said to Anton, "After a few Thursdays in a row of the same order, we worked it out with the pizza place to just deliver the same thing the same time every week unless we call ahead and say otherwise. I always order extra, 'cause I like the leftovers. But you guys dig in. There will be plenty."

Hours later, Brandon lay on the same couch, unable to sleep. Scott and Jake had been stationed across the room from him, and he could tell by their steady breathing that they were already asleep. One of them was snoring. It was past midnight.

Devin was busy doing something upstairs. Justin was stretched out on a pallet of blankets around the corner, and Anton was taking a shower. Everything was still as Brandon tried to recount the events of the day. That morning, he had woken up in Louisiana. He had made his first visit to a military base, heard about hobbits, lashed out at his friends, gotten lost, been chased by a dog, and been found. Now, he was sharing a basement with Justin and Anton, plus three strangers. The strangest one of all was the cowboy.

When Brandon thought of his outburst in the restaurant, he still didn't know how to feel. No one had talked about it since he had gotten into the van. There hadn't been much of an opportunity. Even so, the unresolved argument weighed heavily on his mind. Brandon always felt vulnerable during confrontations. He never had the right comebacks. It was always later when he would come up with the words that had escaped him at the time. And in his moment of vulnerability, Justin had taken not his, but the Christians', side. Justin had backed Brandon into a corner. What had Justin said? That Brandon had finally met a Christian who could defend his faith, and Brandon was losing his footing. Now was the moment that the stroke of genius usually came. *Come on, Brandon. Think.* What comeback would have worked at that moment, besides storming out of the restaurant and getting lost? Nothing came, except shame. Justin was right, and Brandon had been foolish.

"Yo, Brandon," someone whispered. "You awake?" It was Anton.

Brandon sat up. "Yeah, man," he whispered back.

"May I sit down?" Anton moved to the front of the couch. Brandon could smell his fresh shower scent.

"Sure." Brandon swung his legs to the floor, bringing the blanket with him.

Anton sat down. He was wearing a baggy shirt and some

sweatpants. "When you told me about your friend Matt, I didn't pry. I know it's not my business."

Brandon shrugged. He wasn't sure if Anton could see his face in the dark. The only light in the room came from the bathroom light that shone through a slightly open door.

"I don't want you to be mad at Justin, but he thought I should know some of the stuff you've had to deal with in the past couple of years. He really cares for you, and he wants to see some healing in your life. He thought telling me what you've been through would help me understand why you were so upset." Anton paused before continuing. "He was right. You've been through a lot—your mom, your stepdad, and even Matt. It stinks, doesn't it?"

That last phrase didn't sound like something happy-go-lucky Anton would say. Brandon knew Anton well enough now that he was sure he wasn't mocking him. Anton's dark eyes caught the light, and Brandon could see his sincerity. "Yeah," Brandon said, struggling to keep his voice to a whisper. "It does stink. And it doesn't make it easy to hear about some powerful God in the sky who supposedly loves me. Maybe that makes sense for someone who's had a perfect life. But imagine going through something like I've been through, and then someone says that it must have been your loving God's will for it to happen."

Anton was silent. Perhaps he was finally able to see it from Brandon's perspective. After a moment, he said, "I don't have to."

"You don't have to what?"

"I don't have to imagine it." He took a deep breath, his face in the dark betraying some past pain. "I've been there."

Brandon swallowed. What was Anton talking about?

Still whispering, Anton said, "I had a twin sister." He looked down. "Her name was Aaliyah."

Brandon recognized that name. Didn't someone at Aunt Mavel's house mention her?

Anton continued. "She was diagnosed with leukemia when we were seventeen. For the next few years, I watched that cancer destroy her body from the inside out. Not only that, but it also destroyed my parents' marriage and my faith. The only one who seemed at peace with it was Aaliyah." The corner of Anton's mouth curled up, as a tear dropped from his chin. "She died on Valentine's Day three years ago."

Brandon didn't know what to say. He searched for words, but none of them seemed adequate, just like when he had faced Matt's parents after the funeral. He lifted his hand, and after a moment's hesitation, he put it on Anton's shoulder. "That stinks, man," he eventually said. He couldn't believe this entire time he had been in the company of someone who knew what he was going through.

Anton sniffled, and Brandon removed his hand. "I hear that," Anton said. "I knew nothing about leukemia when she was diagnosed. So, I started researching. My research kept showing that it was people who drank alcohol and smoked that were at the highest risk. So, why did Aaliyah get it?" He leaned back on the couch and exhaled. "She never touched that junk. She was healthy." He remained deep in thought. After a moment, he chuckled. "Aaliyah was also a genius. She was the smartest person I ever knew. She had started applying to all the big colleges. Her heart was set on UC."

"The University of Chicago?" Brandon asked.

"Mm-hmm. She was even accepted, but once she graduated high school, it would have been too risky for her to move by herself. She was constantly in and out of the hospital. With our parents' marriage on the rocks, moving the whole family would have been too much. She sacrificed her plans to stay close to us. Well, to stay close to me, I guess."

"UC was Matt's dream college too. He studied all senior

year. Then, SAT scores finally came in, and he was sure they were good enough for a scholarship. He died later that day." Brandon wiped a tear from his cheek.

"That stinks," Anton said.

"Yeah," Brandon said. He narrowed his eyes and asked, "But don't you have to believe that this was God's plan or something?"

"You also know what that's like, huh?" Anton said. "There you are, wondering why God would allow something like that to happen to you and your family, and some well-meaning Christian comes up and tells you that everything happens for a reason, and God must have had plans for your sister…or mom, or friend." Anton wiped away a tear. "How helpful is that?"

"Are you saying you don't believe that?" Brandon asked.

"As I said," Anton began, "when Christians say things like that, they are well-meaning, but they're also presumptuous. The Bible tells us a lot of things about death, but to say it was God's will for a certain person to get sick or die is to speak where God hasn't spoken." Anton paused, perhaps allowing Brandon to say or ask something else. When he didn't, Anton continued. "That's what shook my faith so much. When I was a young Christian, I was pretty arrogant. I probably still have a little bit of that in me." He looked at Brandon with a crooked smile. Brandon smiled back. "I thought everything was black and white—clear cut, easy to understand. I had all the answers, and I thought they were all in the Bible. That's what got me in trouble with Brother Jones and the Christians in Shreveport, by the way—my arrogance. But then Aaliyah didn't get better. She got worse. And in the end, the cancer took her. What happens to a person's faith when he thinks he has all the answers, but then he comes across a question he doesn't have the answer to?" Anton sniffled again. "It crumbles."

"I'm confused," Brandon said. "I thought you believed in the Bible and all?"

Anton nodded. "It turned out, Brandon, that my faith was in the wrong person. I trusted in my own knowledge and perception of the world. I basically had two options. I could do what many people do—blame God and then claim to no longer believe in him. Or I could dig deeper to see what I had missed. And at that point, disbelieving in God was on the table, but I wasn't going to do it out of anger. I did what I should have done much earlier." Anton let the moment hang in the air.

"And that was?" Brandon finally asked.

Anton smiled. "Search."

"And what did you find?" Brandon asked, still whispering.

"The gospel," Anton said.

CHAPTER TWENTY

HE SAID THE WORD AS IF IT HAD WEIGHT. *GOSPEL.* IT DIDN'T strike Brandon the way he thought Anton meant for it to; to him it was just another obscure Christian term. He had heard Anton say the word a couple of times but hadn't considered its meaning. "What's that mean?" Brandon asked.

"It's the churchy way of saying 'good news.' It comes from a Greek word."

"So, you found some good news?" Brandon asked.

"Not just some good news, but *the* good news," Anton said. "There's this misconception that Christianity is simply about shaping people into 'good' people." Anton used air quotes when he said "good." "It is true that Christians should be good people. But I've also known people who don't believe in God, yet they were good people. So, if Christianity isn't just about good behavior, what is it about?"

Brandon wasn't sure, so he shrugged.

"It's about the good news that reverses the curse."

Again, Brandon could hear weight in the word *curse*, but it didn't strike him.

"We've got to backtrack a little bit. My search didn't begin with the Bible. It began with the nature of cancer. I was completely ignorant when it came to it. The first thing I learned about cancer was that it starts with something good and life-giving and basic: cells in the body reproducing. Then, somehow, those cells get distorted and become something bad and lethal. But why?"

Although he paused, Brandon could tell it was more of a rhetorical question. Having no idea why, Brandon couldn't answer even if he wanted to.

"When I was asking that question, everyone around me seemed to have an answer. 'Everything happens for a reason.' 'It was God's will.'"

"God just needed another angel?" Brandon offered.

"Yes!" Anton exclaimed. One of the sleeping bodies grunted, and Anton lowered his voice again. "That's probably the worst one of them all. Completely unbiblical. And if it really was God's will that my sister suffered the way she did, then I wasn't sure I wanted much to do with God anymore. The images in my mind still torment me. She was just flesh and bones when she finally died. But if I was going to give up God and the Bible, what would I believe in their place? What were the options?"

Brandon was starting to catch on—not fully to what Anton was saying, but the way he was explaining things. He was asking questions to keep the conversation going—questions he didn't necessarily mean for Brandon to answer.

"I started surveying alternative worldviews. Some other religions that I came across teach about karma."

"Is that the 'what goes around comes around' thing?" Brandon asked.

"Mm-hmm," Anton replied, nodding.

"I didn't know karma was a religious thing," Brandon said. "I just thought it was a more sophisticated way of saying, 'snitches get stitches.'"

Anton chuckled. "Well, I guess it is. But its origin is religion.

It's a way of answering the big 'why' questions, like, 'Why do people suffer?' Karma teaches that there is no unjust suffering. If you suffer, it's because you did something wrong—either in this life or a previous life. But what's wrong with that picture?"

There was an extra-long pause here. Brandon considered the question. "What's wrong is that you said your sister was a good person."

Anton nodded. "Of course, she wasn't perfect. Who is? But if karma really is about bringing true justice to the world, then cancer shouldn't be for people like Aaliyah. It should be for the scum of the earth—the thieves, murderers, rapists. We wouldn't need prisons or the justice system. Karma should just take care of that for us."

That made sense to Brandon.

"So, I knew my 'why' question couldn't be answered with karma-based religions," Anton said. "What's another alternative? Atheism. No God at all. How does atheism answer the 'why' question?"

Brandon started idly picking at the fibers of the blanket Devin had given him.

"It doesn't, and it can't," Anton said emphatically. "If we truly came from pond scum, and this world is the result of random chance, then nothing has true meaning or value. There's no ultimate meaning to life; there's no meaning to prosperity; there's no meaning to suffering. We've already looked at that."

Brandon remembered his conversation with Anton around the Barrett Strong song about money. People could assign meaning to things, but if there was no God, then there was nothing beyond personal opinion that governed what was good or bad. And disagreeing on such values would be pointless, since there would be no objective, moral law for guidance.

Anton continued. "So, finally, I looked closer at the Bible and God. Granted, I had not surveyed every religion and worldview, but I didn't want to neglect my heritage either. I realized that when I had believed in God, I had listened carefully to my granddad, parents, and preachers about who God is. And I'm thankful for their teachings. But I needed to search for answers myself. I turned a new page—figuratively and literally. The Bible doesn't waste any time telling us about the state the world was in and the state it's currently in. The first pages tell us God created everything good. When you read the entire account, the word *good* is really an understatement. But then humans made some stupid choices and messed everything up. A consequence of those choices is that everything is now under a curse—both the living things and the nonliving stuff are floundering in a world that has the potential to be perfect. But we just won't let it be. We're selfish. We divide. We bite and devour each other. And because that curse didn't just affect the inner man, but also the world itself, things like cancer exist. But my question wasn't, 'Why does cancer exist?' It was, 'Why did Aaliyah get cancer?'"

Brandon let the question hang in the air for a moment. In a way, Anton had been searching for the same answers that Brandon currently sought. Anton obviously believed he had already found his answers, and he was building up to a groundbreaking revelation or punch line. "So, what's the answer?"

"Why did Aaliyah get cancer?" Anton said. "Dunno. The Bible doesn't address that question."

Brandon closed his eyes and exhaled. It was only then that he realized he had moved to the edge of his seat. He had been hanging on Anton's every word. He slumped back into the couch. He couldn't believe Anton had lured him into thinking there was some simple, but profound, answer out there. That was a ridiculous idea. He ran his fingers through his hair. If the Bible could answer that question, Brandon supposed the whole world would believe in Christianity.

Something didn't add up. "Wait a second." Brandon turned his body so he could face Anton a little easier. "You went to the Bible for answers, and you didn't find any. So, how come you still believe in all that stuff? Why didn't you carry on to the next religion?"

"I didn't say I didn't find any answers, Brandon." Anton's eyes found Brandon's in the dark. "I said I didn't find answers to that one specific question. What I did find was much more powerful and much more meaningful." He stood up and walked over to the twin-sized bed Devin had prepared for him. He grabbed something out of his bag and walked over to the bathroom, opening the door a little bit more to let more light into the room. Then, coming back to Brandon, he handed him the object. It was Dean's Bible. "Don't worry," Anton said. "I also have your dad's dog tags in there. You've got to keep track of your stuff." He smiled. Brandon smiled back. "Could I show you a couple of things?"

Brandon accepted the Bible. The last time he'd had it in his hands, he had flung it across the table in a fit of rage. What would happen this time?

Anton sat back down. "I have learned two things about the 'why' question, at least when it comes to asking why someone suffers. The first thing is it assumes, in a roundabout way, the existence of God."

"How do you figure?" Brandon asked.

"As we discussed in the car not long ago, if you say something is bad, you're assuming there is such a thing as good, right?"

"Yeah," Brandon agreed.

"Okay. And if there are good and bad things, they are weighed against a standard. Where does that standard come from if there is no God? I know we've been over this already. Still, I personally needed to keep reminding myself of this, just like I should remind you. I was so frustrated when I couldn't even begin addressing the 'why' question without God. But I finally admitted that God must remain in the equation. Otherwise, nothing has meaning."

Brandon pursed his lips, trying to think of an objection. None came.

"The second thing I learned about the 'why' question is you and I are not alone when we ask it. I know that seems like common sense, but even the Bible admits to it. This book—" Anton tapped the Bible, which was still closed in Brandon's hands, "—deals with real life. It's not just a list of things to do if you want to be a good person. For instance, turn to Job chapter seven."

Brandon tried to hand the Bible to Anton. "Go for it."

Anton pushed it back. "No, I want you to read it for yourself. Plus, I'm not wearing my glasses."

"But I still don't know how to work this thing."

"Neither did I, until I made the effort to learn. Take the training wheels off. You can do this," Anton said gently.

Brandon was tempted to tell Anton to just forget about it. It was late, and Brandon had had a pretty crazy day. But Anton was right. Brandon remembered the little speech he had given in Genevieve's dining room. He was tired of life happening to him. He was going to start doing. New determination welling up inside him, he started flipping the pages of the Bible.

"Job—spelled J-o-b—is in the middle, right before the Psalms," Anton said.

"Found it."

"Good. Chapter seven, verse eleven."

Brandon read it out loud, his voice still a whisper.

Therefore, I will not restrain my mouth;
I will speak in the anguish of my spirit,
I will complain in the bitterness of my soul.

"A little back story is necessary," Anton said. "The guy, Job, has it all. He has a great family. He's rich and healthy. Then, all that changes in one day, and it's Satan's fault. Now, don't you start thinking of some little red man with horns and a pitchfork." He put his index fingers on either side of his head, faking horns. "The devil is real, but the Bible never describes him the way the cartoons do. Instead, the Bible uses words like 'tempter,' slanderer,' and 'accuser.' When we are introduced to Job, the slanderer accuses him of only serving God because everything is going great in his life. That's not a crazy hypothesis, by the way. There are plenty of people who believe in God when things are going great, and then they abandon him as soon as the boat starts rocking. That was almost me not too long ago."

Brandon absentmindedly flipped through the pages of the Bible with his thumbs while he listened to Anton.

"Anyway, Satan puts Job to the test. He destroys his family, his fortunes, and his health—all in one day. It seems the only thing Job is left with is his integrity and intelligence. And with his intelligence, he begins to ask God some deep questions. While reading through the book, we can't help but wonder if Job will ever lose his integrity. Now, read verse twenty."

Brandon found the verse and read.

Have I sinned? What have I done to Thee, O watcher of men? Why hast Thou set me as Thy target, so that I am a burden to myself?

"We have the benefit of knowing that Satan has caused all this," Anton explained. "But Job doesn't know what's going on behind the scenes, so he asks why God did it all. God is patient for a long time, allowing Job to ask all the questions on his heart. You see, Job understands the trilemma."

"Trilemma?" Brandon asked.

"Mm hmm." Anton nodded. "A trilemma is when three options, or three possibilities, are presented, but they can't all be accepted together. The Bible-believer claims that God is all-powerful and all-loving. But suffering still exists. That's the trilemma Job was trying to understand. Now, why is it difficult for people to accept that all three of these are true?"

Brandon was unsure if this was one of Anton's rhetorical questions, but he gave it a shot anyway. "If God loves everyone, and he truly has the power to control everything..." Brandon paused before continuing, "then he would use his power to stop suffering."

"You got it," Anton said. "So, Job wanted to know why God wasn't using his power to stop suffering. Wouldn't you like to know?"

Who wouldn't? Brandon wondered.

"The worst part about the book of Job," Anton continued, "is when some of Job's friends come around and start pretending like they know all the answers. They're also stumped by this trilemma, so they begin guessing why Job is suffering so badly. Some of their answers sound an awful lot like they believe in karma. Through listening to his friends, Job learns what you and I already know—pretending you know how the world works is not helpful. God shows up at the end of the book, and the reader prepares himself to learn from God's own words the answer to the trilemma, which is often the strongest argument against his existence."

Brandon was surprised to hear Anton so candidly admit to that.

Anton continued. "But instead of answering Job's questions, God begins asking his own questions. Through those questions, we find out that presenting this as a trilemma is the wrong way to think. We are limiting God when we put only his love and power against suffering. God is much more than his great love and power. As amazing as those qualities are, God reminds Job and his friends that he's also the creator of the universe. Turn to chapter thirty-eight, and read the first six verses."

Brandon turned a couple of pages and found the passage.

Then the LORD answered Job out of the whirlwind and said, "Who is this that darkens counsel by words without knowledge? Now gird up your loins like a man, and I will ask you, and you instruct Me! Where were you when I laid the foundation of the earth? Tell Me, if you have understanding, Who set its measurements, since you know? Or who stretched the line on it? On what were its bases sunk? Or who laid its cornerstone?"

"What's God doing here?" Anton asked.

Brandon frowned in concentration as he looked at the passage again. "He's definitely asking a lot of questions."

"But what's the point?" Anton asked.

"Well, he's accusing them of being know-it-alls."

Anton smiled. "When my sister and I were growing up, if we complained about something, our parents would say, 'Let's write that down, and when you're grownups, you tell us what we could have done better.'"

Brandon smiled at the thought. "Do you still have that list?"

Anton shook his head. "We never even started it. We didn't see the point—which was kind of the point. Six-year-olds are so limited in their perspective. Their parents are supposed to have more experience and knowledge. If that's true with a twenty-year gap, then how much more with an eternal one?"

Brandon could see Anton's point. It was helpful to see the Christian perspective of suffering, even if Brandon was still hesitant to accept the worldview.

Anton nodded at the Bible. "Read a little bit more, starting with verse sixteen."

"Okay," Brandon said.

Have you entered into the springs of the sea? Or have you walked in the recesses of the deep? Have the gates of death been revealed to you? Or have you seen the gates of deep darkness? Have you understood the expanse of the earth? Tell Me, if you know all this. Where is the way

> *to the dwelling of light? And darkness, where is its place, That you may take it to its territory, And that you may discern the paths to its home? You know, for you were born then, and the number of your days is great!*

"I look around the world, and I see so much suffering," Anton said. "Of course, there's a lot of joy too, which makes me think that if God gave me his power for just a moment, I would fix all this broken stuff in an instant." Anton lifted his hand, which was poised to snap. "But if, with his power, he also granted his eternality, knowledge, and wisdom, I don't think I would change a thing."

That was a good point. Some of the worst villains in the movies Brandon had watched were guys who were good at first, but then they were granted god-like powers. Drunk with power, they destroyed the world, all while thinking they were doing the right thing. If only they had been granted wisdom too…

"God hurts over our suffering," Anton said, "but pain is not always a bad thing. If you didn't know the stove was on, and you put your hand on the burner, what would you feel?"

"Pain, of course."

"But what if you couldn't feel that pain, and for some reason, your hand stayed there?"

"I don't know," Brandon admitted. "I guess it would burn off or melt eventually."

"Something like that. Pain lets you know something isn't right, and it motivates you to change. Even as limited human beings, we admit that some pain—some suffering—can actually produce good results. God, however, with his unlimited knowledge, wisdom, and power, can see the end from the beginning. Does he have the power to stop all this? Yes. But, for whatever reason, his wisdom keeps things as they are. When we lose our friends in a terrible car accident, or when our sisters are diagnosed with cancer, we have every right to ask, 'Why, God?'" Anton's voice cracked as his eyes filled with tears. "But just asking that question reminds us that we are limited in time and space. And one day—" Anton paused as a tear ran down his cheek, "—one day, the curse will be broken, and we will live without any of this junk." He brushed the tear from his face and smiled broadly. "And I will see my sister again."

An uneasy silence descended. Brandon shifted uncomfortably on the couch as he grappled with the idea of an all-loving God who still allowed suffering. To his surprise, he realized he was jealous of people like Anton. Anton had gone through his trials and ended up stronger on the other side. Brandon knew that couldn't happen to him. If there was a God, he didn't care for Brandon the way he cared about Anton and his family. Brandon couldn't help but wonder how it would feel if he truly believed in an afterlife where he could meet his father and be reunited with his mom and Matt.

Anton broke the silence. "Turn to First Corinthians."

Brandon looked down and realized he was still holding the Bible. He came back to reality. "Sorry, where?"

"First Corinthians," Anton repeated. "It's much closer to the end of the Bible." He leaned over and helped Brandon find it the best he could without his glasses. "Now, read the first four verses of chapter fifteen."

He did.

Now I make known to you, brethren, the gospel which I preached to you, which also you received, in which also you stand, by which also you are saved, if you hold fast the word which I preached to you, unless you believed in vain. For I delivered to you as of first importance what I also received, that Christ died for our sins according to the Scriptures, and that He was buried, and that He was raised on the third day according to the Scriptures.

Brandon looked up from the Bible. "What does it mean that Christ died for our sins?"

Anton slapped his forehead. "I'm sorry. I don't mean to take things like that for granted. But you're right; I can't assume you've ever been taught this stuff. It's refreshing."

Brandon shifted his weight on the couch. He had the feeling that he had just asked the dumbest question in all history. Apparently, he was already supposed to know about this. But why would Anton say it was refreshing?

"It's refreshing because a lot of people have heard others talk about these things, but they have never studied it for themselves. They think they know what the Bible says based solely on what they've been told. That's a dangerous thing."

Brandon shrugged. "What's so bad about that? After all, isn't that what you're doing to me right now? You're telling me what you believe."

Anton touched his goatee in thought before saying, "That's true. I am. But the point of difference is that I am asking you to turn to and read the passages where I get my beliefs from. When it comes to something as important as religion, don't just take someone's word for it. Investigate."

Clearly, Anton had taken his own advice. He had investigated and come to his conclusions. But what was the big deal, anyway? Everyone was entitled to their own beliefs, as outlandish as some of them were.

"Anyway," Anton said. "Back to your question. What does it mean that Christ died for our sins? Remember when I took you and Justin to the creek behind Aunt Mavel's house? I told you that's where Granddad baptized me into Jesus Christ. Jesus is his name, but Christ is his title. To say Jesus is the Christ is to say he is the chosen one of God. It says here that Jesus died for our sins."

Brandon felt a yawn coming on. He tried to stop it, but it came anyway. "Sorry," he said sheepishly.

"Okay," Anton said. "We're going to have to study about Jesus' death some other time. But before we catch some shuteye, let me tell you why I asked you to turn to this passage."

"Sure," Brandon said.

"Jesus died, but what happened on the third day?"

"I don't know," Brandon said. "What?"

"Don't ask me. Look back at verse four."

Brandon did. "It says he was raised."

"I could have easily told you that," Anton said. "But one day, I hope you'll appreciate that I had you read it for yourself. Anyway, the Bible claims Jesus rose from the grave."

Brandon resisted the urge to laugh. This was clearly important to Anton. Reminded of his outburst in the restaurant and the sadness in Anton's eyes, Brandon was ashamed at the pain he had caused his new...his new what? Friend? Yes, friend. He had caused his new friend great pain. Regardless, Anton had spent the afternoon searching for him. Even though the two of them didn't agree on some things, Brandon knew he had found a true friend in Anton. So, instead of laughing, Brandon said, "Okay. I guess if you believe in angels and virgins giving birth, it isn't too much to also ask for you to believe that God's chosen one rose from the dead."

"You're exactly right," Anton said. "After all, if the first verse of the Bible is true, everything is possible."

"And what's the first verse of the Bible say?" Brandon asked.

Anton answered by raising his eyebrows.

"Oh, right," Brandon said. "I'll read it for myself." He used his index finger to bookmark First Corinthians fifteen. Then, he flipped to the first page of the Bible and read.

In the beginning God created the heavens and the earth.

"Hmm," Brandon said. "Sure. If this is true, then I guess virgins can give birth, and dead guys can come back to life."

"And that's what that passage claims," Anton said.

Brandon turned back to First Corinthians fifteen.

"Read verses twenty through twenty-two," Anton said.

"Sure."

But now Christ has been raised from the dead, the first fruits of those who are asleep. For since by a man came death, by a man also came the resurrection of the dead. For as in Adam all die, so also in Christ all shall be made alive.

"The resurrection of Jesus was just the beginning of something huge," Anton said. "The Bible calls it the 'first fruits.'"

"First fruits?" Brandon asked.

Anton chuckled at Brandon's thinly veiled skepticism. "Okay, so humor me for a minute and imagine you're a farmer."

"All right…"

"So, you scatter your seeds on your field, water it, fertilize it, and wait. Then, one day, you see the first sprout of the crop. One of your seeds was successful. So, it's reasonable to believe what?"

"That the rest of the seeds are going to be successful?"

"That's right. You have the evidence. Now, you just wait in faith. Verse four tells us that Jesus rose from the grave. What's the next verse say?"

Brandon found it and read.

And that He appeared to Cephas, then to the twelve.

"Jesus didn't just claim he would rise from the dead," Anton said. "He showed himself to people to give them proof. To give them hope. That's the hope I have. The Bible says that those who die in Christ will be raised again when he returns. Not only will I see my Lord, but I will also see my sister again. What's verse forty-two say?"

Brandon looked down and read the verse out loud.

> *So also is the resurrection of the dead. It is sown a perishable body, it is raised an imperishable body.*

"My sister won't have her broken body anymore." Anton smiled at the thought.

Brandon shifted on the couch once more. Again, he felt a tinge of jealousy prick his heart. He wished he could have that type of hope. What had Anton said? Those who died in Christ had it. What did that mean? And what about those who didn't die in Christ? Why should Brandon believe any of this, anyway? A few more questions came to Brandon's mind, but he kept them to himself. He had no idea how late it was. Instead of saying anything, Brandon smiled back wearily.

"Your eyes say it all," Anton said, standing up. "Let's call it a night—or a morning, whatever time it is."

CHAPTER TWENTY-ONE

Brandon turned over on the couch, trying to get comfortable. He opened his eyes to find another face staring back at him, not an inch from his nose. "Whoa!" He shot up with a start.

"Mornin', sleepin' beauty. Hungry?" It was Devin.

"Not cool, man. What time is it?" Brandon asked, rubbing his eyes.

"Nearly nine. Library will be open soon. Better get up if you want a shower and some grub."

Brandon groaned. "I didn't get much sleep."

"Tell me about it," Devin said, walking away. "I had to wait for you and Anton to finish yapping."

"What?" Brandon said, standing up.

"I came down at about one o'clock to go to bed, but I could tell you two were having a serious chat, so I thought I'd wait for the light to turn off. I ended up just crashing on the couch upstairs."

Anton's bed was made, and no one else was downstairs.

"Come on up when you want some food," Devin said. "I'll leave you to it."

Brandon grabbed his stuff and took a quick shower. A few minutes later, he went upstairs to join the rest of the guys. He followed the smell of food to the dining table, where they were all enjoying bacon, sausage, and biscuits.

"It's a pleasure to have you boys." A woman appeared from the kitchen, smiling warmly.

"Meet the best cook in Texas!" Devin exclaimed, putting his arm around her shoulders. "Bet you didn't realize you'd get star treatment when you crashed here. My mom knows a thing or two about how to feed the five thousand." She smiled.

"It's my pleasure. My boy told me you are in need of some good old-fashioned Texan hospitality. That I can do!" She handed Brandon a plate. "Help yourself."

"Thank you, ma'am," he replied, and sat down next to Anton. "Thanks for letting us stay the night," he continued. "And Devin, I'm sorry Anton and I kept you up."

"Not to worry," Devin said with a smile. "Really. I could tell you guys needed some space."

Justin glanced from Devin to Brandon and then to Anton with a questioning look.

"Jake and Scott have things to do after breakfast," Devin said, "so they've gotta skedaddle. The rest of us can head to the library. I've gotta go to work after lunch, so you guys can take Anton's car, and I will lead the way in the van, okay?"

"Where do you work?" Justin asked.

"I'm a lifeguard at the local pool. School's still in session, so it doesn't open till one. But when school lets out next week, it'll be open all day long. One more summer till college. That's what I keep telling myself."

Brandon thought about school and how he and Justin would be in class at that exact moment if they had not gotten themselves suspended. Had it only been two weeks since Matt's death? In one sense, it seemed like yesterday, but in another, it felt like an eternity. Then it hit him. "It's been two weeks," he said to Justin.

Justin put down his fork as it dawned on him too. Not only had it been two weeks since the accident, but tonight, the entire class of 1999—people they had gone to school with for a dozen years—would be walking across the stage to receive their diplomas. The entire class, except for three students.

An hour later, Brandon was in the front seat of Anton's car as they approached the library. Justin had called shotgun with Devin, as he wanted to talk to him about music. Brandon leaned forward in his seat, peering out of the windshield. "It seems a little fancy for a library."

"I hear that," Anton agreed, pulling into a massive parking garage behind Devin. He took his parking stub and followed Devin's van to the third floor.

Justin got out and waited for Brandon behind the van. He joined in stride as Brandon passed. "Guess his genre," Justin challenged.

Eyeing the cowboy hat atop Devin's head, Brandon said, "I'd bet everything on country and western, but I have a feeling there's gonna be a twist."

"You would have lost it all!" Justin said. "Techno."

Brandon stopped. "Like, the electronic stuff? No way."

"Way," Justin said, motioning for Brandon to keep up. "I would never have guessed, but he played some for me. It was kinda catchy."

"Hmm," Brandon said, shaking his head. He jogged to catch up with them, the torn tail of his trench coat flapping behind. The four of them walked to the entrance of the library, accessible from inside the parking garage.

"You weren't kidding when you said they upgraded things!" Justin said to Devin. "You sure this is a library?"

"You bet," Devin said, removing his cowboy hat as they crossed the threshold. On the other side of the door was a long corridor, which led to a set of double doors. The passage was tiled to look like it had a marble floor. Their steps echoed as they crossed.

Brandon glanced out the windows to see they were walking three floors above a busy street. "This is fancy," Brandon said.

"They've got security cameras and everything," Justin said as they approached the end of the corridor.

Brandon looked to where Justin pointed, and sure enough, there were a pair of cameras. One of them was aimed right at them.

The four of them entered through the doors, the scale of the place making Brandon's jaw drop in wonder. Books upon books, shelves upon shelves, stretched as far as he could see. Perhaps all cities had libraries this size, but the only library he had been in was the school library, and that wasn't voluntary. "Who knew so many books even existed?" Brandon said to no one in particular.

"Beyond this, my son, be warned," Devin said, turning to Brandon. He pointed at him with his cowboy hat. "The writing of many books is endless, and excessive devotion to books is—"

"Wearying to the body," Anton finished.

Justin raised an eyebrow.

"Is that another hobbit thing?" asked Brandon.

Anton smiled. "Nope. That's Ecclesiastes."

"Ecclees-e-what-ey?" Justin asked.

Anton chuckled. "It's in the Bible."

Brandon smiled to himself as he remembered the first time he and Justin had met Anton in the Mexican restaurant. Anton had tried to quote the Bible, expecting to make his point quickly and easily, yet Brandon and Justin had been clueless. It seemed

Anton was finally around someone who would get his references.

As Brandon walked with the others among the colossal stacks of books, he marveled at how much things had changed in the past two weeks. Who would have thought that he and Justin would find themselves in a library in the middle of Texas with two Christian guys? He smiled inwardly. Brandon felt much better since his conversation with Anton the previous night. He had a newfound respect for him. Remarkably, Justin seemed to have forgotten the entire episode from the restaurant and was acting as if everything was cool again. He padded behind Devin, and as strange as it was, Brandon was feeling good to be there. Perhaps this was the best he had felt since a police officer and social worker had knocked on his door. Plus, he was about to find out who his grandparents were. He hoped it would help him discover more about himself.

Devin led the three of them to the back of the building. "Here we are." They arrived at a few rows of desks. Each desk had what looked to be a brand-new computer on it. "Take a seat. They're running the latest version of Windows 98," he said to Brandon, motioning to the closest computer.

Brandon assumed he was supposed to be impressed by whatever these computers were running, but it didn't make a difference to him. "I don't know what I'm doing," Brandon admitted.

"I'll walk you through it. Don't worry." Devin showed Brandon how to use the internet browser to navigate to the website they needed to find information about his father's family. After Devin logged into the site with his credentials, Brandon entered "Bason" in the Last Name field and selected "Texas" in the State dropdown menu.

"Now," Devin said, pointing, "click that button."

"Okay. Here we go." Brandon took a breath and clicked

"Search." The screen went white, and the address bar read, "Loading…" While they waited, Brandon reached behind the computer monitor to a stack of blank note slips. He seized a pen from the stationery holder and stared expectantly at the screen. Soon, he would have information about his family on his father's side. To his surprise, a list of 490 people with the last name of Bason appeared on the screen before him. Thankfully, they were in alphabetical order by first name. He scrolled down to D, but there was no one named Dean on the list. Brandon furrowed his eyebrows and double-checked. No one named Dean. He frowned and pushed his chair away from the desk in frustration. Why had he been so optimistic? *Get real,* he thought. *Just because you feel good about something, doesn't mean it's going to happen.*

"He's not there?" Devin asked.

"No," Brandon said, standing up. "Thanks anyway. Sorry to waste your time."

"I'm sorry it didn't work out," Devin said. "Are you sure you spelled the name right?"

Brandon nodded.

"What was his first name?" Devin asked.

"Dean."

Devin leaned in to get a closer look at the screen. "You sure that was his real name and not a nickname or short for something else? This website only works with full names."

Brandon put his backpack on the floor, unzipped it, and pulled out Dean's box. He showed Devin the name etched on the top of the box. "DEAN."

Justin sat at the computer and started scrolling.

Brandon pulled out the dog tags, which Anton had given him that morning, and handed them to Devin to see again. "I'm pretty sure military stuff would use full names too. His name was Dean."

"Wait," Justin said. He pointed to the top of the screen. "You chose Texas as the state. But didn't you tell me your mom and dad met in Tennessee?"

Brandon narrowed his eyes in thought. "Of course!" he yelled. Then, remembering he was in a library, he quietly apologized. "That's it. But not Tennessee. They met in Tennessee, but Genevieve told me my father was from California."

Justin swiveled the chair back to the computer and amended the search. After he clicked the button, another list of names filled the screen. He stood up and motioned for Brandon to sit down. "You have the honor."

Brandon sat down. He found the Ds and scrolled. There it was. "DEAN F. BASON." The other guys had moved in closer. They had seen it too. "But how do I know it's my father? Maybe it's someone else with the same first and last name."

"Click it," Devin said.

Brandon navigated the cursor to the name, and it highlighted, indicating it was a hyperlink. He clicked it. After a minute, the webpage loaded and provided more information for Dean F. Bason. The date next to his name was July 7, 1961, which Brandon presumed to be his birthdate. He was born in Sacramento, California. He enlisted in the United States Army in 1980. Brandon pulled the photo of his parents out of Dean's box. He turned it over and reread the inscription.

My dearest Frankie,

Every moment we're apart will be torture to my soul. But I'll be back. Until then, let us count the minutes.

Your love forever,

Private Dean Bason

The date stamped on the back was November 29, 1980. Was Brandon really tracking down information about his father? He looked at the screen again. There was another date: April 21,

1981. Brandon pointed to a D in parentheses. "What's that stand for?"

"Deceased," Devin said solemnly. "That's the day he died."

"Oh," Brandon said, looking back at the screen. It was all matching up. "I think this is my father." He kept reading. He could feel everyone else staring over his shoulders. Dean's parents' names were George and Paula Bason. They lived at 238 Redwood Street in Willows, California. Brandon couldn't believe how easy it was to find this information, although he was disappointed that there was no phone number listed. What could he do with an address? He could mail them a letter. But what would he put as the return address? Plus, what would it be like for them to receive a message in the mail from a grandson they didn't even know existed? They probably wouldn't believe him, and he wouldn't blame them. He pulled out Matt's map and started unfolding it over the desk and keyboard.

"Whoa, that's nuts!" Devin said.

"Our friend made it," Justin said with pride in his eyes. "It's what's been guiding us on this trip."

Brandon found California, noting how it was the next state over from Arizona. He looked at Anton. "Care to extend our road trip?"

"Sure," Anton said. "But California is a huge state. Where is —" Anton glanced back at the screen, "—Willows?"

Brandon slid his finger west from the Grand Canyon into the California state line, looking for it.

"I'd start with Sacramento," Devin said. "That's where your dad was born, and it's the capital." He pointed at the big yellow star inside California. It was about two-thirds of the way up the state.

After a moment, Brandon spotted Willows. It was a small town even further north than Sacramento. His finger still on Willows, he looked up at Anton. "It's only about a foot and a half away from Arizona," Brandon said with a smile.

Anton chuckled. "You do realize that's the same distance from the Grand Canyon as the Grand Canyon is from here, right?" Anton said. "Ah, don't worry about it," he said, waving his hand. "Let's go meet your grandparents. It'll be another adventure."

Brandon couldn't help but feel a little giddy at the idea. He smiled at Justin.

"Whatever, dude." Justin shrugged and smiled back.

With a new resolve to continue their trip, Brandon jotted down the names and address of his grandparents, stuck the slip of paper in the box, and then returned the box and the map to his backpack. He stood up and looked Devin in the eye. "Thanks, cowboy. We were lucky to meet you."

"Luck?" Devin said. "Maybe. Maybe not." He shot a glance toward the ceiling above them. "I'm thankful to have met you. And it was a pleasure to help." He stuck out his hand, and Brandon shook it.

"What's this?" Devin said. "This isn't a handshake. This is a limp noodle. In Texas, we look each other in the eye and grip the man's hand firmly. Like this." Devin released the handshake and eyed Brandon expectantly. Brandon's ears turned red. He put his hand back by his side. Justin smirked. "Go on," Devin said. "Put out your hand." Brandon did so. Devin continued to hold Brandon's stare and gripped his hand firmly. Brandon tried to do the same, squeezing hard. "Whoa! Not too hard. You don't want to be the guy people call Bone Crusher when you're not around." Brandon eased up. "There we go," Devin said. "Now you're a man." He laughed. So did Anton and Justin. Brandon's ears grew hotter. "Oh, don't be embarrassed, Brandon." Devin put his arm around him. "It's something every boy needs to learn before becoming a man." He pointed at Justin and whispered, "His handshake might be more like a dead fish." They chuckled together as Justin's smirk faded.

Devin looked at his watch. "You guys have to leave now? I

need to grab lunch before work. How about you join me? My treat."

"Sounds great," Anton said.

Devin leaned over the computer desk and logged out. "I know of a nearby place. And we've already got parking taken care of."

"Cool," Brandon said. "But give me a minute. Hey, Anton, can I have your keys?" Anton pulled his keys out of his pocket and tossed them to Brandon. "Be right back." He turned around and retraced his steps to the parking garage. For a moment, he was concerned he wouldn't be able to find his way back. After passing a few rows of shelves, he found his bearings and spotted the door to the corridor. A couple of minutes later, he was walking through the parking garage alone. He thought about the little slip of paper in the box. It was the key to learning who his father was—who he was. Brandon knew that Anton understood what it meant to lose someone so close. But he still had family after Aaliyah's passing. Brandon was left with no one. Now, he had the chance to track down people who were his family, and who were alive. A few yards from Anton's car, Brandon stopped suddenly. *Are they alive?* he thought. There weren't dates or Ds in parentheses next to his grandparents' names on the computer screen. But Dean's dates only showed up after Brandon clicked his name. Distracted in his excitement, he didn't think to click his grandparents' names to retrieve dates for them. He wondered if he should go back and ask Devin to go to the website again. But the cowboy had things to do, and he had already done so much for them. No, even if they were dead, Brandon wasn't ready to learn about it. They would carry on with this road trip to Willows, California, no matter what.

Brandon arrived at Anton's car and unlocked the passenger door. He pulled the Bible out of his trench coat pocket, opened the front cover, and read the dedication.

To our beloved Dean,

Congratulations on the best decision of your life. May the words of life guide you home. We are so proud of you.

Love,

Mom and Dad

June 3, 1978

The handwriting was beautiful. Brandon wondered what his grandparents considered to be the best decision of Dean's life. Soon enough, he would be able to ask them. He placed the Bible in his backpack. Then, he removed his trench coat and dropped it on the floorboard of the car. He swung his backpack over his shoulder and shut the door.

CHAPTER TWENTY-TWO

As Brandon approached the guys, Justin and Anton both raised their eyebrows. "Finally decided it was too hot?" Justin asked.

Brandon dismissed the question with a wave.

Justin turned to Devin and smiled. "Teaching him how to shake hands like a man accomplished more than you thought!"

"Where to?" asked Brandon. He didn't want them discussing his trench coat. The truth was, he was unsure why he shed it. It wasn't the rip in the fabric. He simply didn't feel the need for it anymore. Plus, he was glad he wouldn't be wearing it when they walked in the Texas heat.

Devin led them down the street toward a 1950s-style diner. "It's got great food, but I go there for the milkshakes," he said. Justin lit up a cigarette. "That's something that never made sense to me. People know smoking will kill them, yet they still do it."

Justin took a long drag and said, "So will too many milkshakes." Smoke came out of his mouth with each syllable.

"At least you get some enjoyment out of milkshakes," Devin said with a smile.

A few minutes later, they arrived at Eddy's Diner. The floor was tiled like a black and white checkerboard, and chrome tables and chairs were dotted around the center, with booths lining the walls and a vintage jukebox in the corner.

"This place looks great," Justin said enthusiastically. Brandon knew this was more his style than a seafood grill.

After they ordered their food, Devin told them to find a table while he finished up the order. They sat near the corner, and Devin joined them a moment later. "It'll be ready in about ten minutes," he said, then turned to Brandon. "I was hoping I could get another glance at that map. It's pretty stellar."

"Sure." Brandon retrieved it and unfolded it over the table.

Devin pored over it, unable to hide his amazement. "What's in these pockets?"

"Postcards and smaller maps," Justin said.

"We are here," Devin pointed to Dallas. "Next stop..." He slid his finger south, following the red line. "Austin?" Devin found the number Matt had written next to Austin. "I take it that will be your fifth stop?"

Brandon reached across the map and opened the second pocket, retrieving the three postcards. He handed them to Devin, who moved the Dallas card to the back of the stack to reveal the next one. It had the word *Austin* in a thick, stylized font. The inside of the letters had images of various sites and activities around the city. Below the name, a fancy government building was pictured next to the words, "Capital City of Texas."

"What're you going to see in Austin?" asked Devin.

Brandon shrugged. "Some of the postcards give us an idea of what to do or see. But, like Dallas, this one just has the city on it. Not sure what we'll do."

Devin turned the card over and began reading. "I take it Matthew was the one who made this map? And his map and postcards have been guiding you?" Devin looked up, smirking.

"Then, it appears you're going to a rodeo." He handed the postcard to Brandon. There was a handwritten note on the back.

Dear Matthew,

We were over the moon when you told us of your plans to stop in Austin on your way to the Grand Canyon! Austin is a big city, but don't let that fool you. It's still Texas. Plus, you'll see enough cities on your way. When you arrive in Austin, promise me you'll go to a rodeo.

Brandon turned the card over to look at it again. There was a bull rider in the bottom of the "S" of *AUSTIN*. Brandon buried his face in his hands. "Oh, man. No offense, Devin, but I was hoping your hat was as cowboy as this trip was going to get."

Devin smiled. "Oh, come on. You can't tell me the hat hasn't grown on you just a little? I thought by now you were sure to get one for yourself as a souvenir from the greatest state in the US of A."

Brandon shook his head and looked at Justin. "Sorry. Can't say I would. Besides, me and Justin are a little more cultured than that."

"Give him a break," Justin said defensively. "At least he doesn't like country music!"

"That would be even worse than liking Motown," Brandon retorted, smiling at Anton.

Anton frowned, yet his eyes still betrayed a smile. "And just when I thought my tastes were growing on you."

"We skipped that train museum back in Tennessee," Justin said. "We could skip the rodeo too."

Devin took his cowboy hat off and placed it on top of Justin's head. "Anton, promise me you won't let them off the hook."

As the four guys laughed, Brandon felt a spark of something ignite in his heart. This was the type of banter he used to enjoy with Matt and Justin. Matt always had the best comebacks. And he always teased in such a way that anyone would know he was kidding. It was impossible to take offense. It seemed Brandon and Justin's new friends had similar senses of humor. And to think, Brandon had blown up at the same guys the previous day. Although he was still ashamed of his behavior, he was thankful they were so quick to forgive him.

Devin snatched his hat back from Justin and placed it on an empty nearby chair. Then, he leaned over and pointed at something scribbled on the back of the postcard still in Brandon's hand. "You missed this." It was in Matt's handwriting: "Rock 'N' Rodeo." "What's that mean?"

Brandon grabbed the card back and examined it. "No idea."

"And here they are," Devin said, as a lady with a black and white apron approached the table, balancing a tray with four milkshakes on it. "I took the liberty to order for you," Devin said. He smiled, accepting the milkshakes from the waitress.

Brandon was overwhelmed by the generosity that Anton had shown him and Justin. Now, it seemed Devin was just as generous.

Devin handed out the milkshakes, not asking what their preferences were. No one complained. Brandon ended up with the one called "birthday cake." He returned Matt's map to his backpack just as the food arrived. "Anton," Devin said. "Will you please give thanks for us?"

Anton cut his eyes to Brandon and then to Justin. "Sure." Both Anton and Devin closed their eyes and bowed their heads. Justin bowed his head, but Brandon could tell his eyes were still open. "Our Father," Anton began. "Thank you for the friendship we have developed with Devin. He's been a blessing to us all. Thank you for the gift of food before us now. We pray for clarity of mind to seek and know your will. We also pray for safe passage to Austin. Thank you for the greatest gift of all, the gift of your Son, Jesus Christ. Amen."

"Amen," said Devin. He leaned toward Brandon. "Was that the first time he's done that out loud around you?"

Brandon nodded before picking up his brisket sandwich. "I'm still sorry for what I did yesterday."

"It's okay," Devin said. "I was curious, that's all—maybe too curious."

"I realize that now. I wasn't upset at you, anyway." Brandon looked across at Justin. "Sorry, man."

"Don't worry about it," Justin said. "But next time you do that, let's first work out a rendezvous, okay?"

Brandon smiled. Then, his heart quickened as he remembered how they had gone to the police station to find him. He briefly considered filling them in on what he had seen in the newspaper outside of New Orleans.

Devin dipped a French fry in his milkshake. Then, to Brandon's relief, he changed the subject. "If I recall correctly, you called the Bible a collection of fairytales."

Brandon took a bite of his food.

Devin held up a hand. "It's okay if you don't want to talk about it."

"No, it's fine," Brandon said, pushing thoughts about the police to the back of his mind. "A few days ago, me and Justin listened to Anton talk about angels and a virgin giving birth."

Justin picked up a menu to hide behind. "Not this again."

"Come on," Anton said. "The closest people are three tables away this time."

Devin smiled.

Brandon continued. "Anton had some really good points about design and beginnings. I had never thought about that stuff before. He made a great case for a creator. But even if I accept that there was some creator in the beginning, why should I believe the Bible is true among so many other religious books? It seems every time I learn something new about the Bible, I hear of another hard-to-believe claim."

"Like what?" Devin said.

"When you heard Anton and me chatting last night, he told me he believes Jesus rose from the dead." Anton raised his eyebrows expectantly. "Okay," Brandon said, grinning and raising his hands. "He didn't just tell me, but he also showed me in the Bible where it claims that." Brandon looked back at Anton. "Better?"

Anton smiled as a proud father would.

"Why should I believe what the Bible says about that, or about angels, or virgins giving birth, or anything?" Brandon pressed. Copying Devin, Brandon picked up a French fry and dipped it in his milkshake, then popped it in his mouth. He was surprised at how tasty the sweet and salty combo was.

"Why should you believe what the Bible says?" Devin held up a hand with all fingers outstretched. "I've got five reasons."

Brandon was surprised that Devin seemed so ready for the question. "Five reasons? Do you have a speech prepared and everything?"

Devin snorted. "Maybe. I was raised in a Bible-believing home. I went to church most Sundays, and I've always been active in youth group. But I met someone recently." Devin's eyes seemed to lose focus for a moment.

Brandon looked across the table to Justin. "A girl," they said in unison.

"So what?" Devin said.

"Nothing," Brandon said, taking another bite.

"Anyway," Devin said. "This someone—this *girl*—knows her stuff. When I met her dad, it all made sense too. It's like he's a Bible scholar or something. But he challenged me. Coming from a girl's dad, I don't have to tell you how terrifying that is. But he was cool about it. He started asking me some questions over dinner one night. Most of the questions had to do with whether or not the Bible is reliable. I wanted to impress him, but I couldn't give him anything more than circular reasoning—the Bible is true because it says so, you know?"

Brandon thought about that phrase: *circular reasoning*. That was the perfect way to look at Christianity: believe it because the Bible says it's true.

"Granted," Devin said, "the first of the five reasons—" he began counting on his fingers, "—is that the Bible claims to be from God and claims to be true. Unfortunately, that's the only reason why many Christians believe in the Bible. But before we dismiss it, we need to think about that claim. When Tolkien wrote *The Hobbit*, he wanted his audience to suspend disbelief for a while. When I read his books, I don't put them down truly believing in hobbits, dwarves, and wizards. Why?"

"Because it's fiction," Brandon said.

"You bet. And the author obviously knew he was writing fiction. However, the writers of the Bible believed with every fiber of their bodies that what they were writing was true—including the miraculous stuff. Do you have your Bible with you?"

Brandon took a deep breath, not sure he wanted to get into this discussion right now. But he could tell Devin was passionate about this. Perhaps he had been looking for a test audience for the things he had been researching and was practicing before going back to his girlfriend's dad. "Yeah," he said. Considering everything he'd put Devin through yesterday, he owed it to him. Plus, he admitted to himself, he was curious. What Anton had said last night about suffering made Brandon wish it was all true. He wanted to come out of his pain victorious like Anton, not defeated. He wiped his hands on a napkin before retrieving his father's Bible from his backpack.

"Great," Devin said. He looked at Anton. "Is this okay?"

"Of course," Anton responded.

Justin sipped his milkshake.

"Thanks." Devin turned back to Brandon and asked, "Turn to Second Peter, will you?"

"I'm new to this," Brandon said. "A little help?"

"No problem," Devin pointed to the end of the Bible. "Start flipping this way." Brandon obliged, flipping pages toward the back of the Bible. Devin tapped the back again. "Keep going. Keep going. A little further. Now, you're a bit too far." Brandon turned back a few pages. "There," Devin said. "Now, can you read chapter one, verses twenty and twenty-one?"

Brandon did so.

But know this first of all, that no prophecy of Scripture is a matter of one's own interpretation, for no prophecy was ever made by an act of human will, but men moved by the Holy Spirit spoke from God.

"According to this verse," Devin said, "when the Scriptures were being delivered, the Holy Spirit of God was the one providing the information. These guys truly believed they were delivering God's message. They weren't the writers of science fiction or fantasy. After reading Tolkien, I have no desire to look for hobbits, as the guy who invented them claims to have made them up. But since the Bible claims to be true and authoritative, that's something else. As this is the first of five reasons to believe the Bible is reliable, it also gives us the next four."

"What do you mean by that?" Brandon said.

"Hmm... Let me think about how to rephrase it," Devin said.

"Try to turn it into a question," Anton said. "That's usually helpful for me."

"All right," Devin said. He thought for a moment. "Here's what I mean. If the Bible truly is from the mind of God—the creator of the universe—what other qualities would you expect it to have?"

Brandon blew out his cheeks in an exhale. He looked across

the table at Justin. "Well, Silent One, what qualities would you expect it to have?" he said in a mocking, playful tone.

"I'm just here for the milkshakes," Justin replied before taking another slurp.

"Fine," Brandon said. "But you need to bail me out when you've finished yours."

"I think there are free refills here," Justin said with a smirk.

Brandon turned back to Devin. "You should know that I'm only sounding interested because it's either your cowboy hat or a rodeo right now. I'll take the hat."

Devin raised his hands. "Whatever you need to tell yourself to feel better." He smiled.

"Honestly, I'm stumped," Brandon admitted. "I would just expect the Bible to say, 'This is God speaking. Don't do bad things.'"

Devin thought about that. "That's actually another one of the five. The Bible is authoritative." Devin paused, presumably to give Brandon a chance to respond. When he didn't, Devin continued. "Since the Bible is from God, it doesn't..." he trailed off in thought. Then, he smiled. "It doesn't shake your hand like a limp noodle. It shows up and shakes your hand like a man." Justin laughed, nearly spitting out some of his milkshake. Brandon allowed himself to chuckle. These guys really did know how to joke like Matt. "It doesn't merely give you suggestions on how your life might be better if you follow its advice," Devin continued. "It claims that if you don't obey its commandments, you're asking for trouble—trouble in this life, and trouble at the final judgment."

The idea of a final judgment didn't sit well with Brandon. He had seen movies with passionate preachers warning people about hell. Those preachers were usually con artists in the films, using the scare tactic to get more money. In the end, they got what was coming to them. Plus, the idea of some God judging every decision he had ever made seemed invasive. He put the thought out of his mind, as he felt he had nothing to worry about. At least he wasn't someone like Barry—someone who abused and killed people.

"My point is," Devin continued, "the Bible is every bit as authoritative as you would expect a book to be if it claimed to be from God."

Anton seemed interested in the discussion. Even before Brandon had lost his temper yesterday, he knew religion was one of those topics that was full of tension. It caused people to lose their cool. Anton, however, was relaxed. He even seemed pleased with what Devin was saying. That gave Brandon some confidence.

Devin held up a thumb. "Number one: The Bible claims to be from God." He extended his index finger. "Number two: The Bible is authoritative. Number three..." He looked up in thought. "Ah! Number three: The Bible is grounded in history."

"So, you're just rattling off a memorized list?" Brandon asked.

"You bet! I want to show this girl's dad that I took his assignment seriously. I'll be having dinner at their place again tomorrow night." He pointed at the Bible on the table in front of Brandon. "Anyway, check out Luke chapter three." Brandon picked up the Bible, trying to find the passage. Devin did the tapping thing again, which sped up the process. "Read the first three verses," he said.

Brandon began reading.

> *Now in the fifteenth year of the reign of Tiberius Caesar, when Pontius Pilate was governor of Judea, and Herod was tetrarch of Galilee...*

Brandon stopped. "What's with these names?" he asked. They were hard to pronounce, but there was something familiar about them too.

"These names prove my point," Devin said. "But I get ya. They're weird to our ears. Just do your best."

Brandon continued reading, stumbling a little over the strange names.

> *...and his brother Philip was tetrarch of the region of Ituraea and Trachonitis, and Lysanias was tetrarch of Abilene, in the high priesthood of Annas and Caiaphas, the word of God came to John, the son of Zacharias, in the wilderness. And he came into all the district around the Jordan, preaching a baptism of repentance for the forgiveness of sins.*

Brandon then remembered this was the passage the church had studied when he and Justin went to Bible study with Anton's family in Shreveport. Brother Jones was trying to make the same point that Devin was making—the Bible had its roots in history.

"Not bad," Devin said. "Here's my point. The writer—" Devin pointed to the word "Luke" at the top of the page, "—wanted his readers to know that the events he was about to detail actually happened. And they didn't happen in a corner somewhere. They happened in public squares. By giving these names and dates, he basically said, 'If you doubt it, check the history books.' And guess what?" Devin looked at Brandon expectantly.

Brandon shrugged. "What?"

Devin leaned in and whispered, as if a conspirator with Brandon, "It checks out." Then, louder this time, he said, "The history books we have from the first century agree. All the people Luke just listed existed and filled the roles at the exact time he said they did. The New Testament is full of political, religious, regional, and geographical references showing the culture in which Jesus and his apostles worked. Each one that can be fact-checked turns out to be true. Every single one. Although the New Testament was not meant to be used as an atlas or a history book, it seems to be pretty good at history. That's reason number three: The Bible is grounded in history."

Brandon was reminded that he should never judge by appearances. Anton, with his paint-splattered shirt and strong physique, didn't originally strike Brandon as an intellectual. Devin's cowboy hat never would have given away his interest in Christian evidences. Brandon was impressed, and not just with what Devin was saying and how he was saying it, but also with the content of the Bible. From the moment Genevieve had advised him to try to read it for himself, until now, his view of the Bible had been challenged. No, not challenged—corrected. Everything he thought he knew about the Bible proved to be just an assumption. It wasn't some list from a mean-spirited grandfather in the sky of "Don't do this," and "Don't do that." Instead, it seemed to be more of a collection of stories.

"Now, for number four," Devin said, breaking Brandon's train of thought. "The Bible exhibits supernatural attributes."

Brandon narrowed his eyes. "Supernatural? Really? Like ghosts?"

Devin snorted. "No, not like ghosts. Supernatural, meaning it shows that it's from a source beyond a human's natural ability. If the Bible truly is from the creator of the universe, you would expect it to have qualities that only God can inject into it. It can and has done things humans simply can't do with their own abilities."

"Like what?" Brandon asked.

Devin smiled. "I'm so glad you asked. Now, this reason can get pretty long-winded." He looked across the table. "But it looks like your buddy is about to lose his excuse for not bailing you out." Justin slurped at the remaining drops of his milkshake. "So, I'll try to make it quick. You've probably noticed that the Bible isn't just one long narrative. It's got different books. Sixty-six to be exact."

"I didn't realize that until the other day when Anton started guiding me through it," Brandon admitted.

"Good. These sixty-six books were written by about forty different people over fifteen hundred years. They were written by people of different professions too—from shepherds to kings, prophets to doctors, prisoners to fishermen. And the Bible covers practically every subject under the sun, including any questions we could ask about living moral, upright lives. Here's the part that should surprise you: The writers agree with each other." Devin paused.

Brandon assumed Devin was looking for some big reaction. "So?" he asked.

"So? Forty different people, living at different times, from different backgrounds, agreeing on every subject? Perhaps I can put it into perspective. Take any two people—even people of the same profession and time—and put them in a room. Now, ask them to write about a variety of issues facing mankind. Would they agree on everything?"

Brandon chuckled. "They probably wouldn't agree on a single thing."

"You bet! How do you get forty people to write and agree on everything? The answer comes from our first reason. Although it was people who put pen to paper, the inspiration behind the writing was truly God's Holy Spirit."

Brandon had never considered that. Of course, he had never had enough information to even begin considering it. Justin had moved his empty milkshake glass to the side. He was clearly not going to bail Brandon out of this. Then again, Brandon wanted to know what the final reason was. "So, what's the fifth reason?"

"We'll get there," Devin said. "But there's a bit more to this supernatural one. The forty different authors part is just the beginning. Once you start to read what these guys wrote about, you get to put them to the test again. People have known this for ages and have tried to catch the Bible off guard. But it has always backfired on them."

"What do you mean?" Brandon asked.

"For example," Devin said, "in the book of Numbers, Moses wrote about a group of people called the Hittites. For years, historians accused the writers of the Bible of inventing the Hittite nation. They couldn't find any archaeological evidence of the people's existence."

"I don't blame the skeptics," Brandon said with a shrug. "If the Bible claims it, but there's no proof, why should I believe it?"

"Good question," Devin said. "I guess you'll just have to take the Bible's word for it, huh?" Devin paused. "Unless..." Again, he leaned in to whisper, "There is proof."

"Okay, I'll bite," Brandon said. "What proof?"

"In the 1800s, people found some ruins and artifacts that belonged to a newly discovered civilization. The language was untranslatable, so they were clueless about what they had discovered. Anyone wanna guess who this stuff belonged to?"

"Could it possibly be the people the skeptics were claiming didn't exist?" Justin asked with mock surprise.

"Bingo!" Devin said. "The Hittites. A little less than a hundred years ago, another archaeologist found some tablets with multiple languages on them, including the one on the mysterious ruins. But there were also languages that people did know, which gave them the power to translate. And just like that, the Bible was no longer the only book in history to record the existence of the Hittite people. Archaeological discoveries often force skeptics of the Bible to put their feet in their mouths. The more discoveries people make, the more the Bible is validated, not the other way around."

Was the Bible what it claimed to be? Brandon admitted to himself this was compelling information. But there was no way he would say so out loud.

"This isn't the only example," Devin said. "But I think this one is sufficient for now. I just don't want the order of this to escape you. First, the Bible claimed the Hittites existed. But since no other historical document confirmed that, many people questioned the reliability of the Bible on that fact alone. Then, a non-biblical source confirmed that the people the Bible supposedly invented actually did exist."

It made sense. Brandon searched his mind for an objection, but Devin had already dealt with each one he'd considered. And he knew there was still one more reason left.

CHAPTER TWENTY-THREE

"READY FOR REASON NUMBER FIVE?" DEVIN ASKED.

"I have a feeling you're going to tell me whether I'm ready or not," Brandon said playfully. "So, go ahead and hit me with it."

"Number five: The Bible is relevant. This one is the most important. Check out Hebrews four, verses twelve and thirteen."

With the help of Devin's tapping, Brandon found the passage quickly and read the verses out loud.

> *For the word of God is living and active and sharper than any two-edged sword, and piercing as far as the division of soul and spirit, of both joints and marrow, and able to judge the thoughts and intentions of the heart. And there is no creature hidden from His sight, but all things are open and laid bare to the eyes of Him with whom we have to do.*

"Brandon," Devin met his eyes before continuing, "Jesus will change your life if you let him. And I believe he'll do so with this Bible. I told you I was raised in a Bible-believing home, but I didn't realize how much power the Bible has in transforming people until recently. And I can't believe it happened to me through chasing a girl." Devin leaned back and snorted. "I've been studying the Bible with her and her dad for a few weeks now. I've already seen a change in my life. And my journey's not over yet. But by the grace of God, I am what I am." Devin grinned at Anton, who returned his gaze with a knowing smile.

Brandon looked down at his father's Bible. Was he approaching a crossroads in his life? He wasn't sure. But he did know that he couldn't keep shrugging off the Bible as he had been doing. Devin had given him four good reasons to take the Bible seriously. The fifth one seemed more subjective than the others. "What do you mean, 'the Bible is relevant'?"

"I'll give you a couple of examples. Find Matthew seven and read the first five verses." Devin tapped the side of the Bible in Brandon's left hand. "It's this way."

It only took a moment to find it, as Brandon had been in the book of Matthew before. He read the passage.

> *Do not judge lest you be judged. For in the way you judge, you will be judged; and by your standard of measure, it will be measured to you. And why do you look at the speck that is in your brother's eye, but do not notice the log that is in your own eye? Or how can you say to your brother, "Let me take the speck out of your eye," and behold, the log is in your own eye? You hypocrite, first take the log out of your own eye, and then you will see clearly to take the speck out of your brother's eye.*

"What do you think?" Devin asked. "Do you know many people who struggle with hypocritical judgment?"

Brandon blew out his cheeks. "Of course I do—and the worst ones are Christians," he said, then immediately regretted saying so. He thought back to his time with Anton's family in Shreveport. Anton had mentioned how his outburst years back had to do with a log sticking out of his eye. This must have been the passage he was referencing.

Devin raised his eyebrows.

"Well," Brandon said, "not all of them. I've already talked to Anton about this, and he was pretty good at helping me understand." He looked at Anton. "What is it you said?"

"Even the best people are good at making bad decisions," Anton offered.

"That's a good way of putting it," Devin said. "When Jesus taught this, he wasn't necessarily warning the entire world. He was speaking directly to his followers. Jesus knew his disciples would struggle. In fact, since we hold Jesus up as the perfect standard, we probably struggle with it the most. Anyway, this is one of the examples. The Bible is relevant because it speaks the truth about issues that people struggled with—not just millennia ago—but also today, in the year 1999."

"I see your point," Brandon said.

"Here's another one," Devin said. "James three, verses two through five."

With Devin's help, Brandon found the passage and read it out loud.

> *For we all stumble in many ways. If anyone does not stumble in what he says, he is a perfect man, able to bridle the whole body as well. Now if we put the bits into the horses' mouths so that they may obey us, we direct their entire body as well. Behold, the ships also, though they are so great and are driven by strong winds, are still directed by a very small rudder, wherever the inclination of the pilot desires. So also the tongue is a small part of the body, and yet it boasts of great things. Behold, how great a forest is set aflame by such a small fire!*

"How many times have you said something, only to wish you could take it back?" Devin asked.

Brandon's ears grew hot as he looked up at Anton and Justin.

"Say no more," Devin said. "I don't mean to embarrass you. We've all been there. As the Bible says right here—if any person could say, 'I never regret what I say,' he would be a perfect person. And the point of all this is to answer your question of how the Bible is relevant. If you take the time to read it with an open mind," Devin tapped Brandon's forehead, "and open heart," he tapped his chest, "you would see just how relevant it is." Devin leaned back. "There are a few questions that every person is bound to ask sometime in their life: 'Who am I?' 'Why am I here?' 'What's the meaning of life?' 'Where am I going?' You know what I mean?"

"Yeah," Brandon said. Although he didn't voice them out loud, those questions were what had come to his mind in Genevieve's house the night she gave him Dean's box. Having no answers to them is what led him on this trip across the country. He wondered what Justin was thinking right now. Did he buy into this Bible stuff? *Do I buy into it?* he thought. What would Justin think if he did?

Devin continued. "A lot of people make the horrible mistake of thinking those answers come from within. In other words, they 'find themselves.' Of course, there's nothing wrong with being at peace with yourself. What I'm saying is..." Devin paused to think. "It's not up to us—the creation—to know why the creator made us. If you're truly searching for purpose in life, you'll only find it in the one who created you."

Devin paused again. This time, it was an intentional pause. Brandon regarded him, while the silence strung on, threatening to become awkward. The weight of the moment pressed on him until he yielded to it. "Fine. You want me to ask you how this book answers my questions."

"Yes, I do." Devin smiled.

"What are you waiting for?" Brandon asked.

"For you to ask how this book answers your questions," Devin said, still smiling.

"But I just—" Brandon stopped. No, he hadn't asked a question. He had simply voiced out loud what Devin was wanting to hear. Brandon leaned back in his seat and ran his fingers through his hair. Both Justin and Anton seemed to be waiting for him. He sighed. "Okay. What does the Bible say about my purpose in life?"

"I thought you'd never ask. Turn to the book of Acts. When you find it, read chapter seventeen, verses twenty-four through twenty-eight."

Brandon started flipping pages, expecting Devin to do his tapping thing. He didn't. Brandon kept his eyes on the top corners of the pages while flipping. After several seconds, he finally found the book called Acts. Landing on the passage, he read out loud.

> *The God who made the world and all things in it, since He is Lord of heaven and earth, does not dwell in temples made with hands; neither is He served by human hands, as though He needed anything, since He Himself gives to all life and breath and all things; and He made from one, every nation of mankind to live on all the face of the earth, having determined their appointed times, and the boundaries of their habitation, that they should seek God, if perhaps they might grope for Him and find Him, though He is not far from each one of us; for in Him we live and move and exist, as even some of your own poets have said, "For we also are His offspring."*

"So, how does this answer your question about your purpose in life?" Devin asked.

"It says that I should find God."

"What do you think?" Devin asked. "Have you fulfilled your purpose?"

CHAPTER TWENTY-FOUR

BRANDON COULD HEAR DISHES CLANKING FROM THE RESTAURANT'S kitchen. A few of the patrons chatted on the other side of the dining room. Above the background noise, what Brandon heard the most was the pumping of his heart in his ears. The sound grew louder as he turned Devin's questions over and over in his mind. *What are you searching for? Have you fulfilled your purpose?*

"Devin," Anton began, "I've gotta say I'm impressed."

Devin shrugged. "Most of it was scripted. But who knows? Maybe we struck a chord." Devin smiled at Brandon, who still wore a contemplative face.

Brandon looked back at him. "Isn't it kind of conceited?"

Devin's cheeks flushed. "Sorry. I didn't mean to show off or anything."

"No, not that." Brandon waved a hand. "I mean the claim that our purpose on earth is to seek God. Does God have to have his ego stroked?"

Devin's eyes widened. He glanced at Anton.

"Look again," Anton said.

Brandon regarded the Bible in his hands, which was still open to Acts chapter seventeen.

"Reread verses twenty-four and twenty-five," Anton said.

Brandon did so.

The God who made the world and all things in it, since He is Lord of heaven and earth, does not dwell in temples made with hands; neither is He served by human hands, as though He needed anything, since He Himself gives to all life and breath and all things.

"Good one," Devin said to Anton.

"What does it say?" Anton asked. "What does God need from us?"

"Nothing," Brandon said.

"Although he needs nothing from us, what does it say he does for us?"

"Gives us life and breath," Brandon said.

"When someone gives you a gift that you want, or even better, something you need, what's the proper response?" Anton asked.

Anton had done just that for him and Justin. He had given them something they not only wanted, but also desperately needed. Without Anton, Brandon would be stuck at Grand Junction, tormented by his memories and questions, having tried to honor Matt, but having failed miserably.

Justin was still sitting quietly. Although Brandon had no idea what he was thinking, he was thankful for their lifetime friendship. Justin had forgiven him unquestioningly.

Then, there was Devin. He had taken the three of them in, fed them, and even found Brandon's grandparents' address for him. He thought of his trench coat, still lying on the floorboard of Anton's car. Something had happened in the past twenty-four hours that gave Brandon the courage to come out of his shell. He was indeed making his own decisions, and he was on a journey that he was in no hurry to return from. "Thankfulness," Brandon finally said.

"That's right," Anton agreed. "There's nothing we can do that could add to God's character. However, do you think God knows how we tick? Do you think the creator understands that when we show gratitude, it builds our character?"

Brandon understood what Anton was trying to say. He resisted the temptation to go back to his habit of blaming God for the bad things in his life and reminding Anton there was nothing he owed God—that instead, God somehow owed him. He thought back to their late-night conversation. Anton had been dealt a bad hand, and yet he came out of the situation thankful. "What is there to be thankful for?" Brandon asked.

"The gospel."

Brandon nodded. Justin raised his eyebrows, likely wondering, as he had, what the word meant. Brandon remembered how Anton had explained that the gospel means good news. Something about a curse being reversed.

Justin spoke up. "We should probably get going, shouldn't we?"

Devin looked at his watch. "Yeah, I need to get ready for work." He picked up his hat from the nearby chair and put it on.

"No problem," Anton said.

"Brandon," Devin said, "I hope you and Anton keep talking about this stuff. Remember what I said." He tapped the Bible Brandon was holding. "Jesus will change your life if you let him." Devin stood up and extended his hand. Brandon also stood and smiled. He gripped Devin's hand firmly. Devin grinned with approval, then tipped his cowboy hat in appreciation. "Gentlemen, it's been a pleasure."

"It sure has," Anton said.

"Thanks for giving us a place to stay. And for lunch," Justin said.

"Rise and shine!"

Brandon rolled over in his bed. The previous evening, they had checked into a hotel just outside downtown Austin.

"It's time for our first rodeo!" It was Anton.

Brandon groaned. "Five more minutes."

"That's what you said fifteen minutes ago. To be honest, I'm not excited about this either. But aren't we doing this for your friend?"

Justin came out of the bathroom, dressed and toweling his hair. "We don't even know where this rodeo is."

"We can ask at the front desk," Anton said. "They probably have some info."

A few minutes later, the three of them took the elevator to the lobby. They walked toward the front desk, Brandon trailing behind. While Anton and Justin chatted with the clerk, Brandon made his way toward the continental breakfast. As he reached for the waffle mix, the television above the breakfast bar caught his attention.

"Local authorities are asking the public to help them find two teenagers suspected of running away together."

Brandon froze. A blonde female reporter gave the report. The bottom of the screen had a marquee that read, "SEARCHING FOR BRANDON BASON AND JUSTIN SANDERS." Brandon's breath caught in his throat. He instinctively scanned the room; no one else was having breakfast. Over his shoulder he could see Anton and Justin still speaking with the clerk. He was handing them a brochure. Brandon looked back at the TV.

The reporter continued. "Brandon Bason and Justin Sanders vanished from their homes in Tennessee nearly two weeks ago without a trace." While she spoke, school photos of them appeared on the screen. Brandon dropped the waffle mix back onto the counter, his heart pounding harder with every second. "That is, until now," the reporter continued. "This morning, a library in Dallas has provided a possible ray of hope in this footage of young Brandon and Justin." Black and white footage of Brandon, Justin, and Anton walking to Anton's car in the parking garage after lunch yesterday played on the screen.

Again, Brandon looked back at the counter. He could tell their conversation was wrapping up. But Brandon stayed glued to the report.

The footage on the screen froze and zoomed into Anton's face as he reached for the driver's side door of his car. "This man, who is believed to be Anton Prayther, is now suspected as an accomplice. At this point, authorities have not ruled out abduction. We urge the public not to approach any of the three. Instead, if you have any information on their whereabouts, please call the toll-free number on your screen."

Brandon checked over his shoulder one more time. Anton and Justin were walking toward him. He turned from the breakfast bar and met them halfway, circling around them, so their backs would be to the TV. "So, what did you find out? Is the rodeo close?"

Justin screwed up his face and looked at Anton, who gave him an equally baffled look. "What's with the change of attitude? Something in the bagels?"

"No, no. It's just, uh—" Brandon stammered, "—we've got to honor Matt and all. That's it." Brandon stole a glance at the TV behind them. The screen was now showing images of a school presentation. "Want some breakfast?"

"Don't you want to know about the rodeo?" Anton asked, holding up a brochure.

"Yeah, yeah. Let's talk about it over breakfast." Brandon walked over to the waffle maker and poured some mix into it. The other two started preparing their breakfast. Brandon tapped his toes as he waited for his waffle to be ready. Every few seconds, he glanced up at the TV. After the school presentation, there was a commercial break. *They think Anton kidnapped us*, he thought. When his waffle was finished, he took his plate to the opposite side of the dining room and sat, facing the TV in hopes Anton and Justin would sit with the TV to their backs.

Anton put his food on the table. "Do you mind if I pray out loud again?" Anton asked. As he prayed, Brandon couldn't pay attention to any of the words. He bounced his knee under the table, wondering what to do. Should he tell them what he'd just seen? Probably. But he didn't have the guts. He was afraid Anton would be mad. He had every right to be. Brandon also wouldn't be surprised if he received the news calmly and understandably. Anton would likely insist they call the police. But then what? What kind of trouble would Brandon be in? And what kind of trouble had he now gotten Justin in? Justin was supposed to keep calling his grandmother. Brandon tried to remember the last time he had called her, but he couldn't. He couldn't blame Justin. He had forgotten all about it too. She had apparently called his cousin, who was unable to keep vouching for him. And so Brandon's mind went on, jumping from thought to thought, from question to question. *What should I do?*

"Amen," said Anton.

Justin locked eyes with Brandon. Justin could tell something was up. Brandon turned his attention to his food.

Anton spread a brochure out on the table. The top read, "Rock 'N' Rodeo: The Rodeo for People Who Hate Rodeos." There was a picture of a man riding a bull, and behind him was a stage with a live band on it. "Hey," Anton said, "it might be one of those bands you had me listen to."

Justin laughed through his nose as he took a bite of his waffle. "I seriously doubt that."

"Well, at least it won't be country music," Anton said. He pointed to another picture. "Look at their outfits." A man was swinging a lasso on a horse. He wore a Metallica shirt and stuck out his tongue. Brandon couldn't decide if he thought it was cool or incredibly cheesy. Anton was right. At least they didn't have to suffer through country music. And it was unlikely anyone would recognize them in a big crowd.

After breakfast, they gathered their things and checked out of the hotel, Brandon trying his best to act as though the three of them weren't primetime news. Still, the knowledge weighed heavily on his mind. Several times during the car ride, Brandon had been on the verge of confessing, only to chicken out and vow to himself that he would tell them at some point. *Just not yet...*

Later that afternoon, they pulled into the parking lot for the rodeo. It was packed. They found a spot in the back of the lot. As soon as Brandon stepped out of the car, several smells bombarded him at once. Some pleasant, some not so much.

"Mmm," Justin said. "I smell funnel cakes! Or maybe it's those doughnut things we had in New Orleans!"

"I'm glad you can pick that out," Anton said, putting his wrist over his nose, making his glasses fog up.

They started toward the front, weaving through a sea of people, most of whom wore cowboy hats. Brandon felt conspicuous without one, but at least he'd ditched the trench coat. On their way, they passed market booths and food stalls, selling all manner of mostly meat-related fare. Brandon grimaced as he passed a full pig skewered over an enormous cast-iron coal oven. Justin pointed and made a grotesque face.

It seemed most of the people were still outside the gates, mingling around the outdoor market. Justin stopped and bought a funnel cake. As they neared the front gates, the song "Back in Black" by AC/DC filled the air.

Brandon pulled the Austin postcard out of his back pocket. He held it up in front of him, so the postcard and the gates were both in view. "Well, Matt, I can't believe you ever wanted to do this, but we're here because of you." Brandon felt a hand on his shoulder. It was Justin.

He looked apprehensive, yet he still said, "Let's do this."

"You know," Brandon said, "that could have been a moment —one of those teary-eyed moments in movies. Except..."

"Except what, Brandy?" Justin asked.

"It's hard to take you seriously with powdered sugar around your mouth and on the tip of your nose—not to mention the rotisserie pig staring at us." The three of them laughed and walked up to the gates.

After purchasing their tickets, they climbed up to the top of the bleachers. On the other side of the track, next to the judges' seats, was a stage. As promised, there was a live band setting up their equipment. They wore black shirts and jeans similar to Justin's JNCOs. "Not only is this going to be my first rodeo," Brandon said, "but it will also be my first concert."

"Here's hoping they're good," Justin said. He turned to Anton. "What do you think about all this?"

"It stinks," Anton said. "Literally."

"Want some funnel cake?" Justin held up the cake to Anton. "Get some sugar up your nose, and problem solved."

Anton chuckled. "No, thanks. I don't think I could eat here."

The stands filled up in the next few minutes, and then the band started playing. Their first song was a cover of a Nirvana song. When they started playing "Bullet with Butterfly Wings" by the Smashing Pumpkins, the barrel racing started. All the riders were women, who rode their horses as fast as they could. They zig-zagged around barrels on the field, trying to finish the course in the shortest time possible. Brandon found himself captivated by the sport. He didn't know it would be so intense. The third racer even fell off her horse. The next event was bull riding. This was what Brandon pictured when he thought of a rodeo, just as it was on the front of the postcard. Again, he found himself more interested than he expected to be. As the band performed a Metallica song, cowboys were thrashed and thrown from bulls, inches from injury or death. None of them could hold on for more than a few seconds. Brandon winced every time a bull's hoof nearly crushed a man's skull or ribcage, yet he couldn't take his eyes off the field. When it was over, he could tell Justin had been equally enchanted. When the judge announced the next event as steer jerking, Brandon looked at Justin and Anton. Both of them shrugged.

The band started playing "Freak" by Silverchair. Then, a calf was released from the gates, and a cowboy on a horse chased it. As the cowboy closed the gap between himself and the calf, he threw a lasso around the calf's head and pulled back. Suddenly, Brandon understood why this event was called steer jerking. The calf's legs buckled, and it hit its back hard on the ground. Immediately, the cowboy jumped off his horse and skillfully tied the other end of the rope around the calf's legs. The calf lay on the ground, making a sound that made Brandon feel sorry for the thing.

"I think I've had enough of this," Anton said. Brandon was torn. They had only been there an hour. He felt terrible for the calf, but he was fascinated by the dexterity and speed of the cowboys.

"Say no more," Justin said, standing up.

The three of them exited and made for the car in the back of the parking lot, music fading as they left the Rock 'N' Rodeo behind. Brandon wondered why Anton had felt so uncomfortable in there. Was there something in the Bible about what they'd just seen?

"Hey, Brandon," Anton said, reaching for the handle on the driver's side door. He looked as he had in the news footage that morning. Brandon's stomach twisted at the sight. "Yo! Earth to Brandon!"

Brandon shook himself out of the daze. "Sorry. What?"

"Can you get out the map? What's the plan for tonight?"

"Sure, no problem." The three of them got into the car, and Brandon retrieved and unfolded the map. He followed the line from Austin downward. Next stop: San Antonio. He pulled out the sixth postcard. It had an old brown building on the front.

"The Alamo," Anton said, leaning over. "I remember learning about that in American history. There was a battle fought there. I think Texas lost. San Antonio's not far. It looks like we'll be there in less than two hours."

They left the rodeo behind, heading south. "What did you guys think of all that?" Anton asked after they had driven a few miles.

"I was going to ask you the same thing," Brandon said. "You seemed bothered by the last couple of events."

Anton didn't say anything for a moment. "I didn't like it," he finally admitted. "What did you think?"

"It was cooler than I expected," Brandon said. He fished the postcard out of his pocket. "I still can't believe Matt wanted to go to a rodeo though."

"Hey, it was a cultural experience," Anton said.

"Cultural?" Brandon said. "It seemed like it was more than that to you. What had you squirming so much?" Again, Anton fell silent.

"Don't pry, dude," Justin said.

"No, it's okay," Anton said. "I just can't stand it when people mistreat animals. Now, I'm not saying those animals aren't taken care of. They're probably fine. But the sound that calf made when it fell down and felt trapped..."

"I didn't like it either," Brandon said.

"When I was a boy," Anton began, "I jumped the fence to my neighbor's house, just like I always did. We didn't bother going to the front door to knock. We just invaded each other's yards. His cousins were over, and they had found something to keep them from getting bored. I'll never forget what I saw and heard when I went to the other side of the house." He paused, then sighed. "There was a neighborhood dog that always came and greeted people on their porches. He was a black lab. No one knew who he belonged to. Could have been a stray. But he was so gentle. Anyway, when I rounded the corner, he was cowering in front of the kids with nowhere to escape. They were throwing stones and stuff at him."

"What did you do?" Justin asked.

"I jumped in front of the dog, just as one of the kids released a large stone. It hit me in the shoulder. It hurt pretty bad, but I didn't care. My adrenaline was taking over at that point. I tried to pick up the dog to take him away, but he snapped at me. Who could blame him? So, I walked over to the front gate and let him out. None of the kids tried to stop me. I think when I jumped in front of the dog, they started feeling guilty. That was the end of my friendship with my neighbor. He never apologized. I never wanted to see him again. I knew people rode bulls and stuff at rodeos, but I didn't know people did all those things to the baby cows." He sighed again. "It's just a personal thing, you know?" Anton looked at Brandon. "I think I'll always have that emotional scar."

CHAPTER TWENTY-FIVE

"How about we get some pizza delivered?" Anton asked as they walked into their hotel room in San Antonio.

"But we just had pizza a couple of nights ago," Justin said.

"And your point is...?" Anton asked playfully.

"Um, you can never have too much pizza?" Justin said.

"My thoughts exactly," Anton replied.

Brandon grabbed a phone book from the desk and tossed it to Anton. A few minutes later, he was calling in the order. Afterward, he kept flipping through the book. "What are you looking for now?" Brandon asked.

"It's Sunday tomorrow," Anton said.

Brandon wondered how that answered his question, but then he realized what Anton was saying. "Ah, you're looking for a church?"

"You know that's right," Anton said, poring over the listings. "Just because I'm away from home doesn't mean I'm going to skip worshiping God with his family. You guys want to come?"

Brandon and Justin looked at each other. "Sure," Justin said, answering for them both.

It wasn't until Brandon was getting ready to shower the next morning that he wondered what he should wear. Out of all his clothes, the ones that seemed most appropriate for church were a white undershirt and jeans. Justin seemed to be struggling with the same thing as he turned his black shirt with the Korn logo on it inside out. Anton wore a teal polo shirt with jeans, which struck Brandon as somewhere between formal and informal.

Using a map from the hotel lobby, Anton was able to work out directions to the church. Justin helped him navigate from the passenger seat. On the way, Anton clued Brandon and Justin in on what to expect. Brandon wasn't surprised when Anton talked about prayer, singing, and a sermon. But he was curious about something Anton called "The Lord's Supper."

"What's that?" he asked.

"It's when Christians eat and drink to remember and proclaim Jesus' death. Jesus set up his own memorial the night before he died. When his apostles taught about it later, they said it was also something we should do as we examine ourselves."

Brandon had a lot of questions about that, but he decided to wait and see what it was like for himself.

They arrived at the church twenty minutes later. It was a large rectangular brick building with few outward signs that it had anything to do with God. No fancy windows or ornate statues, not even a cross, as far as Brandon could see. To him, it looked more like a former school building. It had a few steps leading up to some simple glass doors, on which were posted the weekly notices—including Bible study on Wednesday evenings. *That must be a popular pastime,* Brandon thought.

As they entered the church, they were greeted by an elderly man who warmly shook their hands and introduced himself as Harold. On finding that they were visitors, he gave them what he called a bulletin and showed them to a large auditorium filled with pews. It looked like it could hold several hundred people. As Brandon took it all in, he noticed something he knew would please Anton: This church didn't hold on to old-fashioned traditions like Aunt Mavel's church; here there seemed to be an even number of White people and Black people. There were also several Hispanics. Many of the men wore suits and ties, and many of the women were in dresses. But not all of them. Some of the teenagers wore everyday clothes, which made Brandon feel a little more at ease. They found a seat and waited for things to get started. While Brandon and Justin both looked around, Anton examined the bulletin.

After some time, one of the men wearing a suit and tie came to the microphone and announced the order of what was about to happen. There was still some chatter in the room. He said the Lord's Supper would come after a few songs. Then, he said, "Let's pray," and everything hushed. The man started praying. His prayer was laced with thankfulness. He thanked God for practically everything, including the ability to even come to church. His voice came out of the speakers, bouncing off the walls as a small echo. The prayer was punctuated with the occasional "Amen" and "Mm-hmm" from people on the pews. It seemed everyone, except for maybe the children who still chittered, were genuinely involved in praying together. After he said his "Amen," he sat down.

Another guy approached the front and announced a number. Then, all at once, everyone, including Anton, reached for books in the backs of the pews in front of them and turned to that number. Brandon and Justin didn't. It occurred to Brandon that it could be offensive to not participate, but he didn't want to be a hypocrite. He had no idea how to follow along, and he knew his heart wouldn't be in it, anyway. The man started singing, the rest of the congregation quickly catching up to him. Brandon's jaw dropped. He had never heard such powerful singing, each word infused with such raw emotion. But it was more than the four-part harmony that struck him; more than the unity of words that gave him goosebumps. It was the unity of spirit he noticed. As they sang about Jesus, grace, and the church, they sang from the heart. Not everyone had perfect pitch, but it didn't matter; what mattered was the act of singing together with a common purpose. There was a purity there that Brandon almost ached to tap into. The man led the congregation in a few songs, each one just as beautiful as the others.

Based on what the first man had said, Brandon expected the Lord's Supper to come next. He craned his neck this way and that to look for the food. He didn't smell any. Anton had said that Christians eat and drink during this time. "Where do you think the food is?" Brandon whispered to Justin.

"What food?" Justin whispered back.

"The supper. Anton said this is when the Christians eat."

Justin stifled a laugh. "Haven't you ever seen it in the movies?" Brandon shook his head. "This is when the priest, or whoever, gives people little wafers. It's not like a real supper, you doof."

A man with a long beard approached the microphone. "Let's read from Matthew twenty-six, verses twenty-six through twenty-nine." The sound of many Bibles opening and pages flipping all at once filled the room. Not wearing his trench coat meant Brandon did not have his father's Bible so close anymore. He had left his backpack in Anton's car. While the man waited for people to arrive at the passage, Brandon wondered what it was about the book of Matthew that made it so important to Christians. The first time Anton had Brandon read from the Bible he'd chosen that book, yet there were sixty five other ones to choose from. What was with Matthew? The man spoke soberly as he read.

> *And while they were eating, Jesus took some bread, and after a blessing, He broke it and gave it to the disciples, and said, "Take, eat; this is My body." And when He had taken a cup and given thanks, He gave it to them, saying, "Drink from it, all of you; for this is My blood of the covenant, which is poured out for many for forgiveness of sins. But I say to you, I will not drink of this fruit of the vine from now on until that day when I drink it new with you in My Father's kingdom."*

Wait a second, Brandon thought. Was this guy saying bread was Jesus' body? Fruit juice was Jesus' blood? And Jesus' blood was poured out for people's sins to be forgiven? Apparently, everyone else in the room was not disturbed by the idea of pretending to drink a dead guy's blood. The man at the microphone said a prayer, giving thanks for the bread. Then, he started passing it around the pews. It reached Justin, and he passed it to Brandon. It looked more like a tortilla than bread. Brandon handed it to Anton without taking any. Anton broke off a piece, gave the rest to the next person, closed his eyes, and ate the bread.

As much as he was tempted to squirm in his seat, Brandon stayed still and noted how reverent people were at that moment. They looked each other in the eye when they received and passed the bread. Some smiled knowingly. A few, like him and Justin, passed on the bread without taking any themselves. Brandon wondered if they also were a little creeped out by the idea. The people who took some quietly ate as if in prayer.

When everyone had been served, the man with the long beard went to the front again. "Now, we will read from First Corinthians eleven, starting with verse twenty-three."

> *For I received from the Lord that which I also delivered to you, that the Lord Jesus in the night in which He was betrayed took bread; and when He had given thanks, He broke it, and said, "This is My body, which is for you; do this in remembrance of Me." In the same way He*

> *took the cup also, after supper, saying, "This cup is the new covenant in My blood; do this, as often as you drink it, in remembrance of Me." For as often as you eat this bread and drink the cup, you proclaim the Lord's death until He comes. Therefore whoever eats the bread or drinks the cup of the Lord in an unworthy manner, shall be guilty of the body and the blood of the Lord. But let a man examine himself, and so let him eat of the bread and drink of the cup. For he who eats and drinks, eats and drinks judgment to himself, if he does not judge the body rightly.*

Again, questions flooded Brandon's mind. Jesus was betrayed? Christians were to do this until Jesus comes? Jesus was coming?

Justin leaned over and whispered, "Maybe I'll take some this time. It's always wine in the movies." He smiled and rubbed his hands together in anticipation. Brandon elbowed him in the ribs, and he let out an "oof!"

"Don't be so insensitive!" Brandon whispered. "Can't you tell this is like a funeral? The Bible said this is Jesus' blood."

"Since when have you cared?"

"Shh!"

The man at the microphone said another prayer, this time thanking God for the cup, which he called "the fruit of the vine." Again, after the prayer, he started passing something around. Once more, a sense of reverence fell upon the room. When it reached Justin, Brandon was thankful that either he had been bluffing or the sharp jab to the ribs had knocked some sense into him. Both of them passed the crimson liquid.

After the Lord's Supper was finished, another man came to the microphone. He was a short, bald man. Brandon judged him to be in his thirties. "Turn your Bibles to Luke fifteen," he said. He spoke with clarity and purpose. "How many of us can say that we've never been lost?" Brandon could tell the preacher was not looking for a show of hands. The point was clear.

Within the question itself was the assumption that everyone could relate. "We've all been there," he said. Brandon thought back to just a few days ago when he had truly been lost. "Do you remember the feeling of relief when you found your way again?" the preacher asked. "Perhaps someone found you, or you stumbled upon some familiar territory that led you home." Brandon couldn't help but smile and look to his left to Justin, and then to Anton on his right. As much as they teased each other, he knew he was surrounded by friends. "Now, how many of you are currently lost?" Clearly the preacher had shifted from literal to figurative. Brandon could relate—after all, what was this whole journey about? Wasn't he traveling to somehow find himself? He listened carefully as the man read.

> *Now all the tax-gatherers and the sinners were coming near Him to listen to Him. And both the Pharisees and the scribes began to grumble, saying, "This man receives sinners and eats with them." And He told them this parable, saying, "What man among you, if he has a hundred sheep and has lost one of them, does not leave the ninety-nine in the open pasture, and go after the one which is lost, until he finds it? And when he has found it, he lays it on his shoulders, rejoicing. And when he comes home, he calls together his friends and his neighbors, saying to them, 'Rejoice with me, for I have found my sheep which was lost!' "I tell you that in the same way, there will be more joy in heaven over one sinner who repents, than over ninety-nine righteous persons who need no repentance."*

For all the times Brandon had called Christians "sheep," he now realized that it would never have seemed like an insult to them. They saw the head of their religion as their shepherd, who desperately cared for them. When they were lost, he sought them. When they were found, he rejoiced. For Brandon, this truth unearthed more questions. Up to now he had thought of his search as one-way; it was he who was looking for something. But was someone also looking for him? Would he be found? Why should he care, anyway? Did he care? Brandon continued to listen and inwardly question as the man taught his sermon to completion.

After the final amen, they walked through the lobby. The pleasant smell of a long-delayed rain hit them as they navigated through the cluster of jabbering congregants. Looking out the front doors confirmed it had begun raining. They reached the door, and someone called out to them, "Thank you three for visiting this morning!" It was the same elderly fellow, Harold, who had greeted them when they arrived.

"It was great to worship with you, brother," Anton said, extending a hand.

Harold shook Anton's hand. "Shall we expect you for our midweek study?" He then extended his hand to Brandon.

Remembering Devin's training, Brandon looked the man in the eyes and gripped his hand firmly.

"Sorry, brother," Anton said. "We're just passing through. We'll probably be leaving San Antonio tomorrow."

"What a shame. Well, you boys stay safe, okay?"

"Yes, sir," Anton said.

The rain came down as a steady stream. Anton drove them back to the hotel, where some leftover pizza was waiting for them. Justin sat in the front seat, chatting with Anton. With the rain beating against the windshield, it was hard to hear much from the backseat. Brandon watched the raindrops on his window, continually torn in two directions. The force of the air rushing past the moving car pushed the water up, while gravity tried to pull it down. The result was that it went nowhere. Apparently, the vehicle was traveling at the perfect speed to equalize both forces.

In a way, that's how Brandon felt. The questions that he was wrestling with at church still preoccupied him. As he did his best to remind himself he didn't believe this stuff, Devin's "farewell speech" kept entering his mind. He recalled how Devin had looked at him with such earnestness, pleading with him to continue asking questions, reading the Bible, and spending time in study with Anton. He had assured Brandon that doing so would allow Jesus to change his life. It was as though Devin could see that Brandon was at a crossroads and needed some direction.

But why did guys like Anton and Devin bother to care about him at all? He was just a messed up kid who'd had a rough start in life and who stormed out of restaurants because he couldn't control his anger. It dawned on Brandon that maybe their desire to help him was rooted in something bigger—something beyond themselves. He shied away from saying the word at the tip of his tongue—God—but wasn't willing to dismiss it. And that's when he realized something had changed in him; perhaps he'd shed some of his animosity and skepticism along with his trench coat.

Would he forever be like those raindrops, pressed on both sides, resulting in an eternal impasse? No. It was time to make a decision. Justin was still talking to Anton. Where was he on this journey? Did he believe anything Anton or Devin had said?

Anton was right that the fact that something existed, rather than nothing, demanded a logical explanation. The only answer to the design in nature was that there was a designer. And if Brandon, and every other person in history, had been created—rather than the result of some cosmic accident—then it made sense the creator had communicated his will to his creation. Devin had given him five good reasons to believe the Bible indeed was reliable. Did Anton's and Devin's answers satisfy every "but what about" question Brandon could have raised? No, but it was enough for Brandon to reconsider his ideas about Christianity resulting from people blindly following a collection of fairytales. To truly understand it required critical thinking. Of course, he still had questions—plenty of them. Anton had said something about Jesus rising from the dead, which still seemed a bit outlandish to him. Taking Devin's advice seriously, he made a note to ask Anton about that one too.

Regardless of what Justin would think of him, Brandon decided at that moment that he would take the path that led to the truth about Christianity. Today had raised more questions than it had answered, but that didn't bother him. Perhaps the preacher was right. Maybe he was lost, and there was someone else besides the police searching for Brandon Bason.

CHAPTER TWENTY-SIX

It was nearing six in the evening when they arrived in downtown San Antonio and found a parking lot a couple of blocks away from the Alamo. The clouds were giving way to sun rays, the air humid after the summer rain. As they were walking toward the Alamo, a man in tattered clothing stopped Anton, asking for some money.

"Just like downtown Nashville," Brandon said to Justin.

"Yeah."

"What do you need some money for?" Anton asked the man. The beggar's face was grimy. Brandon noticed he was wearing two different types of shoes. The only thing matching about them was how beaten up they looked.

"I'm hungry," he said.

"Well, let's skip the money part and go straight to solving the problem," Anton said. The man looked at him blankly. "What I mean is, we're about to go get some dinner. Come with us." The man's face lit up, shining through the dirt. Anton motioned for Brandon and Justin to follow. Brandon didn't very much like the idea of having dinner with a hobo. He hadn't gotten close enough to confirm, but Brandon suspected he smelled bad. But what could Brandon do? Protest Anton's generosity toward someone else when he himself had benefitted so much from it?

They reached a plaza area near the Alamo, where several food carts were lined up. "What would you like?" Anton asked.

The beggar regarded Anton, likely trying to figure out if he was serious or not. "Is a burger too much to ask for?"

"Certainly not. Are you thirsty too?"

The man grinned.

Anton went to the burger cart and ordered four cheeseburgers and four sodas. He grabbed a stack of napkins and handed them to Justin. "Will you please wipe down that table over there?"

Brandon walked over and took half of the stack, and the two of them cleared the leftover rain from the picnic table and chairs. The table now dry, the beggar came and joined them. The three of them sat down to wait for Anton and the burgers.

"Some friend you've got there," he said.

Brandon watched Anton, who was leaning against the food truck. "Some friend." Brandon breathed through his mouth, trying not to smell the beggar. He shamefully realized how judgmental he was being. He should be more like Anton. He turned to the stranger. "What's your name?"

The sun was setting, casting an orange hue on the limestone walls of the ancient-looking building. Having finished their dinner, they said goodbye to the beggar, who Brandon found out was called Charles, and the three of them walked the neatly laid stone path leading up to the building. They spotted a sign in front of the main door that said, "Closed."

"Sorry guys," Anton said. "If we'd come fifteen minutes earlier, we could have gone inside."

"It's no big deal," Brandon replied. Anton didn't need to

apologize; Brandon knew that to have made it in time would have meant ignoring the chance to serve the hungry man. It was worth missing a tour of the Alamo to help someone in need.

Next to the path were plaques that explained some history of the place. Brandon read them half-heartedly. Nearly two hundred Texans had been besieged inside this former Catholic Mission. Anton was right—out-numbered about ten-to-one, Texas had lost. However, losing this battle seemed to have lit a spark within the revolution. Just over a month later, Texas' independence was won, led by General Sam Houston, who famously cried, "Remember the Alamo!"

Remember the Alamo, Brandon thought. He glanced up at the building. In the middle of a modern city stood this unassuming historical landmark that symbolized a crucial period in American history. When learning about this kind of stuff in school, Brandon had paid only enough attention to get him by without failing. Now he examined the facade of the memorial. It looked as if it hadn't changed for two hundred years. That was probably intentional. If it were a new, polished-looking building, it probably wouldn't conjure up thoughts of the past. Preserving the way it looked during its moment in history was meaningful for those who were not there during the battle. If it had been renovated with the times, it would hardly be worth remembering.

Brandon thought back to the church service that morning, when the man with the long beard had read from the Bible. Jesus had told his friends to eat and drink in remembrance of him. He looked across the courtyard to Anton, who was reading a different set of plaques. "Hey, Anton!"

Anton looked over. "What's up?"

"Why did Jesus tell his friends to remember him?"

Anton smiled. He looked up at the Alamo, likely making the connection. "Great question. Got your dad's Bible?"

"Yep," Brandon said.

Anton walked across the street to a half wall by the sidewalk. Justin stomped out a cigarette and followed. Brandon put his backpack on the ground, and the three of them sat. He fished the Bible out of his bag.

"I think it was great that the guy who led the Lord's Supper this morning read from Matthew twenty-six and First Corinthians eleven," Anton said. "Each one tells us some new information about that night when Jesus was betrayed."

"I remember hearing about that," Brandon said. "Who betrayed him?"

Anton frowned. "It was his close friend named Judas. I guess we should backtrack a bit. We already covered Jesus' birth when we studied about Mary conceiving Jesus as a virgin." Anton leaned forward to grin at Justin, who was sitting on the other side of Brandon.

Justin grinned back. "I think we've covered that enough!"

"Now, let's look at John seventeen, verse five." While Brandon took the time to find the passage, Anton said, "What we are about to read took place the same night Jesus was betrayed and gave the bread and the fruit of the vine. In this passage, he was praying."

Brandon landed on the verse and read it.

And now, glorify Thou Me together with Thyself, Father, with the glory which I had with Thee before the world was.

"Jesus asked the Father for the glory he had before what event?" Anton asked.

"Before the world was created," Brandon said.

"Ah, so you're admitting there was a creator now, huh?" Anton said.

"Well..." Brandon looked back at Justin, who remained silent. "Let's just say I'm not going to be so difficult anymore. I want to know the point of all this."

"I'll accept that," Anton said with a smile. "And you're right. Jesus, although he was born on the earth, existed for an eternity before then. Check out what he said to his contemporaries in chapter eight, verses fifty-six to fifty-nine."

Brandon turned back a couple of pages and read.

> *"Your father Abraham rejoiced to see My day, and he saw it and was glad." The Jews therefore said to Him, "You are not yet fifty years old, and have You seen Abraham?" Jesus said to them, "Truly, truly, I say to you, before Abraham was born, I am." Therefore they picked up stones to throw at Him; but Jesus hid Himself, and went out of the temple.*

"It says here that Abraham was their father," Anton said. "What is meant is that Abraham was their ancestor—both physically and religiously. He had lived centuries before this day. But Jesus said before Abraham was born, what?"

"He said, 'I am.' But that doesn't sound right."

"You don't have to be a grammar guru to know something is off in that sentence. 'Before Abraham was born, I am,'" Anton repeated. "Jesus didn't misunderstand the rules of grammar; he was making a point. The point was, before Jesus came to the earth, he lived outside of time. Remember our conversation on our way to Aunt Mavel's house? Who has the same attribute?"

"God does," Brandon said.

"That's right. This title—I Am—is the title that belongs to the God of the universe in the Old Testament. But Jesus applies it to himself right here, which explains why people picked up stones. They weren't just trying to annoy him by throwing little rocks at him." Anton kicked at a few pebbles on the ground by his feet. "This is the way people executed others in the Bible. It was called stoning, and they threw huge rocks at the victim until he died. They knew the implications of Jesus' words. He was claiming to be God, and they didn't like it."

"But why should we believe it?" Brandon asked.

"Good question," Anton said. "And it shows I'm not doing a good enough job backtracking. So, Jesus came to the earth. We don't know a lot about his childhood. In fact, the book of Mark jumps straight into his ministry as an adult. He's baptized at the beginning of chapter one, and then he starts performing miracles, like healing people with infectious diseases. Anyway, we get a glimpse of his priorities in verse thirty-eight. What does that verse say?"

Imitating Devin, Anton tapped the part of the Bible in Brandon's left hand, indicating Mark was before John. Brandon found chapter one and read verse thirty-eight.

> *And He said to them, "Let us go somewhere else to the towns nearby, in order that I may preach there also; for that is what I came out for."*

"What was his priority?" Anton asked.

"It was to preach."

"Yep," Anton said with a nod. "But everywhere he went preaching, he also performed amazing miracles. People saw his compassion and ability to heal and feed people, and they followed him. Now, read the first seven verses of the next chapter for us." Brandon did so.

> *And when He had come back to Capernaum several days afterward, it was heard that He was at home. And many were gathered together, so that there was no longer room, even near the door; and He was speaking the word to them. And they came, bringing to Him a paralytic, carried by four men. And being unable to get to Him because of the crowd, they removed the roof above Him; and when they had dug an opening, they let down the pallet on which the paralytic was lying. And Jesus seeing their faith said to the paralytic, "My son, your sins are forgiven." But there were some of the scribes sitting there and reasoning in their hearts, "Why does this man*

speak that way? He is blaspheming; who can forgive sins but God alone?"

"Why do you suppose these guys brought their paralyzed friend to Jesus?" Anton asked.

"I guess they thought he could heal him," Brandon said.

"But before Jesus even addressed his physical state, what did he do?"

Brandon looked down at the Bible to find the answer. There it was in verse five. "He forgave his sins."

Anton leaned over. "Justin, what do you think this says about Jesus' priorities?"

Justin was looking at the sun-drenched Alamo, leaving Brandon to assume he wasn't paying attention to the conversation. He surprised Brandon when, still looking off into the distance, he said, "Jesus must be interested in our health. Otherwise, he wouldn't have healed people. But he apparently thought forgiving sins was more important."

Anton smiled. Brandon didn't mind thinking out loud, whereas Justin was always the silent thinker. Anton continued. "After Jesus said his sins were forgiven, how did the crowds respond?"

Brandon found the answer in the Bible once again. "They said he was blaspheming—whatever that means."

"To blaspheme simply means to say something false about God, which is pretty serious. In this case, what did they think Jesus was doing?"

"They thought he was putting himself in place of God."

"Why?"

In any other situation, this constant back and forth of questions would have annoyed or angered Brandon, but he knew Anton was doing it for a purpose. Brandon was reminded of their late-night conversation in Devin's basement and how Anton emphasized the value of Brandon learning this stuff on his own, rather than having someone just tell him. That way, when Brandon either rejected or accepted it, he was rejecting or accepting the source of the information—God—and not just his friend. "They said only God can forgive sins."

"What do you think about that?"

Brandon thought for a second, then said, "Well, considering everything God is, that seems right. If Devin is correct, and there is a final judgment, then it seems God should be the one judging people's actions."

"That's exactly right. And these people saw a man, albeit a preacher, proclaiming someone's sins were forgiven. I think if you and I were in that situation, we would have responded the same way. Even the most righteous preacher on earth doesn't have the authority to forgive another man's sins."

"Then why did Jesus try to do it here?" Brandon pointed to the passage in front of him.

Anton smiled. "I thought you'd never ask. Read verses eight through twelve."

Brandon was intrigued. He read.

> *And immediately Jesus, aware in His spirit that they were reasoning that way within themselves, said to them, "Why are you reasoning about these things in your hearts? Which is easier, to say to the paralytic, 'Your sins are forgiven'; or to say, 'Arise, and take up your pallet and walk'? But in order that you may know that the Son of Man has authority on earth to forgive sins"—He said to the paralytic —"I say to you, rise, take up your pallet and go home." And he rose and immediately took up the pallet and went out in the sight of all; so that they were all amazed and were glorifying God, saying, "We have never seen anything like this."*

"Why were these people so amazed?" Anton asked.

"Because Jesus healed this man just by speaking to him," Brandon said.

"Do you believe he did that?"

Brandon shifted on the half wall, suddenly aware of how uncomfortable it was. The sun had sunk low on the horizon, casting long shadows across the sidewalk. Although the temperature had cooled considerably, the humidity remained. He thought back to the raindrops on the car window and felt the pressure of his past urging him to scoff, to stand up and walk away, to do anything but give in to this mumbo jumbo. Then, he considered the whirlwind of a trip this had been. Two weeks ago, he and Justin were still in Tennessee. Now, they were halfway to the Grand Canyon. He had learned much so far. He had also gained a couple of friends. *There is a creator,* he thought. *There is a shepherd.* "Yes, I believe that," Brandon said, surprising himself. He couldn't help but feel like a hypocrite at that moment. How long had he given Anton a hard time over this? How long had Anton patiently endured? Brandon resisted the urge to look at Justin, who was probably rolling his eyes.

Anton smiled. It wasn't just his mouth, but his whole face contributed to the look of joy he gave Brandon—his eyes, his cheeks, and every tooth that gleamed in the evening haze. Then, he nodded slowly. "That's pretty cool." A moment later, he asked, "What does verse ten say Jesus' miracles proved?"

Brandon reread the verse silently. "He said that we can know he has the authority to forgive sins."

"That's right. And who alone has that authority?"

"God."

"Therefore, Jesus is..."

It hit Brandon. Just as realization dawned, confusion also arose. "Jesus is God?"

"It seems you're getting it, but I can tell you still have questions," Anton said, still beaming.

"Totally," Brandon said.

"I hear that," Anton agreed. "The Bible was not written for our curiosity. It was written for other reasons, like to give us a history of God's works on earth, and to show us his plans through the family of faith in the Old Testament. Ultimately, the Bible shows us God through the person of Jesus Christ. There's a lot more that can be said, but the point I want you to get now is this: If you know Jesus, you know God. If you see Jesus, you see God. That's why Jesus, on the one hand, said that only God is worthy of worship; on the other hand, he accepted worship. Jesus is not just the founder of Christianity. He's the creator of the world, and he's worthy of our service and thanksgiving."

Brandon nodded slowly, the confusion fading from his face.

"Let's go to Matthew one," Anton said.

Brandon was getting used to the location of Matthew. He found it in a couple of seconds.

"Now, read verse twenty-three." Anton leaned over and added, "And Justin, brace yourself."

Brandon read.

> *"Behold, the virgin shall be with child, and shall bear a Son, and they shall call his name Immanuel," which translated means, "God with us."*

"I know we've been over the virgin part a few times," Anton said with a smile. "Here's a new point. What is Jesus called in this passage?"

"Immanuel," Brandon said.

"Which means?"

"God with us."

"Putting all this together," Anton began, "we understand Jesus was with the Father even before the world existed. The book of Luke tells us that because he had no earthly father, but the Holy Spirit miraculously conceived him in his mother's womb, he was called the Son of God. Then, he was born on the earth as God with us. While he was here, he did things that only God has the power to do, proving the things he said about himself, including calling himself the God of the Old Testament." Brandon nodded again to show Anton he was following. Anton continued. "We have a record of about three and a half years of his ministry on earth. We saw the beginning of it when he healed the paralyzed man. Another thing he did at the beginning of his ministry was to call twelve men to be his close followers. He had a lot of ground to cover, so he trained these men to help him. As he sent them out, the Bible calls them apostles."

"I've heard that word a couple times in the past few days."

"Great." Anton leaned forward to look at Justin, who now seemed more interested in what they were discussing. Anton stood up. He positioned himself in front of Brandon and Justin and sat on the sidewalk. "While Jesus was with these twelve guys, he taught them a lot of lessons. One of the most important ones is found in Mark eight."

Brandon leaned in subconsciously.

"Well, what are you waiting for?" Anton said.

"Oh!" Brandon started flipping the pages in the Bible, seeking the passage. "Got it."

"Good. Verses thirty-four to thirty-eight."

> *And He summoned the multitude with His disciples, and said to them, "If anyone wishes to come after Me, let him deny himself, and take up his cross, and follow Me. For whoever wishes to save his life shall lose it; but whoever loses his life for My sake and the gospel's shall save it. For what does it profit a man to gain the whole world, and forfeit his soul? For what shall a man give in exchange for his soul? For whoever is ashamed of Me and My words in this adulterous and sinful generation, the Son of Man will also be ashamed of him when He comes in the glory of His Father with the holy angels."*

"According to Jesus, what is the most important thing you

have?" Anton asked, pointing to Brandon with one hand, and Justin with the other.

"Our souls," Justin said.

Brandon smiled, seeing his silent friend starting to contribute.

Anton shrugged. "If I may be bold enough to say so, I believe the three of us have grown close on this trip. And I think we've learned a great lesson about possessions. Between the three of us, I don't think we could fill a single suitcase with the stuff we've got with us. And I know I haven't missed anything I've left back home. Why should I? I've got friends. I've got experiences." He turned and gestured toward the Alamo behind him. Now, the orange hue was gone entirely. Floodlights in the forecourt had just turned on, making the Alamo look every bit of a fortress. "But this truth about the soul also applies to the wealthiest person in the world. As tempting as it would be, if we were ever offered all the riches in the world for our soul, what would we gain from that deal?"

"Nothing," Brandon said.

"Nothing," Anton repeated. "This passage reminds us that Jesus will return in his glory. The book of Hebrews says it's appointed for all of us to die once, and after that will come the judgment. On that day, we will not care how much money we made in our lives. We won't care about anything at that moment, except for the answer to this question: Did I deny myself and take up my cross?"

"What's with this judgment we keep hearing about?" Justin said.

"I'm glad you asked," Anton said. "Remind me, and we will come back to that."

Justin nodded, satisfied for the moment.

"For now," Anton continued, "let's explore this question: What does it mean to deny yourself and take up your cross?"

"Beats me," Justin said.

"Brandon, turn a few pages to chapter ten, and read verses forty-two to forty-five."

Brandon found the passage, then he offered the Bible to Justin. "Wanna read?"

"No, thanks."

Brandon held the Bible in both hands and read.

> *And calling them to Himself, Jesus said to them, "You know that those who are recognized as rulers of the Gentiles lord it over them; and their great men exercise authority over them. But it is not so among you, but whoever wishes to become great among you shall be your servant; and whoever wishes to be first among you shall be slave of all. For even the Son of Man did not come to be served, but to serve, and to give His life a ransom for many."*

The longer he read, the closer he held the Bible to his face. "It's getting dark. It's hard to read in this light."

Anton looked around. "There's got to be a café or ice cream shop around here somewhere."

CHAPTER TWENTY-SEVEN

THEY STROLLED SILENTLY DOWN THE LAMPLIT STREETS OF downtown San Antonio, heading away from the Alamo toward the river, until they found a café that still had an hour before closing. Anton purchased brownies for each of them, and they found a booth in the corner. Knowing what was coming next, Brandon held his father's Bible at the ready.

"Picking up where we left off," Anton said, "Jesus told his disciples that his mission was to give his life as a ransom for many. As soon as the New Testament announced Jesus' coming, with no uncertain terms, it claims Jesus' primary purpose was to save people from their sins. Now, if I recall correctly, Brandon, when we were in New Orleans, you called Jesus' offer of forgiveness a crutch."

Brandon cringed. "I did." He looked down. "I didn't know much back then."

"Back then? It wasn't that long ago."

"I know. Sorry about that."

"It's encouraging that you're changing your attitude as you learn more."

Brandon smiled at Anton's compassion. He truly cared about

people. A lesser man would be so wrapped up in his own beliefs that he would jump down anyone's throat who didn't conform to his ideals. Most people would respond that way, thinking it was somehow the way to change their opponent's mind. The irony was that just as outspoken, hypocritical Christians turned Brandon off Christianity, Anton's demeanor and lack of offense drew Brandon in.

"When Jesus was on the earth," Anton began, "he spent time with the sick. He ate meals with sinners. He healed the broken-hearted. He never busied himself trying to get rich or climb social ladders. And every step of the way, he was training his close friends to do the same. The problem was, however, there was one of the twelve who loved the approval of men."

"Judas?" Brandon asked.

"Yes. He also loved..." Anton extended his hand and rubbed his index finger and thumb together.

"Money," Justin said.

"Exactly. Check out Matthew chapter twenty-six, verses fourteen and fifteen."

Brandon turned to the passage and read.

> *Then one of the twelve, named Judas Iscariot, went to the chief priests, and said, "What are you willing to give me to deliver Him up to you?" And they weighed out to him thirty pieces of silver. And from then on he began looking for a good opportunity to betray Him.*

Anton said, "Since Jesus was not what the religious leaders expected him to be, they were jealous. If God had granted any one of them the power of Jesus, they would have used it to flaunt their positions in their religion. Jesus, on the other hand, stayed humble. So, the proud people quickly saw Jesus as their enemy, and they sought to kill him. When Jesus was eating with these twelve guys—you know, when he took the bread and called it his body—he predicted that someone would betray him, and all those jealous religious leaders would torture and kill him. Most of the disciples didn't understand. But Judas saw his opportunity. He left the room and told the priests where to find Jesus later that night. Judas got his money, but at what cost? He betrayed the one who had come to save him. He betrayed his friend. Jesus, the only man to have lived a perfect life, was turned over to the self-righteous religious leaders who treated him as a criminal. The next day, he was executed on a cross."

"What do you mean by a cross?" Brandon asked. "I know it's a symbol of Christianity, but I don't get what this cross was."

Anton finished a bite of his brownie and sighed. "I grew up knowing this stuff. So did most of my friends. The fact that you even have to ask about the cross shows me that I've taken a lot of things for granted."

"I know about the cross," Justin said, but not arrogantly. "I don't remember where, but I picked it up. Probably in a movie or something."

"It's important that you both get a good, biblical idea of what happened to Jesus after Judas betrayed him." Anton held out his hand toward the Bible. "May I?"

"Sure." Brandon handed it to him.

"I'm going to read from John chapters eighteen and nineteen. I'll stop now and then to give you an idea of how they would have done things back in Jesus' day." Anton proceeded to go through the passage, explaining some of the politics of the time, and how the Romans were occupying Israel. Brandon and Justin listened to how people treated Jesus that night. They broke laws so that they could put him on trial in secret. They passed him around between religious and political leaders who disagreed on what to do to him. The soldiers saw him as just another criminal to mock, although the governor believed he was innocent. It was clear he indeed was innocent by the desperate measures the priests took to get him executed. Although they had no real evidence against him, they still cried for him to be killed on a wooden cross, even taking the place of a previously convicted criminal.

Brandon marveled at the composure of Jesus. He knew if he were in that position, he would plead for his life. He would continuously proclaim his innocence. He would demand a fair trial. All the while, however, Jesus stayed silent. Adding injury to insult, the soldiers beat him and put a fake and painful crown on his head. Hoping it would appease the religious fanatics, the governor presented the bloodied Jesus. Instead, their bloodlust grew, and they demanded that he be crucified. They truly were motivated by their passions and jealousies. Anton explained how crucifixion involved a man being stretched over two beams of wood—a cross—having spikes nailed through the wrists and ankles to hold his body in place. They then dropped the structure into a pre-dug hole in the ground, causing the cross to stand upright as if it were a roadside decoration. They crucified the victim backside down, and in Jesus' case, they crucified him after his back had been shredded by whips designed to tear human flesh. Jesus was executed with other criminals, who were suffering the same fate. While he endured such great agony, his family and friends who still dared to approach him were left to watch him die a slow, agonizing death. Some soldiers mocked him. Others gambled over the only possession he had left—his clothing. Once he died, one of Jesus' friends offered his own tomb to bury Jesus' body.

Even though Anton already knew all this, he was still visibly shaken by revisiting the details. His voice cracked toward the end of the reading. When he finished, he swallowed hard and removed his glasses. The three of them sat in silence for a moment, until Anton said, "When he told his disciples to eat the supper in remembrance of him, this is what they were supposed to remember and proclaim."

Then, Justin asked, "What was the point? That was pretty gruesome. Why did he have to die?"

"Great question," Anton put his glasses back on and turned the Bible to First John chapter three. He slid it across the table to Justin. "Will you please read verses four and five?" He pointed to the verses on the page.

Justin cut his eyes at Brandon.

"Don't look at me," Brandon said. "You didn't bail me out the other day."

"Fine," Justin said. "Why not?" He looked down and read the two verses.

Everyone who practices sin also practices lawlessness; and sin is lawlessness. And you know that He appeared in order to take away sins; and in Him there is no sin.

"So, what was the point?" Anton asked Justin.

"It says what you've been saying all along. Jesus came to take away sins. Good for sinners. What's that got to do with me?"

Anton touched his goatee in thought. "Who are sinners?"

"I don't know," Justin said with a shrug. "Murderers, rapists, people who deserve to go to prison."

"Those things are definitely against God's law," Anton said. "The second sin the Bible highlights is when one man murdered his brother. But what was the first sin?"

"No idea," Justin said.

"That's fine. Let's read about it." Anton eyed the Bible. "The first book of the Bible, chapter two."

Justin hesitated, then flipped to Genesis two.

"Verses sixteen and seventeen, please."

Justin read.

And the LORD God commanded the man, saying, "From any tree of the garden you may eat freely; but from the tree of the knowledge of good and evil you shall not eat, for in the day that you eat from it you shall surely die."

"The commandment here is simple, right?" Anton said. "Don't eat a specific fruit. But in the next chapter, both Eve and Adam eat from it. The murderer in chapter four broke God's law, but so did these people by eating the fruit."

"Sure," Justin said. "But you're not about to tell me that eating fruit is as bad as murder."

"No, I'm not," Anton said. "But that also doesn't mean God is going to turn a blind eye to 'small' disobedience, either. After the woman and man ate from the fruit, God cast them out of his presence. Second Thessalonians tells us that will be the same fate for all those who will not obey the gospel today." Anton paused. "The book of James says that we are all tempted by our own lusts. Yes, some people give in to the temptation to murder. Others are tempted by drugs, sex, the love of money, or simply selfishness. I think everyone is tempted to lie. At this point, the question isn't which one is worse. It's who has given in? And the answer is, we all have—somehow or another." Still speaking to Justin, Anton said, "I think we will come back to this. But before I lose my train of thought, remember the first passage you read for us said Jesus came to take away what?"

"Sins," said Justin.

"That's right," Anton said. "A moment ago, we also read that the last three words Jesus uttered on the cross were, 'It is finished.' Jesus' death accomplished his task."

"That reminds me," Brandon said. "You were supposed to teach me about that. In Devin's basement, we read about Jesus dying for our sins, and I asked what it meant. You said we would have to discuss it some other time."

"Looks like now is that time," Anton said with a smile. "Of course, this raises another question. How does Jesus' death take away sins?" Anton said it in the tone of voice he used when he didn't expect anyone to answer. By now Brandon understood that he was setting up the question so that the Bible could answer it. "The other day, when Devin said the Bible is relevant,

I thought he made a great point. Every time God has commanded someone to do something, it was for their best interests. It's not like God is on some ego trip and wants to show everyone who's boss. Just like a loving parent who warns children of the consequences of disobeying them, God—from the beginning—has been warning people that breaking his commandments comes with a consequence."

"And what's that?" Justin asked.

"Turn to Romans chapter six."

Justin slid the Bible over to Brandon. "It's your Bible."

Brandon was about to remind Justin that it was his father's Bible, but he stopped himself. His father was dead. His mother had wanted Brandon to have it. *This is my Bible,* he thought as he picked it up. With a resolve to understand his own Bible, he started turning the pages to find the book of Romans.

"Chapter six, verse twenty-three," Anton said.

Brandon found it. Before he read, he asked, "Why are you going to preaching school? The preacher this morning was great, but you seem just as good as any preacher I've ever heard of."

Anton arched an eyebrow. "How many preachers have you heard of?"

"Well," Brandon began, "What I mean is—"

"I know what you mean. And what you said means the world to me. Thanks. And you're right. I don't have to go to school to be a preacher. I told you once before that Jesus' first preachers were uneducated, for the most part. And ever since I caused that huge fuss among the Shreveport Christians, I knew I needed more than just an attitude adjustment. I've spent every day with my nose in the Bible, trying to learn as much as I can. I've spent time with my elders to learn hospitality. But I can always learn more, like Greek and Hebrew, as well as geography. It'll be good for me."

"Fair enough," Brandon said. He read the passage.

For the wages of sin is death, but the free gift of God is eternal life in Christ Jesus our Lord.

"This sentence has two clauses," Anton said. "The first one tells us the consequence of sin. What is it?"

Brandon met Anton's eyes. "Death."

Anton nodded. "What do you see after the word 'death'?"

Brandon looked down. "But?"

Justin chuckled. "You see a *what* in the Bible?"

Anton rolled his eyes. "Control yourself, little boy. No, Brandon, you've gone too far. Between the words 'death' and 'but.'"

Brandon looked closer. "A comma?"

Anton hammered his hands on the table, causing Brandon and Justin to jump. They both stared at him expectantly, not caring if others in the café noticed the sound. He looked back with seriousness. "Never forget to praise God for that comma," he said slowly. "There is more love in that single punctuation mark than anything ever expressed by you or me or in the history of mankind." Brandon blinked at Anton. He was trying to grasp what Anton was saying. He knew this was an important point, but he didn't want to ruin the moment with a foolish question. Thankfully, Anton elaborated. "Ever since God created humans, he has been warning them of this simple fact: sin results in death—from the 'smallest' to the 'biggest' of sins. Therefore, he had every right to put a period at the end of that clause. If that were the case, we would be up the creek without a paddle. What does a comma mean?"

"Pause," Justin said.

"Take a breath," Brandon said.

"Why should we pause or take a breath?"

Neither Brandon nor Justin answered.

Anton planted his hands on the table again. "Because there's more to the story! Sorry for the theatrics, fellas. You just need to get this point. The consequence of sin is death." He pointed at the Bible. "But instead of death, God offers what through whom?"

Brandon looked down again. "Eternal life through Jesus."

Anton curled his hands into fists. He smiled and closed his eyes. "Father, thank you for that gift."

Brandon looked at his new friend across the table. He imagined himself being as thankful as Anton was in that exact moment. He yearned to know more.

Anton opened his eyes. "Turn backward to chapter three and read verse twenty-three."

Brandon did so.

For all have sinned and fall short of the glory of God.

"You probably didn't need the Bible to tell you as much, did you?" Anton asked.

Justin dropped his eyes in thought. Then, he shook his head.

"No," Brandon agreed.

Anton grabbed a napkin out of a dispenser and placed it on top of the Bible. "Use this as a bookmark, and turn to Isaiah fifty-nine, verses one and two. It's in the Old Testament."

Brandon fumbled with the pages for a few seconds until he found the passage and read.

Behold, the Lord's hand is not so short that it cannot save; Neither is His ear so dull that it cannot hear. But your iniquities have made a separation between you and your God, and your sins have hidden His face from you, so that He does not hear.

"Isaiah was prophesying to a group of people who were determined to live in sin," Anton said. "They also wanted to draw close to God. The question on their minds was, 'What's the problem?' Tell me. What was the problem?"

"Apparently," Brandon began, "sin separates people from God."

"You know that's right," Anton said. "Think about it this way. A little boy wakes up and looks out his window. He sees it's raining. He's itching to get outside and play. His mother, however, says that they've got plans later, and he should stay inside. He grabs his clothes from his closet, puts them on, and completely disregards his mother's instructions. He goes out and plays in the mud. He splashes, he runs, he jumps, he has a blast. Then, he starts to feel cold. He also thinks about how upset his mother is going to be. Shivering, and getting colder by the second, he returns to the house and opens the door to go inside. There she is, looking down at her filthy, freezing boy standing on the doorstep. How do you think he feels?"

"Regretful," Brandon said.

Anton nodded. "Was it fun?"

"Sure," Justin said. "For a few minutes, at least."

"How do you think she feels?" Anton asked.

"Mad," Brandon said. His mother had never lashed out at him when he disappointed her, but he knew too well what an angry stepfather would do.

"She's probably feeling bad for him too," Justin said. "He's freezing."

"Now, before he can get on with his day, what needs to happen?" Anton asked.

"A shower," Brandon said.

Anton nodded. "And he needs to be reconciled to his mom. Reconciled—that's a fancy way of saying they need to get on good terms again." To illustrate, Anton clasped his hands together. "That's what God does for us. We mess around with sin. Why? Because it's fun, at least for a while. The Bible doesn't mask that fact, by the way. In Hebrews eleven, the Bible says sin brings pleasure. Otherwise, we wouldn't be tempted to do it."

He suddenly changed tack. "Hey, Justin. I've got some clam chowder for you. Would you like some?"

Justin scrunched up his face. "No way, dude."

"My point exactly. We're not tempted to eat the foods we hate. But we are tempted to sin since it brings happiness—at least for a few minutes. God knows what's best for us. That's why he tells us not to lie, not to steal, to treat our neighbors with the utmost respect, and to take care of the needy. But we've all given in, myself included. We show up at his doorstep, asking to come back into his grace. What needs to happen?"

"A shower," Brandon said.

"Yes. And?" Anton clasped his hands together again.

"The r-word," Justin said.

"Reconciliation," Anton said. "Turn to the napkin bookmark."

Brandon turned the Bible back to the book of Romans.

"Now, read chapter five, verses six through ten."

Brandon did.

> *For while we were still helpless, at the right time Christ died for the ungodly. For one will hardly die for a righteous man; though perhaps for the good man someone would dare even to die. But God demonstrates His own love toward us, in that while we were yet sinners, Christ died for us. Much more then, having now been justified by His blood, we shall be saved from the wrath of God through Him. For if while we were enemies, we were reconciled to God through the death of His Son, much more, having been reconciled, we shall be saved by His life.*

"In verse eight, how did God show his love?" Anton asked.

"Through the death of his Son," Brandon said.

"In verse ten, what reconciles us to God?"

"The death of his Son," Brandon repeated.

"And that's why that comma is so important. Without the

death of Jesus, we would be stuck in our sin, stuck to face the consequence—death. Look again in chapter three. This time, read verses twenty-three through twenty-six."

> *For all have sinned and fall short of the glory of God, being justified as a gift by His grace through the redemption which is in Christ Jesus; whom God displayed publicly as a propitiation in His blood through faith. This was to demonstrate His righteousness, because in the forbearance of God He passed over the sins previously committed; for the demonstration, I say, of His righteousness at the present time, that He might be just and the justifier of the one who has faith in Jesus.*

"This passage has two of God's attributes in view," Anton said. "His justice and his mercy. A just judge always gives criminals what they deserve. Now, if God is just, what is he going to give us?"

"Death," Justin answered.

"But because he is also merciful, he doesn't want to condemn us. In every case, a judge has to decide between justice and mercy. You can't give both. Unless..." Anton paused. Brandon was unsure if he was waiting for him and Justin to finish his sentence. When they didn't, he continued. "Unless someone else pays the penalty. Let's suppose the three of us are in God's courtroom. We know it's useless to claim innocence, so we plead guilty to sin. We deserve death. So I say to God, 'But Brandon and Justin are my friends! Let me die for them!' Do you think God would allow that?"

Justin shook his head.

"Why not?" Anton asked.

"You said it yourself. You're also guilty," said Justin.

"But in walks Jesus," Anton said. "Can he pay the penalty?"

"I guess so," Justin said.

"You guess so? Turn to Hebrews four," Anton said to Brandon. "Read verses fourteen through sixteen."

Brandon found the passage and read.

> *Since then we have a great high priest who has passed through the heavens, Jesus the Son of God, let us hold fast our confession. For we do not have a high priest who cannot sympathize with our weaknesses, but One who has been tempted in all things as we are, yet without sin. Let us therefore draw near with confidence to the throne of grace, that we may receive mercy and may find grace to help in time of need.*

"This passage says Jesus has something in common with us: He's been tempted just like we have. But what's unique about him?"

"He never sinned." Brandon imagined what it would be like to have never done anything wrong, never done anything he regretted.

"Justin, you said I can't die for you," Anton began, "because we're in the same sinking boat—we've both sinned."

Justin leaned in, clearly engrossed in the conversation. Brandon smiled again. He and his best friend were on two journeys together—one to the Grand Canyon and one to understand the Bible. He shook his head, thinking how unlikely it was.

"While we are all sinking together, Jesus comes along and offers a ride in his perfect, hole-free boat. You gonna take that offer?" Brandon didn't have to think about that for long. Anton continued. "After Jesus died, he rose from the grave a few days later. Soon afterward, he returned to heaven with the promise he would come back to judge the world. On that day of judgment, God will be able to do what every good judge wants to do—be both just and merciful. The death of Jesus paid the consequence of sin. Therefore, he can let us—the sinners—go free of charge. Our case is legally dismissed."

They were quiet at the table for a minute or so, until Justin spoke up. "Hang on. That sounds good and all, but how come people still die?"

Anton adjusted his glasses. After a moment, he nodded and said, "Turn to Revelation twenty." He looked at Brandon. "It's the last book of the Bible." After Brandon found it, he instructed him to read verses eleven through fifteen. Brandon read.

> *And I saw a great white throne and Him who sat upon it, from whose presence earth and heaven fled away, and no place was found for them. And I saw the dead, the great and the small, standing before the throne, and books were opened; and another book was opened, which is the book of life; and the dead were judged from the things which were written in the books, according to their deeds. And the sea gave up the dead which were in it, and death and Hades gave up the dead which were in them; and they were judged, every one of them according to their deeds. And death and Hades were thrown into the lake of fire. This is the second death, the lake of fire. And if anyone's name was not found written in the book of life, he was thrown into the lake of fire.*

Brandon swallowed hard. "Well, that's scary."

Anton had his head down. He nodded. "I hear that." He looked at Brandon and Justin across the table. "The end of Hebrews chapter nine says that every person is going to die, and after that comes the judgment. That's what we just read about here, and it's going to happen when Jesus comes again. When the Bible talks about the wages of sin being death, death is contrasted with eternal life. The discussion of where physical death comes from is a long one, and it goes back to the first sin. But the passage you just read, Brandon, talks about a second death. You and I can't change the fact that we will die physically. But the question remains: At the judgment, will we receive eternal life, or will we receive the second death, which is called the lake of fire?"

Brandon didn't know what to say.

"What's the criteria?" Anton asked. "Reread verse fifteen."

Brandon skimmed the verses he'd just read. "If our names aren't in the book of life…"

Justin sat back in his seat and stared blankly out the window. Brandon kept his eyes fixed on the Bible.

"Brandon, do you remember the hope I have about my sister?"

Justin wore a puzzled expression. Brandon nodded but didn't say anything. He feared Justin would feel left out since he hadn't been part of that conversation in Devin's basement.

"There's a future resurrection coming," Anton said. "In John five, Jesus told the people of Jerusalem that some would be raised to life, and some would be raised to judgment. I don't know about you, but I want the resurrection of life."

Justin turned away again and crossed his arms over his chest.

Anton cleared his throat. "Brandon, will you please read Matthew chapter eleven, verses twenty-eight through thirty? By the way, this is my favorite passage."

Brandon did so.

> *Come to Me, all who are weary and heavy-laden, and I will give you rest. Take My yoke upon you, and learn from Me, for I am gentle and humble in heart; and you shall find rest for your souls. For My yoke is easy, and My load is light.*

"Jesus knows what it's like," Anton said. "He was tempted in all the ways we are, yet he never sinned. In life, all of us are tempted to outdo each other. We want to look good. We want the praise of people. But with those desires comes the oppressive burden of self-righteousness. It's the old, 'I can do it myself' attitude. Devin was right—the Bible is relevant to all generations of people. But let me ask you: How do you feel about this offer of Jesus to throw off the weight of self-righteousness and simply submit to his will?"

Brandon watched Justin. Something was up. At that moment, Brandon realized what he was doing—by instinctively turning to Justin, he was looking for the approval of someone else, albeit his best friend for as long as he could remember. But what did Brandon think of this offer? He sighed. "You know, Anton," he said slowly. "We've had a lot of conversations about things. Most of them have been you giving a lot of logical answers to my questions."

"I did my best." Anton grinned.

"You did great," Brandon reassured him. "I've thought a lot about it. But I've gotta admit that listening in church this morning and learning about Jesus tonight has caused the biggest difference."

Anton smiled at Brandon, but there was also sadness in his eyes. "That's really cool."

"You seem kind of bothered by that," Brandon said.

Anton shook his head. The sadness faded. "I'm ecstatic at what you just said, Brandon. It just proves the Bible right."

"What? The fact that I am starting to believe this proves the Bible is right? Devin was right when he called that circular reasoning."

"No, it's not that," Anton said. "Check out Romans chapter ten."

Before Brandon began flipping pages, he could sense that Justin was still somehow disconnected from the conversation. He was pushing brownie crumbs around the otherwise empty plate in front of him.

"Verses fourteen through seventeen, please," Anton said. Brandon read the verses out loud.

How then shall they call upon Him in whom they have not believed? And how shall they believe in Him whom they have not heard? And

> *how shall they hear without a preacher? And how shall they preach unless they are sent? Just as it is written, "How beautiful are the feet of those who bring glad tidings of good things!" However, they did not all heed the glad tidings; for Isaiah says, "Lord, who has believed our report?" So faith comes from hearing, and hearing by the word of Christ.*

"There's a progression mentioned here," Anton said. "The end goal is faith."

"Two weeks ago," Brandon said, "I had never heard any of this stuff."

"Right. And verse seventeen says faith comes from what?"

"Hearing," Brandon said.

"Yes, which is what you're proving true. Faith doesn't come from perfectly constructed arguments about the world having a creator. It comes from the gospel of Jesus being taught and heard."

"I see that," Brandon said. "But I probably never would have heard anything you taught us about Jesus tonight if you hadn't done a good job defending the creator concept. And Devin's five reasons to believe the Bible speech didn't hurt either."

"I guess you're right. But I wish I would have spent more time showing you Jesus this entire time, rather than depending on my crafty speeches." He gave a sheepish smile. "I told you I still have a little arrogance in me."

"What are you talking about, man?" Brandon said. "Let's see, the Jesus I've heard and read about today is patient toward jerks." Brandon started counting on his fingers. "Compassionate toward sinners, humble, sacrificial, gentle..." Brandon paused and smiled. "Jesus was a true friend." Then, he pointed to Anton. "See my point?"

CHAPTER TWENTY-EIGHT

THE NEXT MORNING, BRANDON GRABBED HIS BACKPACK AND headed down to the continental breakfast. Justin and Anton were still getting ready. Brandon hadn't slept much, his brain in overdrive after the conversation in the café.

He sat down with some fresh-made waffles and thought more about yesterday's church service. Christians ate plain bread to remember Jesus' body. And the dark fruit juice in the cup reminded them of Jesus' blood. Now, it made a lot more sense to Brandon. Jesus was not just a martyr. He was also a savior. His sacrifice provided life to billions of people. But how many would not take the time to learn about it? How long had Brandon ignored these things? Even worse, how long had he dismissed them as fairytales? It would be easy to justify himself by citing his ignorance, but ignorance was no excuse. Everything he had learned in the past several days had always been available. He simply had never sought more information. Although he'd never searched, others had, and Brandon had been fortunate enough to meet a couple of them. He took a bite of waffle and smiled. Anton was a true friend. Brandon wished he'd had some more time to get to know Devin too. Then, he frowned, thinking of Justin. Something had bothered him last night. What was it? Hopefully, Brandon could talk to him soon.

He allowed his mind to drift again. This time, he thought of the sermon about the shepherd who searched for his single lost sheep. *Searching.* A television hung in the corner of the breakfast room, which aired a morning show. Brandon glanced around. No one else was nearby. He stood, crossed the room, and turned it off.

As he was walking back to his seat, Justin entered, rubbing his eyes. "Whatcha doin'?"

"Nothing," Brandon said, sitting down. "You gonna get some breakfast?"

Justin poured a bowl of cereal. For a few minutes, they ate in silence.

"Anton still showering?" Brandon asked.

"Nah. He's just finished packing up. He said he'll be down after he prays."

"Cool. So, what do you think of Texas?" Brandon asked as he poured some extra syrup on his waffles.

Justin raised his eyebrows. "It's hot," he replied flatly. "Since when have you and I done small talk?"

Brandon shook his head. "Sorry. I really wanna know what you think of all this. The trip, the sights, the car rides, and…"

"And?" Justin said, still looking at Brandon.

"You know, Anton and the stuff we're learning. What do you think? As usual, you've been quiet."

"Just taking it in," Justin said. "I find it interesting, just like you." He took a bite of his cereal.

"I don't think you're seeing it just like me," Brandon said.

"What do you mean?"

"Something bothered you last night at the café. What was it?"

Justin took a deep breath and sighed. "Look, dude, I know you're getting a lot out of this. I don't want to be a buzzkill."

"Just tell me."

"Fine." Justin put down his spoon. "I can tell you're really soaking this up. And yes, I also find it interesting. But there's one major thing that bothers me. And it makes it worse that it doesn't seem to bother you."

"And that is?"

"Let me see if I can do this like Anton. I'll use some questions to help you see what I mean." Justin paused to think. "Why are we on this trip?"

"To get to the Grand Canyon."

"Why do we want to go there?"

"To honor Matt."

"Right," Justin said. "And why aren't we doing this with Matt?"

"You know why."

"And so do you. So why don't you say it?"

"Because Matt's dead!" Brandon blurted, the words seeming to pierce him with their finality. Brandon stared down at his half-eaten breakfast and composed himself.

Justin picked up his spoon. He started pushing the cereal around in his bowl. "That's right. Now, what did Matt think about all this Jesus stuff?"

"The same that we did a couple of weeks ago."

"And what did your Bible say yesterday about dead people?"

"What do you mean?" Brandon asked.

"It said something about names not written in a book." Justin paused and met Brandon's eyes. "And a lake of fire."

A lump grew in Brandon's throat as it hit him. Last night, he had been so caught up in trying to apply what he was learning to himself that he didn't think of the implications. His stomach lurched.

Justin pursed his lips. "Looks like you get it." He stood up and walked out of the room, leaving Brandon to contemplate another question.

Not just Matt. What about Mom?

Brandon sat silently in the front seat next to Anton. When he had studied the map earlier that morning, he could see that today was going to be the longest leg of the trip so far. That was okay with him. It would give him plenty of time to think, and it would be good preparation for their much longer stretch of road after the Grand Canyon to his grandparents in Willows, California.

Justin hadn't said anything since breakfast. Brandon didn't like leaving things unsettled. He resisted the urge to look at Justin in the back seat. He knew if their eyes met, he would feel sick again.

Brandon tried to distract himself by enjoying the sights out the window. But after a few minutes, he felt like he had seen it all. Did the view ever change from San Antonio to El Paso? Nothing but flat, dusty fields. Every now and then, some trees or windmills broke up the monotony. In its own way, it was beautiful—certainly different than Middle Tennessee. Anton tried to start a conversation a couple of times. With each attempt, Brandon replied with the shortest answer he could find, and Justin contributed nothing. Anton eventually gave up, and they drove in unsettled silence. Was Brandon upset at Anton? No. At least, he didn't think so. Perhaps Brandon was upset at himself for getting so wrapped up in all this. If he had just ignored the things Anton had said, then he wouldn't have to care about any of it. But that wasn't right either. Just because he denied something didn't mean it was not true. The fact that he was now on national television proved that point. He wanted to deny what he'd seen in the newspaper outside of New Orleans, to ignore the broadcast he'd seen in the hotel. But ignoring it didn't help the problem. The police already knew he was in Texas, and Justin and Anton were with him. He needed to tell them, but at that moment he'd rather do anything else than that—except maybe have a conversation about the eternal fate of his mom and Matt. He thought of those raindrops from yesterday. He envied them. He hadn't known the bliss of being torn in two directions at once until he experienced being torn in many directions at once.

Brandon had seen hell depicted on television a few times, usually in cartoon form. It involved fire and the devil cackling maniacally, as unsuspecting people dodged jumping flames. But hadn't Anton said the movies got the devil wrong? Maybe the movies got hell wrong too. *Is it really a lake of fire?* Brandon tried to think of a time Anton had even used the word "hell." He couldn't remember. Regardless, images of his mom and Matt being tortured continued to torment him.

Just over four hours later, they stopped for fuel and a late lunch in a town called Fort Stockton. Anton pulled the car into a gas station–restaurant combo. "You guys go on in while I fill up," he said.

The restaurant was a sandwich and soup deli. While Brandon and Justin studied the menu, Brandon said tentatively, "We need to talk more about what you said this morning, but now I've got to talk to you about something else." Justin glanced at the menu board. Brandon could tell he was still upset. Was he mad at Brandon? Anton? Or was it just the facts that bothered him?

"Know what you're getting?" Brandon asked.

Justin nodded. "What do you need to talk to me about?"

Brandon took a deep breath. His heartbeat quickened. "I need to go to the bathroom first." Brandon knew he should tell Justin and Anton that they were wanted by the police. But how would they react? And how would it affect the rest of their trip?

Coming out of the restroom, he saw Anton standing next to Justin at the counter. "Whatcha getting?" Anton asked, handing Brandon his backpack. They all placed their order and sat down.

"So?" Justin asked.

Brandon took a deep breath and shook his head. "Later."

Anton cut his eyes from Brandon to Justin. "Let's check the map while we wait for our food," Anton said.

Brandon fetched the map and spread it out on the table, thankful for the distraction.

"This has been a long four hours, huh?" Anton said. "It wouldn't be so bad if there was something more interesting to look at. Or talk about." Anton met Brandon's eyes.

"I saw my first wild cactus." Brandon gave a weak smile.

Anton pointed at the map. "We are here. It looks like we're about halfway to El Paso. Can we see the rest of the postcards?" Brandon opened the pockets and spread the rest of them out in order: El Paso, Albuquerque, Four Corners Monument, Monument Valley, Flagstaff, and the Grand Canyon. Anton looked at each one. Then, he placed his finger on El Paso. Tracing the red line, north at first, he stopped his finger at each location. "I'm going to guess we have…" Anton thought for a moment, "… roughly fifteen to twenty more hours in the car before we get to the Grand Canyon. If we stop at each location for the night, we have five more nights until we arrive." Leaving the Grand Canyon, he trailed his finger west. "Then, we probably have another fifteen hours on the road until we get to your grandparents."

Genevieve was right. This trip was a lot longer than Brandon had ever envisioned. He regarded the map as a whole and realized they were currently only about halfway between Nashville and Willows, California.

"I don't think we've said it in a few days," Brandon began, "but thank you very much for what you're doing for us."

Anton smiled. "It's no problem, fellas. I'm getting something out of it too. It's been an amazing journey so far."

Justin chuckled. "Even if our car had not broken down, I

doubt we would have made it this far. We were clueless and license-less."

"Hey!" Brandon said. "You didn't have to tell him that!"

"You mean to tell me that you two were going across the country without even knowing how to drive?"

"Oh, we know how to drive," Brandon said. "We made it from Nashville to wherever it was we met you just fine, didn't we?"

"Just fine? You were about to turn back." Anton pointed to the map. "It was in Winona, Mississippi. So, you don't have your licenses. Who gave you permission to go on this—"

"I think we should speed this up," Brandon said, cutting off Anton.

"Really?" Anton said.

The more he thought about it, the more Brandon was itching to get to the Grand Canyon. Now that they were not just in the newspapers, but also on national television, he didn't want to risk being found before they reached Willows. "Let's skip this place." Brandon pointed at Albuquerque. "And this place won't take long." He pointed at Four Corners. "We shouldn't have to stay the night there." Next, he picked up the Monument Valley postcard. "And this place—"

"No," Justin said. "We can't skip that place. Don't you recognize those rocks? They're in every western movie and social studies book."

Anton arched an eyebrow. "Brandon cringes at a cowboy hat. But you watch westerns?"

"Of course not!" Justin said. "My grandma does. But we've gotta see this place. Plus, we might be able to ride in a hot air balloon." He pointed at the balloons on the postcard.

"Sorry, guys," Anton said. "That'll probably break the bank. I've heard those things are expensive."

"Okay, fine. We'll go to the rocks," Brandon said with a shrug. "Tonight, we stay at El Paso. Then, tomorrow, we spend all day in the car. We stop at Four Corners, and we stay here." He pointed to a small town outside Monument Valley. "Then, we should be able to go to Monument Valley on Wednesday. That night, we can stay in Flagstaff. And Thursday..." Brandon smiled at Justin, then flipped the folder over and pointed at the big, bold words Matt had written.

"GC-bound, baby!" Justin exclaimed, smiling back. Matt would finally be honored.

As the server arrived at the table with their food, Brandon replaced the postcards into their pockets and folded up the map. If everything went well, they should be in Willows within a week. They'd be moving fast, which would make it more difficult, Brandon hoped, for the police to track them down. It might just be okay after all.

"Sounds like a plan," Anton said after thanking the server for the food. "We should be in El Paso by sunset tonight."

As Anton bowed his head in a silent prayer, Brandon closed his eyes too. If there was a God out there, he hoped he was looking out for him now.

CHAPTER TWENTY-NINE

OTHER THAN THE TREES STEADILY BEING REPLACED WITH CACTI, and the distant silhouette of mountains appearing on the horizon, the roadside attractions didn't improve much. They were still about two hours away from El Paso. Anton had been playing Motown since their stop in Fort Stockton. Brandon hadn't complained, but he was getting tired of it. The only way to get Anton to turn down the music was to approach a conversation. Still, it took Brandon several minutes to work up the courage to speak. When he did, he just blurted out the question. "Anton, is Matt going to be thrown into the lake of fire?"

"Sorry, what?" Anton lowered the volume.

"Are my mom and my friend going to hell?"

Anton didn't say anything, but Brandon was sure he heard him. Finally, Anton said, "There are three things about that question that comfort me."

That was not the reply Brandon had expected. "How could anything about that question comfort you?" he asked.

"You've got a point." Anton paused. "What I mean is every single person who considers Christianity eventually asks questions about the implications of it. Can you get your Bible out?"

Brandon sighed. "Can you not just tell me the answer? I don't know if I'm ready for another one of these studies."

Anton nodded. "I understand. But I want you to see it from my perspective too. I could just give you an answer, but I don't want you to hear it from me. I want you to see it…?"

"In the Bible," Brandon finished, getting Anton's point.

"Yesterday, it seemed you were quite interested in what the Bible says about Jesus. Don't you want to read for yourself what it says about this question?"

"I guess so." He pulled the Bible out of his backpack. "Where to?"

"Hebrews chapter five, verses eight and nine."

While Brandon flipped the pages of the old book, he marveled at Anton's encyclopedic knowledge of the Bible. Certainly, not all Christians knew the Bible as well as Anton, or Devin for that matter. Otherwise, there wouldn't be so many of them who were hypocrites. Brandon found the passage and read.

> *Although He was a Son, He learned obedience from the things which He suffered. And having been made perfect, He became to all those who obey Him the source of eternal salvation.*

"This passage is talking about Jesus," Anton said. "And it says that Jesus brings eternal salvation to whom?"

"Those who obey him," Brandon replied. He stole a glance behind him to find Justin looking out the window, presumably not paying any attention. Brandon knew he could hear them.

"When someone learns and believes this, what's the proper response?" Anton asked.

"I guess, to obey him?" Brandon said.

"You've got to break that habit."

"What habit?"

"Did you, or did you not, just read the truth from the Bible?"

"I did," Brandon admitted.

"Then, why are you guessing? If it's true, then you can say it with confidence, can't you?"

Brandon shrugged. "I guess so." He couldn't help but smile a little at that.

"You're hopeless," Anton said with a chuckle. "So, if I follow through with this and obey him, what should I expect? What does the verse say exactly?"

"Eternal salvation."

"Because that's offered to whom?"

"Those who obey him. Are we going in circles here?"

"No," Anton said. "We're emphasizing a point. By believing this with all my heart and following through, what am I implying about those who don't obey?"

Brandon looked down at the verse and thought for a moment. "That they don't have eternal salvation?"

"Let me give you a different example. Let's pretend we stop the car in a few minutes to stretch. We wander away from the road a bit to get some fresh air."

Brandon surveyed the barren landscape around them. "I'm not sure if I'm ready to stop the car out here," he said. "What if it doesn't start back up?"

"We'd probably fry in the sun. Just bear with me. We wander out there—" Anton pointed at a dusty field with a few cacti and trees, "—and Justin and I get bitten by a snake. You panic and get us into the car, and you drive us to the hospital, however long that would take. We've also got to assume I pass out, 'cause there's no way I'm letting you drive my car now that I know you don't have your license." He winked knowingly at Brandon.

Brandon turned to see Justin still staring out the window, but his face betrayed a hint of a grin.

"Okay," Anton said. "We get to the hospital, and the doctor tells you that Justin and I have to take an anti-venom, or we will die from the snake bites. Justin believes the doctor and gratefully accepts it. But for some silly reason, I reject the doctor's advice and don't accept the anti-venom. Now, what is Justin doing by accepting the medicine?"

"I'm not sure I'm following," Brandon said.

"By agreeing with the doctor and accepting the antidote, Justin is also agreeing with the implications—that since I don't accept it, I will die."

"But it's true," Brandon said. "And Justin shouldn't prevent that from saving his own life."

"My point exactly," Anton said. "And if Justin somehow thought it was compassionate to deny the anti-venom for the sake of those who didn't know about it or didn't want it, would the doctor side with Justin, or would he still urge us to take the medicine?"

Brandon understood Anton's point.

"We should be motivated to follow Jesus for many reasons," Anton said. "His love, his compassion, his sacrifice. We should also be motivated by our sorrow. Why did Jesus die?"

"For our sins," Brandon said.

"Yes, and if we had never sinned, then Jesus would never have had to do what?"

Brandon thought about that for a moment. He felt a prick in his heart when he understood Anton's point. "If I had never sinned, Jesus never would have had to die."

Anton frowned. "Same here. My sins also put him on the cross. We should talk about that more later. My point right now is that this fact should motivate us to accept his forgiveness. Jesus also talks about a coming judgment. I think a healthy fear of that judgment is a good motivator. The Bible says our names must be in the book of life if we want to avoid the lake of fire. But if we follow through, what are we saying about those who don't? You don't have to answer that. I know you know. Otherwise, you wouldn't be asking this question."

Brandon pursed his lips in thought.

"Turn to Second Corinthians, chapter five. When you get there, read verses ten and eleven."

Brandon found the passage and read.

> *For we must all appear before the judgment seat of Christ, that each one may be recompensed for his deeds in the body, according to what he has done, whether good or bad. Therefore knowing the fear of the Lord, we persuade men, but we are made manifest to God; and I hope that we are made manifest also in your consciences.*

"But here are the things that...comfort me, for the lack of a better word," Anton said, his eyes still on the near-empty road. "Number one: I will not be the judge of your mom's, Matt's, or anyone's soul on the day of judgment." Anton paused while Brandon considered that fact. "Number two: Jesus will be the judge of everyone on that day. That means I don't have to feel the burden of other people's decisions. But it also motivates me to not just accept Jesus' message myself, but also try to tell others about it—like you, and like Justin." Anton glanced up at the rearview mirror. He smiled. Brandon wondered if Justin had met his eyes. "And the third thing, which is the most important one for us to understand, is: God will only do the right thing. That's always true, and it will be true on that day."

There was silence for a few minutes. Brandon wondered what Justin thought about all this: Was this helping or hurting? Anton was right. Even though this was a challenging topic, leaving the decision to Jesus did somehow comfort him.

Anton broke his train of thought. "I know what Jesus requires for those who want to live with him in glory. It's plainly taught in the Scriptures. But I never knew your mom or Matt. Let's just leave it with God, okay?"

This seemed like too easy of a solution to Brandon, but he couldn't think of any reason not to agree with Anton. The things Brandon had learned about the creator, the Bible, and

Jesus were starting to make sense. Why question it all as soon as something Jesus said hurt?

"Plus, there's one more question to consider," Anton said.

"What's that?" Brandon asked.

"No matter where your mom and Matt are now—" Anton looked away from the road for long enough to peer into Brandon's eyes, "—no matter how Jesus will judge them on that day, would they encourage you to follow Jesus, or would they tell you to reject his offer of salvation?"

The mountains were much closer now. Soon, after a quick dinner at a fast-food joint, they could see signs of city life, the mountains serving as a backdrop. By the time they reached El Paso, the mountains were drenched in the same orange hue that had coated the Alamo the previous evening. It was a welcome burst of color after hours of nothing but brown scrubland. "Let's see if we can get up there," Anton said, pointing ahead. He did his best to navigate around the city to get to a good vantage point. A half-hour later, they were following signs up Scenic Drive, anticipating the views that were promised.

They arrived at a small parking lot and stepped out of the car. They had known they were not going to be disappointed on the drive up, but nothing really prepared them for what they could see from up there. For miles, the land stretched before them. In the far distance lay more mountains, much like the ones behind them. The bottom of the hills yielded to a bustling metropolis. "Let me see the map," Justin said. Brandon retrieved it and handed it to him. He spread it out over the hood of Anton's car and studied it. Then, he turned and pointed. "These are called the Franklin Mountains; they reach all the way into New Mexico. And from here we can see two countries."

"Really?" Brandon asked. "Is that Mexico?"

"I've never seen another country before," Anton said, taking in the sight. "And look at those mountains and sunset." He paused. "God truly is an artist."

"It's amazing," Brandon said. If God had not created this, then what other options were there? No, this was not the result of a series of cosmic accidents. Someone thought about it and had decided to show it to Brandon at that moment. "It is amazing," he repeated.

For several minutes, they looked on in silence, leaning on the railing. As the sun dipped further into the horizon, the lights of the city started turning on one-by-one. It was a nice reward for such a long day in the car.

"Hey," Brandon said to Justin, trying to sound casual. He knew he had failed. "Um, when was the last time you called your cousin?"

"I'm not sure. A few days ago, I guess," Justin said, also trying to sound casual, but Brandon saw a flash of panic in his eyes before he concealed it.

"A few days ago? Let me guess—the last time was at the mechanic's shop before we left with Anton."

"It was about then," he admitted sheepishly. "Why?"

Brandon cleared his throat and glanced over at Anton. "Just wondering." Anton got the hint and wandered away, apparently taken in by the sights further down the sidewalk. Once he was out of earshot, Brandon said, "I think your grandma told the police that you're missing."

"What?!"

"Shh!"

Quietly, Justin said, "What do you mean? How do you know?"

"When we were in New Orleans, my picture was in the newspaper. It was a national one—not just a New Orleans one."

Justin's draw dropped. "What did it say? And why are you just now telling me this?"

"It said the police were searching for me. Like a runaway or something. I kind of thought if I ignored it, it would work itself out." Brandon laughed at his hypocrisy. "I figured the Grand Junction people would call your grandma, and your grandma would call your cousin, and, well…I don't know."

"But I never even told my cousin you were with me. He was just supposed to vouch for me."

"Oh—I didn't realize that."

"You said I shouldn't mention your name, remember? You said you hadn't exactly worked things out with the Grand Junction people. What did you tell them?"

Brandon shrugged. "Nothing. I just left. The police said I'm old enough to make my own decisions. Plus, I assumed they'd figure it out and be happy. One less mouth to feed. I know that was a stupid thing to do now. But I just kept ignoring it."

"What are we going to do?"

"I don't know," Brandon said. "It gets worse."

"How so?"

"The other day, at the Austin hotel, we were on the news—all three of us." Brandon cringed.

"On TV?"

"It was footage from the library parking lot in Dallas. Remember when you, Devin, and Anton went to the police station in Dallas to look for me?" Justin slowly nodded. "You said they changed their tune after you submitted the missing person paper with my name on it. That's what must have tipped them off that we were in the area."

"Hang on—you're not pinning this on me, are you? How was I to know? Of course I went to the police—"

"No, I'm not blaming you. Don't have a cow." Brandon paused, then said, "The news made it sound like Anton kidnapped us."

"No!" Justin said, not bothering to hush his voice.

Brandon looked warily in the direction of Anton and nodded silently.

"Hey, fellas," Anton called from a distance. "We should probably start looking for a place to stay for the night." Only a sliver of the sun remained above the horizon.

"You've gotta tell him," Justin urged.

"I will."

"When?"

"I don't know."

"He'll want to go to the police and sort things out."

"I know," Brandon said, fidgeting with his fingers. "But then the police are gonna send us home." He paused, regarding the vista that lay before them. "Then what?"

CHAPTER THIRTY

"I DON'T UNDERSTAND WHY WE SUDDENLY NEED TO RUSH," ANTON said.

"Now we're this close, I'm getting anxious to get there, you know?" Brandon said. Justin gave him a sideways glance across the hotel room.

Anton grabbed his dirty clothes and stuffed them into his bag. "I know this trip is all about getting to the Grand Canyon, but can't we at least stop and smell the roses? What was on the El Paso postcard?"

"Just another cityscape. No rodeo this time," Brandon said.

"Okay," Anton said. "Let's take some time on the road, at least. It'll be another eight hours or so in the car today."

After a quick breakfast, they checked out of the hotel and headed north. An hour later, Justin pointed to a sign. "Check it out! New Mexico is just a few miles away." He looked back at Brandon. "Is that four states so far?"

"And later, it'll be three more."

"Sweet."

Without warning, Brandon's body jolted forward, his seat-belt suddenly taut. His body lurched to the side, and something slammed against his head. As if moving in slow motion, he felt nothing but saw everything. Justin braced himself against the dashboard. Anton struggled to get the car under control. The world passed across the windshield sideways. The car continued to skid, making a horrible screeching sound, until it slipped off the road onto the dirt. Dust rose up outside Brandon's window, and the car slowed to a stop.

For a moment, the only sounds were tiny stones hitting the side of the car and everyone taking in deep breaths. Then, the ringing in Brandon's head started.

Anton turned to Justin and said something. He turned around and said something to Brandon. Slowly, the ringing gave way to a muffled voice. Anton repeated himself. "Are you okay?"

Brandon blinked back at him. That's all he could do. He looked out the window. "What happened?" he finally managed. He tried to figure it out himself, but the only thing he could see out of the car was a dust cloud.

"Anybody hurt?" Anton asked.

Brandon's head throbbed. He reached up to find the source of the pain and felt a warm, sticky patch of matted hair. He pulled back his hand to find blood on his fingertips.

Anton said something else, but Brandon couldn't concentrate. Dizzy and confused, his mind couldn't decide what to focus on—the ringing, the pain, or doing anything about it. His door opened, and someone reached over his lap to unlatch his seatbelt. Brandon blinked again, and Anton's face was inches from his. "Can you hear me?" Brandon nodded. "Can you stand?" Anton reached between the front seats to retrieve his glasses. He ducked out of the car, and Brandon swung his legs to the ground. Anton helped him up, and he had to brace himself against the car. "Stay here," Anton said.

Brandon looked around to see Justin leaning against the hood. He seemed fine. Remarkably, so did the car. The dust was settling, and Brandon watched Anton run toward the road. Just past Anton, Brandon saw the wreckage—two cars twisted together, smoke billowing from one of them. Brandon spotted another car nearby. It was also totaled. The image of Matt's Chrysler flashed into Brandon's mind. He rubbed his eyes, still confused.

Justin took off after Anton, leaving Brandon still leaning against the car. The engine made a popping sound as it cooled off in the desert heat. Brandon watched as Anton and Justin helped people out of the other cars. The ringing in Brandon's head intensified. He vomited. He rubbed his eyes again. Then, he heard sirens. *That was fast,* he thought. *Or was it? How long have we been here?* Attempting to clear his foggy head, he blinked a few more times and looked back at the road. An ambulance had backed up to the wreckage, and some paramedics were putting someone on a stretcher. Another paramedic was pointing and saying something to Anton.

Justin left the scene and ran toward Brandon. "Come on. They want to look at your head."

Brandon blinked.

"Dizzy?" Justin said. "Here." He lifted one of Brandon's arms and helped him walk toward the road.

"Wait!" Brandon stopped walking.

"What?" Justin said. "What hurts?"

"Nothing. It's just I don't want to talk to the ambulance people."

"Why not? You're delirious. Come on."

"No. They'll take my name, won't they?"

"I don't know. So what?" Then, he understood. "Oh, I see."

"I'll be fine," Brandon instinctively touched his sore head with his free hand.

"No, I'm taking you to them. They need to look at you. I've got your back, dude." Justin helped him walk to one of the ambulances, where a paramedic was waiting. Anton was still helping the other two paramedics.

"Sit him here," the paramedic said to Justin. She gestured to the back step of the ambulance. "What's your name?"

"Matt," Justin answered for him.

Brandon caught a knowing look from Justin.

"Hello, Matt. My name is Rachel. It looks like you took quite a hit. We'll get that cleaned and wrapped up soon, okay?" The paramedic started testing Brandon's reflexes, while his mind drifted. She shone a flashlight in his eyes. After a few more tests, Rachel said, "Can you hear me?"

"Uh-huh."

"Here, hold onto this." Rachel guided Brandon's hand to a handlebar. Then, she jumped up in the back to retrieve some supplies. A few moments later, his head was bandaged up. Rachel turned to Justin. "He has a minor concussion and will likely feel sick for a couple of hours. If his symptoms do not worsen, he can sleep if he wants to. His head doesn't need any stitches, but here." She handed Justin some aspirin and some gauze. "Change the bandage as needed. If his nausea doesn't go away by this evening, take him to a hospital to see a doctor." Justin agreed. The paramedic explained a few more things, then left to help the others.

"Hey, Matt," Justin said with a wink. "You're just paranoid."

Brandon groaned.

"Looks like I'll be your nurse." He shook the aspirin package.

Brandon forced a smile. "Aren't nurses supposed to be pretty?" He was thankful his friend had his back, even if it did turn out to be unnecessary.

A moment later, Anton joined them. "You okay?" he asked.

Justin filled him in on what they learned from the paramedic. "What's going on over there?"

Anton hung his head. "Looks like the two kids are going to be fine. But they're going home without a mother tonight." A tear slipped down his cheek.

"What happened?" Brandon asked.

"The two cars in front of us had an accident," Anton said. "Not sure what caused it. We barely missed slamming into them. But the driver behind us didn't react fast enough. Can you walk?" Brandon stood up. Anton tossed the car keys to Justin. "I'm pretty sure the car is fine. Go ahead and start it and get the AC going. I'll join you in a minute. I want to see if I can pray with any of these folks."

Brandon and Justin slowly made their way back to the car. Anton was right; the car started just fine, and the air conditioning felt terrific. Although he still found it difficult to concentrate, as Brandon watched Anton go from person to person, he marveled at his friend's living faith.

A few minutes later, the police arrived. An officer emerged from his car and approached Anton. Brandon's heart quickened.

"Don't worry," Justin said. "They probably just want a statement about what happened. As Anton said, he doesn't even know what caused the accident, so this'll be quick." All Brandon could do was trust that Justin was right.

"Wake up," Anton said. "We're almost there."

After lunch and some medicine, Brandon had felt much better, but he was very sleepy. He opened his eyes, but everything was still dark. He started to panic, thinking his injury had worsened, but then he realized it was dark because it was nighttime. "What time is it?"

"Nine-thirty," Anton said. "We're not going to make it to Four Corners today, but we'll stay nearby. We can be there first thing in the morning."

Brandon sat upright and rubbed his eyes. His vision had cleared, and the only discomfort was the bandage that had dried to his head. He looked forward to a shower.

After checking into a hotel in Shiprock, New Mexico, Anton

gave the key to Justin and sent them up while he ventured out to find some food.

By the time Anton returned, Brandon had showered and replaced his bandage.

"Refreshed?" Anton asked.

"Much better," Brandon said. "And I'm not tired anymore!"

"Excellent." Before they ate, Anton led an extra-long prayer, thanking God for preserving their lives. He also prayed for those who fared much worse by the crash. Brandon thought about the kids that had lost a mother. Anton ended the prayer with thanks for the future resurrection.

A few minutes and a few bites later, Brandon said, "You never finished telling me about this resurrection stuff."

Anton wiped his mouth with a napkin. He touched his goatee in thought before saying, "Romans one, verse four, claims that God declared some major things with Jesus' resurrection." He took a bite of his chicken sandwich, but Brandon could tell he was still thinking. "For a couple of reasons, the resurrection of Jesus is the most important claim Christianity makes. First, it's unique among religions. Most other religions have a story on how their god or gods were involved in bringing the world to order. But of all the founders of religions, Jesus is the only one still alive. In fact, he proved his religion true by his resurrection. Second, since Christianity is based on the resurrection of Jesus—a historical event that can be proven—it remains the most credible religion of all time. Third, if the resurrection is false, it doesn't matter how much else of Christianity is true. If the resurrection is a fairytale, Christianity offers nothing to anyone, and it should be thrown away. The apostle Paul put it this way: 'If Christ has not been raised, your faith is worthless; you are still in your sins. We are of all men most to be pitied.'"

"Those are some big claims," Brandon said. "What do you think?" he asked Justin.

Justin took a drink of his soda. "What proof is there?"

Anton smiled as if that was exactly what he wanted Justin to ask. "When people claim things, it's not other people's job to disprove it. The person who claimed it has the burden of proof on his shoulders." Anton paused. "But we know each other well enough now that you're not just going to believe something is true just because I say it is. I was just setting this up." Anton took another bite while he thought. "All right, I know where to begin. Let's go back to why people killed Jesus in the first place."

"He was disrupting the religious status quo," Brandon said.

Anton nodded. "Neither the Jews nor the Romans wanted this disruption anymore. After he was killed, Roman soldiers were stationed at his tomb. The tomb where they laid Jesus was public, and they didn't want any funny business going on. They even sealed a huge stone across the opening to ensure no one could get in—or out. We will read about a lot of this later." Anton showed his greasy hands to them. "But let's not get your Bible all dirty. Anyway, the Bible says the soldiers who had been stationed at his tomb went to the Jewish priests to report that Jesus had risen from the dead. Now, you probably remember when we read John eighteen and nineteen that the Jews and Romans were not friends. They didn't work together. So, why do you suppose the Roman soldiers reported this to the Jewish priests, instead of their superiors?"

Brandon shrugged.

"Their job was to guard the tomb," Justin said. "But they failed. They would have been fired."

"You know that's right," Anton said. "There would have been severe consequences. But it would have been more than losing their jobs—they likely would have lost their lives. They knew the Jews had a vested interest in all this, and it paid off literally. The priests bribed the soldiers to keep their mouths shut. But it didn't work. Somehow, news got out that Jesus had risen from the dead. Think about that. After everything Jesus had endured—the beatings, the nails, the blood loss, the dehydration, everything. Still, people were saying he was walking around? Brandon, remember what we discussed the other night in Devin's basement?"

Brandon thought back and remembered the story of Anton's sister.

"The Bible says Jesus' resurrection is like the first crop you see after planting seeds in a field," Anton said. "It's vitally important that Christians believe in the resurrection of Jesus. But God did not leave us without evidence. The New Testament is full of witnesses who saw him alive after his death. And once they saw him, they couldn't keep quiet about it. I'd guess you and I wouldn't be able to either." Anton took a drink before continuing. "This rumor was now threatening to destroy everything the Jews and Romans thought they had accomplished by killing Jesus a few days prior. It was in their highest interest to discredit this claim as soon as possible. If some celebrity died in the public square today, and then suddenly people started claiming he had risen from the dead, what's the fastest way authorities could prove them wrong?" He took another drink.

"Take the news cameras to the graveyard, I guess," Justin said.

"And do what?" Anton said.

"Dig up the body and show the world."

"That's right!" Anton said, pointing his drink bottle at Justin. "We think that to be pretty disgraceful. We're taught to respect the dead, which is a good thing. But the Romans wouldn't have thought twice about disgracing a body—especially the body of someone they had killed as a criminal. They could have stopped the spread of Christianity right then and there. They were happy to display his death on a public road. Why not display his body in the middle of town to prove he had not risen from the dead?"

"They didn't have it," Brandon said.

"They didn't have it," Anton repeated. "And they never would, despite their best efforts. In addition to that evidence, we also see the conversion of thousands of people in the book of Acts. In Acts chapter two, it says that thousands of devout Jews came to Jerusalem. After spending time with men who were eyewitnesses of the resurrection, they left Jerusalem as devout Christians. In that context, of course, Christianity was not a contrasting religion. It was simply God's next step of redemption."

Brandon gave a puzzled look.

"Let me try to explain that quickly. In the Old Testament Scriptures, God told his people that he was going to do something big in the future with his chosen one—his Christ. He would take away people's sins, he would establish a kingdom, he would welcome people from every nation to be part of his family. Christ would come from Abraham's lineage, which meant he would be a Jew. He would be David's descendant. The promises kept coming throughout the ebb and flow of Israel's faithfulness until the Old Testament Scriptures closed. After the Israelites had read Malachi—the last book of the Old Testament —they were left wondering when God would keep his promises. Jesus, of course, fulfilled them. So, if someone was a devout Jew, and they learned what Jesus did, it only made sense to become a devout Christian. But still, there were many Jews who didn't believe in Jesus and his resurrection. And it wasn't easy to go against your family's beliefs, especially in that culture. The point is this: A few weeks after Jesus' death, in the same city where he died and was buried, thousands of people converted to Christianity from Judaism. If there was ever a time and a location for skeptics to be satisfied, it was then and there. Yet, their skepticism gave way to belief."

Anton paused. Brandon and Justin continued their dinner. When they offered no questions or objections, Anton continued. "The disciples of Jesus were so convinced of his resurrection that they were willing to die for their faith. For years, critics of Christianity have been claiming the disciples made it all up for fame, money, or whatever. Their faith in the resurrection brought them nothing but trouble. Not only did they not get rich off it, but most of them lost everything. Even so, they continued to believe and profess. For instance, in Acts seven, a disciple named Stephen was killed. He was the first person to die for his faith in the resurrected Jesus. He had plenty of opportunities to recant, yet he continued to confess until his dying breath. In Acts twelve, Herod killed one of the original apostles. For the rest of the New Testament, apostles and other disciples were imprisoned, beaten, and killed. We don't have a single record of any of them going back on their claim. Tell me, if you had made something up, and the law threatened you because of it, would you keep spreading the lie, or would you eventually swallow your pride and admit you made it up?"

"It wouldn't make sense to keep spreading the lie," Brandon said.

"What if they were brainwashed?" Justin asked.

Anton lifted an eyebrow. "Are you serious, or are you grasping at straws here?"

"It's possible, right?" Justin said.

"Sure, it's possible," Anton agreed. "But completely unlikely. When we are searching for truth, we are looking for the information that best explains reality. The Old Testament prophesied that his body would not see corruption. Jesus himself predicted his resurrection. Then, mentally stable people started claiming they saw him—from all pockets of civilization. Then, more mentally stable people evaluated the evidence and also believed. When people are brainwashed, it usually happens in private, cult-like meetings. But these people were converted in public squares after surveying evidence."

"Hmm," Justin said.

"It gets better. Brainwashing is successful among vulnerable people who are predisposed to believe. We also see Jesus' enemies believe in his resurrection. The best example is a man named Saul. This is the same guy that I've talked about who was also named Paul."

"Huh?" Brandon said.

"I know it's confusing. A lot of people in the Bible were known by multiple names. But we don't need to get into that now. This Saul guy was there when Stephen was killed in Acts seven. In the next couple of chapters, Saul led a frontal assault on the church of Christ. He dragged men and women off to prison. Educated at the highest levels, his plan was to stamp out any claim that this so-called Christ had risen from the dead. He was on his way to a place called Damascus to arrest some Christians. Then, he himself witnessed the resurrected Christ. He did a one-eighty in his beliefs, and instead of arresting believers in Damascus, he ended up preaching about the Christ, trying to convince others to believe. Again, this stuff didn't happen in dark corners in the first century. It publicly turned the world upside down, and the religious and political leaders didn't know how to deal with it, except kill anyone they could find who believed it. But even that didn't stop the truth from spreading." Anton wiped his hands and his mouth with a napkin. "Now, shall we get the Bible out and look at some of this?"

Brandon cleaned his hands and fetched the Bible. They spent the next half-hour reading. In chapters twenty-seven and twenty-eight of Matthew, Brandon and Justin learned more about Jesus' death, burial, and resurrection. Those chapters also showed the great efforts the Romans took to keep the resurrection quiet. It didn't work. In First Corinthians fifteen, they read how Paul dealt with a skeptical audience. In addition to providing further proof of the resurrection, the passage also gave implications of the resurrection being false. Brandon read that the Christian hope is entirely wrapped up in the bodily resurrection of Jesus. If the resurrection was false, Christianity was a hoax, and Christians were still in their sins. "Not only is Jesus' resurrection worth believing in," Anton said, "but so is our future resurrection. Remember that Jesus said one day all people will be raised—some to a resurrection of judgment, others to a resurrection of life. Which one would you like?"

Justin was silent.

"The resurrection of life sounds pretty good to me," Brandon said.

"We need to get to bed soon," Anton said. "Big day tomorrow. Plus, you need to recover." He leaned over to look at Brandon's bandage. "But before we do, I want you to read one more passage."

Brandon picked up the Bible, readying himself to turn to wherever Anton directed.

"Acts seventeen, verse twenty-nine."

Brandon found the verse and read.

> *Being then the offspring of God, we ought not to think that the Divine Nature is like gold or silver or stone, an image formed by the art and thought of man.*

"Remember the former terrorist, Saul?"

"Mm-hmm," Brandon said.

"That's him preaching here." Anton pointed at the passage. "He's guiding their minds through a logical process. Point number one is the God who created the world isn't some god you can form out of stone or wood. Of course, we live in the twentieth century. We're too sophisticated to bow down to statues." Anton held his nose high in the air in mock conceit. "But are we really? We fool around in life, creating gods in our own image all the time. Money, sex, accomplishments. And if we don't say it out loud, by our actions, we're constantly thinking, 'God would never punish someone like me,' or 'I know I've done something wrong, but at least I'm not like so-and-so.' When we create gods from our own imaginations, we're just as bad as the people Paul was preaching to on this occasion. In other words, we ought to listen to what he has to say just as much as they did."

Brandon swallowed and leaned back. He considered how Anton had also taken him and Justin through a logical process. Creation demands a creator. Design requires a designer. That designer must be relational and loving. The love of the creator was best exemplified in the death of Jesus. The death of Jesus offers forgiveness. The resurrection of Jesus provides hope. Was Brandon ready for whatever was coming next? What was coming?

"Brandon, Justin," Anton looked at them in turn. "How would you describe your attitude toward Christianity when we first met?"

"Indifferent," Justin said.

"Pssh. Hostile," Brandon admitted.

"What about now?" Anton asked.

Brandon looked down in thought.

"Indifferent," Justin said.

"Really?" Brandon said. "You can't possibly—"

"Yes, I can," Justin said defensively.

"Have you not listened to anything Anton has taught us?"

"I have, and I'm indifferent to it. What's it to you?"

"But you're the one who told me to listen to him. You're the one who told me to have an open mind. Where's your open mind?"

Anton held out a hand to stop Brandon. "Justin, thank you for your honesty. Brandon, Christianity isn't something you can force someone to believe in. Instead of focusing on his answer, let's hear yours. What do you think of Jesus?"

Brandon reached up to run his fingers through his hair but stopped short when he remembered his bandage. He then realized his head was beginning to throb again. He wondered if it was from his small outburst. Anton was right. Brandon needed to stop worrying about what others thought. What did he think? Finally admitting there was a creator lifted a burden off his shoulders. Now, he felt a new weight: sin, which brought the pain of death. He had been surrounded by death for too long. Even today, he had been within inches of it. Jesus was willing to take it all away—worry, sin, death. The creator indeed was relational and loving. He looked up at Anton. "I believe him."

Anton smiled. "Now, read verse thirty."

Brandon leaned in and read.

Therefore having overlooked the times of ignorance, God is now declaring to men that all everywhere should repent.

"What does God demand of you?" Anton asked.

"I need to repent," Brandon said. "What's that mean?"

"It means you need to die."

Brandon widened his eyes. "Excuse me?"

"You need to die to sin and your own righteousness. The other day, we read my favorite passage. It's where Jesus says, 'Come to me, all who are weary and heavy-laden, and I will give you rest.' I know what it's like. We walk around thinking we're good enough. But eventually, we come to grips with the fact that we're not, and we need help. Help is not found from within. It's from without. But to accept Jesus' help, the Bible says you need to deny yourself and take up your cross."

"Meaning?" Brandon asked.

"What did the cross mean to Jesus?"

"He died on it."

"Yep. And you need to die on yours. Thankfully, not physically. Jesus already did that for you. You need to let go of your own way of doing things and let Jesus instruct your way." Anton went silent to give Brandon a moment to think. Justin stood and headed to the bathroom. Brandon couldn't tell if that was an act of kindness to give him a moment with Anton, or if Justin was upset, or if he simply needed to go. Again, Brandon had to shake the thought out of his head. Right now, Justin's opinions shouldn't matter to him. What Anton was saying was that Brandon needed to personally commit.

"This is a big decision," Anton said. "Don't make it lightly. And it might be best if you don't decide on the day you received a concussion. But even that should add some weight to your decision. The three of us came this close to a fatal accident today." Anton held his fingers a half-inch apart. "But I don't think you need a reminder of the frailty of life. Instead, I'll leave you with a different reminder. It's in the next verse. Can you read that?"

"Okay."

Because He has fixed a day in which He will judge the world in righteousness through a Man whom He has appointed, having furnished proof to all men by raising Him from the dead.

"The logical process is this: God is alive and well; he declares all people should repent, because he will judge us all. How do we know? The proof is in the resurrection of Jesus." Anton and Brandon locked eyes for another moment before Anton stood up and began cleaning up their food containers.

Brandon also stood to get ready for bed. He closed the Bible. He recalled the first time he had picked it up, sitting on the stone bridge on the way to Genevieve's house, when he thought it was a poetry book. He laughed at the memory. How far he had come with this Bible—both physically and spiritually. Was he following in the footsteps of his father—his dad? Indeed, this was what Dean wanted. And how cool would it be to be able to identify with his grandparents in this way when—if—he met them? But what did Brandon want? He readily admitted he wanted the blessings Jesus offered him, but it wasn't as easy as holding out his hand. He needed to commit.

He looked across the room. Anton was reclining on his hotel bed, reading his own copy of the Bible. Brandon had not wondered until then why Anton never used his Bible in their studies. It was likely because most of the studies began in the car, and Brandon's Bible was always at hand. There was probably another reason, such as the benefit of having Brandon read stuff for himself. Anton seemed wise beyond his years. Without him, Brandon would be rotting away in Grand Junction, likely being torn apart by his grief, and ignorant of the man who died for him and the God who loved him. The thought of that pricked his heart. Anton was right that if Brandon had not sinned, there would be no reason for Jesus to die. There was no denying that Brandon had rejected God's riches at Christ's expense. He had betrayed his creator.

Justin came out of the bathroom. "What's the plan for tomorrow?"

"We should be able to get to Four Corners first thing," Anton said. "Then, we'll go see your rocks." He smiled.

"Why are they *my* rocks?"

"You were adamant about seeing them," Brandon said. "I didn't know you paid that much attention in social studies."

"I didn't. You've just gotta admit they're cool."

"They are," Anton said.

Something else was tugging at Brandon's heart. Not only had Brandon betrayed Jesus; he had also betrayed Anton. Justin was right. He needed to tell him.

Maybe tomorrow.

CHAPTER THIRTY-ONE

BRANDON'S HEAD POUNDED AS THEY GOT INTO THE CAR THE NEXT morning. He wondered how much of it had to do with the concussion, and how much was due to having barely slept. The resurrection of Jesus. The coming judgment. The lake of fire. His mom. Matt. Justin's reaction. Repentance. The Grand Canyon. His grandparents. It was almost too much. But he'd heard the paramedic tell Justin that inability to focus was a short-term effect of a concussion. "Hey, nurse!" Brandon called. "Hand me some of that medicine."

It didn't take them long on the road before they started seeing signs for the Four Corners Monument. "Man, this place is in the middle of nowhere," Justin said. They arrived just as the monument was opening, which was a good thing, according to the keeper. Usually, the crowds showed up an hour later. As it was, they were the only three there.

The monument comprised a large circle divided into four parts by two intersecting perpendicular lines. At the center of the circle, the lines crossed at the exact point where the boundaries of four states met. As Anton continued speaking with the keeper, Justin hung back and let Brandon be the first to step into the four corners. He moved forward, crossing over the "NEW MEXICO" sign. A couple of more steps brought him inches away from the middle. One more step unceremoniously added three more to the list of states he had visited on this trip, and in his life. He was now standing in New Mexico, Colorado, Utah, and Arizona at the same time. Etched in the ground beneath him were the words: "FOUR STATES HERE MEET IN FREEDOM UNDER GOD." The irony was not lost on him. As he stood there, not only was he in four of the free United States under God, but he was also in four states of distress, feeling imprisoned: Die to self, or forget it all? Tell Anton about the news report and risk the entire trip, or wait just a little longer? He blew out his cheeks and stepped into Colorado to give the other guys their time in the middle.

A few minutes later, they were back in the car, Justin in the front with Anton. "Well, that was an interesting ten minutes," he said.

"It was a hot ten minutes," Brandon said. "And it's only just past eight."

"The guy at the monument told me it's supposed to get over a hundred and ten degrees today," Anton said. "He said something about frying an egg on a rock. We'll stock up on water and snacks at the next gas station." Anton pulled the car back onto the road, and they crossed over into Arizona. The sky was clear, and they could see for miles over the plains. "We'll be there in a couple of hours."

To pass the time in the backseat, Brandon pulled the Bible out of his bag. He opened the cover and read the inscription once more.

To our beloved Dean,

Congratulations on the best decision of your life. May the words of life guide you home. We are so proud of you.

Love,

Mom and Dad
June 3, 1978

Again, Brandon was left to wonder what Dean had done in June 1978 that made his parents so proud. Now, he guessed it had something to do with committing to follow Jesus. How proud would Dean be of Brandon if he knew how far he had come? But there was something else written under the inscription he hadn't noticed before. It was a passage of Scripture.

John 8:31–32

How had he missed that? Perhaps he had seen it before, but his ignorance kept him from realizing it was a Bible passage. Brandon flipped until he found it. He read silently.

Jesus therefore was saying to those Jews who had believed Him, "If you abide in My word, then you are truly disciples of Mine; and you shall know the truth, and the truth shall make you free."

Abide. That seemed like another commitment word. But the payoff sounded worth it. *Truth. Freedom. Freedom from what?* Brandon continued reading and found Jesus' original audience had the same question.

They answered Him, "We are Abraham's offspring, and have never yet been enslaved to anyone; how is it that You say, 'You shall become free'?" Jesus answered them, "Truly, truly, I say to you, everyone who commits sin is the slave of sin. And the slave does not remain in the house forever; the son does remain forever. If therefore the Son shall make you free, you shall be free indeed."

Brandon closed the Bible and returned it to his bag. He picked up Dean's box and opened it. Staring back at him were his father's dog tags. "BASON." "CHRISTIAN." Where first he was disgusted at discovering his dad had been a Christian, now, as he ran his fingers over the inscription, a sense of peace washed over him. Were the words *Bason* and *Christian* going to be put together again? He reached for his grandparents' address. In a couple of days, he would be able to meet them and ask more about their son and their faith.

Looking into the box, he smiled at the photo of Matt, Justin, and him posing in their jean jackets. He picked up the picture of Dean and his mom. What Brandon would give to go back in time to either of those two moments. He wanted to experience the happiness, to get to know his father, to hear Matt's laugh. He wanted to tell his mom that they could get through anything together; that there were other ways to escape the pain and guilt of life. Jesus offered freedom.

Brandon recalled their time in the café in San Antonio, when Anton was so thankful for a single comma. That punctuation mark separated death and the gift of eternal life. Brandon wanted to accept it and be as thankful as Anton was.

"Getting closer," Anton said.

Brandon looked out the window to see some gigantic red rocks jutting out of the horizon—the contrast of red against the clear blue sky striking in its simple beauty. Brandon took out the Monument Valley postcard. Above some similar rocks shaped like hands on the card floated three hot air balloons. More and more rocks appeared on the horizon. Brandon spotted a sign that said, "HOT AIR BALLOON RIDES." He imagined himself in a basket, floating over the valley. Justin had also liked the idea, but Anton said it would be too expensive. Brandon frowned. This trip was possible entirely due to Anton's generosity. Of course, they couldn't ask Anton to shell out any more than he had. *Wait!* he thought. At the bottom of the box he found it: the envelope. How could he have forgotten? "Pull over."

"What?" Anton said.

"Pull over for a second, okay?"

Anton put on the brakes. Brandon held up the envelope. "What's that?"

"Money. I had forgotten about it. It's almost five hundred dollars. I want to give it to you." Brandon passed the envelope to Anton.

He raised a hand in objection. "I can't take this. I won't take this. Remember, I'm the one who offered this trip—on my bill."

Brandon pointed to the hot air balloon sign. "Fine. Then let's go in a balloon."

Justin and Anton looked at the sign. "Who's afraid of heights?" Anton said. Brandon thought he detected a note of hesitation.

They followed the sign to a small building. "Are you sure you want to do this?" Anton asked.

"Completely." The impulsive decision excited Brandon. He jumped out of the car.

"Wasn't yesterday's spin-out adventure enough for you?" Anton called out of the car's window.

Brandon waved for Justin and Anton to follow. The trip in a balloon for the three of them was going to be four hundred dollars for a one-hour flight. The sign by the front door promised unforgettable views. "Let's do it!" Brandon said, bouncing on his toes.

Anton hesitated, then pulled open the door. The man behind the counter was a heavy-set guy. With his white beard and overalls, he looked every bit the stereotypical prospector. "Howdy," he said as they entered. "I'm Danny. Going up?" He gave a husky laugh, as if that was the funniest joke ever.

A few minutes later, they were giving Danny some money, and Anton was signing a waiver. "How high do these balloons go?" Anton asked.

"Our balloons are equipped to reach five thousand feet, but

we won't take you that high. We'll probably float around a thousand. A lot of people think the higher, the better—"

"I don't!" Anton said with a nervous laugh.

When Anton had asked who was afraid of heights, Brandon had no idea Anton was. "Sorry. I didn't know you were afraid. We don't have to—"

"Afraid? Let's call it a healthy respect. Don't worry about me. It'll be fun," Anton said before swallowing hard.

Danny cleared his throat. "Monument Valley is best seen from a minimal height. We'll get you close enough to the rocks to see the bushes growing on top and the jackrabbits running from your shadow."

Anton took a deep breath and finished signing the waiver. "It'll be fun," he repeated.

Danny led them to a room in the building with a TV. "This is the safety briefing. You boys watch this while Jeff works on filling the balloon."

After the briefing, Danny opened the door and led them out the back to a large, open field. In the distance, a man—presumably Jeff—was directing a massive fan to blow air into the opening of a balloon the size of a house. Not far away was another open space. There must have been another balloon launch earlier that morning. Danny walked over to the security cable, which held the balloon in place. Jeff jumped into a sideways basket attached to the balloon and turned on a torch. A flame about six feet long shot into the pathway of the fan.

"You inflate the balloon with cool air!" Danny yelled over the sound of the fan and torch. "You lift the balloon with hot air!"

Just then, the balloon began lifting off the ground. As it erected, the basket started to flip onto its bottom. Once it was level to the ground, Jeff turned the torch down low. "All aboard!" Jeff said. Danny motioned for them to get into the basket.

Justin made for the balloon, and Brandon followed, while

Anton hung back. Brandon turned to see Anton eyeing the top of the balloon that towered over them. Brandon returned to Anton's side. "Massive, isn't it?" Brandon said. He put an arm around Anton's shoulders and walked him to the edge of the basket. "This'll be fun. Don't worry." Danny reached out a hand and hoisted Anton in. Justin did the same for Brandon.

"I'm Jeff. Today's voyage will take just over an hour. Look up. Do you see an engine?"

Anton shook his head, the edge of the basket in his death grip.

"Do you see a propeller or a rudder?"

"Nah," Justin said.

"That should tell you, then, that I do not have complete control over everywhere we go. But rest assured, I am an experienced and licensed pilot. I will do my best so that you can see the Three Sisters, Big Indian, Castlerock, and all the famous monuments up close. You remember everything from the safety video?" Brandon gave two thumbs up. "Okay! Let's go!" Jeff said as he pulled a rope that was dangling above his head.

Brandon's throat went into his stomach. He instinctively grabbed the side of the basket, as did Justin. Anton sunk down to the floor, groaning. Brandon smiled and gave him a reassuring look. "This is gonna be great!" Brandon peered over the edge of the basket and watched the ground retreat from beneath them. Soon, the building they were just in looked tiny. Then, Jeff turned off the torch, and everything was silent, except for the occasional creak of the basket.

"It's so quiet," Justin said.

"It never gets old to me," Jeff said. "And it never ceases to surprise the customers. When people are this high in the air, they're usually in a busy skyscraper or a noisy airplane."

"I've never flown," Justin said.

"Me neither," said Brandon.

"Well, both those things were created for a busy world," Jeff said. "But she was created to remind us to slow down." He patted the side of the basket.

Brandon looked out, amazed at what he saw. He had thought he could see far when they were on the road. Now, he was expecting to be able to see the Grand Canyon from where he stood. The sky was a perfect blue, the ground a clay red. Just ahead lay the first monument.

"Anton, get up," Brandon said, extending his hand. "You've got to see this."

Anton closed his eyes and took a deep breath. He stood up on shaky knees. Letting go of Brandon's hand, he grabbed the edge of the basket. He slowly opened his eyes and let out his breath. "Wow," he breathed.

"Coming up just below us is the West Mitten," Jeff said. It was the formation that was in the foreground of the Monument Valley postcard. "Just beyond it is the East Mitten. To our left is the Sentinel Mesa." They looked to where Jeff was pointing. A long plateau of red rock dominated the horizon.

"Just like the social studies books," Justin said with a smile. "This is incredible." He lifted his fist. "Thanks for doing this, dude."

Brandon bumped Justin's fist. "Thank my dad. It was his money." Again, he felt that word in his mouth. Dean was not just his father. Even before Brandon was born, he'd had his physical and spiritual interests in mind. Without his Bible—and cash—none of this would have happened. Dean really was his dad. "I figured if Anton wouldn't take it, what else should I use it for?"

"Wasn't that the money we were going to use to fix Genevieve's car?"

"Oh." Brandon had forgotten about that. "You're right." *He's right,* Brandon repeated in his head. *Now what?* There was no going back on this now. It's not like they would give him a refund because he was careless. *It'll work out,* Brandon told himself. After all, they had already put down half the money to pay for the car's repairs. *What's the worst that could happen?* Brandon tried to forget about it for now. He was a thousand feet in the air with a couple of the best friends someone could ask for. *If only Matt could be here.* Brandon pulled the Monument Valley postcard out of his back pocket, alternately looking at the image on the card and the vista below them. *Then again, maybe he is.* Brandon stole a glance at Anton, still gripping the basket tightly but managing a weak smile. Yes, Anton was the best kind of friend someone could have.

But what about Brandon? What kind of friend was he?

CHAPTER THIRTY-TWO

"We are less than two hours from the Grand Canyon," Justin said. "Do you realize that?" He ate the last spoonful of his oatmeal. Brandon had come down first again to check out the dining room of the Flagstaff hotel. Thankfully, there was no television. They could have their breakfast in peace. Justin had quickly followed.

"Aunt Genni was right. This has been a long trip."

"And you're up for even more after today?"

"Yeah," Brandon said. "We'll only technically be halfway done with this trip once we reach my grandparents. At least we won't have to take the scenic route on our way back."

Anton entered the room with his bag in hand. "I'll check out, and then I'll join you guys."

Nearly in a whisper, Justin asked, "Do you really think we will still go to California? When you gonna tell him?"

"Today," said Brandon. "I've been wanting to tell him, but I keep chickening out. I know he'll want to go straight to the police."

"And so we should," Justin said, before taking a drink of his orange juice. "You told me the TV people said he kidnapped us."

"No," Brandon said. "No, I didn't. They said they haven't ruled it out yet. Big difference."

"Big difference? Same difference. Look, if you don't tell him, I will."

"Don't you dare."

Justin shook his empty orange juice glass. "Look. He's on his way now. And I need a refill." He stood up just as Anton sat down.

Brandon poked idly at the food on his plate. "Hey, Anton."

"Hmm?"

"I've been thinking a lot about the repentance stuff."

Anton smiled.

"It's not easy denying yourself," Brandon said.

"I hear that. And there's another thing I need to talk to you about," Anton said.

Brandon looked over Anton's shoulder to see Justin pointing to Anton across the room and mouthing, "Tell him!"

"When it comes to converting to Christ, repentance is only part of it," Anton said. "As I said before, it's dying to sin. But you can't stay dead, just like Jesus didn't. You've got to be raised. And that's what I want to talk to you about."

No, Brandon couldn't be distracted by this. Whatever Anton had to say could wait. "That sounds great, Anton. But first—"

"Hold that thought. I'm famished. I'll be back in a sec."

Brandon sighed.

Justin returned. "Well?"

"I'm working on it, okay?"

Justin shot him a frustrated look and walked out of the room.

Anton sat back down. "The lady at the counter said we should get on the road as soon as we can. For one, it's gonna be another scorcher. It'll only get hotter as the day goes on. She did think that calling it a dry heat seemed to make it sound better. And for another, we should probably get there before the hordes of tourists do. Apparently, half the people who stay at this hotel do so because they're on their way to the Grand Canyon."

"Just like us," Brandon said. About a dozen other people were also eating their breakfasts.

"Yep," Anton said between quick bites.

Brandon stood up and walked over to the juice station. This was harder than he expected.

"What's Matt's folder say?" Anton called. "'GC-Bound,' right?"

"Yep," said Brandon.

"Let's make it happen," Anton said.

As soon as they finished eating, they piled into the car and headed north. The road was lined with pine trees—a welcome change from the barren landscape of the past few days. Above the trees they could see a high mountain peak. Brandon squinted and did a double take. "Is that snow on top of the mountain? In this heat?"

"It's much colder up there," Anton said.

"Hmm. Anyway, Anton, what I was going to say during breakfast..."

"Right, we were talking about being raised. Got your Bible?"

Brandon sighed. Anton seemed determined to finish this discussion—more determined than Brandon was to break the news. *Okay,* Brandon thought. *Once Anton finishes saying what he has to say.* Hopefully, Justin would be patient enough.

Brandon retrieved his Bible. "Got it."

"Great. Turn to Acts chapter two." Brandon found the passage. Anton continued. "In the previous chapter, the resurrected Jesus had told the apostles to go out and be his witnesses. Comparing this with other accounts in the New Testament, they were to go preach the gospel and make disciples, baptizing them."

"You've mentioned that before. I think the first time was behind Aunt Mavel's house."

"Yes. Granddad baptized me into Christ in that creek I took you to. That's what I want to talk to you about today."

"How long will this take?" Brandon could feel Justin's eyes boring into the back of his head. Not only was Justin putting on the pressure, but the longer Brandon delayed, the more personal guilt he felt. The weight was almost too much to bear.

"How long? I don't know. As long as it needs to take for you to understand God's will. What's the rush?" Brandon didn't say anything. What would Anton say if he knew that at that very moment, Texas authorities were looking for him, and his picture was circulating national television? "Well," Anton continued, "it's pretty straightforward, anyway."

"All right. Acts two," Brandon said half-heartedly.

"Right. So, Jesus had sent these fellas out to preach about his death, burial, and resurrection. That's what they began doing in this chapter. A bunch of people had gathered to honor God, and Peter broke it to them that they were guilty of killing the man God sent to save them. Read verse thirty-six."

Brandon did so.

Therefore let all the house of Israel know for certain that God has made Him both Lord and Christ—this Jesus whom you crucified.

"Peter didn't pull any punches," Anton said. "They were guilty, and he let 'em have it. Read the next verse."

Brandon continued reading.

Now when they heard this, they were pierced to the heart, and said to Peter and the rest of the apostles, "Brethren, what shall we do?"

"How do you think these people felt?" Anton asked.

"Guilty?" Brandon said, the irony not lost on him.

"You know that's right. They came to Jerusalem on this occasion to honor God. Instead, they killed God's son. They asked what they needed to do to remove the guilt of this sin. No matter what Peter said to answer that question, what do you think their desire would motivate them to do?"

That was a long-winded question. Brandon thought it through again. *Oh, great,* he thought. *He doesn't even know he's rubbing it in.* "They would have done anything Peter said, I'm sure."

"And I would too. Grab a bookmark."

Brandon looked around and eventually stuck the photo of his parents in Acts two.

"Second Corinthians seven," Anton said.

Brandon turned to it.

"In this passage, Paul was writing to some people who had also changed for the gospel. What does he tell them in verses nine and ten?"

Brandon's Bible was feeling more and more familiar in his hands. He found the verses and read.

> *I now rejoice, not that you were made sorrowful, but that you were made sorrowful to the point of repentance; for you were made sorrowful according to the will of God, in order that you might not suffer loss in anything through us. For the sorrow that is according to the will of God produces a repentance without regret, leading to salvation; but the sorrow of the world produces death.*

"These people felt really bad for what they had done," Anton said. "And the weird thing is Paul wrote this letter to tell them how happy he was that they felt bad. In this passage, he explained why. It wasn't just that they got caught sinning and said, 'Rats, we got caught.' No, they realized the consequences were far-reaching. What kind of sorrow did they have?"

Brandon looked down. "It says they had godly sorrow."

"So, what do you think godly sorrow is all about?"

Brandon took a deep breath and thought about the times he had felt guilty in life. He didn't have to think long; the best example was the current one. Why was he feeling guilty? It wasn't just the prospect of getting caught that weighed on his mind; it was also the consequences—losing the rest of the trip, getting sent back to Grand Junction. He looked at Anton, who had proved to be such a good friend. He had sacrificed much for Brandon and Justin. Then, his heart ached even more. That was it. Despite Anton's grace, Brandon had betrayed him. Someone else was about to face the consequences of Brandon's foolish decisions. Then, it hit him harder. *Isn't that what Jesus' death is all about?* Brandon had sinned, yet Jesus was willing to take the punishment. One difference was Anton had no idea what he was facing, whereas Jesus went to the cross knowingly. "It's about realizing sin is serious," Brandon said finally, adjusting the bandage on his head. "Both the 'big' sins and the 'small' sins. Godly sorrow is about hurting over what you've done to God through your decisions."

Anton looked at Brandon, eyes wide. "I don't think I could have said that better myself. You got it. And godly sorrow produces what?"

"Repentance."

"And repentance leads to?"

"Salvation."

"Let me give you one more example," Anton said. "In the middle of the Bible, you'll find the book of Psalms. Go to Psalm fifty-one and read the first four verses." Brandon found the passage. Before he read it, Anton said, "David had sinned terribly against God. His friend came over and slapped some sense into him. Afterward, David wrote this Psalm." Brandon read.

Be gracious to me, O God, according to Thy lovingkindness;

According to the greatness of Thy compassion blot out my transgressions. Wash me thoroughly from my iniquity,
And cleanse me from my sin.
For I know my transgressions,
And my sin is ever before me.
Against Thee, Thee only, I have sinned,
And done what is evil in Thy sight,
So that Thou art justified when Thou dost speak,
And blameless when Thou dost judge.

"When someone has godly sorrow," Anton said, "what does he want more than anything else?"

"To be cleansed. For God to forgive him."

"Right. To use the Corinthians as an example again, in First Corinthians six, Paul listed a bunch of sinful lifestyles that people participate in. He said people who live like that will not receive an inheritance from God. Then, in verse eleven, he said, 'And such were some of you; but you were washed, but you were sanctified, but you were justified in the name of the Lord Jesus Christ, and in the Spirit of our God.' Notice the progression of things: They lived, never considering God's grace. Then, they changed. And then, they were washed. Converting to Christ involves a change and a cleansing." Anton must have anticipated Brandon's next question, as he added, "So, what do you think that washing is all about?"

"It sounds nice," Brandon admitted. "It reminds me of your story about the little boy getting muddy."

"Turn to Romans five," Anton said. "Read verses eight through ten."

Brandon found it and began reading.

But God demonstrates His own love toward us, in that while we were yet sinners, Christ died for us.

Brandon stopped. "I remember this one. We read it in the café in San Antonio."

"Right, that's where we were. A lot of these days are blurring together for me."

Justin spoke up from the back. "What else happened in San Antonio, Brandy? Did you learn anything? Maybe from a television program?"

Brandon pursed his lips and resisted the urge to look back.

"What's he talking about?" Anton asked. "I don't think we even turned on our TV in that hotel."

"I'll tell you later," Brandon said. He glared at Justin. "In case you didn't hear that, I will tell him later."

"Better sooner than later," Justin replied bluntly.

"O-kay," Anton said suspiciously. "Let's continue, then." Anton focused on the road for a moment, then said, "Keep reading. Two more verses."

Brandon cleared his throat and continued.

Much more then, having now been justified by His blood, we shall be saved from the wrath of God through Him. For if while we were enemies, we were reconciled to God through the death of His Son, much more, having been reconciled, we shall be saved by His life.

"This washing that we are studying about comes through the blood of Jesus," Anton said.

"I've gathered that much," Brandon said.

"What does Jesus' death provide us?"

"Reconciliation. Remind me again what that means?"

Anton rested his forearms on the steering wheel and clasped his hands together as an answer.

"Got it."

"And reconciliation is through?"

"Jesus' death," Brandon said.

"Yep. In Ephesians one, the same apostle says that when we

are in Christ, we have forgiveness of our sins through his blood. The next chapter of Romans says that eternal life is also in Jesus. It also says that it's only when we are made in the likeness of his death."

"Huh?"

"I know it doesn't sound like something we would say in any other context. And I also know I'm beating around the bush. But I want you to have this image in your mind. When someone is placed into Christ, that person is fused with the death of Jesus. And Jesus' death provides what?"

"Washing. Reconciliation."

"Christianity is not just about believing in the crucifixion of Jesus. It's about participating in his death—being crucified with him. And now—" Anton said, lifting his index finger in the air, "—for the big reveal. Read chapter six, verses one through seven."

Brandon turned a single page in his Bible and read.

> *What shall we say then? Are we to continue in sin that grace might increase? May it never be! How shall we who died to sin still live in it? Or do you not know that all of us who have been baptized into Christ Jesus have been baptized into His death? Therefore we have been buried with Him through baptism into death, in order that as Christ was raised from the dead through the glory of the Father, so we too might walk in newness of life. For if we have become united with Him in the likeness of His death, certainly we shall be also in the likeness of His resurrection, knowing this, that our old self was crucified with Him, that our body of sin might be done away with, that we should no longer be slaves to sin; for he who has died is freed from sin.*

As Brandon waited for Anton to say something, he mulled the passage over in his mind. *Die to sin,* he silently repeated. Anton had talked about that before. *Repentance.*

Anton finally spoke up. "What state is someone in after they've repented?"

Brandon continued to think as he stared ahead. The snow-capped mountain was nowhere in sight. They must have left it behind. The roadside had become more barren, except for some stubby trees and cacti. It resembled the roads near Monument Valley. Clouds rose out of the horizon in the distance. Finally, he said, "They're dead."

Anton waited a moment before saying, "Are you dead or alive to sin?"

"To be honest, I'm not sure."

"As my mama always said, honesty's the best policy—especially when it comes to your relationship with God. You can't kid yourself into his grace. What do people do with dead bodies?"

"What?" Brandon said, somewhat shaken out of his stupor.

"What do people do with the body after a funeral?"

Nearly three weeks ago, Brandon had helped carry Matt's casket to a hole in the ground. On that rainy day, Genevieve had given him Dean's box and the Bible he now held. In a sense, Matt's death was the beginning of this journey. Matt had guided them to the middle of Arizona. Anton had guided Brandon to this crossroads.

"Well?" Anton said.

"Dead bodies are buried."

"That's right. Just like Jesus was buried after he died. So, when someone dies to sin, what do you think needs to happen?"

"A funeral?"

Anton chuckled. "That's one way to look at it. What do verses three and four say?"

Brandon reread the verses.

Or do you not know that all of us who have been baptized into Christ Jesus have been baptized into His death? Therefore we have been buried with Him through baptism into death, in order that as Christ was raised from the dead through the glory of the Father, so we too might walk in newness of life.

"When does God consider someone buried with Christ?" Anton asked.

"When they're baptized."

Anton smiled. "I'm not going to make the same mistake I made a few days ago. I'll proceed to assume you don't know what this Bible word is all about." Brandon was thankful for that. His best guess at this point was it was a strange Christian ritual involving water. Anton continued. "I told you I was baptized in a creek. So, you can probably guess what baptism requires?"

"Water."

"The word 'baptism' comes from a Greek word that means to submerge. Bible baptism is when someone is immersed in water. So, someone dies to sin, is buried in water. Then, what happens?"

"They're raised," Brandon said.

"Just like Jesus. Check out verse seventeen."

Brandon read the verse.

But thanks be to God that though you were slaves of sin, you became obedient from the heart to that form of teaching to which you were committed.

"Someone provided the pattern, and these people had obeyed that pattern to be set free from their sins. That pattern was Jesus' death, burial, and resurrection. When they died to sin, were buried with Jesus in baptism, and raised out of baptism to a new life, they were made in the likeness of Jesus' death. What's the promise in verse five?"

Brandon read the verse silently and then answered, "If I am

made in the likeness of his death, then I will be made in the likeness of his resurrection."

"Exactly, Brandon. You can't just change your habits. Technically, if a thief is caught and thrown into prison, he's no longer stealing, right?"

"Right," said Brandon. An image of Anton being thrown into prison flashed in his mind's eye. *I'll tell him soon*, he reminded himself.

"But does that necessarily mean he's repented?"

"No. He'll probably just go back to stealing once he serves his time."

"Maybe," Anton said. "For repentance to happen, someone has to have godly sorrow. That often follows when someone truly learns and appreciates what Jesus has done for him. That sorrow will drive him to repentance, seeking God's forgiveness. He needs to bury that old person of sin, so he can be raised with the new life God offers him. Matthew twenty-eight says that happens in the name of the Father, the Son, and the Holy Spirit. God changes that person from the inside out."

"It sounds like a huge commitment," Brandon said.

"The most important one anyone could make."

Brandon breathed in deeply while thinking about himself as Anton was—a follower of Jesus. Anton had proven all of Brandon's previous prejudices against Christians wrong. Sure, as Anton had said, even the best people were good at making bad decisions. Brandon should be patient with those who didn't truly represent Jesus. However, if Brandon was going to become a Christian, he wanted to be like Anton. Brandon imagined himself in a casket, dead to sin, dedicated to receiving the washing from Jesus' death. Just as Matt's coffin was lowered into the ground, he pictured himself falling into water. As soon as his body was submerged, however, he imagined God doing an amazing transformation inside him. And with the creator's strength, he saw himself bursting out of the water, just as Jesus had risen from his tomb. The guards around Jesus' grave were shaken to see new life in a formerly dead man's body. If Brandon went through with this, everyone who ever knew him would also be aware that there was something undeniably new about him.

"I'm glad you're taking this time to think," Anton said. "Jesus knew the weight of this decision. That's why he told people to count the costs before following him. Jesus also knew what his mission would cost. But he still went through it for you and me. Check out one more passage. First Peter two, verses twenty-one to twenty-five."

Brandon took his time finding the passage. It was nearly at the end of the Bible. He read.

> *For you have been called for this purpose, since Christ also suffered for you, leaving you an example for you to follow in His steps, who committed no sin, nor was any deceit found in His mouth; and while being reviled, He did not revile in return; while suffering, He uttered no threats, but kept entrusting Himself to Him who judges righteously; and He Himself bore our sins in His body on the cross, so that we might die to sin and live to righteousness; for by His wounds you were healed. For you were continually straying like sheep, but now you have returned to the Shepherd and Guardian of your souls.*

After Brandon finished reading, Anton asked, "What will it cost you to entrust your soul to the Shepherd, Brandon?"

A few minutes passed while Brandon turned that question over and over in his mind. In one sense, it wouldn't cost him anything. Jesus wasn't asking for money. Brandon didn't have any possessions to give up. On the other hand, he knew it would cost his own identity. But what identity was that? One of the reasons he wanted to go on this trip was to learn who he was. So, who was he? No one. But, with Jesus, he could be who he was meant to be. Where would they find water for Brandon to be buried in? He didn't know, and at this point, he had something else to take care of. It was bad practice to bury the living. First, he needed to die. And he wasn't dead to sin until he came clean with the truth. *Just tell him!* He took a deep breath and nodded to himself. This was it.

Just then, Anton exclaimed, "Fellas! We're here."

CHAPTER THIRTY-THREE

ANTON PULLED THE CAR TOWARD A BOOM GATE NEXT TO A BOOTH. A sign above the booth said, "WELCOME TO GRAND CANYON NATIONAL PARK." Anton rolled down his window, and a woman in a brown park ranger's uniform explained the entry fees and a few rules about the park.

Brandon rubbed his eyes in disbelief. *We're here,* he told himself. He turned around. "We're here," he said to Justin. "Can you believe it?"

Justin was craning his neck to see out the windshield. He looked back at Brandon, and the corner of his mouth curled up. "We made it."

The boom gate rose, and Anton handed Brandon a map the woman had given him. Brandon looked around outside. Puffs of cumulus dotted the sky, crisscrossed by the thin white streaks of a plane's contrail. He couldn't see a canyon yet. Glancing down at the map, he noticed several viewing spots were highlighted.

A few minutes later, they pulled into a small parking lot, which Brandon assumed was for the first viewing platform. Other visitors were leaving their cars and walking toward a paved trail, cameras draped around their necks. "Must be it," Anton said.

Brandon unlatched his seatbelt, grabbed his backpack, and opened the car door. Justin was opening his too, but Anton wasn't moving. "You coming?" asked Brandon.

Anton shook his head. "Not yet. I'll give you guys some time first."

Brandon hesitated. He considered insisting Anton come, but Anton was right. This was something Brandon and Justin should experience together first. "Okay." He stepped out of the car. Although the sun was hot, he was surprised at how cool the air was. It was refreshing. Justin joined him in front of the car a moment later. "You ready for this?" Brandon said.

Justin held out a fist, and Brandon bumped it. They stepped toward the tree-lined trail. As they walked, Brandon still couldn't see the canyon. The trail zigged and zagged for a few minutes; then, suddenly everything opened up. No more trees. No more bends in the path. Just open views of the Grand Canyon. Brandon's breath left him as he approached a railing and took it all in—layer upon layer of intricately carved rock, a seemingly endless rainbow of reds, browns, and yellows. And beneath it all, he could just make out the winding path of a river—the Colorado River, he had learned from Matt's map—that had shaped the canyon over millennia. In the distance he saw thick, dark clouds rolling over the other side of the canyon; from where he stood, in brilliant sunshine, it seemed incongruous to think that there was a storm raging just a mile away. Brandon inched forward, his heart quickening with each step. It wasn't the height. It was the beauty. The expanse. The depth. The implicit declaration of the creator's majesty. "My God, this is incredible," Brandon finally said. Out of all the times Brandon had used the word "God" to express himself, this was the first time he did so with intention. God was no longer just a swear word. Without a doubt in his mind, God was the one to whom all worship was due.

Justin peered over the railing with wide eyes. "Now we know what Matt was going on and on about." His voice cracked. "How stupid we were to shrug it off."

Then, Brandon's vision became blurry as the tears welled up. One by one, they began to fall. And for the first time since Matt's death, Brandon wept; he truly wept. Soon Justin began to cry too. They wept together in complete disregard of the other visitors. Brandon put an arm around Justin, and they hugged. For how long, Brandon didn't know. "I wish he was here," Justin said.

"Me too. Come on." Brandon led Justin to the shade of a nearby tree just off the main trail. They sat. Allowing the tears to fall, Brandon unzipped his backpack and took out the photo of the three of them. Still holding out the picture, he said, "Remember that time we were at his house, and we were jumping on his trampoline?"

"When the neighbors came over, there were like seven of us on there at once," Justin added.

Brandon chuckled. "We were taking a rest, and all of us conspired against Matt."

"On the count of three, let's jump on him!" Justin said. "One, two, three..."

"The trampoline must have lost a dozen springs in one second. Most of them ended up in the other neighbor's yard." Brandon let himself laugh again.

"And one of them ended up in the neighbor's house."

"Oh, that's right!" Brandon said. "He stormed over and pounded on Matt's door. Mrs. Steele came out holding a trampoline spring demanding to know how in the world it smashed through Old Man Taylor's window." They smiled weakly through the tears.

Pulling out the folder, Brandon ran his fingers over Matt's

name. "We made it, buddy." He unfolded the map. Starting from Nashville, he moved his finger slowly along the red line, remembering various moments of the trip: trying to figure out how an interstate worked, Sun Studio, riding in the tow truck, meeting Anton. He smiled at the impact Anton had made on him and wondered where Justin stood now with all the Bible study stuff. His finger crossed over Dallas, and Brandon was reminded of Devin, the cowboy hat-wearing, video game-playing computer aficionado. *I wonder how dinner went with his girlfriend's dad?* As he neared the New Mexico border, he reached up and touched his bandage. The wound was still tender, but all the concussion symptoms were gone. He crossed into New Mexico and noticed an unfamiliar town on the map. He looked closer. "Did we go through here?" he asked Justin.

Justin leaned in. "I'm pretty sure we did. But I think it was when you were conked out from the concussion. Interesting name, huh?"

"What could have happened that led someone to name a town 'Truth or Consequences'?" Brandon wondered aloud.

Justin pursed his lips. "Maybe someone is trying to tell you something."

Brandon gave a quick nod, folded up the map, and returned the stuff to his backpack. "Truth or consequences. I'm going to tell Anton everything. And if I put it off again, you tell him."

"Let's go," Justin said, standing up. He offered a hand to Brandon. They took a single step forward when Justin suddenly stopped and pointed at the trail. "Hey, isn't that…"

"Ronald?" Brandon whispered.

"Your caseworker?"

There was no doubt about it. From the freckled face to the bright orange shirt, not to mention the police officer next to him, Brandon knew it was him.

"My grandma must have called the police," Justin whispered.

"Wait, you told your grandma?"

"Of course I did. I called her last night," Justin said. "I knew she must have been worried sick. I couldn't keep waiting for you to tell Anton."

"Anton!" Brandon made for the path and bolted toward the parking area, Justin on his heels.

They could see the clearing. Then, a hand gripped Brandon's shoulder. "Brandon! Stop!"

Brandon didn't stop. He ducked out of the grip and took a few more steps. Blue flashing lights shone through the trees. "No!" Brandon yelled. Someone grabbed onto him again, and he threw his elbow back hard. It landed into something soft—a stomach. Brandon glanced behind him just enough to see Ronald doubled over.

Brandon ran toward Anton's car, and another police officer stepped in front of him. "Whoa, whoa! Brandon Bason? Don't worry; you're safe."

Brandon tried to get around him, but he couldn't. He stretched his neck and saw another officer putting handcuffs on Anton. "What are you doing! He's done nothing wrong!"

The officer in front of Brandon looked back. "If that's true, he'll be fine. But you let us do our job." He stuck out his hands, trying to calm Brandon. "And it would be a lot easier if you settled down."

Another officer was doing the same to Justin. They met eyes for a moment, and Brandon's blood boiled. How could Justin call his grandma and do that to him? How could he betray them like that? He looked back at Anton, and Brandon's anger turned to shame. This wasn't Justin's fault. If Brandon hadn't been such a selfish coward... Brandon sighed in surrender.

"Are you okay?" The officer in front of him was looking at the bandage around his head.

In the distance, Brandon could see an officer leading a handcuffed Anton away from his car to a police car. Anton didn't struggle. He didn't curse. He simply submitted. He looked over, and his eyes met Brandon's. Brandon looked away and began crying again.

Ronald caught up with them. "Brandon! Thank God you're safe."

"Of course I'm safe!" Brandon said. "And you need to tell these cops that Anton didn't do anything wrong."

"We'll get it worked out. Right now, our priority was to find you and Justin. You have no idea how much we've been searching for you." He shook his head. "And you have no idea how difficult it's been."

CHAPTER THIRTY-FOUR

"He didn't do anything!" Brandon yelled at the closed door. A half-hour ago, an officer had stuck him in a room in the police station and ordered him not to go anywhere. They said they would send Ronald in soon. Brandon wondered whether Justin had also been shoved into a room with nothing but two chairs and a desk. He and Justin had traveled to the station in separate cars, which was fine with Brandon, as he had nothing to say to Justin anyway. Why couldn't Justin have waited another day to call his grandma? Didn't he know what that phone call would inevitably lead to?

What was Anton facing at this exact moment? *They didn't have to handcuff him,* Brandon thought. He could only imagine how humiliating it must have been for Anton to be cuffed in front of tourists and led away in a patrol car.

"Let him go!" Brandon screamed, pounding on the door. *What good is it doing?* He had spent the majority of his time in the room yelling. But now his voice was giving out, and nobody had paid him any attention. Defeated, he sat down and waited.

Brandon filled with shame as he recalled the last time he'd met Anton's gaze on the canyon. Despite being handcuffed unjustly, Anton had looked so calm; Brandon had seen no trace of anger in his eyes, just bewilderment. It was all too much for Brandon; he had turned away.

He stood up and began to pace. *What's taking so long?* He kicked the desk hard. Brandon knew, of course, that there was only one person to blame—and it wasn't Justin.

Guilt stabbed at his heart. *It's my fault.* Anton had lived like Jesus, and Brandon had been his Judas. Brandon was to blame, yet Anton took the fall. He thought back to the last passage he had read in Anton's car. What did it say? Although Jesus was mistreated, he entrusted himself to God—the one who always judged righteously. That's probably exactly what Anton was doing—entrusting himself to God. Brandon wished he had that kind of faith.

He stopped pacing, trying to picture what Anton would do. Although he knew he was alone, Brandon instinctively scanned the room. Then, he closed his eyes and bowed his head. "God," Brandon began, "if you can hear me, keep Anton out of trouble. This was my fault. Let him know I'm sorry." Brandon opened his eyes just as a tear slid down his cheek.

CHAPTER THIRTY-FIVE

BRANDON HAD NEVER FLOWN IN AN AIRPLANE BEFORE, BUT THERE he was, three hours later, sitting at gate fifteen, waiting for his flight to Nashville. Ronald sat between him and Justin. Brandon still hadn't said anything to him.

Ronald had assured Brandon that Anton would be okay. He had no criminal record, and both Brandon and Justin were adamant that he had not abducted them. He would be released sometime that afternoon. Still, Brandon knew if he were Anton, he would be furious. *He probably never wants to see my face again.* But he also knew that Anton would practice what he preached and would be willing to forgive him. Brandon wondered if he would ever get the chance to apologize in person. *Probably not.* Brandon had no idea which preaching school Anton was planning to go to or where it was. Perhaps if he could get ahold of a Shreveport phone book, he could find Aunt Mavel. Then again, he couldn't even remember if Aunt Mavel's last name was the same as Anton's.

Brandon briefly considered telling Ronald about his grandparents, but he decided to keep that information to himself. He recalled how Ronald's system had no record of his dad's family.

He'll probably think it's some sort of trick, he thought. *Who am I kidding? My grandparents are probably dead, just like everyone else.*

The overhead speaker called for them to board the plane. As Ronald stood up, Brandon's instincts told him to run—down the corridor, into the airport lobby, and out the doors into the hot, Arizona sun. And if he knew for sure where Anton was at that moment, he probably would have done it. Instead, he slowly stood, picked up his backpack, and followed Ronald and Justin to the plane.

Brandon took a seat next to the window and buckled his seatbelt. Ronald sat next to him, and Justin sat across the aisle. At the airport, Ronald had tried to speak with Brandon about everything that had happened, but Brandon made it clear he was not ready to talk about it. Ronald insisted they would eventually have to. Before sliding his backpack under his seat, Brandon pulled out his Bible. Ronald raised an eyebrow at the old, beat-up leather book. Was that a look of approval? Judgment? Brandon didn't care. He started flipping through the pages, wondering what he should read.

"This is your pilot speaking," a voice called through the intercom. "Due to the weather, you will feel some turbulence during the first few minutes of our flight. Once we get above the clouds, things should settle down."

Some turbulence? Brandon thought, as if he needed a reminder of the chaos he had caused. A moment later, a flight attendant began a safety briefing. He tuned out the voice as he held the Bible, considering what he should read. He turned to the book he was most familiar with—Matthew—and began reading about the life and ministry of Jesus on earth. He recalled his surprise at learning that the name "Matthew" appeared in the Bible; now, here he was, taking the initiative to learn from the gospel-writer first-hand. Three chapters in, Brandon read about how Jesus was baptized.

And after being baptized, Jesus went up immediately from the water; and behold, the heavens were opened, and he saw the Spirit of God descending as a dove, and coming upon Him, and behold, a voice out of the heavens, saying, "This is My beloved Son, in whom I am well-pleased."

Brandon couldn't help but wonder why Jesus—God's Son—needed to be baptized. What did it mean? Perhaps, he concluded, it was another way Jesus led by example.

In the next chapter, when Jesus chose his disciples, Brandon noticed Jesus was not interested in the high and mighty. He wanted basic people, broken people, faulty people.

The book of Matthew challenged Brandon the most when he read chapters five, six, and seven. Jesus' disciples came to him, and he taught them. As he read, it struck Brandon how different Jesus' teachings were to anything he had come across in movies and history classes. The world was full of motivational speakers who taught people to follow their hearts, to pursue their dreams no matter the cost, and to look out for number one. Jesus, on the other hand, taught his disciples to be poor in spirit, telling them greatness came by loving their neighbors as themselves. If someone hit them, they were not to hit them back. They were to give to the poor liberally. Instead of trying to gain riches, Jesus taught his disciples to be content with what they had right then. The more Brandon read of Jesus' teachings and example, the more his trust in him grew. The first time he had read this Bible, he had flipped to a random spot. It didn't make sense to him. Now, he had started with the beginning of a book. He wondered what his reaction would have been if he had done that at first. He continued to read.

Enter by the narrow gate; for the gate is wide, and the way is broad that leads to destruction, and many are those who enter by it. For the

> *gate is small, and the way is narrow that leads to life, and few are those who find it.*

Was Brandon on the road to destruction or life? Jesus' use of "many" versus "few" was startling. It seemed to Brandon as if Jesus were saying the people who felt comfortable in the world were the ones heading the wrong way.

Then, Jesus gave his disciples a challenging warning.

> *Not everyone who says to Me, "Lord, Lord," will enter the kingdom of heaven; but he who does the will of My Father who is in heaven. Many will say to Me on that day, "Lord, Lord, did we not prophesy in Your name, and in Your name cast out demons, and in Your name perform many miracles?" And then I will declare to them, "I never knew you; depart from me, you who practice lawlessness."*

Midway through the passage the plane shook violently. Brandon struggled to keep his place in the Bible as he gripped the armrests, then turned to Ronald for reassurance. Ronald placed a comforting hand on his forearm and told him not to worry. Brandon glanced across the aisle and noticed Justin looking equally frightened. The pilot's voice cut in. "We're just passing through a pocket of high pressure, as expected. Please stay in your seats with your seatbelts fastened. We should be out of this in a few minutes."

Brandon took a deep breath and tried to turn his focus back to the Bible passage. Was he prepared to call Jesus his Lord? And if so, that clearly was not enough. He had to do the Father's will, which, he assumed, must mean he would have to follow through with what he read and had studied from his Bible. What struck Brandon the most was that there would be many people on the day of judgment who would be in for a shock. They thought they were good servants since they did good deeds in Jesus' name. Two other things were also true: Jesus didn't know them, and they practiced lawlessness. Brandon had heard that word before. *Lawlessness.* In the café in San Antonio, Anton had shown them a passage that explained what sin was. *Sin is lawlessness,* Brandon recalled. *That's why repentance is so crucial; you can't inherit the kingdom of heaven while also in your sin.*

The turbulence subsided and Brandon started to relax again. It dawned on him how far he had come: Here he was, reading the Bible on his own—and he understood it. And with every word, his faith grew. What had Anton said? Faith came from hearing the message of Christ.

He looked out the window, expecting to see fields and rivers like the movies showed. Instead, he saw the top side of clouds—puffy white clouds. The storm was behind them. In a matter of hours, this plane would have crossed over what had taken them days to travel. The roads, hotels, and landmarks below the plane all told a story. According to the police, it was the story of a runaway teen on the cusp of adulthood trying to escape grief and a foster home—that was one version of the truth. But to Brandon, it was not as much a story of escape as it was a journey of searching.

Hungry for more, Brandon read the end of chapter seven. Jesus contrasted two people—the wise and the foolish. The wise were those who heard and obeyed Jesus. The foolish were those who heard, yet disregarded his teachings. What would Brandon be? Justin, it seemed, was the foolish one—he had also heard almost everything Brandon had heard on this trip. But when asked what he thought, he shrugged it off. "Indifferent," Justin had said. Brandon shook his head. *Don't be so judgmental,* he thought. But what could he do? Maybe he could do what Anton did—lead by example. In the short time Brandon had known Anton, he had observed more compassion than he had ever witnessed in anyone. Not only had he unquestioningly helped him and Justin in their time of need, but he had also fed the poor, befriended a stranger, prayed over the injured. Where could that compassion come from, other than Jesus?

Next to him Ronald had closed his eyes, and across the aisle Brandon saw Justin fidgeting with the tray in front of him; what was he thinking now? He was probably terrified about what his grandma would say to him when he got home. For a selfish moment, Brandon thought, *At least he has a grandma.* If only he had made it to Willows to meet his grandparents. That could have changed everything. Maybe he would never have had to see Tennessee again.

The pilot's voice interrupted his thoughts again, telling them there was an hour left in their flight, and they would soon begin their descent. Brandon was in no rush to finish the book of Matthew. He read the words and sentences slowly, sometimes reading them a second time to ensure he understood them. He had reached chapter twenty-eight. Once again, he read how Jesus defeated death. Jesus had known what was coming, yet he faced it head-on. He didn't rail at his accusers. He didn't hit them back. He allowed them to nail his body to a cross. He prayed. He submitted. He died. Three days later, however, he turned the world upside down by walking out of his grave. For what? For sinners like Brandon. At the end of the chapter, Jesus commissioned the remaining eleven apostles to finish his work.

> *And Jesus came up and spoke to them, saying, "All authority has been given to Me in heaven and on earth. Go therefore and make disciples of all the nations, baptizing them in the name of the Father and the Son and the Holy Spirit, teaching them to observe all that I commanded you; and lo, I am with you always, even to the end of the age."*

This passage reminded him of something Anton had said.

The book of Acts was where these men carried out this mission. Brandon flipped a few pages forward and found chapter one. It didn't take him long to realize the beginning of Acts was an overlap of what he had just read at the end of Matthew. Sure enough, soon after Jesus left the earth, the apostles busied themselves teaching thousands of people about his death, burial, and resurrection. As soon as the guilt set in, the crowds asked, "What shall we do?"

> *And Peter said to them, "Repent, and let each of you be baptized in the name of Jesus Christ for the forgiveness of your sins; and you shall receive the gift of the Holy Spirit."*

Peter told this to a group of people who were personally guilty of the crucifixion of Jesus. How many times in the past couple of days had Brandon also felt that guilt? The shame of betraying Anton returned and pricked his heart. Would Peter tell Brandon to do the same thing—repent and be baptized in Jesus' name for the forgiveness of his sins? He continued reading.

> *For the promise is for you and your children, and for all who are far off, as many as the Lord our God shall call to Himself.*

It seemed so. Was Brandon ready to follow through? He adjusted the bandage on his head. *Yes,* he thought. *I want to die to sin.* His heart had been heavy for a few days, yet he hadn't truly repented. The one thing that had held him back was not revealing the truth to Anton. Now, he faced the consequences. It was too late. He prayed he would have a chance to tell Anton he was sorry.

The death of Jesus weighed on his heart, as he felt the pages of his Bible in his hands. He was reading other people's questions, but he had not applied the answers to himself yet. *Yes,* he thought again. *I am dead to sin. I want to be on the path that leads to life. I want to know Jesus and do his Father's will. I want to be the wise person who built his house on the rock.* Brandon swallowed hard and continued reading.

> *And with many other words he solemnly testified and kept on exhorting them, saying, "Be saved from this perverse generation!" So then, those who had received his word were baptized; and there were added that day about three thousand souls.*

A beep sounded, interrupting Brandon's reading. "This is the pilot speaking. We are approaching our descent toward Nashville. I want to thank you personally for flying with us..."

Again, Brandon tuned out the voice and trained his eyes out the window. This time, he could see the city he used to call home. Sure, he had been born and raised there, but he was still searching for somewhere he truly knew as home.

An hour later, the sun low on the horizon, he and Justin sat in Ronald's car, heading toward Grand Junction. They still hadn't spoken to each other since Arizona. Justin stared idly out the window, seemingly uninterested in initiating conversation. Brandon silently pulled out his Bible and picked up where he left off, not caring what Justin thought.

The church in the first century was a family. They worked together to make sure no one was in need. They worshiped God together. They clung to the teachings of the apostles as if they were teachings directly from Jesus.

Reading faster than before, he reached chapter seven. He learned about intolerant people who closed their ears to prevent them from hearing any more of the gospel from Stephen. Then, they killed him. Although Brandon didn't remember ever doing the same thing literally, he certainly was as intolerant as Stephen's audience at one point. He hadn't wanted to kill anyone, but he had been quick to judge. He had been spiteful. He had been dismissive of anything that related to Christianity. Brandon marveled at how a simple, gentle approach from Anton had softened his heart in a matter of days.

Brandon continued reading. He smiled as he learned about a disciple named Philip taking the gospel of Jesus Christ to a place called Samaria.

> *But when they believed Philip preaching the good news about the kingdom of God and the name of Jesus Christ, they were being baptized, men and women alike.*

One thing was clear to Brandon: The proper way to respond to the gospel of Jesus was to be baptized into Jesus. That was what Anton had been trying to explain that morning as they drove to the Grand Canyon. To repent was to die. But what needed to happen to that dead person? Burial. Brandon looked out the car window. He began to recognize the streets. They were near Genevieve's house.

He read more. The narrative told how Philip met a man from Ethiopia. The man was traveling home from Jerusalem and was reading from the Scriptures.

> *And when Philip had run up, he heard him reading Isaiah the prophet, and said, "Do you understand what you are reading?" And he said, "Well, how could I, unless someone guides me?" And he invited Philip to come up and sit with him.*

Brandon smiled at the memory of meeting Anton. He had seen Brandon and Justin with a Bible and assumed they understood it. He tried quoting from Scripture, but they were clueless. Brandon allowed a chuckle to escape, and Justin turned to him with an expressionless face. Brandon gave an apologetic look. He kept reading.

> *And Philip opened his mouth, and beginning from this Scripture he preached Jesus to him. And as they went along the road they came to some water; and the eunuch said, "Look! Water! What prevents me from being baptized?" And Philip said, "If you believe with all your heart, you may." And he answered and said, "I believe that Jesus Christ is the Son of God." And he ordered the chariot to stop; and they both went down into the water, Philip as well as the eunuch; and he baptized him.*

Brandon looked up from reading to put the pieces together. The connection was uncanny. The Ethiopian was on his way home after a long journey, and someone taught him about Jesus. Believing in the message, he wanted to respond right away. Brandon felt the Bible in his hand. He wondered what percentage of it he had read. Maybe five percent? But thanks to Anton, he seemed to know just as much about Jesus as this Ethiopian, the Jews in Acts two, and the Samaritans in Acts eight. What did they all want to do as soon as they had heard the message? Die to sin, be buried in Christ's death, and be raised to new life by the power of God. Did Brandon want the same? "Stop the car!" he shouted.

Ronald jumped and slammed on the brakes. He turned around. "What? What's wrong?"

Brandon didn't answer him. He turned to Justin. "I'm sorry. I'm sorry for everything!" he blurted. "This isn't your fault." His voice cracked. "You did the right thing by calling your grandma. It was my fault for not telling Anton. We can just hope the police were right that he'll be free to go and free of charge." He paused.

"Can you please explain why we are stopping?" Ronald asked.

Brandon held up an index finger to tell him to wait. He continued locking eyes with Justin. "Look, I know this doesn't mean to you what it now means to me." He held up the Bible. "And I'm not asking you to believe anything. But I need your help." Justin grunted. That was enough for Brandon. He continued. "First, I need you to find it in your heart to forgive me. If not today, then someday. Second, I need you to admit that this has been one heck of a journey." Brandon smiled. The corner of Justin's mouth turned up. "Good," Brandon said. "One more thing." He looked at Ronald. "Will you please drive us down there?" Brandon pointed down Genevieve's street.

"I'm sorry, Brandon. I can't do that. This fiasco has already put me on thin ice with my boss. I need to take you back to Grand Junction."

"And you will," Brandon said, his voice laced with sincerity. "Very soon. This won't take long."

"I'm sorry, Brandon—"

"Why do you work with Social Services?" Brandon interrupted.

"To help people," Ronald said.

"Good," Brandon said. "If you really want to help me, take us down that street for just a minute. I'm not gonna pull a fast one, if that's what you think. We'll be back on our way to Grand Junction before you know it."

Ronald didn't say anything. He looked down the street and sighed. "How long is this going to take?"

"Ten minutes, tops."

"What is this about?" Justin finally asked.

Brandon didn't respond. "Please," he said to Ronald.

Ronald put the car in drive and turned the wheel. Relief washed over Brandon. They drove over the old stone bridge, where he had sat when he first opened the Bible. They passed three houses, then Brandon said, "Here." Ronald stopped the vehicle. Brandon jumped out.

"Wait!" Ronald said, but Brandon was already running up Genevieve's driveway. Justin got out and followed him, Ronald in his wake. The three of them stepped onto the porch, and Brandon knocked. The door opened.

For a moment, Genevieve seemed too stunned to speak. "Brandon!" She threw her arms around him, then pulled back. "You've been all over the news. They were searching for you. I didn't know what to do," she spluttered. Then, she spotted Ronald. "Wait, who's that?"

"Don't worry, Aunt Genni. I came to say thanks. And to tell you your car is in Winona, Mississippi."

She had a puzzled look on her face. Then, with a dismissive wave, she said, "Thank God you're safe!"

"I do," Brandon said.

"You do what?"

"I thank God I'm safe."

Again, she looked at him, puzzled.

"And I thank you, Aunt Genni." Brandon held up the Bible. "Thank you for getting this to me. Thank you for telling me about my dad."

"Did you find your grandparents?"

Brandon dropped his head. "No. Well, kind of. I have their address, but we didn't make it there before the police caught up to us. But we did make it to the Grand Canyon."

"You did?! How was it?"

"Later," Brandon said. "There's something more important right now." Brandon turned and looked at Justin and Ronald. "Follow me. All of you."

Brandon stepped off the porch and walked back the way they had come in Ronald's car. With purposeful steps, he closed the distance between them and the bridge. He stopped and turned. Holding up the Bible again, he said, "Aunt Genni, you were the first person to give me the advice to read this on my own to learn what my dad believed. Thank you for that advice. Thank you for your car. Thank you for telling me about my dad. And because I read this on my own and listened carefully to a good friend, I believe Jesus is the Son of God."

Brandon then turned to Justin. "Here's the last thing I need your help with." He pointed to the creek below the bridge. "Baptize me."

"Baptize you?" Justin said incredulously.

"That's what I said. I don't expect you to agree with me or even understand. But I need this to happen now."

Justin stared back at him, mouth agape. Brandon opened his Bible and found the passage he was reading. He read the account of the Ethiopian for all to hear. Pointing at the water again and echoing the Ethiopian, he said, "Look! Water! What prevents me from being baptized? Are you going to prevent me?"

"I have no idea how to baptize someone. And don't you need a priest or someone to do it?"

Brandon shook his head. "Every time someone was baptized in here—" he lifted his Bible for emphasis, "—the passage hardly says anything about the person doing the baptizing. Instead, the Bible focuses on the heart of the person being baptized. I admit I haven't read it all. And if I find out later that you're right, then I'll find someone to do it for me properly. But I don't want to wait anymore. If Anton were here, I would ask him to do it. But he's not." Brandon's voice cracked, and tears began falling. How many tears had he shed that day? "Help me out, okay?"

Justin looked at Ronald, who didn't object, then at Genevieve, who gave a shrug.

"Aunt Genni and Justin, you two and Anton are the people that mean the most to me," Brandon said.

"Who's Anton?" asked Genevieve.

"Later," Brandon said. "This is the most important decision

of my life. And I want you to do it, Justin, and I want Aunt Genni to see it happen."

"Fine," Justin said. "But again, I have no idea how this works."

"It's pretty simple, I think," Brandon said. He read from the passage again.

> *And he ordered the chariot to stop; and they both went down into the water, Philip as well as the eunuch; and he baptized him.*

"I think we both need to go down there," Brandon said. "You need to push me under the water, and then I come back up. The Bible calls it a burial and a resurrection—like Jesus."

"Fine," Justin said.

Ronald looked like he was going to say something.

"It'll only take a moment," Brandon reassured before Ronald could speak.

Brandon handed the Bible to Genevieve and started walking down the bank. Stepping carefully over weeds and vines, Justin followed until they were at the water's edge. Brandon kicked off his shoes and peeled off his socks. Justin did likewise. Then, Brandon walked into the water. He didn't care about his jeans. He didn't care about his shirt or his bandage. All he cared about at that moment was being made in the likeness of Jesus' death, burial, and resurrection. He was a dead man walking, and it was time to do away with his old, sinful life. He took a few more steps and turned around to face Justin, who was right behind him. They were in the middle of the creek, which was about three feet deep.

With an awkward smile, Justin said, "Okay. Here we go. Wait, do you go forward or backward?"

"I don't know. Surprise me."

"Okay." Justin planted his hands onto Brandon's chest and began to push.

Brandon closed his eyes and took a deep breath. He fell

backward, and just like the car crash the other day, everything went in slow motion. The water inched up his back until it reached his neck. Brandon remembered the handful of dirt the preacher had thrown on Matt's casket. That was just the beginning of a complete burial. A second later, Brandon's face was underwater, including the bandage. He was completely buried while he thought of Jesus telling his disciples to baptize in the name of the Father, the Son, and the Holy Spirit. He felt Justin's hands retreat, but his body remained underwater, suspended. Although it was a physical act, Brandon didn't expect the wound on his head to be healed. He knew God was doing something at that moment to transform him on the inside. He remembered the comma in Romans chapter six.

> *For the wages of sin is death, but the free gift of God is eternal life in Christ Jesus our Lord.*

Thank you, God, Brandon prayed, *for that comma.* Brandon was being baptized into Jesus, where he could find eternal life. God was forgiving him of all his sins by the blood of Jesus. Even though he had been in police custody, he was not being carted away to prison. However, he was in just as much need of God's grace as the worst criminal. *Thank you, Father,* he prayed again. *Thank you for the gift of your Son.* He lifted his hands out of the water. Justin grabbed them and began hoisting him up. Brandon thought of Jesus, the Good Shepherd, who went away searching for that single lost sheep. When he found the sheep, he lifted it and carried it on his shoulders. Jesus had been searching for Brandon Bason. As Brandon's face broke out of the water, he rejoiced. Recalling the inscription in his Bible, Brandon now understood with perfect clarity what the best decision in Dean's life had been. On the exact date, twenty-one years later, Brandon had followed in his dad's steps by following Jesus.

"Can we take you both home now?" Ronald called from the top of the bank.

Brandon lifted a dripping fist to Justin. "Today is the first day—"

Justin collided his fist with Brandon's, "—of the rest of our lives."

EPILOGUE

"CAN YOU GET THAT?" GENEVIEVE YELLED FROM THE BACK ROOM.

Brandon looked up from his math book. "Sure!"

Nearly six months had passed, and the first thing he did after turning eighteen in July was to accept Genevieve's offer for him to move in. The group home couldn't keep him anymore, and he was so busy with schoolwork that holding a job was impossible. Therefore, an apartment was out of the question. Although he was old enough to make his own choices, including making the best decision of his life, he knew there were a lot of life skills he needed to learn. He was grateful for Aunt Genni's generosity.

Brandon stood up and answered the front door. "Hey, Ronald. Happy Thanksgiving!"

"Happy Thanksgiving, Brandon. I came to drop off a gift." He held a wrapped package in his hands.

"Thanks. Wanna come in?"

"That'd be great."

Brandon stepped aside and motioned for Ronald to take a seat at the dining table.

"Are you listening to Motown?" Ronald asked.

Brandon flushed. "Uh, yeah." He turned down the volume on the CD player and sat down.

Upon noticing the math book, Ronald asked, "How's your schoolwork going?"

"It's going well. Aunt Genni's helping a lot, and it looks like I'll be able to graduate at the beginning of next month."

"That's really good to hear. Be sure to thank Principal Vernon. You know he didn't have to allow this."

"I've received a lot of grace these past few months. Hey, I'm sorry again for all the trouble I caused."

Ronald gave a dismissive wave. "You've been a real success story, Brandon. It was worth traveling across the country on a wild goose chase, then getting elbowed in the stomach, to see how far you've come," he said with a twinkle in his eye.

Brandon winced. "I never apologized for that blow to the stomach, did I?"

Ronald rubbed his stomach in mock agony. "I was not ready for you to throw an elbow, that's for sure. But fortunately it wasn't a fatal blow."

"Hey," Brandon said. "Did you hear? We got Aunt Genni's car back last month."

Ronald pointed at Brandon. "Don't even think about it. You still don't have your license."

Brandon smiled and changed the subject. "Aunt Genni took me to see Barry a few days ago."

By the look on Ronald's face, Brandon could tell he was impressed.

"It was awkward," Brandon admitted. "Small steps, you know? So, what's that?" He pointed at the package on the table.

"Something a stranger dropped off at the office. He thought you might like it back."

Brandon looked at it, puzzled. He reached for the package. "Do you mind?"

"It's yours. Open it."

Brandon tore the packaging to reveal his trench coat. His trench coat? He looked at Ronald, confused.

"The stranger said you left it in his car."

"Wait. He dropped this off? Anton? Where is he?"

Ronald nodded at the door and winked.

Brandon stood up so fast, the chair he was sitting in dropped to the floor. He yanked the door open to find Justin and Anton casually chatting on Genevieve's front porch. "Anton!"

"Hey, brother!" He stood up and gave Brandon a bear hug. "Happy Thanksgiving!" The noontime sun provided a pleasant warmth.

"How in the world did you find us?" He looked at Justin. "How long have you known?"

"Just since this morning." A toothpick stuck out of Justin's mouth. "Ronald and I have been planning this surprise for a while."

Brandon turned to Ronald. "Thank you!"

"You're welcome." Ronald smiled.

Genevieve stepped onto the porch.

"Don't tell me you were in on this too!" Brandon said to her.

She tilted her head and smiled. "Now you know why I'm cooking such a big turkey."

"I'll get out of here to give you guys some time to catch up." Ronald stepped off the porch toward his car.

"I've got to take care of the rest of dinner," Genevieve said, then went back inside.

"So, how did you find us?" Brandon asked.

"After the police in Arizona released me, I kept exploring the West a little bit. Then, I started back home. I stopped in Dallas and found Devin. We worked together to track you down. I made a few calls, followed some advice to wait until you turned eighteen. But then I had to start school. We're on Thanksgiving break now. I worked things out with Ronald, and here I am."

"Here you are." Brandon's smile faded. "Anton, I should have told you people were searching for me. Justin wanted me to tell you. I was just so scared. I'm sorry—"

"Apology accepted, brother. Don't worry about it. All charges were dropped after your testimony cleared. Plus, we had a great time." Anton smiled.

"You know that's right!" Justin said, adopting Anton's phrase as his own.

"I hear that!" Brandon said.

"So, Justin tells me you were baptized."

"Just down there. It was on the last day we saw you. We had just left the airport. And did Justin tell you he quit smoking?"

They spent the next couple of hours laughing and catching up. Anton was doing well in preaching school. Brandon had read through the New Testament twice, and he had just started the Old Testament.

"What about church?" Anton asked.

"I've gone a couple of times," Brandon said. "Justin even came with me once."

Anton raised his eyebrows at Justin. "Still indifferent?"

Justin shrugged. "Maybe."

"That also means maybe not." Anton winked. "I'm proud of you for going a couple of times, Brandon. That's another thing I'd like to talk to you about." Anton looked at his watch. "I think we've got time." The sun was much lower in the sky now.

"Time before what?" Brandon asked.

"There's something else I've got to do today."

"What do you have to do in Nashville?" Brandon said. "And I thought you were staying for dinner?"

"I am. Don't worry."

Brandon narrowed his eyes.

"I'm also proud of you for taking the initiative to read your Bible," Anton said, disregarding Brandon's confusion. "When you did, what picture of Jesus' church did you get?"

Brandon thought back to the book of Acts. He had been

surprised to learn that the church wasn't a building like he had always assumed. It was a people—the people of God. In the second chapter of Acts, as people were baptized, the Lord added them to the number of disciples. Once added—no matter their age, race, social class, or gender—they were part of the family. They took care of each other. They served each other. "It's a beautiful picture."

"It sure is," Anton said. "The apostle Paul's favorite way to talk about the church is to call the church the body of Christ. What do you think the significance of that illustration is?"

Brandon smiled. He had missed these conversations and studies. Again, he thought about what he had learned from the New Testament. Paul said in the book of First Corinthians that the body was to be united—with no divisions—because each member was valuable, just like each part of a human body. "To show that every Christian has a part to play in the family."

Anton smiled. "That's absolutely right. Justin, how many different churches meet around here?"

"I don't know. Dozens."

Brandon was thankful Anton was including Justin in the study too. For the past few months, Brandon didn't know how to engage in spiritual conversation with Justin without making it seem like he was forcing stuff onto his best friend. At least Justin had come to church with him, but Brandon didn't know how to take the conversation further. It was strange not having the most valuable part of his life in common with him.

Anton dropped his head. "Dozens. Dozens of different churches. But that was never part of God's plan."

"What do you mean?" Brandon asked.

"We see all these denominations today. They've done a great job dividing the body of Christ. So many of them look so different from the church in the Bible, it's a wonder they still call themselves Christians."

"Who are we to judge?" Brandon asked.

"We're no one to judge," Anton said. "It's not our call. It's God's call. And he has already told us what he expects from his church. Keep reading your Bible, Brandon. It will tell you what the church is supposed to look like, how the church is supposed to worship, and what the Bible truly teaches on salvation. Use the words of God to always ask if you're on the path to life. When you do that, you're not making the judgment. You're using the revealed judgments of God to help you make important decisions."

"Fair enough," Brandon said. Not a day since the Grand Canyon had gone by without Brandon thinking about Anton. But somehow he had forgotten how wise Anton was. Although the air was getting colder by the minute, Brandon felt a warmth swell inside.

"But that brings me to my next point." Anton glanced at his watch again. "You said you've gone to worship a couple of times since you became a Christian. Why not several times?"

"I don't know. Don't get me wrong. I like church. I like the preaching and singing and Lord's Supper. It's just that I never grew up doing that. And this is kind of between me and God, you know?"

"Yeah, I know. But is that the picture of Christianity you get from the New Testament?"

Brandon had to admit it wasn't. The only times Christians didn't share their faith with fellow believers in the Bible were when they were imprisoned or exiled. But even then, they were busy writing letters to each other. Brandon could see where this conversation was going. "No. The church should be a family."

"A family. We are the body of Christ. We are members of one another. Don't forsake your family." He smiled. "How about tomorrow we call the local church's elders and get you plugged in?"

"Tomorrow?" Brandon asked. "How long are you staying?"

"Aunt Genni said I could stay as long as I want." Anton

grinned.

Brandon raised an eyebrow. "Aunt Genni? How long has she been involved in this?"

"Long enough. I have to go back to preaching school before Monday. I'll probably get on the road after worship on Sunday. By then, Devin should be back on campus."

"What campus?" Brandon asked.

"Devin's going to college a couple of hours west of here. Thought I'd stop and see him on my way home." Anton gave a mischievous smile. "Wanna come?"

Brandon would give anything to be on the road with Anton and Justin again. He looked at Justin. "Think your boss will give you some time off?"

"I'll call him now." Justin stepped inside.

"But Brandon," Anton began with a grin, "just promise to not get me arrested this time." Brandon's ears grew red. Before he could apologize again, Anton brought the subject back around. "So, tomorrow, let's get in touch with the elders of the local church," Anton said.

What Anton was saying made sense. And Brandon didn't mind that Anton was not giving him an option here. The Bible didn't either. "That sounds really good."

Then, an unfamiliar car stopped in front of the house. Anton checked his watch. "Just in time. Good thing Aunt Genni prepared for more than just me this evening."

"What's going on?" Brandon asked.

"Come on." Anton stepped off the porch toward the car. "Our trip was cut short, remember? We still had one more stop to make." Brandon trailed behind him. He tried to look inside the car, but the evening sun was reflecting off the windows so that he couldn't see in. Anton reached for the door handle to the passenger side. "Brandon, meet your grandparents."

THE END

A NOTE FROM THE AUTHOR

Thank you for reading *Searching for Brandon Bason*. One of my early readers asked, "Is Brandon's story based on your life?" The answer is yes, and no. Brandon's story came to my mind in mid-2017 when I was ministering to a friend who was going through yet another traumatizing event in life. Where many people in similar situations would say they had been dealt bad hands, he looked back and saw how God had used such cases to search for him.

With my friend's attitude as inspiration, I began crafting Brandon Bason's story. I couldn't help but inject some of my own experiences in there too. I know what it's like to be the gothic kid in school. I was the one the popular kids (who usually claimed to be Christians) laughed at in the hallways while yelling things like, "Watch out! He'll put a curse on you!" On the other hand, I also know what it's like to be on the receiving end of indescribable Christian generosity. I know what it's like to both search and be searched for. Although I currently live in Porirua, New Zealand, I've been on most of the roads Brandon, Justin, and Anton traveled (I mean that both figuratively and literally). I was born in Arizona, and I spent most of my life in

Tennessee. Those who know me best would probably say I'm much more like Justin and Anton than Brandon. I love talking to anyone about music (like Justin) and the gospel (like Anton). If you're interested in learning more about my story, I encourage you to read my first book, *Transformed: A Spiritual Journey*. And if you do, you'll get a chance to meet the real cowboy Christian from Texas named Devin.

Thank you to my editor, alpha readers, beta readers, and Launch Team. Without you, this story would not be what it is. I especially thank God for my sensitivity readers, who helped me turn Anton and his family into relatable characters. From the beginning, it was important to me that I did not write Anton's character based on stereotypes, or in a way that could be perceived as racist in any way. My sensitivity readers helped me achieve that goal.

Again, thank you for supporting my writing. If this story (or any of my writing) has inspired you at all, give God the praise and glory. I would love to hear from you. Reach out to me at lancemosherbooks.com.

God bless you. If you are a lost sheep, stop wandering, and allow the Good Shepherd to find you.

LANCE MOSHER
July 2020

I [Jesus] said therefore to you, that you shall die in your sins; for unless you believe that I am He, you shall die in your sins.
(John 8:24)

Therefore having overlooked the times of ignorance, God is now declaring to men that all everywhere should repent, because He has fixed a day in which He will judge the world in righteousness through a Man whom He has appointed, having furnished proof to all men by raising Him from the dead.

(*Acts 17:30–31*)

Everyone therefore who shall confess Me [Jesus] before men, I will also confess him before My Father who is in heaven. But whoever shall deny Me before men, I will also deny him before My Father who is in heaven.

(*Matthew 10:32–33*)

And now why do you delay? Arise, and be baptized, and wash away your sins, calling on His name.

(*Acts 22:16*)

PLEASE TURN A FEW PAGES FOR A SPECIAL REQUEST.

ABOUT THE AUTHOR

Lance married the love of his life, Kristen, in 2008. He earned his bachelor's degree in fine arts in 2009 and his master's degree in ministry in 2011 from Freed-Hardeman University. In his free time, he enjoys being with his family, reading, writing, the outdoors, photography, music, and movies. Lance and Kristen moved to New Zealand in June 2012 to spread the gospel of Christ. They have two sons, Silas and Asher.

Other books by Lance Mosher:

- *Transformed: A Spiritual Journey* (2013)
- *Clouded by Emotion: Studies on the Holy Spirit and Miracles* (2019)

So, what did you think?

While it's fresh on your mind, will you please take a moment to leave a review for *Searching for Brandon Bason* on Amazon, Goodreads, and other retailers?

Thank you for reading and reviewing!

Audiobook coming soon.

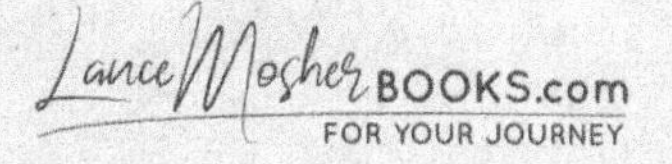

Made in the USA
Monee, IL
21 August 2020

39147941R00225